BOOKS BY TIM FRANKOVICH

Heart of Fire
Until All Curses Are Lifted
Until All Bonds Are Broken
Until All the Gods Return
Until All the Stars Fall

Dragontek Lore
Viridia
Incarnadine
Auric
Onyx
Amaranth
Atramentous

TIM FRANKOVICH

THE
CERTAINTY
OF
BLOOD

In memoriam
Tommy Frankovich

Table of Contents

Part One

ROCHINBAL

CHOSEN

"Clanless! Clanless! Clanless!"

The crowd chanted his title as the warrior held his blade aloft, coated in the invaluable blood of his opponent. He could spare only a few seconds for their adulation. The kill strike had been a chest wound. He had only moments to gather his portion.

"Blood is life. Blood is precious. Blood is power," the warrior quoted to himself. He knelt beside the dead body. Corlis of clan Dendsu. Clanless couldn't imagine what had possessed Corlis to challenge him, but he vowed to remember him, though it seemed little comfort for the dead. Corlis. The second-to-last step to freedom.

Clanless snatched the Siphon from the back of his belt. A quick glance showed the attendants already on their way across the sand, pressed to hurry by the priest accompanying them. Clanless took the punch tube and jammed it into the dead man's heart. Blood shot up through the tube and the attached hose, flowing into the bladder. Heart-blood: the most valuable of involuntary blood donations.

"Come on, come on," he muttered. The attendants' feet approached in his peripheral vision, their sandals slapping against the arena sand in their rush.

"Enough, Clanless. You have your share. Step away." The voice of the blood-priest, slightly out of breath, grated on his ears.

Clanless pulled the Siphon free at an angle, making sure he obtained every drop possible. He sealed the punch tube and re-attached the Siphon to his belt. After picking up his blade, he stood and gave the blood-priest a curt bow. In return, he received a hostile glare. Clanless tightened his grip on the blade's handle. It would be so simple. One quick thrust, and he'd never have to hear that voice again.

But one quick thrust would doom him forever. So close. So very close. He could wait. Maybe.

"Clanless!" the crowd roared again. Having siphoned his portion, he turned in a circle for them, holding both arms aloft. Let them cheer while they could. They would only see him fight one more time. The final step to his freedom.

He paused in his turn, facing the royal box. In a slow and practiced move, he took blood from his blade and drew a line across his forehead, paying homage to the Hawk King. Such a waste of the precious liquid, but he followed the expected protocol and bowed.

To his surprise, the Hawk King stood and approached the railing. He raised his hand, and the crowd noise dwindled.

"Well done, Clanless!" His mighty voice, enhanced by blood-magic, boomed across the arena. "You fight as you always have, like a man possessed by the goddess herself!" The king gestured upward to the moon in her constant position.

The crowd cheered their approval of his words. Clanless lowered his head again in deference.

"We recognize you as the greatest of all our arena fighters! Perhaps the greatest of all time!" The Hawk King paused, smiling that arched smile Clanless had grown to despise over the past two years. "Though, of course, we still disapprove of your… less-than-honorable weapon choices."

Hoots and hollers came from the crowd. Most of them didn't care. His moonblade gave more of a show than most of the others who fought here.

The king waved to the crowd. "Tomorrow, High Winter begins. The sun surrenders fully to the goddess. But it is also the thirtieth such winter, which means the chaos moon will appear in the sky."

The crowd made their disapproval known. Those who'd been alive thirty years ago knew the horrible weather soon to come. Those younger, like Clanless, had heard the stories.

"And so we celebrate one last time, before the weather drives us all into hiding. Tomorrow's festival will be the greatest of this generation!"

Louder cheers shook the arena. Everyone knew this, of course, but they were already excited. Hearing from the Hawk King himself, after witnessing the epic arena fights, spurred them almost to a frenzy.

"Clanless!" The Hawk King's fierce gaze bored into him. "Will you be my champion tomorrow for one last battle?"

He'd expected something like this, though he hadn't been sure whether the Hawk King would announce it to the crowd. The ruler understood the significance of the next fight. After all, this was the immortal Hawk King, beloved of the moon goddess, and he held the one thing that mattered to Clanless right now: his bloodbond. Of course he would know. Even so, why bother telling the crowd? What would that accomplish?

"Clanless? Do you keep your king in suspense?"

The crowd laughed, and Clanless realized he'd stood silent for longer than he'd intended.

"It would be my honor and privilege to fight on your behalf, great king!" he shouted. His voice wouldn't carry anywhere near as well as the king's, but the crowd got the message. They roared their approval.

The Hawk King raised his hand again and waited for the noise to subside. "My people, tomorrow night, as the chaos moon appears, you will see our champion, the clanless one, strike a mighty blow for all of us!" He stretched both hands wide, his white cape spreading with them. "For tomorrow, our champion will fight and defeat the greatest enemy of us all: the so-called Hero of Dolkot… Daviland!"

The crowd exploded, going far beyond their previous frenzy. People jumped in the air, threw clothes into the arena, and climbed onto the railings. Clanless watched at least two fall into the sand below. If they didn't survive the fall, the blood-priests would claim them. Involuntary though their blood might be, it was still blood.

Clanless stood in the midst of the cacophony, unsure of his feelings. He knew the name, of course. The rebel. The hero of the people. He'd made quite a name for himself in his opposition to the Hawk King's rule. Word of his capture had reached the arena fighters the night before. Everyone expected him to be executed, but the Hawk King, true to form, wanted more drama. And what higher drama could there be than for the greatest arena champion of all time to fight this rebel in the capital arena?

Clanless needed only one victory to purchase his freedom, after all these years. And this hero, regardless of his deeds, was no warrior of the arena. The fight should not be difficult. Still, it felt… wrong. Clanless wanted out, but to end his career with what amounted to a showy execution… what a waste.

The Hawk King waved to dismiss him and turned away. Clanless bowed one last time, then hurried to the exit. Hagh met him there. Clanless handed him the blade while he toweled the sweat from his body. He nodded to the waiting healer, unneeded this time. With Hagh at his side, he moved on to the waiting room.

"It augers ill," Hagh said, followed by a deep, hacking cough that went on longer than it had any business doing.

"What is that supposed to mean?" Clanless demanded, once he'd finished with the towel.

"This fight. The chaos moon. Daviland." He shook his head. "It's not good. Not good at all."

"It's a glorified execution," Clanless shot back. "A waste of my skill. But it's still my last fight. I buy my freedom with his blood."

The blood-priest's voice broke into the conversation. "The tithe, Clanless. I've come to collect."

"I'm not even dressed yet, priest! You couldn't wait five minutes?"

The priest lowered his head, but his narrow face held its usual sneer. "You know the way of things."

"Gotta stop leaving that door open," Hagh muttered.

Clanless sighed. He picked up the Siphon and tossed it to the priest. "Take your tithe. Bad enough you won't let me fill the thing. And then you take more."

"It is the way of things," the priest repeated. He held up the Siphon, murmured a few words over it, then poured a portion into a crystal vial. As always, Clanless fought the urge to ignite the stolen blood. Such an easy thing to do, but the priest would know. When they discovered the blood to be tainted, they'd know exactly who had done it.

With another lowered head, the priest returned the Siphon and glided away. Now that he'd gone, Clanless's stress and frustration faded.

Hagh coughed. "I am telling you, Clanless. I've heard of this hero. You shouldn't fight him."

Clanless wrapped a robe around his body and collapsed into a chair. "Why, Hagh? Why would I avoid an easy kill?"

Hagh shook his head. "It won't be so easy. They say…" He looked around, then leaned closer. "They say he's… the chosen one."

TAINTED

Clanless left the waiting room, on his way to the baths. In the hall, he stopped to hand the Siphon to Yesun, one of the arena attendants.

"To my room, Yesun. For the last time." He smiled at the boy.

"Last time for him too!" the second attendant chimed in. "Yesun becomes a man next week!"

"Is that so?" Hagh asked. "Manhood ceremony coming up, Yesun?"

"Yes, sir. In three days' time."

"You won't have any problems," Clanless told him. "Good luck to you, Yesun. What will you do after that?"

"Find a better job," Yesun said. "My family needs the blood." He hurried away with the Siphon.

As Clanless continued toward the baths, his mind went back to the day he came of age. His memory troubled him at times, but he remembered every detail of that day, the day everything changed…

Then

On the dawn of the last day of his twelfth year, Aldan of clan Tokuur rose from his bed with a thrill of anticipation… and, if he were honest, a small bit of fear. Today, he would become a man. Today, he would shed his own blood in front of his entire clanhold and offer it to the moon goddess in payment for his manhood.

He'd waited so long for this day.

"Aldan!" his mother called from the next room. "Prayers!"

He shouldn't neglect prayers, today of all days! He hurried past his still-sleeping little sister and into the living space of their home. Father and Mother waited there for him, both smiling. He joined them and looked up through the circular window in the roof. The moon stared back at him, as it did every day, as consistent as his parents' love. If he squinted, he could make out the entire circle, faded in the light of day. The early morning shield the moon generated toward the sun, a crescent on the lower left, always looked a little pink to him at this hour. With the start of Low Spring, the roof window would be open every day now, letting the cool air inside.

"This is a special day," Father said. "And so, I have asked the rest of the family to join us as the sun begins its pursuit." He stepped to the open door and beckoned.

Uncle Sejikdi crossed the courtyard from his adjacent home, along with his wife and Aldan's cousin Borde. She smirked at him. If they were alone, she would have made a sarcastic comment about his transition to manhood. And he wouldn't have minded. Three years older than Aldan, Borde defined youth and beauty to him. She would be married within the next month, much to Aldan's disappointment. The betrothal had been announced only two days ago. Little sister Ot would be the only child remaining within their connected homes, too young even to be included in the prayers.

Aldan closed his eyes and gave a low nod to his uncle. "Here is the new man!" Sejikdi exclaimed, tousling Aldan's hair. At least it wasn't anything more embarrassing than that.

"Not until the ceremony," Mother chided. "Come, come. Gather under the moon. It is time."

The family assembled in a tight grouping and looked up. Father, as the Patriarch of this family—his own father having died two years ago—recited the prayer:

"Goddess above, watch over us today. Let our blood pulse for you. And should it flow, let it flow for you as well. Bless our work and our growth."

"Blood is life. Blood is precious. Blood is power," they all joined in to declare. At the familiar words, Aldan shivered. Today, those words would be more true for him than ever.

Mother clapped her hands. "And now for breakfast!"

After breakfast, Aldan set about his morning chores. At least he would not have to work in the field today. He hadn't had a day away from the fields since… the last Sun's Surrender, come to think of it. Now that had been a party. Caught up in his memories, he didn't notice Borde until he almost ran into her in the courtyard. She swirled gracefully out of his path, an empty basket in her hands.

"Oh!" Aldan stumbled back. "I'm sorry."

Borde smiled: not quite the smirk she'd worn at first seeing him, but not devoid of playfulness either. "Real men should watch where they are going," she teased.

"I won't be a real man until the blood spills," he answered without thinking.

His cousin cocked her head. "Will you be all right with that? I've seen a couple of boys pass out when they see their own blood. Do you remember Buqu last year?"

"I can handle it." Aldan squared his shoulders. "Father helped me practice two week ago. It doesn't hurt much."

"And will you be married soon after?" Borde swept her hair back. "Do you have your eye on any of the young ladies of the hold?"

Aldan wrinkled his brow. "I don't know if I'll ever get married."

"Why not?"

He shrugged. "Marriage is good for some people, like our parents. And you! I just don't know if it is for me."

Borde looked down at her basket. "You think it is good for me?"

"Yes, of course. Monge is part of a fine family. He will treat you well. Their back wall is the strongest in the clanhold!" Remembering his own chores, Aldan bent and lifted a large rock from a pile.

"Back wall, back wall," Borde murmured. "Is that what you are doing now?"

Aldan nodded. While working the fields, he and his father would bring any stones they found to the courtyard. Each morning, as the sun began its pursuit of the moon, Aldan would place one of them on the back wall of the family's home. All of these back walls linked together to form the outer wall of the clanhold.

"Don't you get tired of silly things like that?" Borde sat on a stool and dangled the basket from her fingers, tilting it back and forth.

Aldan's eyes widened. "The back wall is not silly! It protects us from the High Winter winds. Without the walls, the clanhold would be destroyed. And, and what if barbarians were to attack? We cannot be the weak spot!"

"When was the last time barbarians actually attacked a clanhold?"

"I… I don't know."

"Because they don't do that any more! It's pointless! Just another silly clanhold tradition. Remember when you broke your arm trying to carry a rock too big for you?" Borde jumped back to her feet and spun in a circle. "I want to get away from this, Aldan. I'm so tired of this life."

"W-where would you go?"

"To one of the cities!" Borde's eyes sparkled. "That's where real life happens. No more working in the fields. No more of the same old food every day. No more back walls!"

Aldan frowned. "Is that what Monge wants too? Will he take you away from the hold?"

"I don't know." Borde sighed. "I don't know him at all. What kind of man is he, Aldan? Do you know him?"

"I've worked with him in the fields a time or two." Aldan shifted the stone in his arms. He considered setting it back down, but as long as he held it, he could claim to be working if one of the adults came out. "He is a good worker."

"That's not what I'm asking." Borde caught Aldan's eyes with her own. "What kind of man is he? Is he… kind? Like you?"

"Kind?" Aldan echoed.

"You know what I mean." Borde reached past the stone and brushed Aldan's chest with her fingers. "You have a kind heart within, Cousin. Not like—" She broke off with a quick glance back at her home.

"I-I'm not sure." Aldan swallowed. No one had ever called him kind before. He didn't know what to think.

"Borde!" Uncle Sejikdi emerged and waved at them. "Do not keep the priests waiting!"

"I have to go!" Borde whispered. "Be a kind man, Aldan. Don't change." She swept out through the gate.

Sejikdi gave Aldan a large smile. "Strengthening the back wall, eh Aldan? Good, good. A man's work." He glanced after Borde as she hurried away. "Tonight, after your ceremony, we will celebrate, you know. We will show you how a man celebrates after a man's work!"

Aldan didn't know what to think of that either. He shifted the stone in his arms again and hurried back through the house to find a place for it.

❨❨❨❨●❩❩❩❩

The blood-priest, clad in his bright red robe, stepped away, holding the ritual knife as if it were a precious thing. Aldan watched blood ooze from his arm. The cut hurt, but not even as much as the practice cut his father had given him. The texture of the blood itself fascinated him, as it always did. The thickness of the red liquid reminded him of syrup more than water. It flowed in a slow trickle down over his hand, between two of his fingers, and into the ceremonial bowl.

What would happen to this blood, his blood no longer? The priests would take it away, but what would they do with it? Would they offer it to the goddess? Would they use it to create magic? Borde said they could do miracles if they had enough blood. The Hawk King himself might use this very blood in his rituals to protect the Empire. The possibilities were endless and fantastic. "Blood is power," he whispered.

He spared a quick look at the crowd here at the temple, the central gathering place of the entire clanhold. His mother beamed at him, holding little Ot on her hip. Beside her, Borde smiled, but her eyes wandered the room. He saw childhood friends (and antagonists) among the crowd, many who still waited for their turn at manhood. How would his life with them change now? Would they still talk as they always did, or would it be different? Could he only talk of men things now?

Father stepped up beside him then, along with Uncle Sejikdi and three other men of the clanhold. As one, they cut their arms and let their blood flow into separate bowls, making their own sacrifice in honor of his.

Aldan's eyes darted from one bowl to the next. All of the blood looked so much alike, even from men of different ages and sizes. The goddess truly made them all equal, all possessed of the same liquid life within.

"Blood is life. Blood is precious. Blood is power," the priest declared, lifting both arms in the air, letting the sleeves of his robe fall loose. Aldan compared the robe with his blood. They weren't the same color at all, were they? Shouldn't blood-priests have blood-colored robes?

"Blood is life. Blood is precious. Blood is power," the crowd recited again and again. Aldan joined in, but on the third recitation of the words, he experienced a change within.

Something swept over his entire body, like the time he'd been sick with the sand cough and run such a fever he could feel the temperature changes passing over him. But this wasn't a temperature. Light-headedness followed. He struggled to stay erect. Passing out during the ceremony would be the worst thing possible. He'd be like Buqu. He'd never live it down!

He focused on the blood, each drop pooling in the bowls. As the other men continued the chant, his eyes wandered again from bowl to bowl. Something had changed. Something was happening with the blood. He didn't know how he knew, but he did. Something altered within the blood itself.

A burning sensation erupted behind his eyes. He blinked repeatedly with no relief. Someone in the crowd murmured something about "eyes." Others joined in. Trying to ignore the odd feelings, he re-focused on the blood in his own bowl. He stared at it, trying to repeat the words, or at least mouth them. A spark flew out of his bowl. How could that be? Blood didn't burn; it—

In the exact same moment, all five of the other men broke off their chanting and cried out. They seized their bleeding arms with the other hand. "Burns!" his uncle gasped.

The heat behind Aldan's eyes spread throughout his head and neck. Pain—a burning sensation—exploded, first in his bleeding arm, then shooting up into his chest and cascading throughout his body. He opened his mouth, but couldn't scream.

One by one, four of the men fell to the ground. "Aldan," his father gasped, "what—" He fell forward, knocking the bowl of blood from its pedestal, spilling the precious liquid across the platform. Spectators shrieked in horror.

As his father collapsed, Aldan himself could bear it no longer. His vision turned dark. A sensation of falling added on top of everything else. Before he hit the ground, he heard a feminine voice, low but distinct over the sound of the crowd. It seemed to come from within him somehow.

"Oh, well done. Very well done."

(((●))))

Aldan woke to find himself still inside the temple. Two temple guards stood near him, holding their maces at ready. Aldan pushed back against the wall and jumped to his feet. His eyes bounced around the temple, his heart beating faster than he ever remembered. An enormous bandage covered his arm, hiding the cut and preserving any more blood.

"Aldan! Son, stay calm!" The voice of his father drew his attention past the guards. Father and Uncle Sejikdi stood with one of the blood-priests almost exactly where the ceremony had taken place. The rest of the temple was empty.

"This is ridiculous," Sejikdi grumbled. "He's only a boy."

"He spilled his blood. He is now a man," the priest answered calmly.

A second priest charged into the chamber from a side door, waving an arm. "The Taint!" he shouted. "It is the Taint! All of the blood is tainted. All of it!"

The three other men gasped. "Are you certain?" Father demanded. "It can't be," Sejikdi said at the same time.

The priest leveled a finger at Aldan. "And it is all his doing! He bears the Taint!"

"You don't know that." Father pointed at the bandage on his own arm. "It happened to all of us."

Aldan wished he could hide. None of this made any sense.

The blood-priest drew himself up. "The rest of you have all given before, and regularly. Nothing untoward has ever occurred. His presence is the only difference!"

"He's just a boy!" Uncle Sejikdi argued. "Whatever happened, you can't hold him responsible."

"He completed the ceremony." The priest folded his arms and glared. "He is a man by the law. And responsible for his own actions."

"What action did he take?" Father demanded. "You were right there. Did you see him do anything?"

"Yes."

"He was right beside me!" Sejikdi pointed at Aldan. "I would have seen it."

"Did you look at his eyes?" Before Aldan's uncle could answer, the priest went on: "No, of course not. You were beside him. Both of you. The rest of us, all of the crowd, everyone else: we saw his eyes. We all did. They glowed red."

"My eyes turned red at my first offering too," Father said. "It's a common ailment—"

"They did not 'turn' red!" the priest snapped. "They glowed! Red light shone out from them! It is the Taint, and nothing less."

Father and Uncle Sejikdi did not answer. Aldan lifted his fingers to touch his eyelids. They felt fine now, but he recalled the burning sensation. What did it all mean? What was wrong with him? What was this Taint? His body trembled with each breath.

"And the blood is now tainted. Ruined," the priest continued. "He did it. He is unholy, tainted."

"But the goddess spoke to me!" Aldan exclaimed, remembering.

The three other men all turned to him, eyes wide. One of the guards murmured something and lowered his mace.

"What did she say, son?" his father asked.

"Don't be ridiculous!" The priest threw both hands out in dismissal. "The moon goddess would not deign to speak to a mere boy!"

"I thought you said he was a man." Uncle Sejikdi's observation earned him another glare.

"She said 'well done,'" Aldan said. "I heard her. I swear it!"

The blood-priest mimed putting his hands over his ears. "So now he blasphemes as well. When the Daghilch hears of this, there can be only one outcome."

"No," Father pleaded. "Have mercy, please."

"There is no mercy for blasphemers and those who taint the holy blood offerings." The priest drew himself up. "It is only a matter of a new ceremony being completed, but once it is done…" He paused, then pointed at Aldan. "This one will be clanless."

"You would banish him for an accident?" Aldan's uncle looked dangerously close to attacking the priest. One of the guards turned away from Aldan and took a step closer to the men.

The first priest raised a hand. "Brother, perhaps they do not know our history as well as they should. The Taint is not something we can allow, regardless of how it manifests itself."

The ranting priest scowled and nodded. "Then educate them."

"Hear and observe," the first priest said. He put both palms together and looked up toward the moon. "Long ago, clan Tokuur held honor within the Empire. We were warriors first and foremost. But in a battle with the barbarians, we went too far. In our zeal to overcome our enemies, we chose dishonorable ways of fighting. We shed their barbarian blood into the sand. Gallons and gallons of that which is precious to the goddess spilled out into the hungry earth, wasted and worthless. This was a grave sin."

He turned and looked toward Aldan. "On the same day, though we knew it not at the time, four children were born with the Taint, the ability to destroy the value of spilled blood. It is the curse on our clan. The Taint appeared in dozens of children that year, but as we sacrificed more and more to appease the goddess, such births decreased. There has not been a child born with the Taint now in several ten of years."

"Because we wasted blood, the goddess cursed us with a way to waste more blood?" Father asked. "How does that make sense?"

Both priests glared at him. "Do you wish to join your offspring in the penalties for blasphemy?"

"It was an accident," Sejikdi repeated. "Whatever he did, we can teach him not to do it. It doesn't have to happen again."

The priests shook their heads. "All of the clanhold witnessed it. He cannot stay," the first said.

"We cannot allow this to remain within our clan," the second continued. "Either we kill him, or we banish him. The Daghilch will decide, and now that your son has blasphemed as well, he will be lucky if he lives another day."

Father looked toward Aldan. His eyes, red with tears, said more than his words ever could. He was giving up. "Aldan. Son…" He covered his face with his hands.

Uncle Sejikdi put a hand on his brother's shoulder. "We… we understand. Will you allow his family to say farewell at least?"

"That will be the Daghilch's decision as well. He will be summoned and be here within two to three days."

Aldan's uncle nodded. He helped Father turn away. The two of them walked slowly out of the temple. Aldan opened his mouth to call after them, but didn't. What good would it do now?

One of the priests looked at him again. "Take the blasphemer to the unused cell," he commanded the guards. "Feed him as necessary, but allow no one within with him." He paused. "And shed no blood in his presence. Not even a drop."

☾☾☽☽ ● ☾☾☽☽

The temple's "cell" grew cold that night. Without a blanket, Aldan shivered and slept little. The cell itself was little more than a tiny room made entirely of stone, with a circular window viewing the moon high above Aldan's head. He heard one of the priests muttering that the room was intended for prayers, not prisoners.

Curled up in the corner, Aldan stared up at the never-moving moon. "I know I heard you," he whispered. "Why? Why is this happening to me?" He didn't receive an answer… and didn't know how he would have reacted if he did.

What did the "Taint" mean? The priest's explanation didn't help: it made the blood useless, somehow. His own blood had felt like it burned within him. Did that mean all of his blood was now tainted? What about Father and Uncle Sejikdi and the other men? Would their blood be tainted forever? None of it made much sense. Whatever it meant, he could not change it, apparently. He would always bear this curse.

Maybe he deserved it. Or maybe the Taint explained why some other unpleasant things happened in his life before now. Either way, he found no comfort that night.

In the morning, the guards allowed Borde to deliver water and some food: bread, cheese, and a little bit of dried meat. Under the watchful eye of the guard and his threatening mace, the cousins embraced and exchanged a few quick words.

"Your father is doing everything he can," Borde whispered, "but no one wants to go against the priests."

"Tell him not to get in trouble for me. The family needs him!"

Borde sniffed and wiped an eye. "See there? A kind man. Just like I said."

Aldan looked down at the food. The flatbread looked delicious, especially considering how long it had been since he ate, but… it hadn't been made by his mother. Her bread always held a certain golden tone. This bread looked like someone trying to imitate it, but not quite achieving the same results. He picked up a piece. "Who made this?"

Borde smiled with a lowered head. "I did."

"Is Mother all right?"

"She's—"

"That's long enough," the guard interrupted. "Time to go."

"She's taken it hard," Borde said in a rush. "And she admitted she's been feeling ill the past few mornings."

The guard stepped between them, and Borde backed out of the cell. As the door swung closed, she called a few more words: "My mother thinks she's with child!"

The door shut. Aldan sat alone again.

"With child." At first the words thrilled him. His mother would have another baby! He would have a new little brother or sister! And then the reality of the situation settled upon him: he would never meet this new sibling.

As he ate Borde's bread—not as good as his mother's—and the rest of the food, his mood sank even further. His family would give up on him. And then they would forget him. They would have a new child to take his place. A new son, perhaps. One without this "Taint." Ot would be the older sister to this boy. He would be loved by all of them.

And Aldan would be forgotten.

He drank some of the water the priests provided, then scooted back into the corner. He pulled his knees up to his chest and hugged his legs.

For all that day, he sat alone with nothing to do… nothing save staring up at the moon and wondering. What would happen to him? What did it mean to be banished? To not belong to a clan? Obviously, he would have to leave the clanhold. But where would he go? To another clanhold, maybe belonging to a different clan? Or would they drive him out into the wilderness, where he might meet wild animals or barbarians or beastmen?

Maybe it would be better to die. At least then he wouldn't have to think about the wilderness. Or his family replacing him.

But he had no way of ending his own life. He knew people could die from lack of food or water, but he'd just eaten and drank. He didn't know how long it would take to die that way, but it couldn't be easy. He didn't know if he could refuse sustenance while his body demanded it.

And of course, his captors had made sure he had no way of cutting himself. The cell was empty. Even the basket Borde brought was a thick woven fabric. The hardest substance in the room might have been the bread he'd eaten. Borde definitely needed more practice.

No. He would have to face the fate the priests intended for him. Maybe once he knew more, he could find a way to escape, or end his own life.

After another cold night in the cell, the Daghilch arrived. Aldan knew little of the priestly structure, but he understood enough to know the Daghilch had authority over many temples in clanholds throughout this region.

When the door to the cell opened, Aldan didn't move. The guard stepped aside and let the Daghilch enter. The two local priests remained outside the door.

The Daghilch stared at Aldan from dark eyes under pronounced brows. The religious leader was a tall, thin man wearing red robes much like the other priests. He wore a purple sash across his chest, the only indication of a differing rank. Other than his haircut, that is. The regular blood-priests shaved the sides of their heads, leaving only a circle of short hair on top, presumably in the shape of the moon. The Daghilch's hair, Aldan noted when he bent lower, had been cut into a half-circle, leaving the front half of his head bald.

"Stand up, boy," the Daghilch said in a coarse voice.

Aldan's first inclination was to insist he wasn't a boy, but he stood nonetheless.

"Bring a bowl of blood," the Daghilch instructed the priests.

The priests' mouths dropped open. "Sir, he could taint it!"

The Daghilch's eyes rolled before he turned back to them. "Of course he could. I must confirm the Taint. It is the law."

"You've seen the already tainted blood. Surely—"

"I have only your word for its origin," the Daghilch interrupted. "Bring me a bowl. NV blood, if you must."

One of the priests hurried away. For the first time, Aldan experienced a glimmer of hope. If the power or Taint didn't work again, would they let him go? Maybe it only happened the one time. Maybe...

"Tell me of your heritage, boy," the Daghilch said.

Aldan blinked. "My... what? Sir?"

The Daghilch sighed. "Your bloodline. Are you pure Tokuur clan?"

"Oh. Yes, sir. As far back as I know, sir."

He nodded as if he'd expected the answer.

A moment later, the priest returned, holding a small bowl of blood. The Daghilch took it, murmured something Aldan couldn't hear, and then held it out toward him. "Show me!" the Daghilch commanded.

Aldan looked at the blood. "I, I don't know what to do. What happened at the ceremony was… it was an accident." His father had called it that, anyway.

"Hold your hand out over the blood," the cleric instructed.

Aldan licked his lips and obeyed.

"Now. Look at the blood. Imagine it burning, on fire." The Daghilch's voice grew sterner with each phrase. "You want it to burn. You want to ignite it. Burn it. Taint it. Let the power flow through you!"

Aldan gasped as the burning sensation exploded behind his eyes again. In the same moment, a bubble burst from the blood, as if it were boiling. The Daghilch drew the bowl back in a swift move and handed it to one of the priests, both of whom gasped and muttered about Aldan's eyes.

The burning sensation faded as quickly as it had come. Aldan blinked. It hadn't hurt him that time. He didn't lose consciousness. What did it all mean? Only then did he realize he'd condemned himself. He looked up at the Daghilch.

The cleric nodded. "We have our confirmation. He has the Taint."

"What is to be done?" one of the priests asked.

The Daghilch dipped his thumb in the tainted blood. He reached forward and drew a line across Aldan's forehead with it. Fear kept Aldan from resisting.

"In the holy and hidden name of the goddess of the moon," the Daghilch intoned, "I banish you from clan Tokuur. I remove you from the clan's bloodline. You have no part in this or any other clan beneath the moon's gaze. You have no relations, no family. I strip you of your name."

"My name?" Aldan exclaimed.

"Should anyone need to refer to you from this day onward, it shall be as Clanless. Should the goddess have mercy on you, and you attain adulthood, you are forbidden from marriage or the fathering of children. Let it be known throughout the Empire and under the moon's gaze."

"Let it be known," the other priests echoed.

"He must be marked," the Daghilch proclaimed. "See to it, and then have him ready for departure. I have other duties." He handed the bowl of tainted blood to the nearest guard and turned to go.

"But… but I heard the goddess!" Aldan cried. "Surely that has to mean something!"

The Daghilch paused. "What do you mean?"

"She spoke to me. At the ceremony!"

"A blasphemous claim," one of the priests hastened to put in. "We did not wish to trouble you with it, sir."

The Daghilch held up a hand. "I must investigate all such claims. Tell me, Clanless, what did she say to you?"

Aldan swallowed. "She said 'well done.'"

"After you used the Taint?"

"I guess so. I didn't know what was happening."

"What did she sound like?"

Aldan shifted and tried to remember. "I, I don't know. Like a woman. Young. Not old."

"The goddess has many voices," the Daghilch murmured. "But her voice can be discerned by what she says, and she would not say such a thing." He shook his head and walked from the cell.

"What will be done with him?" a priest asked as the door began to shut on Aldan's last hopes.

"Brand him. He is for the arena."

SUMMONED

Clanless sank deeper into the bath and let his muscles relax. The fight had not been a difficult one, but life and death still danced a delicate balance in each battle. He could never take anything for granted.

Only one fight left. Only one more man he must kill. And then he would be free. After eight years, he would finally be a free man. He would still be without a clan, but at least he could leave all of this behind.

Hagh and Sugh entered the bath, grimy and sweaty from their own battle. They stripped off their gear and climbed down into the water, sighing with pleasure.

"Good to fight early," Sugh declared. "We can have a good night in the city still."

"May as well," Hagh said. "Big fights tomorrow night for the festival."

Sugh ducked under and shook the water from his bare head. "Except for Clanless here. He gets the easy one."

Clanless grunted in response. He'd seen Daviland before, and Sugh might be right. He wasn't an arena warrior. A leader of men? Certainly. Courageous? Sure. But when it came to wielding a weapon, the so-called hero didn't appear to have much experience.

"I wouldn't be so sure," Hagh said. He coughed and splashed water in his face.

"Why, Hagh?" Clanless stared up at the ceiling. "Why do you call him the Chosen One? What does that even mean?"

"They say he's destined to overthrow the Hawk King, to bring freedom from the blood-priests. Chosen by the goddess herself, some say."

"You're moonbent." Sugh snorted and laughed. "How's he gonna overthrow the king when he's a prisoner?"

Hagh shook his head again. "I'm telling you: he's not like other rebels we've had. He's got a following. The entire city's on edge right now."

"The king wants him killed in front of everyone," Clanless said. "The only risk is if any of his followers start something after he's dead." He stood up and reached for a towel. "And by then, I won't care."

"You won't care if the whole Empire comes crashing down?"

"Why should I?" Clanless wiped the water from his back. "What has the Empire ever done for me?"

"If Suirel has his way, everything will fall," Hagh said, his eyebrows narrowed.

"What is that?" Sugh asked. "I don't know anything about this other moon, this… chaos moon."

"You're too young," Hagh said. "You don't remember the last time it appeared."

"But you do?"

"I was a child." Hagh stared down into the bath waters. "When the second moon appeared, it started a winter like no other."

"High Winter is always horrible," Clanless protested.

"Not like then. The winds… the winds were much worse." Hagh lifted his face, but didn't look at either of them. "And it would deceive us. One day would be warm; the next frozen. You never knew whether it was safe to go outside." He took a deep breath. "Once every thirty years, Suirel comes. The Sar Empire is fortunate to survive his coming."

Neither Clanless nor Sugh said anything else. Hagh didn't often speak this way. It was disconcerting.

Yesun the young attendant ran into the bath. He glanced at the other fighters, then approached Clanless. "The Hawk King requests your presence at once, Clanless."

"Maybe the Empire wants to do something for you now!" Sugh called.

Clanless tossed the towel at him. "Let me get dressed, and we can go," he told the boy.

BRANDED & SOLD

Then

The branding hurt more than anything Aldan had experienced thus far. The blood-priests used a hot iron to burn some kind of mark into his right shoulder. Once he stopped screaming, he tried to turn his head to look down at it.

"It is the half moon without a clan symbol," one of the priests told him. "It shows that you have no clan."

"Leave it exposed to the air," the other said. "It will heal quicker. From this day forward, in fact, you must never wear a sleeve on that arm. If you are caught hiding the brand, your life is forfeit."

"What about when it's cold?" Aldan continued to arch his neck to view the brand.

"Never," the priest repeated.

The next step baffled him. A priest removed the bandage from his arm and opened the cut again. He squeezed some of Aldan's blood onto a thin sheet of metal no larger than a hand's width. The other priest returned with the hot iron and held it at ready. Aldan eyed it and swallowed. They wouldn't brand his other shoulder too, would they?

"Do not use the Taint!" the first priest warned. "You would only hurt yourself now."

Even if he could, Aldan didn't want to use it again. The power confused and repulsed him.

"Place your hand here," the priest instructed, holding out the metal plate.

"Why?"

"Do as you are told," the other said, gesturing one of the guards to step closer.

Aldan placed his hand on the metal sheet, feeling his own blood. The priest placed his own hand on the opposite side of the sheet.

"Repeat after me," instructed the other priest. "This is my bloodbond."

"My what? Why would I say that?"

"You have two choices here," said the priest holding the metal sheet with him. "You either give me your bloodbond, letting you live as an arena slave, or"—he nodded toward the guard—"you die here and now."

The guard adjusted his grip on his mace. Aldan shivered. Beaten to death like that would be horrible. "This is my bloodbond," he said.

"My blood is the pledge," the priest said.

"My blood is the pledge."

Aldan continued, swallowing hard as he repeated the words that followed: "I will serve the owner of this bloodbond until death takes me, or I purchase my freedom. Should I break this oath, may the goddess burn my blood and that of all those I love. Let it be known throughout the Empire and under the moon's gaze."

"It is done." The priest pulled the metal sheet away from Aldan. The other priest impressed the hot iron's tip against it. The blood sizzled beneath its burning point.

"How do I do that?" Aldan asked. "Purchase my freedom?"

The priests glanced at one another. "It is possible for someone to earn enough to buy their bloodbond for themselves," one admitted. "But it is almost never done."

"Why not?"

He leveled Aldan with a smug look. "Because no one lives long enough to earn that much."

((((●))))

The priests sent Aldan back to the cell under guard while they readied the transportation for him and the Daghilch. He held out hope that Borde or someone else from his family would come again, at least to say farewell.

No one did.

One thing had changed in the cell. The guard apparently hadn't wanted to deal with the bowl of tainted blood, so he left it on the floor. Aldan sat down, picked it up and stared at the red liquid. How was this tainted? It still looked like blood. Yet somehow, the Daghilch immediately knew it had been changed. During both uses of the Taint, Aldan believed the blood changed; somehow, he could sense it in a vague way. But it looked no different. He swirled it around the bowl. It moved like any other liquid.

He set the bowl back onto the floor. The blood stirred. Aldan blinked. It had stirred after he set it down, while the bowl wasn't moving.

"Aldan…" whispered a female voice.

At first, he thought it came from outside the cell. "Borde?" He got to his feet.

"No. Over here."

He turned back and looked around. Only the bowl of blood… which moved again. Aldan dropped down beside it.

"Is it you?" he whispered.

"Stay… strong." He knew the voice now: the same one he'd heard at the ceremony. The goddess spoke through the blood? Considering her demands for sacrifice, it made sense. "We have much to do," the voice said, fading with the last word.

"What—?" Aldan began.

At that moment, the cell door flew open again. "Come!" the guard demanded.

"But… the goddess. She—"

"Now! The Daghilch is tired of waiting!"

Aldan got to his feet and followed the guard outside the temple. The blood-priests waited beside the Daghilch's wagon. The Daghilch himself gave Aldan a brief glance and climbed aboard. The two-wheeled wagon, pulled by a single ox, included a small enclosed space, large enough for a single person. The Daghilch entered and closed a curtain behind him. One of the guards climbed up to a narrow space in front of the enclosure. He took the reigns, then patted a small spot beside him. "Here," he said to Aldan.

Aldan took a quick look around the clanhold. Aside from a few young women running errands, he saw no one else outside of their homes. Most of the men would be in the fields by now. Seeing no other options, Aldan climbed up onto the narrow seat.

The guard flicked the reins, and the ox started forward. The wagon turned and circled the interior of the clanhold. Aldan watched for his family home on the right. The driver could have taken the wagon around the other side and left him without any last view of home. Either he didn't know, or… it was a mercy.

Aldan always thought oxen were slow-moving animals, but this one got the wagon moving faster than he liked. His family home could be seen ahead on the right. He lifted himself up in the seat to see better.

"Don't try anything," the guard growled.

Wild thoughts did enter Aldan's mind: thoughts of jumping free of the wagon and running away. But what good would that do? His family couldn't shelter him from the priests and their guards, and they would all suffer for his sin. Once outside the clanhold, maybe he could run away into the wilderness. He could live like Otkerel the Wild in the stories Father used to tell him every evening. But Okterel had friends to help him survive against the threats of wild animals, barbarians, and beastmen—not to mention High Winter! He also had a wolfhound at his side. And a magical sword. Aldan had nothing… except the Taint, the power that made bad things happen to him.

As the wagon passed by the home he'd known his entire life, Borde emerged from the house, holding little Ot. Both of them waved to him. He lifted a hand to wave back as a deep, wrenching tightness filled his stomach. It moved rapidly up into his throat. His eyes welled up.

He twisted around in his seat to keep watching the girls. His father and uncle would be out in the field, but why didn't Mother come out? Was she too sick? Too heartbroken? Or had she already given up and forgotten him?

Borde waved harder. She shouted something, but Aldan couldn't hear it. He started to stand up, to call something back to her.

"Sit down!" The guard grabbed his shirt and pulled. Aldan plopped back onto the seat. He craned his neck to look back at Borde as she lifted Ot on to her shoulders. The tiny child waved from her new perch. Aldan couldn't hear it, but he knew she laughed with delight from her high position. She'd always laughed when he lifted her in the same way.

The wagon moved on, rolling through the gates of the clanhold and out. Aldan straightened in his seat and looked ahead. For the next couple of miles, at least, they would be passing through the fields belonging to the clanhold. Already, he could see the men of the hold moving here and there, doing the farming they'd done for hundreds of years. Somewhere out there, he might see the men of his family. But even if he saw Father, what good would it do?

His family was gone. He was going to the arena, whatever that meant. He had a vague recollection of his uncle talking about witnessing a fight between great warriors in an arena once. Maybe he would become one of those warriors.

Or maybe he should still run away into the wilderness. He could cut through the fields right now, there to the left, where no one worked. The wagon would not be able to pursue him. He glanced at the guard. He could outrun this man. He was sure of it.

The curtain behind him swept open and the Daghilch leaned out. "Did the priests bother to explain the bloodbond to you?" he asked. "Do you know what it is?"

Aldan shook his head. "No, sir."

The Daghilch held up the metal sheet from the odd ceremony. "Whoever holds this plate is your master. The master decides how much you are allowed to do and where you are allowed to go. Should you violate his will in any way, the blood-magic will stop you."

Aldan wrinkled his brow. What did that mean?

"For example," the Daghilch went on, "I desire that you stay with this wagon until our journey reaches its end. If you were to try to run away from it… it would not go well for you. Your very blood would fight against you, constraining your arms and legs, forbidding you to move." He cocked his head and raised an eyebrow. "Do you require an example?"

Aldan shook his head. The Daghilch nodded and closed the curtain again, muttering something about the lack of imperial roads.

The wagon moved on, soon leaving the fields behind and taking Aldan beyond the furthest point he'd ever traveled. He shifted on the hard wooden seat. "How far are we traveling?" he asked either of his companions.

"The trip will take two days," the Daghilch said from behind the curtain.

"Where are we going?"

"To the city of Rochinbal, where arena fighters are trained." The Daghilch pulled the curtain aside a few inches to peek back out. "We will be very curious to see how long you survive."

☾☾☾●☽☽☽

On the evening of the second day, as the sun gave up the night sky to its steady guardian, the moon, the slow-moving wagon reached the outskirts of Rochinbal. Aldan was curious to see an actual city for the first time in his life, but the wagon did not enter it. Instead, they turned aside before reaching the city gates and followed a rougher road toward a large structure set about half a mile from the city itself. Aldan watched the tall walls of Rochinbal pass behind them, so much higher than the back walls of the clanhold. No haphazard filling in with random rocks and dirt here. These walls were made of carefully-interlocking quarried stone. The people inside the city would be well protected when High Winter came with its winds. If he'd been alone, Aldan would have spent far too long marveling at the wall construction.

He tore his attention away and looked ahead to their apparent destination. It appeared to be an enormous circular building, larger than his entire clanhold. He glanced back at the city. Surely, it was larger still, but he couldn't see where it ended. How many people must live inside such a thing?

Aldan could tell little about the circular building. The bottom half appeared to be made of stone, much like the city walls, while a wooden plank structure made up the top half. If he hadn't just seen the city, Aldan would have thought it the tallest construct he'd ever seen.

The wagon came to a stop at the base of the building. A pair of metal doors awaited them, set into the stone. Combined, the doors were wider than the entire front of Aldan's old home.

The Daghilch opened his curtain. "Let's get this over with and return to the city. I am in desperate need of a bath and a real bed."

The guard grunted and hopped down. Aldan followed him. He staggered a little, his muscles cramped from the hours of riding. The Daghilch followed them with more deliberate movements, grumbling. At least he'd had cushions for his seat and a shade from the sun. Why was he complaining?

The cleric led the way along a cut stone pathway to the doors. As they approached, the last light of the retreating sun illuminated faded etchings in the metal. Each door depicted a warrior of some kind, mouth open in a shout, weapon raised and shield at ready. One held aloft a mace, while the other wielded a sword. Grime and weather had taken their toll on the etchings, rendering them barely visible. They must have been spectacular when first engraved.

The Daghilch nodded his head toward the door. The guard stepped past and rapped on it with his mace. The clank of metal on metal reverberated. Aldan heard an echo somewhere within.

"Again," the Daghilch ordered. The guard repeated his knock and stepped back.

They waited for what seemed at least ten minutes. The sun continued to retreat, almost disappearing over the distant hills. The Daghilch tapped his foot impatiently. Aldan ran a finger over the brand on his shoulder, convinced he felt blisters forming.

At last, they heard sounds behind the doors. A pair of clanks were followed by a grunt, and the door on the right swung outward. A hunched man draped in heavy clothes held up a lantern. "It's late," he said in a rasping voice.

"We are well aware of the time," the Daghilch responded. "Take us to Kan at once."

"He won't like it." The hunched man turned away, leaving them to follow. The Daghilch gave an exasperated sigh and went after him. Aldan glanced at the guard, who motioned him in.

The hunched man's lantern didn't reveal much about their surroundings. They walked along a hallway as wide as the double doors for a little while before turning off at an open door leading into a smaller hall. After following it for at least a hundred yards, the hunched man turned left and descended a stair to a solid wooden door. He knocked once. "New one!" he called, followed by several coughs from the effort of raising his voice.

This door opened much sooner, letting light from the inside spill out around the silhouette of a large, shirtless man. "Daghilch!" he exclaimed. "What do you have for me now?" He stepped out of the room, and Aldan got a good look at him.

For his entire life, Aldan had been around strong men, men who did backbreaking labor in the fields all day every day. His father and uncle impressed him with feats of strength on a regular basis. With this man, Kan, Aldan saw a new type of strength. His muscles, no less defined than Father's, might be a bit smaller, but tighter somehow. And there were more of them, spreading across both arms and chest, all the way down to his firm stomach.

"Kan," the Daghilch said. He offered the bloodbond plate. "Here is another one for you. My blood is already there. Let it be known throughout the Empire and under the moon's gaze."

Kan took the plate. He took a dagger from his belt and cut his palm. He smeared some of his own blood on the plate and declared, "I take ownership of this bloodbond." Setting it aside, he turned his attention to Aldan. His eyes swept over the boy's frame, lingering briefly on the brand. "Farmer stock, I see, from one of the outer clanholds. Excellent. They breed them much tougher out there. Better than the city brats you usually bring me. Is he Tokuur or Ghamkiin?"

"Clanless now, as you can see. But I believe he can serve you well, with the proper treatment."

Kan snorted. "No doubt. What horrendous crime did you commit, boy?"

Aldan opened his mouth, but the Daghilch answered first: "It is irrelevant and immaterial. This is a new beginning."

"A new beginning? Aye, it's that all right." Kan grinned, revealing two missing teeth in his lower jaw. "Just a moment." He entered his room and returned only a moment later with a cloth bag about the size of Aldan's head. He tossed it to the Daghilch, who caught it with an annoyed grunt. Something inside clinked together with a tone Aldan didn't recognize.

"Your timing is impeccable, Daghilch," Kan said. "My new class starts tomorrow. All of the other boys arrived within the past week. It will be a full class with this one now."

"I am gratified to hear it." The Daghilch's tone implied much less interest than his words. "We'll be going now." He turned on his heel, then paused a moment. His head turned to take one last look at Aldan. "Another time, Clanless," he said in a low voice. He and the guard went up the stairs and hurried away.

"Well, well." Kan turned back to Aldan. "Clanless, eh? Do you have any idea what you're in for here, boy?"

"No, sir."

"Ha! 'No, sir.' Very good. Show me that respect on a regular basis, and we might just get along. Nukai! Take him to the bunk room. Try not to wake the other boys. I told them to get their sleep tonight." He nodded to Aldan. "You'd better do so as well. We start when the sun's pursuit begins."

"Yes, sir."

Kan chuckled and waved them off. Nukai, the hunched man, headed back up the stairs, and Aldan followed him. They walked down several more halls, taking a couple of turns. At one point, they passed a wide entrance on the left that seemed to lead out into some kind of enormous open space under the twilight. Aldan paused to look, but Nukai grunted for him to keep moving.

Aldan hurried to catch up. "Why do you wear so many clothes?" he asked. "Does it get very cold here?"

Nukai snorted. "I'm a cold person. Hurry up."

Aldan wasn't sure why he'd said to hurry, as the hunched man moved with a shuffling gait his baby sister could have outrun. A few minutes later, Nukai opened another door, then stood to the side.

"Take the first empty bed you find," he said. "Good luck to you."

Aldan stepped into the dark room. As his eyes adjusted, he saw a row of crude beds along the wall of a rectangular room. Most of the beds were occupied, but the third one from the door looked empty. With a last glance at his guide, Aldan tip-toed to the bed and climbed in. Nukai shut the door, taking the dim light of the lantern with him.

Whispers came from some of the other beds. Aldan ignored them and pulled a rough coverlet over himself. It wasn't much of a bed, but it was better than the ground he'd slept on the night before. Of course, his bed back home had been much nicer.

Thinking of home brought a lump to his throat. He would never hear little Ot stirring in her bed again, or crying for Mother. He would never hear the low tones of his parents speaking in the next room, sometimes serious, sometimes laughing. Instead, he heard the whispers of strangers, wondering who he was and why he'd come so late.

Aldan let a few tears slip out and roll down his cheeks to the coarse cloth pillow. He pulled the coverlet tighter and swallowed against the lump. "Lock it away," he told himself. He knew how to do that, how to take something painful and hide it in a dark place in his mind. He'd done it before. But did he want to forget the past three days? Maybe he should hold on to it for now. "A new beginning," the Daghilch had said. Tomorrow, he'd find out what that meant.

FOR THE ARENA

Then

Aldan opened his eyes to find another set of brown eyes staring down at him. "He's awake!" shouted the mouth below those eyes. Aldan pulled himself up, blinking. The other boy backed away from his bed to join two others who waited at the end.

"Who are you?" asked the boy who'd been staring at him. He stood a few inches taller than the other boys, who all appeared around the same age and size as Aldan.

"Ask the important question, idiot." The second boy cocked his head. Though smaller than the first, he held himself with a strength and readiness that demanded attention. He pointed at Aldan's shoulder. "What did you do to get that?"

Aldan got to his feet. He needed to relieve himself, but he didn't want to start out wrong with these boys. "It was an accident," he said.

"What kind of accident?"

A fourth boy, smiling and slightly overweight, pushed past the first three, stumbling a little. He held out his hand toward Aldan. "I'm Tunt. Ignore those guys. You don't have to tell them anything you don't want to."

Aldan reached out his hand and took Tunt's. The other boy's hand was surprisingly soft, not the hands of someone who'd grown up working the fields. "I'm Al—"

"He doesn't have a name," the second boy interrupted. "He's Clanless."

"Oh, silence yourself, Yeltek," Tunt said, still with a friendly tone. "Let the boy speak."

"Assembly on the sands in five minutes!" someone called from the doorway. Yeltek and his two companions scrambled past each other to run out.

"Kan doesn't like it if we're late," Tunt explained. "Do you know where to go?"

"I don't know anything." Aldan looked around the bunk room. "I got here when it was dark."

"Come on." Tunt beckoned, heading toward the door.

"Wait." Aldan caught up with him. "Where do I go to, uh, pee?"

Tunt's smile never faded. "Right! That's kind of important too. I'll show you on the way. We'd better hurry!"

After stopping at the appropriate location—which Tunt called a "latrine"—the two boys hastened on their way to the assembly. Aldan followed Tunt through the wide entrance into the open space he'd noted the night before. He slowed as they entered, staring.

They stepped out onto sand, coarse and solid, packed tight without any wind to disturb it. From the doorway they entered, walls curved out on either side, encircling an empty space several hundred feet in diameter. The walls reached about ten feet high, while behind and above them, angling upward, sat row after row of benches. All of the people of Aldan's clanhold could sit on those benches and not even take up half of it!

"Clanless over there has never seen an arena!" someone said, followed by laughter.

Aldan brought his view back to the sands. Counting Tunt, there were seven other boys waiting in a loose group. Tunt pointed to them and spouted off their names: "You've already met Yeltek. The loud one with him is Duurald. The other is Uyan." Tunt pointed to the smallest of the boys, who gave a short wave. "That's Jik over there. The tall, brooding one in the back is Shool Baina, but we all call him Bain." The seventh boy, larger even than Duurald, stood apart from the others, moving his arms and legs in some sort of exercise technique that bewildered Aldan. "That's Nerlesen. We don't know what he's doing either."

"Thank you. I'm Aldan."

"You're Clanless," Yeltek said. "You don't have a name."

"How could he not have a name?" Tunt snorted.

"It's what happens when you're banished," Yeltek sneered. "They do it so no one will know what clan you came from."

"Names don't tell your clan," Jik said with a wrinkled brow.

"Of course they do," Yeltek shot back. "Every clan uses different types of names. You're obviously from clan Zavi with a name like Jik."

"How do you know that?" Uyan asked, scratching the side of his head.

Yeltek rolled his eyes. "Because I've studied. I had an education, not like most of you sand-eaters."

"What's a sand-eater?" Jik asked.

Before Yeltek could answer, the tall figure of Kan strode out onto the sand behind Aldan. "Line up! Facing me!" he barked.

The eight boys obeyed, managing to maneuver themselves into the semblance of a straight line. Aldan found himself on the end, next to Tunt. He wondered how many of these boys were "city brats" like Kan had complained about. From his quick looks, at least half of them would have been fine working in the clanhold fields. The others, like Tunt especially… not so much.

Kan walked down the line, his eyes examining each one of them. "With the arrival of Clanless here, we have our full class," he announced. "And so your training begins today. My job is to make the eight of you into arena fighters, skilled enough to survive and dramatic enough to entertain."

He reached inside his cloak and pulled out a cloth bag. When he held it up, they all heard metal-on-metal clanking. "This is your only reminder. I hold your bloodbonds. All of you. According to the laws of the Empire, that makes you my slaves."

Aldan shifted his feet. His shoulder burned. Somewhere down the line, one of the other boys sniffed.

Kan put the bag away. "Let me explain what that means for you practically." He continued to walk back and forth as he spoke. "You belong to me, but I am not interested in the details of your life outside this place. Right here and right now, you are here to be trained. So you will do whatever I tell you to do, and when I tell you to do it. Please me, and you will be awarded some freedoms. Annoy me—or worse, disappoint me—and your lives will be absolutely miserable. Until such day as I sell your bloodbond to the master of another arena, this is how it will be. And should you gain any ideas because of your ignorance, let me relieve you of it: if you try to kill me to get this bloodbond back, you will fail. As time progresses, and you gain strength, you may even think to gang up against me. You will still fail. Even if, by some miracle, you kill me, the bloodbond is both magical and sacred. You cannot escape it."

Jik started to lift his hand, but stopped.

"Do you have a question, Jik?" Kan asked, stopping his walk.

"Uh, yes, sir. If we are to be arena fighters, sir…" He glanced at the boys around him. "Are we going to kill each other?"

At least two of the boys laughed, but Aldan couldn't tell which ones from his position.

"That's a good question. I don't mind questions if they are good questions. Not foolish ones," Kan answered, his tone silencing the laughter. He looked up and down the line. "The answer is no. You will train with each other, and you will train against each other. But it would be absolutely pointless for me to train boys who are going to kill each other. By the time the class was over, I'd have only one or two left!" He raised a finger. "But do not take this lightly. You will be called on to kill. Just not any of the seven people in line with you right now. When I am through with you, another class from a different trainer will arrive. You will be pitted against each other in a series of fights right here"—he waved at the seats above—"to entertain the good people of Rochinbal and surrounding areas. And those fights will be to the death. Sixteen boys will fight that day, and eight will become true arena fighters. The other eight will be buried in the ditch behind the arena."

He paused to let that sink in.

"If you follow my training, none of you will end up there." Kan tapped his own chest. "I am Kan. And I am the greatest arena trainer in the Empire. Listen to me, boys, and all eight of you will live."

"How many lived in your last class, sir?" someone asked. Aldan thought it was the biggest one: Nerlesen?

Kan studied him with a stern gaze and didn't answer for a few moments. The boys shifted their feet and glanced at each other. "Four boys in my last class failed to observe my instruction," he said at last. "Four men went on to become the latest heroes of the arena."

Aldan inched forward a little and took a quick look down the line. He'd just met these seven, and now Kan said four of them would probably be dead whenever this ended?

"You'll notice that I call you 'boys.'" Kan resumed his walk. "I know that most of you have already gone through the ceremony at your temples, shedding a few drops of your blood for the goddess. Let me be clear: that doesn't make you a man. Not in my eyes. You're not a man to me until you kill someone on these sands. Do you understand?"

The boys murmured quiet affirmation.

"How long is the training, sir?" Nerlesen asked. "How long do we have to prepare?"

Kan nodded at another good question. "You will be under my instruction from now until the end of High Spring. Nine months."

"Like a woman with child!" Duurald exclaimed.

Kan turned his head with a look that made Duurald cower.

"How can you be so big and yet possess so little brain?" Shool Baina asked in a low tone.

"Yes, Duurald," Kan said in a condescending voice. "I am carrying you all like a heavy whore, burdened with the unwanted consequences of her employment. I will carry you around until it's time to fart you out onto this sand in a spew of blood and water. Any other foolish observations?"

No one dared speak. The reference to a woman with child made Aldan's chest ache with thoughts of his own mother. Before he finished this training, she would have a new child to take his place. Would it be another boy or a sister for little Ot?

"Sands." Kan said it as if it were a curse. "Let's see if any of you have any brain. I'll ask you a question. What is the most important thing in the arena?"

"Strength!" Duurald answered immediately.

"Wrong."

"Weapon skill," Yeltek said.

"Also wrong."

No one else said anything.

"Nothing?" Kan strode down the line. "None of you? No brains in the entire lot?"

"Speed," Shool Baina said at the same time Aldan whispered, "Blood."

Kan stopped. "Who said that?"

"I said 'speed,'" Shool Baina repeated.

"Not that, but I'll come back to it." Kan's eyes darted along the line.

"Blood." Aldan lifted his hand a few inches.

"Clanless is exactly right." Kan made a show of clapping his hands. "Blood is power. Blood is precious. Blood is life. You've been taught these things since you were infants."

Aldan was sure all the boys noticed that Kan had reversed the order of the incantation. But at this point, none of them dared point it out.

Kan smacked his fist against his own chest. "Never lose an awareness of the blood beneath your flesh. Feel it pound within your chest! It is your life force. Your source of power. Blood is everything!" He pointed at them all. "In the arena, something changes in your blood. It grows hot when you fight. Let it! Let it sweep over you in those moments of danger. You will find your senses sharpened. Sometimes, even time itself seems to slow down. I call it the bloodrush. You'll understand it soon enough."

Kan lowered his hands. "But that is a lesson that will take time to learn. For now, we turn to the second-most important thing in the arena: speed."

One or two boys chuckled.

"Behind you, on the far side of the arena, is another set of doors. I want all of you to run to those doors, touch them, and run back here as fast as you can. Now. Go!"

Aldan spun around and started moving before his eyes located the doors. The other boys, with varying reaction speeds, joined him. All eight sprinted across the sand with whoops and challenges to each other. Aldan discovered running on packed sand to be different from the earth he knew. His felt and leather boots, so practical for the rocky ground around his clanhold, dragged at his feet. Some of the other boys wore heavier boots, which proved even worse. Aldan slowed long enough to yank off the boots and renewed his pace with bare feet. His toes dug into the coarse surface with each stride, propelling him faster than most of the others.

Nerlesen slapped his hand against the far doors first, followed by Yeltek and Aldan. The three leaders passed by the other five on the way back. Tunt trailed well behind the rest.

Aldan never saw the trip. One moment, he was matching Yeltek stride-for-stride. The next, he slammed both palms into the sand, tearing skin from both, but narrowly avoiding doing the same with his face. Laughter burned his ears as the others passed him. Tunt slowed, but Aldan scrambled back to his feet and raced after the others. Heat flushed his face. He pushed himself to the limit and made it back to Kan in fifth place.

Kan waited until all the boys made it back, then clapped his hands again. "Some of you weren't horrible. That's good. We'll work on it. You'll be running door-to-door every day, many times. Get used to it."

Many times? Some of the boys groaned. Most were bent over, hands on knees, panting.

"Clanless is the only one to discover another secret of the arena."

Aldan looked up.

"Shoes are unnecessary here." Kan shook his head. "In most cases, they slow you down. And if you're slow… you're dead."

Yeltek and his two friends glared at Aldan.

"But he also left his shoes in the middle of my clean arena." Kan pointed. "Go get them."

Aldan turned and started jogging to the boots.

"Run!" Kan bellowed.

Aldan sprinted to the boots, grabbed them up in his bloody hands, and raced back.

"Some of you also discovered the joys of competition," Kan went on as Aldan returned. "That's good. Competition is good. Push each other. Fight each other for every inch. Any one of you not trying to beat out all of the others is not doing his best."

Someone's stomach growled loud enough for all to hear. Yeltek shoved Uyan. "It wasn't me," he protested.

"Ah yes, breakfast," Kan said. "I agree. Breakfast is waiting for you." The boys straightened with hopeful expressions. Kan raised a finger again. "After you run door-to-door again."

((((●))))

Breakfast—which was far too short—took place in a common room not far from the bunk room. Aldan wanted to talk more with some of the others, but Kan interrupted. The boys barely had time to scarf down the food before their master ordered them back out to the arena.

Nukai, still wearing multiple furs over his regular clothing, pushed a rolling rack of weaponry out onto the sand. The hunched man muttered to himself and retreated to the wall as Kan approached. The boys formed themselves into the semblance of a line, whispering to each other about the weapons.

Kan gestured to the rack. "Before we begin the more serious aspects of your training, I wanted to show you some of the common arena weapons." He took a mace from the rack and tapped the end against his palm. "The mace is by far the most common weapon throughout the Empire, not just in the arena. Why is that, do you suppose?"

"It's honorable," Yeltek said at once.

"It is honorable," Kan agreed. "But again: why?"

None of the boys answered. Aldan had a vague idea, but kept his thoughts to himself.

Kan took a short sword from the rack and held it in his other hand. "What is the difference between these two weapons?"

"One of them cuts, and the other, uh, bashes?" Duurald answered.

"Close enough." Kan lifted the sword. "Swords and other bladed weapons are designed to slash and stab. In short, they shed blood. A lot of blood." He lifted the mace. "Maces and other bludgeoning weapons break bones and do damage without a lot of blood. This is the difference between honorable and dishonorable fighting."

"Because… the blood-priests get more blood from someone killed by a mace," Shool Baina said.

"Exactly. And… most of the time. Maces can still draw blood, of course. But they're not designed to do it, like a sword."

Aldan didn't want to draw more attention to himself, but the question had to be asked: "Why do we need to fight honorably if we're slaves?"

The other boys all stared at him with wide eyes… except Shool Baina, who gave him a knowing smile and nod.

Kan pursed his lips and put the weapons away. When he turned back, he gave them all a grim smile before turning his attention to Aldan. "We will all train to fight in both ways. When your training is complete, you will be equally proficient with the sword and mace." He frowned and looked over them all. "Let me be absolutely clear to you all. I am charged with training arena fighters. Some of you will likely die in your first fight. Some of you will go on for a year or so and then die. Some—a very few—will keep fighting for years to come. If you succeed above all odds, and end up fighting as one of the Hawk King's Dohor, his elite personal fighters, then you may even have the opportunity to buy your freedom."

Aldan sucked in a breath through his nose. The Daghilch said no one survived that long. Yet here was hope.

Kan shook his head. "In all my days, I've never seen anyone do that. Not only would it require being the best of the best, it would require careful financial control, something arena fighters are not known for. And so, I prepare you to fight either way, so that you can survive the longest. It is your choice how you fight. But if you want to reach the top, angering the blood-priests is not the best method."

For a moment, Aldan thought he saw a vulnerability in Kan. What must it be like to train groups of boys over and over and watch half of them die? What kind of man could do that without emotion?

Then Kan straightened, and his face grew stern. "And I get paid based on how far you go. So it's in my best interests to see you succeed!" He pointed a finger at them, drawing it down the line. "Do not think that I am your friend! Within one week, you will all be cursing my name and wishing the worst death you can imagine on me! You will hate me with greater hatred than you can imagine right now." He lowered his arm. "And that's good. Let that hated drive you. Beat my training. Prove to me that you can fight." He shrugged. "Or die. Your choice."

Kan turned back to the weapon rack and took up a round piece of metal with a handle on one side. "This is a buckler," he announced, turning to face them again. "It's your defense. We could equip you with larger shields, to protect more of your soft bodies, but we don't. Large shields only slow you down. And as I told you this morning, speed is the most important way to keep yourself alive in the arena."

He removed the buckler from his hand and tossed it to Nerlesen. "There are sixteen bucklers here. Everyone, take two."

Aldan joined the others around the rack. He took one buckler and slipped it over his left hand. The weight was significant, but not more than he expected. He picked up a second one with his right hand and stepped back from the others. He swung both arms back and forth, testing.

"Feel that weight?" Kan asked. The boys murmured in agreement.

"Good. Keep them on. Now run door-to-door again. Go!"

ᛟᛟᛟᛟ●ᛞᛞᛞᛞ

That night, Aldan struggled with his thoughts. After a full day with Kan and the other boys, his perspective had changed. Through all of Kan's demands, it quickly became apparent which of the boys were well positioned to succeed, and which ones weren't. Faster than most of the other boys, but about average on strength, Aldan found himself in the middle of the pack. He might be able to survive all of this. But did he want to?

The day had rushed past from one grueling exercise to another. But at night, in his bed again, the reality of his new life overwhelmed him. He wasn't the only one, either. He heard sniffling coming from at least one other bed, until Yeltek griped out loud about the noise.

From the ceremony in the temple until now, Aldan had struggled to accept the reality of all this. It wasn't some horrible dream. He would never see his family again. And even if he could find the strength he needed to survive Kan's training, he would probably die in his first battle. The Taint would see to that. What was the point of even trying? No one would mourn him if he died. No one would even care. The blood-priests who sent him here would probably breathe a sigh of relief at the news.

He should fight dishonorably. Use a sword instead of a mace. What difference would it make? If he was going to die, why do it in a way that pleased the blood-priests who put him here? The face of the Daghilch filled his mind.

In the dark, one of the larger boys got up from his bed and stumbled near Aldan's. Fear seized him. He rolled off the other side of the bed, sprang to his feet, and ran out of the door. The other boy might not have even been coming toward him specifically, but Aldan couldn't help it.

He ran into the latrine and slumped down in an empty corner of the room. The smell assaulted his nostrils, but he ignored it. At least here he could be alone for a little while.

All of this started with the Taint. He remembered the heat behind his eyes and how it felt like his own blood burned. He'd knocked down all of the grown men with him. In its own way, the Taint was powerful. If only he could use that in the arena!

If only. But why not? He'd used the Taint against the bowl of blood the second time, without hurting himself. Could he control it? Use it as a weapon?

Aldan removed the bandage from his arm. The cut from the ceremony had scabbed over long ago and was on its way to healing. He picked at it until the scab tore off. A spot of blood oozed to the surface of his skin.

He squeezed the cut, turned his arm, and let several drops of blood fall on to the floor. He squeezed a little harder, producing some more. In any other circumstances, it would be a horrible waste, or so he'd been taught. Blood should never be squandered like this. But he no longer cared about the priests and their beliefs. They hated him. The moon goddess probably hated him too, since he corrupted her sacrifices. But then… hadn't she spoken to him? He knew he'd heard a voice, a female voice. Twice now. Maybe the Taint came from her, and maybe it didn't.

He stretched out on the dirty floor and stared at the tiny pool of his own blood. He tried to focus on it and not on the rest of his blood within his body. The familiar burning sensation grew behind his eyes. According to everyone else, they glowed red when he did this. Someday, he needed to see that in a mirror.

A spark appeared above the tiny pool of blood and vanished as quickly as it came. So he'd been successful in focusing his power, keeping it from affecting the rest of his blood, but the results were… underwhelming. Then again, what had he expected? He'd only tainted a few drops. The pool stirred, as if something shook it.

"Not much to work with, but I'll give it a try," a female voice whispered.

Aldan gasped. The voice again! The tiny pool shifted and shaped itself into a vague approximation of a face.

"Next time, use more than this, if you want me to show more of myself."

Aldan put his face into the floor, bowing to the blood. "Forgive me, goddess. I didn't know."

The tiny voice laughed, almost a tinkling sound. "I'm not the goddess, silly. I'm a part of you."

He lifted his face and watched the blood. "Part of me? How?"

"Your power. Your bloodright. When you use it, you summon me."

The blood-face was so tiny, he couldn't tell much about it, but the mouth appeared to be moving as she spoke.

"The Taint?"

"Is that what they call it now? Ridiculous. It's your bloodright."

"Who are you?"

"Who do you want me to be? No, who do you need me to be?"

He thought about that one. "I need… I don't know what I need. A way to survive, I guess."

"I've already begun to help you with that. You'll make it through this. Anything else?"

He shrugged. "And someone to talk to, I suppose. The others—"

"Yes, I know," she interrupted. "They don't understand you, more's the pity."

"And you do?"

Again with the tinkling laughter. "Dearest, I know all about you. I've watched you your entire life."

A feeling of dread, like the wrong kind of food clumped up in his stomach, settled into him. His entire life? Then she'd seen… everything. Even…

"Please know I'm your friend," she said. "I'm always on your side, even when those close to you aren't. You and I are going to do great things together."

"How?"

"They're making you into an arena fighter, yes?"

He nodded.

"Then we will make you into the greatest arena fighter this world has ever seen. Crowds will chant your name in worship. You will be more revered than the Hawk King himself, second only to the goddess."

"They won't chant my name. They took it away from me."

"Your title then. Clanless. It's intended as an insult, a way of mocking you. We will make it into a name of glory."

"Glory," he repeated.

"So much glory." The voice appeared to sigh. "But this little bit of blood won't allow me to be here much longer."

Aldan reached for his left hand. "I'll spill some more."

"Not now, dearest. Wait until you have a more serious wound, then collect some of it in a bowl or something."

He nodded eagerly. "I'll do that."

"Good. Then we can talk some more."

"Why not now?"

"You're weak, little one. You've been through a lot. It wouldn't do to lose more blood right now. Rest. You need to sleep before another day of training. And then work hard to grow stronger. Don't worry. You will see me again, I promise."

"Thank you."

"Thank me? No. Thank you, Clanless. You brought me into this world."

"I did?"

The face faded, along with the blood itself.

"Later…" The voice also faded away.

Aldan stared at the dark spot on the floor where she'd been. Had it been real? Or was he losing his mind as well? Maybe the Taint was making him imagine things now. He'd heard of people going insane that way: seeing things that weren't there. But even if that were true… if the blood-woman weren't real… he didn't care. The Taint got him into this. Maybe he could use it to fight his way out.

((((●))))

The next day, Aldan and the other boys got a clearer picture of what their daily routine would be like. Kan summoned them into the arena when the sun's pursuit began. Once there, he would have a few words for them while they prepared themselves. Then the running started. Aldan could see no consistency in the amount of running each day. Some they ran door-to-door once or twice. Sometimes, they ran for what seemed like hours.

After that came breakfast. Aldan spoke little at the meals, letting Tunt do most of the talking. Jik often sat with them as well. Aldan soon understood the sorting of the boys. Yeltek dominated, supported by the duo of Duurald and Uyan. Nerlesen kept mostly to himself, the most focused of them all. Even during break times, he exercised his body. Shool Baina lurked on the outskirts of the groups, sometimes sitting with Yeltek's group, but just as often sitting in the middle or even near Aldan.

Only Tunt called him by his name. The rest followed Kan's example and referred to him as "Clanless." Aldan accepted the title, remembering what the blood-woman had told him. Yeltek and his flunkies mocked him, though not as much as he'd expected. The exhaustion of their training often left them with little desire to waste their breath in speaking.

The meals contained high amounts of protein and bread, Aldan noted. On the one hand, it felt luxurious to have so much meat available. On the other, he missed his mother's cooking, especially her flatbread. The thick, hard stuff that came with his meals now did not even compare.

When breakfast ended, the boys returned to the arena for the morning's strength training. Kan ran them through various exercises of lifting, pulling, and pushing. The boys' least favorite involved picking up large rocks, though that one didn't bother Aldan as much. He'd been lifting rocks as far back as he could remember. Admittedly, these rocks were larger than the ones he used for his home's back wall, but as time passed, they didn't feel as heavy any more.

Kan allowed two or three breaks throughout the morning sessions, but never longer than a few minutes. He pushed their strength and endurance on beyond what any of them thought possible.

Lunch was the largest and longest meal of the day, giving them a real break as the sun met the moon for their daily dance. Afterwards, weapons training took place—or at least, training with weapons in hand. Kan did not teach them how to use the weapons at first. He spent hours drilling them in stances and movements while holding a weapon and a buckler. He chastised anyone who let a buckler drop away from a protective pose and often sent them to run door-to-door with weapon and buckler as punishment.

Aldan took the buckler training more seriously than anything else. Protecting himself from attacks sounded like the best way to survive. He worked harder at positioning the buckler than he did the weapon.

By the time the boys reached their very late supper, some of them were too tired to eat. They slunk away to the bunk room, needing sleep more than anything. No matter his exhaustion, Aldan made sure to always be the last one in bed. He didn't trust the others.

He had good cause for his worries.

THE HAWK KING'S PRESENCE

Now

The boy led Clanless to the Hawk King's royal box overlooking the arena. The king himself had left his seat at the edge, no longer interested in the fights. Instead, he lounged on a couch next to a table laden with fruits and meats. A handful of other officials, family members, and religious leaders also occupied the royal box as his guests. Most of them crowded at the edge, discussing the conflicts below.

Yesun bowed and scampered away, his job done. Clanless stood before the Hawk King and waited. The king appeared engrossed with a bowl of dates. Several of the other residents of the box, intrigued by the warrior's arrival, drifted over beside the couch to watch. Two of the women whispered to each other as their eyes roamed over his body. At last, the Hawk King looked up and feigned surprise.

"Ah, Clanless! Thank you for coming. I suppose this is quite a different position for you, looking down on the arena instead of within it."

The women tittered, though it didn't seem like a joke to Clanless. "I've been here before, sire," he answered.

"Of course you have, of course you have." The king picked out another date and tossed it into his mouth. "Tell me: what do you think of the fight I have arranged for you?"

"I will win."

"He will win. You see, Ghouk"—the king gestured to a scowling young man behind the couch——"he will win. Nothing to worry about. Oh, Clanless. Have you met my son?"

Clanless gave a short bow to the future king, paying little attention to his face or appearance. All of this seemed like nothing more than a king's idle fancies… in other words: completely pointless. He would play his part and leave as soon as allowed.

"I still say execute the traitor," Prince Ghouk growled. "Don't give him even the slightest chance!"

"But Clanless here is so much more entertaining than our executioner," the king protested. "The people love him."

"Too many of them love Daviland also." Ghouk folded his arms over his chest. Clanless finally took notice of him, observing his musculature and the way he stood. The future king clearly had some martial training. He might even be a capable warrior, though not on the same level as the best arena fighters.

"Which is why they need to see another one of their heroes deal with him." The Hawk King tossed the half-empty bowl on to the table. "If I merely execute this Daviland, I prove his point about being some sort of evil emperor." He stood and shook crumbs loose from his voluminous sleeves. "But by putting him in the arena, I give him a fair chance." He chuckled. "Except it won't be a fair chance at all, will it, Clanless?"

"I do not believe he has such a chance, sire."

"Have you ever met Daviland, Clanless?"

He hesitated only an instant. "No, sire. Though I may have seen him from a distance."

"Yes, yes. Ah." The king pinched the bridge of his nose. "Be sure to stop by his cell on your way out and fully evaluate him, then. We wouldn't want any surprises."

"Then we shouldn't be doing this," his son mumbled.

"Something else, something else." The king tilted his head, as if thinking hard. "Oh, yes. Now I remember." He stepped out from behind the table and gestured toward the viewers still looking down into the arena. "Clanless, I want you to meet my new Ghamba Lam."

Ghamba Lam? The religious leader of the blood-priests? Why meet him?

A tall, thin man in the usual red robes turned from the arena and smiled. He wore a golden sash across his chest and a large necklace bearing the emblem of the moon. His hair had been cut into a crescent moon shape at the back of his head. Clanless bowed as he approached.

"Ghamba Lam here says he watched some of your earliest fights,

Clanless." The Hawk King waved off in the distance. "Somewhere out there, in the far reaches of our empire. Where was it, Gamba Lam?"

"Rochinbal, your highness," the religious leader answered with a smile. Clanless straightened and looked in his face. Many years had passed since he last saw that face, but he knew it now.

"I was but a Daghilch then," Ghamba Lam went on, confirming it. His eyes were locked on those of Clanless. "We have both come a long way."

The brand on Clanless's shoulder almost burned at the sound of the voice. This was the man who had banished him, cast him out from his clan, his family, his home, stripping him of even his name. And then there were the other things he'd done. The threats to the few people Clanless cared about. A wave of heat swept over him. Wild thoughts erupted in his mind: thoughts of rushing forward, seizing the holy man, and throwing both of them over the edge down into the arena below. It would be the end for both of them, but the desire still tempted him. He wondered what Zektel would say about that.

"Ghamba Lam has plans for increasing the blood donations and their uses," the Hawk King said. He yawned, as if bored with his own words. "All very interesting. But I thought the two of you should be reacquainted, at the least." Beneath the apathetic appearance, the king's eyes darted back and forth between them, missing nothing. Clanless knew quite well the brilliance—and ruthlessness—of the man hiding behind the masquerade of an idle ruler.

"The clanless one was no more than a boy when I first laid eyes on him," Ghamba Lam said. "Even then, I could see his potential." The smile never left his face. "I knew I would see him again someday and somewhere more… regal."

"There! You see?" The Hawk King slapped the priest on the back. "Potential cannot be hidden by those with eyes to see."

Clanless said nothing, eyes unmoving. Why did the priest lie about their first meeting? Why didn't he reveal what he knew? Why not tell the Hawk King of the Taint and how Clanless became branded? Most disturbing of all, this wasn't the first time the king had brought in someone who knew Clanless from the past. Was this one intentional too?

"The goddess moves in unusual ways to our eyes," Ghamba Lam said. "She chooses who she will for what purposes only she knows. The voice of her will comes to those who will listen."

Clanless tried not to flinch. The Hawk King might not have noticed, but the priest put a touch more emphasis on the word "voice." He hadn't forgotten.

"Yes, well, let us hope her voice doesn't come to Daviland," the king said, "unless it is to tell him of his death." He waved to Clanless. "You are dismissed, Clanless. We look forward to your fight tomorrow."

"As you command, sire." Clanless bowed again, then gave another short bow to the religious leader. "Ghamba Lam."

He nodded in return. "We will speak again, Clanless. I am sure of it."

TAICHIN

Then

For six days, Aldan fell asleep as soon as he hit the bunk, and no one disturbed him until Kan's summons. Everyone else felt the same way. Sleep had become a precious commodity after their strenuous workouts.

On the seventh night, things changed. Aldan fell into the bunk as usual and slipped off to sleep. He jerked awake a short time later when someone seized his left arm. Fear clamped hold of his heart. He started to swing around when someone else grabbed his right arm with both hands and pulled back on it. In a moment, two dark figures had him pinned. He strained against their hold and kicked his legs, terror giving him a rush of energy.

"Don't waste your energy, Clanless." The low voice came from a third figure in the dark, standing out of reach of Aldan's kicks. "We just want to talk."

"Yeltek! Let me go!"

Only Yeltek. Aldan closed his eyes in relief. He'd imagined something worse, though he couldn't say why. The two holding his arms must be Duurald and Uyan. They weren't all that smart, but Yeltek was. He'd have Duurald holding Aldan's right. Uyan, the weak link, would be on the left. Aldan stopped kicking and relaxed his arms. He tried to slow the racing of his heart. He could get out of this. He wasn't trapped. He wasn't. He opened his eyes. The only light in the room came from a soft glow at the door. It didn't provide much illumination, but at least he could make out the shapes of the boys around him.

"Why were you branded?" Yeltek demanded.

"Why are you an idiot?" Aldan shot back.

Duurald twisted Aldan's arm. He grunted, but wouldn't give them the satisfaction of any cries of pain.

Yeltek stepped closer. Aldan could barely make out his shaking head. "You may as well tell us. We're going to find out eventually."

"Why do you care? We're all slaves here now."

"We're slaves, yes." Yeltek came closer. "But you? You're lower than that. Lower than us. And don't you forget it. The only thing lower than a slave is a clanless slave. You barely rank higher than those goats you clan-holders raise."

Aldan flexed his left arm slightly. Uyan responded by shifting and tightening his grip. Aldan resisted the urge to smile, even though he knew they couldn't see his face.

"I want to know all about you, Clanless," Yeltek went on. "You've got a story to tell, and I'm sure it's moonbent. So come on. Tell us. It can't make things any worse."

Aldan tried to remember some of the worst curse words his uncle had used when he was angry. But the only ones that came to mind were: "You blood-damned fool!"

Yeltek gave an exaggerated sigh. "We tried doing it the easy way. I'll give you one more chance, sand-eater. Or else Duurald will wrench your arm out of its socket."

"I can do it too," Duurald said from his right.

"And then how will you do in Kan's training?" Yeltek asked. "And if that's not enough, we'll think of something else... something that might hurt worse... and be more embarrassing..."

"What's going on?" another voice asked groggily from across the room.

"Go back to sleep, Jik!" Yeltek hissed. "Or I'll put you back myself."

Jik didn't respond.

Aldan took in a deep breath and let it back out. "All right, all right. I'll tell you my secret. But only you, Yeltek."

"You still think I'm an idiot. They're not letting you go."

"All right. Whatever you want. I'm still only telling you. Lean in close, and I'll whisper it to you." Aldan swallowed, hoping this would work.

Yeltek paused, considering, then leaned in.

"Closer." Aldan glanced toward Uyan, who had also tried to get a little closer. Perfect.

"What's the secret?" Yeltek growled, getting a little closer.

"The reason I was branded…" Aldan whispered.

"Yes?" Yeltek leaned in to hear.

Aldan threw his head forward, smashing his forehead against Yeltek's face. The other boy staggered back, grabbing at his nose with a sharp exclamation. The sudden movement threw Uyan off balance. Aldan jerked free of him and rolled off his bed into Duurald.

"You bastard!" Yeltek shouted. "Crush him, Duurald!"

Even in the darkness, Aldan knew: Yeltek's nose was bleeding profusely. A few drops decorated his own forehead. His skin prickled from the dampness of the liquid, and his other senses exploded. He could smell the blood, even taste it on the tip of his tongue. His entire body seemed attuned to the detection of blood—or at least, blood exposed to the air.

"Burn," Aldan whispered. He struggled against Duurald but also focused the Taint. His eyes burned.

"Ahhhh!" Yeltek screamed. "What is this?"

The other boys, if they'd been asleep before, woke up now, exclaiming over the noise.

Yeltek flailed about. "It hurts," he whimpered, before collapsing.

Duurald wrestled against Aldan. "What did you do?" he demanded.

"Let him go!" Tunt barreled into Duurald. It wasn't much, but it gave Aldan the chance to break free. He took several steps back from the other boy.

Someone lit a lantern and held it up, illuminating the crowd of boys standing around their beds. A cacophony of questions and murmurings filled the room.

Yeltek lay unconscious on the floor. Uyan crawled over to him. Duurald shoved Tunt away and spun back to Aldan, fists clenched. "What did you do to him?"

Aldan pointed at Duurald, his finger shaking. In the faltering light of the lantern, he knew he must look deranged, but he couldn't help laughing. "Maybe I'm a sorcerer, Duurald. Maybe that's what got me branded."

Duurald took a step back.

"What is all this?" Nerlesen asked. "Save the fighting for the arena."

"Yeltek?" Uyan shook him. "Wake up!"

"Or maybe I made a pact with a demon," Aldan went on, rushing his words. "And it strikes out when I'm in danger."

"He's waking up!" Jik said, pointing at Yeltek.

Yeltek moaned. Uyan pulled him up and helped him sit against the end of Jik's bed. Everyone stared. Aldan stepped back next to his own bed, watching Duurald.

Yeltek's eyes wavered across the room. He blinked and focused on Uyan's face.

"Yeltek?" Uyan said. "What did he do to you?"

Shool Baina held the lantern up higher to get a better look.

Yeltek's bloody face spun toward Aldan. "It burned," he said in a low voice.

"He's a taichin!" Duurald yelled. Several of the boys murmured. Aldan had never heard the word before.

"Goddess," Jik said, like a prayer.

"Help me up!" Yeltek ordered. Uyan obliged.

Aldan pointed at him. "You can call me whatever you want. But leave me alone, or worse things will happen to you." He chuckled. "Something more embarrassing, maybe."

Yeltek glared, but he didn't say anything.

"Stay away from my bed!" Aldan climbed into it and adjusted his pillow before putting his head down. "Are we going to sleep tonight?"

"Everyone back to bed!" Nerlesen ordered, as if he were in charge. But the others moved to obey, possibly because he wasn't Aldan.

Shool Baina waited until most got to where they were going, then put out the lantern. Only then did Aldan allow himself to relax. As soon as he did, he started to tremble. He'd been forced to reveal his secret, but without naming it. Would any of the others know? Did it matter?

Only one thing he knew for sure: none of them would look at him the same way again.

☾ ☾ ☾ ☾ ● ☽ ☽ ☽ ☽

Aldan tried not to obsess over their looks the next morning. Yeltek, his face improved by the enormous bruise around his nose, glared at him with open hatred now. Duurald and Uyan were no better, though Aldan thought he detected a touch of fear in their gazes too. Nerlesen glanced at him and shook his head a little. Jik stared and did not come near. Tunt tried being his usual friendly self, but he'd clearly been shaken by the night's events.

Shool Baina's actions were the most perplexing. He came up behind Aldan as they entered the arena, patted him on the back and murmured, "Nicely done last night." He walked on as if he hadn't said anything, and took his place in the line.

When Kan joined them, he took note of Yeltek's nose. His eyes scanned the line and rested briefly on Aldan.

"Hm. Took an entire week, I see." The trainer folded his arms across his chest and gave hard stares to each one of them. As he'd predicted, most of them now hated him, but they also feared him. "Let me be clear about something. I am not training you to be a team. You will not be fighting together. And so, you don't need to like each other. That's fine. Should you move on from here, there's even the remote chance that you may end up fighting against one another in an arena far from here."

He paused and continued moving his eyes down the line. Each one of the boys squirmed under his relentless gaze. "But for now, you are not to fight each other anywhere other than on these sands. Out here, under my supervision, you will get the chance to knock the eternal moon-blood out of each other." He pointed toward the door. "But not once you cross that line. Is that understood?"

"Yes, sir," they all murmured.

"Good. Now behind you, you will find eight large stones. Pick them up."

Aldan turned, found the stone and lifted it. Heavy, but nowhere near his limit.

"For every bruise or other injury I see in the morning that wasn't there the night before, you will carry these rocks…" Kan smiled in a smug way they'd all grown to hate. "…and run door-to-door. Go!"

☾ ☽ ☾ ☽ ● ☾ ☽ ☽ ☾

"This is not your permanent partner," Kan warned.

Aldan found himself paired with Shool Baina. Kan had broken them up into pairs and armed them with bucklers and wooden practice weapons.

"You'll be practicing with this partner for the next week or two, depending on how I see you progressing. Then we'll change partners. Eventually, you will spend time sparring with everyone else in this class. Who knows why I'm doing this?"

Nerlesen lifted his weapon. "To be sure we learn from a variety of opponents, sir."

"Yes." Kan nodded. "And from a variety of opponents, you will learn different things. You will learn the strengths and weaknesses of seven other boys here. This is important, because every single opponent you face in the arena will be different. The more opponents you face, the less you'll be surprised by one."

To Aldan, it seemed so obvious as to not require explanation. But Kan had been doing this for years. He probably grew tired of answering the same questions and gave out answers before they could be asked.

Shool Baina tried to spin his practice weapon in his hand. It looked awkward, and he almost dropped it. Aldan examined his own weapon. It didn't look like a particular weapon. It wasn't much more than a stick the length of his forearm. A swelling partway up divided the handle area from the "weapon" area.

"These weapons can substitute for either maces or swords," Kan went on. "For now, pretend they're maces. Their weight is close to the real thing." He paused. "And they will hurt. For now, I want you to practice the form of your attacks, rather than the strength of them. And, of course, the use of your bucklers. Block everything, and you won't go to bed with any new bruises today. Begin!"

Aldan dropped into the defensive stance Kan had taught them. He and Bain circled each other. After Kan had drilled them in the circling walk for hours, Aldan believed he could do it in his sleep.

"You try to attack me a few times, and then we'll switch," Bain suggested.

Aldan agreed. He lunged in with a quick swing. Bain blocked it and kept moving. Aldan tried a few more of the attack forms they'd been learning. Bain managed to deflect each one, then took over the initiative.

"Yeltek won't forget what you did to him," Bain said as he circled.

"Good. I want him to remember." Aldan kept his eyes fixed on Bain's face, watching for indications of which way he'd strike.

Bain executed a half-hearted slash from left to right. Aldan blocked it with ease.

"Be careful when you're matched up with them out here," Bain suggested. "They'll look for ways to hurt you now."

"Then I'll hurt them." Aldan surprised himself with the statement. When had he become so vengeful? Maybe when his life was taken from him, he told himself.

"If you use that power in the arena, people will talk. I don't know if they'll let you keep fighting." Bain's next attack also didn't come very strong. Aldan stepped out of the way without even using his buckler.

"What will they do to me? Sell me into slavery where I'll most likely die?"

"I don't know. The blood-priests have the power, you know, even in the arenas. Clan Dalbai runs the system, but the priests influence a lot of it."

Aldan cocked his head. "You know a lot about the way things run, then?"

Bain shrugged before launching a simple thrust attack. "I've paid attention. I've learned things."

"I know nothing about the Empire," Aldan confessed. "My whole life was spent in a clanhold."

"I know nothing about life in a clanhold. Let's exchange information."

"Let's see some movement!" Kan shouted at them. "I didn't bring you girls out here to talk!"

Bain smiled. He slashed in from the right while stepping forward with his left foot. Aldan blocked the slash with his buckler. But at the precise moment of impact, Bain pivoted on the ball of his left foot and spun in a complete circle. He brought his weapon down in an overhand arc right at Aldan's head. Aldan managed to get his own weapon up for a parry, but the surprise and impact of Bain's attack knocked his weapon from his hand. He staggered back a foot.

"Good form, Bain!" Kan called.

Aldan retrieved his weapon. "You set me up with those weak attacks."

Bain smiled again. "Kan said we're supposed to learn the strengths and weaknesses of each other. I have no intention of showing my true weaknesses to anyone. You might consider doing the same."

Aldan nodded. "But to hide your weaknesses, you have to know what they are," he pointed out.

"True. Your turn to attack."

Aldan tried changing up his attacks, but couldn't surprise his opponent with any of them. Bain deflected each one. "Ask a question," he suggested, after Kan moved on to watch a different pair.

Aldan thought for a minute. "The Hawk King rules the Empire," he said. "Does he control the priests?"

"Good one! You're thinking about the top layers." Bain returned to his own seemingly weak attacks. "No one is really sure about that. I think he does, because no one's ever seen the priests defy him on anything. But who knows what happens inside, where no one else can see?" His weapon bounced off Aldan's buckler yet again. "My turn. Are you a taichin?"

"I don't even know what a taichin is."

"Heh. You used the word sorcerer last night. It's kind of the same thing. Nobody believes in sorcerers, though. They only show up in children's stories. Taichin, on the other hand…" He shook his head. "They're real."

"They use magic?"

"The blood-priests use magic. That's what the blood they take is for… That and other things. And the Hawk King, of course." Bain staggered back from Aldan's blow, even though Aldan knew it hadn't been very hard.

More deception. "But taichin operate outside of that. They corrupt the blood-magic."

Aldan wrinkled his brow. "How so?"

Bain shrugged. "That's all I know. I've never seen one myself." His quiet little smile came out again. "That I'm willing to say at this time, anyway."

Kan came their way again. "If neither of you manages to put a bruise on the other before I call time on this session," he growled, "you'll both be running door-to-door throughout supper. Let's see some action!"

Aldan narrowed his eyes and lunged forward.

(((●)))

Over the next eight weeks, Aldan saw the progress from Kan's training. His muscles grew harder, his reaction times faster, and his endurance stronger. Around him, the other boys grew in the same way, more or less. With the practice weapons, they each soon learned to accept pain and keep moving. Kan didn't give them any other choice in the matter.

Every day, they woke up with bruises from their previous day's training. Every day, they stretched out and kept going. What else could they do? They were slaves, after all.

At the six-week mark, Jik gave up. Or at least, he tried to. One morning, he refused to leave his bunk. Kan sent the other boys running and went to find Jik himself. Aldan and the others did not hear what passed between them. They only saw Kan drag Jik out into the arena and throw him into the sand. A few moments later, Jik was running door-to-door with everyone else, tears streaming down his face. Not even Yeltek dared mock the smaller boy that day. For the most part, everyone pretended it hadn't happened.

Plenty of mockery took place the rest of the time, of course. Yeltek's hatred toward Aldan only grew after the nighttime incident. He never passed up an opportunity to make some cutting remark or insult. Aldan wasn't his only target, though. Yeltek distributed his mockery to Tunt, Jik, and occasionally even his own friends. Aldan wondered why they stuck with him.

When Yeltek and Aldan were paired in weapon practice, the competition became its fiercest. The two boys fought harder against each other than anyone else. Kan approved and enjoyed their bouts, often pausing the other boys to watch. In those fights, Aldan came closest to experiencing the "bloodrush" Kan talked about. He did feel a thrill and maybe a sharpening of the senses, but not to the degree he expected.

Shool Baina continued to be an enigma. At times, he appeared friendly to Aldan, exchanging information about how each grew up. He seemed to know a lot about many aspects of the Empire, things for which Aldan had no knowledge at all. But sometimes, he would behave like one of Yeltek's crew, joining in the shunning of Aldan and his friends.

One by one, Aldan learned the stories behind each of the boys. Virtually all of them were slaves because of a debt owed by their parents. The debts must have been enormous, because as Bain explained, debt-slavery ordinarily could only last for seven years. But arena slavery was for life, except for the remote promise of buying one's own freedom. As for Bain, he gave the same story of debt, but Aldan could tell he didn't mean it. Curious… but to get the truth, he'd probably have to tell his own story, and Aldan wasn't ready to do that for anyone.

Once a week, Kan gave the boys what he called a "rest day." He still kept them busy almost all day, but the exercise wasn't as strenuous, and he dismissed them early for supper. Those nights, the boys sat long around the table, boasting about their future arena fighting careers or telling stories they'd heard from their parents. The stories almost always included evil beings of some kind, like the beastmen of the high hills. Aldan knew about them, but some stories included monsters he didn't recognize, like a pair of stories Shool Baina told of creatures called blood-wraiths who would devour men's souls. Several of the boys told stories about sinister taichins, which always ended with a few sidelong glances at Aldan. Despite that part of it, Aldan loved the story-telling. Most of them he'd never heard before. Upon prompting from Tunt, he even joined in a few times, telling some of the tales of Otkerel the Wild his father used to tell.

Every two or three days, Aldan would find time to sneak off alone, usually when the boys were in bed, and speak to the blood-woman. Even though he'd found some measure of friendship with Tunt and Jik, he still couldn't share parts of his life with them. They would never understand the Taint. He couldn't trust them with that knowledge. But the woman knew everything about him. She even knew about his life before the Taint. He could talk with her about anything. She didn't volunteer much information about herself, but she listened to him. Aldan valued the opportunity to talk with someone who understood him so well.

Obtaining enough blood to make her appear became easier, as well. Someone returned bleeding from training almost every day. Aldan would help "clean up" the blood, but keep it for himself instead. For such a precious commodity, blood did not seem very valuable in arena training. Aldan wondered that a blood-priest never came to the arena. Did their status as slaves prevent them from making donations?

He asked Nukai, the hunched assistant, about this one night. He often asked Nukai the questions he feared to ask Kan. Nukai grumbled, but always gave answers. He obviously knew even more than Shool Baina, but in different areas.

"It's only during your training," he explained, pulling one of his furs up over his shoulder. "Once you become a real fighter, the priests will be there, demanding their share, every step of the way." He glanced around, as if afraid someone might hear him. "This spot, this training ground, is considered a neutral ground for the blood collection. Kan and the other trainers argued hard to obtain it." He shrugged, and one of the furs fell back off the shoulder. "If we had to deal with the priests in here, the training would take twice as long. It's in their best interests to get more fighters trained faster."

"How?"

Nukai appraised him from under dark eyebrows that almost—but not quite—met in the middle of his face. "Blood. It's all about the blood." He shook his head and walked away, muttering to himself.

As it turned out, Aldan soon learned a little more about the value of blood within the Empire.

KEKEEN

Then

Kan strode out before the line of boys after lunch. They had already exchanged whispers to each other about the missing weapons rack. Were they not training with weapons today? Uyan woefully predicted running door-to-door throughout the sun's retreat. No one had a better theory.

"You've been here two months," Kan announced. "In just a few days, we begin your training with real weapons. And then everything changes."

Aldan and several others shifted their feet. With real weapons would come the possibility of more serious injury. They might soon miss the days of going to bed with only bruises.

"And so, today is different. Today…" Kan drew it out as long as he could. "Today, you have the sun's retreat and evening to yourselves."

For a moment, the boys did not know how to respond. Half a day to themselves? Completely? What would they do?

"In the city," Kan added.

The boys exploded with thanks and questions. Kan lifted a finger with a glare, and they all fell silent at once.

"I do not need to remind you of your current position as slaves of the arena… but I do it anyway. You know what will happen if you try to run away." He took a large bag from his belt and swung it back and forth absently while he spoke. "You have until midnight. Anyone who is not in their bunk by then will be running door-to-door all day tomorrow, and then stay up cleaning the latrines. Is that understood?"

"Yes, sir!" The chorus was more unanimous than any they'd given him prior to then.

Aldan watched curiously as Kan opened the large bag and took out smaller bags. He walked down the line and handed one to each boy. "This should be enough. Go. Have fun. But remember your place."

With a whoop, Yeltek led the way, rushing out of the arena, through the hallways and out through the front gate. All of the others chased after him, shouting and cheering. A couple of dozen yards down the road, they slowed to a walk. Some dug through the contents of their bags, counting or muttering to themselves.

Aldan's bag clinked with several small objects. He opened it and reached inside. He pulled out a tiny ovoid vial made of some kind of crystal glass. Within the vial, blood glistened. "Why do they give us blood?" he asked aloud.

"You really do come from the sands, don't you?" Uyan hooted. Yeltek and Duurald joined him in derisive laughter.

Aldan ignored them, turning the tiny vial over and over in his hand. It couldn't be more than an ounce of blood inside. The vial had a narrow opening, sealed with green wax.

"I'm going to find the brothel!" Duurald announced loudly.

"Ha!" Yeltek shoved him. "Hand them that bag of NV and you can buy enough for a quick kiss… on the cheek!"

Jik moved next to Aldan. "You really don't know what they are?" he asked in a low voice.

Aldan shook his head.

"In the cities, you use blood to buy things," Jik offered. "What do you use to buy things in the clanholds?"

Aldan shrugged. "We trade for things. My father and uncle would give the farmer a lamb or a goat in exchange for vegetables."

Jik giggled. "You can't walk through a city carrying sheep. If you want a hot meal at an inn, or a place to sleep, or something else, you have to pay for it." He shook his own bag. "This is how you pay."

Tunt came alongside, listening to their conversation. He walked slower than the others, due to a bruised knee suffered in a fight with Duurald.

Aldan furrowed his brow. "But it's just blood. Why would anyone want it?"

Jik took one of his own vials out and held it up. "See that seal on the end? That comes from the priests. That makes it official. The green wax means it's NV—involuntary blood. You know, like the blood from someone who gets killed in the arena."

"I thought the priests used the blood for magic." Ahead, Aldan could see the gates of the city of Rochinbal. The boys continued down the road, most of them boasting over what they would do in the course of the evening.

"They need V-blood for that. Voluntary. When people donate it. But you can use that for buying stuff too. If the wax seal is gold, that means it's V, and it's worth a lot more."

"I still don't understand." Aldan shook his head. "Why do the priests let it go, if they need it?" And why was voluntary blood more powerful and rare, if they obtained so much of it through sacrifices? Wouldn't involuntary blood be rarer?

Jik shrugged. "It's the way things work. I don't know." He laughed. "I guess it's to keep everyone from having to carry sheep around all the time!"

"We didn't just trade sheep," Aldan answered, irritated. He glanced around for Shool Baina. He would probably be able to explain this better… but Bain was walking with Yeltek and friends.

"Yeah, look." Jik shook his bag. "Of course Kan didn't give us much here. It won't buy hardly anything. Least of all"—he pointed ahead at Durald—"anything at a brothel."

Aldan stopped himself from asking what a brothel was.

"Tell you what," Jik went on, pointing at Tunt, "if the three of us combine our NV here, we might be able to get ourselves a nice meal somewhere. What do you say?"

Aldan nodded. "Sure. Why not?" He had no idea what he would have done on his own, anyway.

"I could do that," Tunt agreed.

"Great!" Jik slapped Aldan on the back… lower back, anyway. "Come on, Clanless. Let us show you what life in the city is like!"

As they drew near the gates, Aldan paused and stared down the road stretching away into the wilderness. Somewhere in that direction lay his clanhold, his family.

"Don't even think about it," Tunt warned. "You know what will happen."

"Do we know? I mean, we only have Kan's word for it." Aldan took a slight step down the road.

"Don't you remember what happened to Uyan?" Jik asked.

"He wasn't here yet," Tunt said. "He showed up that night."

"Oh, right."

"What happened to Uyan?" Aldan turned back toward the city.

"He tried to run," Tunt said. "Kan went after him and brought him back."

"When Kan left us alone, Uyan said he made it about half a mile down the road," Jik added. "And then"—he hugged himself—"the blood in his body just froze up. He couldn't move at all! He said he stood at the side of the road like a statue until Kan picked him up."

Aldan grunted and joined the other two in heading back to the city gates. The other boys entered far ahead of them: Yeltek and his friends, with Nerlesen trailing behind.

Tunt pointed. "Should we ask him if he wants to join us?"

"That guy? He scares me," Jik said. "Out of all of us, he's the one I bet becomes a big-name arena fighter."

"Not you?" Tunt elbowed him.

Jik shook his head. "I've probably got less than seven months to live, if I'm honest." He picked up his pace and waved at them to keep up. "All the more reason to enjoy life now. Come on!"

((((●))))

Once they passed through the gates of the city, Aldan couldn't help but stare around him. The concept of buildings set close together was nothing new, but these buildings were so different. Most of them looked like two buildings stacked on top of each other. Some even had another level on top of that! The temple at the clanhold had been taller than homes, of course, and the arena contained more areas than he'd yet discovered, but the idea of houses with rooms on top of rooms surprised him. After considering it, he realized families didn't have much ground space, so they built up instead of out. In a tightly-packed city, it made sense. Perhaps the oldest family members lived on the ground floor, and younger ones on the secondary levels, like turning a clanhold home on its side.

"I'll be right back," Jik said. He ran over to speak with one of the gate guards. Aldan turned to watch. The guard, a short man, reminded him of the temple guards who'd watched him back home. He carried a mace, the weapon of choice for most of the Empire, apparently. As he talked with Jik, he waved it around and pointed down the street.

Jik returned with a satisfied smile. "Always ask soldiers for the best place to eat," he said. "They're the ones most likely to have eaten lots of places."

"Lead the way," Tunt replied with a gesture.

The three boys walked down the street, talking and laughing. Or at least Tunt and Jik laughed. Aldan kept staring at everything, unused to… all of it: the sights, the sounds, and the smell. "It smells like a latrine," he said, interrupting another conversation.

Jik chuckled. "Yeah, cities don't always smell nice. Sometimes the waste gets dumped out into the street." He pointed to a pile of what Aldan had assumed was dirt. The boys made a larger circuit of anything suspicious on the streets after that.

As they kept walking, they encountered more and more people. The voices grew louder, though it didn't sound like fighting, necessarily.

"It's the marketplace," Jik said. "We'll pass through it on our way."

Aldan understood the concept of a marketplace, but what they encountered next took his breath away. So many people. So many shops and booths and stands. The cacophony of sounds overwhelmed him at first, but as they continued to work their way through it all, he began to understand the rhythm and flow of the merchants' calls. Many of them tried to get the attention of the three boys directly, but Jik steered them on.

As they rounded a corner onto a different street, one of the last carts caught Aldan's attention. On top of the cart, full of various items of decoration—cheap-looking necklaces and such—stood a wooden rack on which dangled a number of colorful scarves. The plainest one, mostly sand-colored, drew Aldan's eye. He pulled it out from the others to examine an embroidered design: a crude figure carrying a rock toward a grey wall.

"Ah, you're clanhold!"

Aldan looked past the cart and saw a young girl, perhaps eight years old, smiling at him. He pointed at the scarf. "Back wall?"

"You know what it is! That makes you clanhold." She wrinkled her brow, looking at his brand, then shook her head. She came around the cart and took the scarf. She removed it from the rack and held the entire cloth out for display. "I stitched it myself. You like?"

Aldan hesitated. He didn't need a scarf, but the imagery reminded him too much of home. "How much?"

"Three greens," she answered without hesitation.

Aldan reached for his bag. Jik appeared beside him all of a sudden. "Hey, hey. I thought we had a plan!"

"I want this," Aldan said.

"Sands, you never give them what they ask!" He looked at the girl and the scarf. "You want three for that piece of nothing? You're moonbent. It's not even worth one."

The girl put a hand over her heart with a shocked look. "Moonbent, am I? You're trying to take food directly from the hands of my poor old mother, sick these three weeks. Have you no heart, boy?" She gave an exaggerated sigh. "It will probably mean we get no supper tonight, but I'll take two if I must."

"We'll give you one," Jik countered. "It doesn't even have a seam around the edges. This thing could fray in the winter winds in minutes." He shook his head. "What good would it do my friend then?"

"I like you." The girl pointed at Jik, then shifted to Aldan. "But I like him better. He has an honest face. He looks like my little brother would look… if he ever reached your age. Unfortunately, he doesn't get enough to eat unless I sell enough out here." She lowered her gaze to the ground, and her shoulders slumped.

"I'll give you two," Aldan said. Jik threw up his hands and stepped out of the way.

Aldan dug into his bag and took out two of the tiny vials of blood. He handed them to the girl, who smiled and placed the scarf across his hand. "Goddess bless you, sir. Enjoy your evening!"

Jik pulled Aldan by the left sleeve. "Come on, before you spend the rest of our vials." They joined Tunt and continued down the road.

"It's not worth two," Jik insisted, looking at the scarf. "It's barely worth one, if that."

"I don't care," Aldan answered. He examined the embroidery again, then stuffed the scarf into his pocket. "Where are we going now?"

"Not far."

A few minutes later, Jik turned down a third street and pointed to the second building from the corner. "There."

To Aldan, the building had little to make it stand out from those around it. A solid wood construction, the building sported a pair of frayed banners drifting lazily in the breeze. One of the banners depicted a goat walking on two feet. The second showed the moon passing in front of the sun.

"What makes this place so special?" Tunt asked.

"The guard said they have great food, and the storyteller is second to none. Let's find out if he was right." Jik pushed the door open. Aldan and Tunt followed him in and stopped just inside the doorway.

Though the sun shone bright outside, the banners hanging in front of the windows kept most of the light from reaching the interior of the eating-house. Oil lanterns scattered about the room gave it a warm glow, not unwelcoming. Rough tables and chairs filled most of the large room. But the far side of the room drew Aldan's eyes. To the left, he saw a tall bar, behind which a thickset woman stood, counting something in a bag. To the right, an empty stage stood next to an equally empty fireplace.

The woman finished her counting and looked up at the boys. "You're quite early," she called across the room. "But we can get you started, if you like."

Jik turned to the other two. "Give me your vials," he said. Aldan and Tunt obeyed and watched him head across the room. While he engaged the woman in a lengthy conversation, Aldan wandered near the stage.

"What's this for?" he asked Tunt.

"Oh, I know this much! It's for a performer. You know, someone to entertain people while they're eating."

"Is that what Jik meant by a storyteller?"

Before Tunt could answer, Jik left the bar and beckoned them toward a table next to the stage. Jik sat down on a bench facing away from it, while Aldan sat facing him. Tunt slid in next to Aldan.

"We're pretty early for dinner," Jik observed, "like she said. But they don't mind if we just hang around here, and we'll get the very first food when it's ready." He slid two vials across the table to them. "Here's all we have left."

Aldan picked up one and toyed with it. "Why are we spending this on food when we get so much food at the arena?" he wondered.

"We get plenty to eat, certain," Jik answered. "But it's bland as the open sands. I don't think Nukai's ever seen any spices. He sure doesn't use any on our food. Didn't your mother use spices in the clanhold?"

Aldan nodded. He hadn't spared much thought for the flavor of the food, but Jik was right.

The woman from the bar set a tall pitcher of water and three mugs on their table. "I'll have some bread for you in a little while," she said before hurrying away.

Tunt laughed. "Water, Jik? This is what you got for us?"

"After the food, I couldn't afford to pay for good drinks! If someone hadn't spent two vials on a rag, we might have had enough."

Aldan's face grew red. But before he could respond, four more vials slid down the table next to his. "Use mine. Water's hardly good enough for our purposes, now is it?"

All three of them stared as Shool Baina sat down next to Jik.

"Bain! Where did you come from?" Tunt exclaimed.

He shrugged. "Yeltek wouldn't know a good eating-house if it fell on him." He pointed at Jik. "But he grew up in clan Zavi. I figured he'd know how to find the right spot."

"You followed us?"

Bain sighed. "When I explain everything, it destroys the fun. No, I saw you talking to the guard, so I asked him where he sent you."

Jik gathered up five of the vials. "This should be enough." He hurried back to the bar.

Aldan picked up the remaining vial and turned it around in his hand. "I still don't understand this," he said. "If blood is how you buy things, why don't people just pour their own blood into a bottle and buy whatever they want?"

"It has to have the seal and the ribbon from the priests," Tunt pointed out.

Aldan frowned. "Ribbons are easy. Wax shouldn't be too hard."

Bain leaned in. "But what is the vial made of?"

Aldan held it up in the dim light and turned it back and forth. "I don't know. It's not ordinary glass, is it?"

"It's some kind of crystal." Another vial appeared in Bain's hand, which Aldan could have sworn was empty. "Wherever this particular crystal comes from, only the priests know. You can't find it anywhere on your own."

"Then it's the crystal that's valuable. Not the blood."

"Maybe." Bain shrugged. "Someone once told me that it's the combination of the crystal and the blood that lets them do magic."

"Have you—"

Jik plopped down a new pitcher. "Zokin! This is better than water!" He started pouring the mugs. "Thanks, Bain. They know to make four meals now, instead of three." With the drinks distributed, Jik lifted his mug into the air. "To surviving the arena!"

The others agreed and drank. Aldan didn't know what to make of it. The zokin was bubbly, but had a wild fruity flavor with a touch of honey. He took a long drought.

"Hey, hey! Don't drink too much this early!" Jik exclaimed. "It's got to last us, you know." The boys laughed, and Aldan joined in.

They fell into the easy camaraderie they often enjoyed at the breakfast table, when they had the most energy to make jokes and enjoy each other's company. Aldan hadn't felt this relaxed since the ceremony where everything went wrong. He didn't say much, content to let the other three meander on through various topics. Without the threat of mockery from Yeltek and company, Tunt and Jik talked more than they ever had. Bain joined in as well, but Aldan noted his contributions to the conversation often seemed right on the edge of being insulting. His words, if Aldan listened carefully, could usually be taken two different ways.

"Bread." The announcement came simultaneously with the descent of a large platter onto the table. To Aldan's great delight, steam rose from fresh flatbread. The boys all seized a piece, then dropped it from one hand to the other.

"Hot, hot, hot," Tunt muttered.

The serving woman smiled and set down a small plate with a knife and a big square of butter. "Enjoy."

Aldan grabbed the knife before anyone else. He carefully cut a small piece of butter and placed it on his flatbread.

"You don't like butter?" Jik asked.

"I love butter!"

"Then take what you want! We paid for this, remember?"

Aldan's eyes widened. At home, he'd always been warned about taking too much butter, because of its value. He took a much larger chunk and added it to the first.

"Now you've got it!" Jik took the knife and cut off some butter for himself.

Aldan folded the flatbread in half and massaged the butter inside it, spreading it around. He lifted it and took a bite. Butter spilled out of his mouth and ran down his chin, but he didn't care. He closed his eyes and savored the simple flavor. Yes, he was looking forward to the spices Jik promised, but the salt of the butter and the light floury warmth of the flatbread made the trip worthwhile right now. For a moment, he almost felt home again.

"I don't know," Tunt said. "I think I like my bread with more… what do you call it? Thickness? But not real thick, you know? Not hard."

"This is the best," Aldan said. "I don't care what you say." He put the rest of the bread into his mouth and snatched another one.

Across the table, Jik's eyebrows went up. "We found something Clanless likes!"

"A significant accomplishment," Bain agreed.

Aldan ignored them and reached for the butter again.

While they enjoyed the bread, a few more people entered the room, taking some of the other tables. By the time the bread (and butter) was gone, the crowd had grown to over a dozen. A younger woman joined the first one in delivering drinks and bread to each table. Aldan caught snippets of conversations from the other tables. Most seemed to be related to business and work with occasional references to family. As the crowd grew, so did the noise. Soon, Aldan could barely hear the conversation at his own table, let alone any others.

As promised, the boys were first when the food arrived. The serving girl set a huge platter on their table, filled with some kind of meat pastries, cheese squares, and a scattering of boiled vegetables.

"I love these!" Jik exclaimed, seizing one of the pastries. He let it cool in his hand a few moments before taking a small bite. "Ahhh. Now that's flavor! Why can't they find onions at the arena?"

Aldan took one and also took a small bite. The seasoning filled his mouth, masking even the taste of the meat. He thought it might be sheep, but he couldn't be sure. He definitely tasted onion and a number of other strong flavors he couldn't identify. His tongue burning, he took a quick drink to cool it.

"Give it time," Tunt said quietly. "You'll get used to it."

Aldan found alternating bites of the flatbread and cheese with the pastries helped his mouth acclimate to the spices. Within a few minutes, the four boys consumed most of the food, talking and laughing the whole time.

While they were eating, a man walked on to the stage. He set a rough wooden chair in the center and then left. A minute later, he returned, carrying a strange instrument. He settled on the chair and bent over the device. The largest part of the instrument looked like an inverted bowl covered with some kind of animal skin. A long wooden neck stretched up from it, making the whole thing almost four feet long. Three tight strings were stretched from the top of the neck to the bottom of the bowl. The man plucked one of the strings and a musical tone echoed through the room.

Aldan stared as the man began to pluck the strings repeatedly, moving his other hand up and down the neck. He'd never seen or heard music played like this. He'd heard drums at the temple, and one of his neighbors sometimes played music by blowing through a tube with holes carved in it. But nothing compared to the sweet sounds that came from the stage. Jik and Bain abandoned what was left of the food and turned around to watch the player.

The cacophony of conversation faded as the man continued to play. By the time he played his last note, not a single voice could be heard.

"Good evening, friends and fellow travelers beneath the moon!" He greeted them with a rich voice that resonated through the silence left by his music. "My name is Koland of clan Dendsu, and I will be your storyteller this evening."

With the music stopped, Aldan finally paid attention to Koland himself. A man of average height, his upper body showed signs of some kind of regular physical exertion. His hair, black with streaks of gray, swept back from his forehead, complemented by a narrow beard and mustache which contained much more gray than the rest of his hair.

Koland plucked a single string. As the note reverberated, he asked, "What sort of story shall I tell tonight? Should it have a hero?"

"Yes!" Jik cried, followed by an echoing agreement from most of the room.

Koland plucked another string. "Should it have a romance, perhaps? A story of true love?"

"Yes!" came the majority chorus, along with a few who protested "No!"

"Ah, but adventure!" Koland exclaimed. "Surely you want adventure!"

The crowd agreed.

"And what about a villain? Should there be evil to face?"

More agreement. "The worst!" someone shouted.

"Ah. The worst. Very well. Let's see what we can tell..." Koland strummed a few notes. "Once, long ago, before the Hawk King's reign, before even the Empire itself existed, there lived a young man." His eyes flickered across the four boys at the front table. "Along with three of his friends, he learned the way of the warrior. Every day, he strove to improve himself at whatever task he found to do."

"It's us!" Tunt whispered a little too loud.

"As the goddess would have it, this young man"—Aldan felt certain that Koland's eyes locked with his own—"met and fell in love with a beautiful young woman."

The crowd murmured, mostly in approval.

Koland plucked a string, releasing a discordant note. "Seeking to impress her, the young man made a rash vow, declaring that he would find and slay a death worm. The woman cared nothing for such a feat, but the vow was made. Accompanied by his three friends, the young man set out into the wilderness."

"What's a death worm?" Aldan whispered to Tunt.

"A death worm, rarely seen these days," Koland, his eyes twinkling, went on before Tunt could answer, "lived beneath the sands of the northern desert. It burrows through the sand, creating waves upon the surface. Most are little longer than a man's leg, but few survive an encounter with them. Bright red their skin, and they can spew forth venom from ten feet away. So poisonous are they that even to touch one could kill.

"But our young hero was determined to kill one and bring back its body to win his lady love. Alas, what he did not know was that he had an enemy... among his friends! One of those he considered his fellow warrior did not wish for him to succeed. In fact, this enemy loved the same woman and wanted her for himself! And so, this enemy determined in his heart that regardless of how the hunt proceeded, the young hero would die in the attempt."

Koland continued to play a note or two every few sentences of his story, matching the tones with the story's progress. The crowd, thoroughly hooked by his skill, hung on every word, exclaiming and reacting to each twist and turn of the tale.

Aldan tore his eyes away from Koland, thinking about the young man in the story. Facing betrayal by a trusted friend would be horrible. Had been horrible. A memory slid away before he could catch it. Uncomfortable, his eyes wandered away from the stage. He noticed a young woman leaning against the wall between the stage and the bar. At first, he took her for one of the serving staff, but she never left her spot to deliver drinks or food, as the other women were doing. Instead, she watched the storyteller, arms folded, with a delighted smile on her face.

Captivated, Aldan's interest in the story wavered. He missed large pieces of it, watching the girl. She reminded him of Borde, at least in facial structure and general body size. But while Borde had long black hair, this girl's, braided on the sides, was a light brown, almost pale. He'd never seen that color hair before. She wore a simple brown dress, trimmed in a lighter brown near her hair color.

Tunt elbowed him and pointed to a half-eaten meat pastry in front of him. "Are you going to eat that?" he whispered. Aldan shoved the food to Tunt and tried to re-focus on the storyteller. Somehow, the young hero, though terribly wounded by his enemy, had managed to overcome both enemy and death worm. But the death worm, also terribly wounded, escaped into the sands, never to be seen again.

"And so our young hero returned home with his two remaining friends," Koland went on. "His beloved, despite her doubts about his mission, rushed to care for his wounds. And as she did so, our hero recognized her true value: not as a prize to be claimed or some kind of ruler to impress with his deeds, but as a companion, to come alongside him and work together as companions for the rest of their days." Koland strummed a quick series of notes. "And thus our story ends... for now."

The audience erupted in applause. The boys at the table might have been the loudest. "A song!" someone shouted. Others took up the cry.

Koland held up a hand. "Of course, of course. A song that follows a story is always a welcome thing. But alas, dear friends, my singing voice does not equal my telling voice." A few groans came from the crowd. "Fortunately, my daughter's voice more than makes up for it!" He gestured to the side, and the young woman Aldan had been watching bounded onto the stage beside her father.

Koland played while he waited for the audience to quiet down again. The girl, showing no lack of confidence, gazed out at the crowd, her eyes flicking from one table to the other. She smiled at the boys before opening her mouth and starting her song.

Aldan sat transfixed. He could remember his mother singing little Ot to sleep, and maybe doing the same for him in his earlier years. But as much as he loved his mother's voice, it paled in comparison to the woman on stage. Her tone, light and airy, didn't match the strength of his mother's, but made up for it in enthusiasm. The words of the song said something about stories and their nature, but Aldan didn't catch very many of them. The young woman swayed as she sang, sometimes gesturing with her hands, but she kept her eyes above the heads of the crowd.

As the song crescendoed, she stretched out one hand, as if trying to get to something just beyond reach. The chorus of the song, by now familiar enough to even Aldan, repeated one last time:

"Touching a story,
Grasping a cloud,
Reaching for songs that
Are never too loud…"

She ironically echoed the last line in a quiet and low tone: *"Never too loud."* Koland plucked two more notes and let his music fall silent as well.

The crowd sat quiet for a moment or two before erupting in even louder applause. "More, more!" they shouted.

Koland stood and raised both hands. "Friends, friends. Allow my daughter to rest a bit! For now, sit back, enjoy your meal, and I'll tell another story in a few minutes." The crowd quieted down. Koland sat and plucked a few strings. His daughter bent and gave him a quick kiss on the cheek. Then, to Aldan's shock and delight, she stepped off the stage, grabbed a chair from nearby, and pulled it to the side of their table, between Jik and himself.

"Pour me a mug, boys, and tell me your stories," she said, breathless. Jik leaped to his feet, ran to the bar, and grabbed another mug for her. Aldan, Tunt, and even Bain stared at the girl.

"What's the matter? Did the death worm steal your tongues?" She took the mug from Jik and drank several huge swallows, before wiping her mouth with the back of her sleeve. "Tell me your names, at least. Mine's Kekeen."

"I am Jik, my lady. The one beside me here is Shool Baina." Jik gestured, his voice squeaking a little.

"Call me Bain," he said with a short nod, regaining his full composure before the others.

"I'm Tunt."

"And you?" Kekeen turned to Aldan, looking at him over the top of the mug with deep brown eyes.

He opened his mouth to answer, but Jik spoke first. "Don't you see his brand? He's Clanless."

She raised her eyebrows. "So?"

Aldan lowered his gaze to the table. "They took my name," he mumbled.

Kekeen set the mug down. "That's silly. No one can take away your name. That's like saying someone took away my song just now. I sang it. It's my words. Nobody can take words away from me." She reached over and tapped his brand with a finger. "Come. What's your name, clanless one?"

"Aldan." He looked back up at her.

"Aldan," she repeated. "See? You do have a name." She looked around at the other boys. "I'm sure you three, being his friends, all knew that too, right?"

"I did," Tunt offered.

"Then I guess you're not the enemy of the story, are you?" She took another drink and smiled again.

"The story wasn't about us," Bain said with a chuckle.

"Wasn't it?" Kekeen's smile teased all of them.

"Bain is clearly the enemy," Jik declared.

"Then which one of you is the hero?" Her eyes drifted across the group and stopped on Aldan.

"Out of this group?" Tunt asked. "It's got to be Aldan."

"Why is that?"

Tunt shrugged. "He's the best fighter here."

"Fighter?"

"We're arena fighters in training," Jik explained. "We train at the arena outside the city."

"Bain's probably better than me," Aldan put in.

"Modesty too," Kekeen murmured. Then in a louder voice: "What does that mean? Arena fighters? You're training to kill each other?"

"Not each other," Jik said. "But we will have to kill someone else at the end of the training." He paused and lowered his head. "And keep on killing, if we want to live."

Kekeen's eyes widened. "That's horrible! Is this what you all want?"

"None of us asked for it," Bain said. "We're slaves, bought and sold."

Kekeen looked from one to the other of them. "And there's nothing you can do? No way out?"

The boys were silent. "They hold our bloodbonds," Aldan said. "We can't leave." For the first time in weeks, he found himself thinking of Borde's words about being a kind man. He couldn't be a kind man now. The option wasn't open to him any more. At least not in the arena. But here and now?

"So we fight," Bain concluded. "Or die."

"I'm going to die," Tunt said. "There's not much doubt of that."

"How can you say that?" Kekeen exclaimed.

Tunt shrugged. "I've accepted it. I'm not very good at fighting, so I don't have a chance." He paused. "This is probably the last time I'll get to do something like this, unless Kan lets us out again near the end. At least I got to hear you sing."

Kekeen's face fell. She looked around. "And the rest of you? Have you no hopes for the future?"

"I'm going to live," Bain said. "I'm too stubborn to die."

"I don't know," Jik said, still looking down.

"Aldan?" Kekeen turned her eyes on him.

He stared back at her for a moment. "If it means I get to hear you sing again, I'll live."

Did he actually say that out loud? And was he imagining it, or did she actually blush?

Bain snorted. "And now we know which one is the romantic."

Kekeen shot him a look and patted the table. "If you recall the story, that means he's the hero too."

No one said anything. Aldan looked up toward Koland and tried to pretend nothing had happened. The storyteller caught his eyes and winked. Then he bent over and plucked several notes in a row. "Time for another story!" he proclaimed.

Kekeen turned to watch her father, as did everyone else. Aldan caught himself glancing at her repeatedly throughout the next story. And then when she jumped up and joined her father on stage again, for another song… Aldan didn't even pretend not to stare. Fortunately, almost all other eyes in the room were on Kekeen at the same time.

This time, she sang a slow ballad, telling of a lost love. It must have been a well-known song, because some of the crowd joined in on a few lines. When she finished, and the crowd roared its approval, she slipped out a side door behind the bar.

Aldan felt like all of his energy collapsed down into the floor. Would she come back? Had they scared her away with their talk of dying?

"Sands," Jik said. "You really are struck, aren't you?"

Aldan looked up to see the other three boys watching him. Bain's smirk irritated him. "What do you know?" He started to stand.

Kekeen appeared beside the table, almost out of nowhere, holding a new pitcher of zokin. "Are you leaving already?"

"No!" Aldan dropped back onto the bench. Jik snickered.

Kekeen laughed and sat down again. "All right, then I'll stay as well." She raised a finger and grew stern for a moment. "But no more talk of dying. Are we agreed?"

The boys agreed, and the conversation turned to more pleasant topics. One by one, Kekeen drew more life details from each of the boys than any of them had shared with each other. Aldan knew Jik and Tunt were slaves because of family debt, but nothing about Bain's past. As they talked, he went into great detail about his father, a merchant, who wanted only the best for his family, but made foolish decisions, losing everything. In the end, he killed a man to cover up one of his debts, but the man's partner killed him in return. Bain volunteered to be sold to save the rest of his family.

Kekeen studied him for a moment when he finished. "How much of that is actually true?" she demanded.

"How much of your father's stories are true?" he countered.

She rolled her eyes and shook her finger at him. "You're a sneaky one. I don't trust a word you say."

"You shouldn't. I keep telling everyone that."

"And what about you, clanless Aldan?" She turned and leaned her head on her fist, watching him.

For a brief instant, Aldan almost told everything. He wanted to. If anyone would understand, this girl would. But... no. She might have heard of the Taint; she might be horrified and turn against him. He lowered his gaze. "I don't talk about it."

"Certain you had a life before coming here, no?"

He smiled a little. "I can tell part of that."

"Then by all means!"

Aldan began hesitantly, but grew more confident as he talked, explaining life in a clanhold. None of the others knew much of that life. Jik grew up in a city, Tunt in a small town near a city, and Bain... he talked like he knew cities, but who could tell? Aldan told of his family—father, mother, little Ot, cousin Borde—and their home. He talked about his mother's flatbread, inspiring Jik to take one of their last vials to request more for their table. And he talked about work in the fields and in maintaining their house. Kekeen appeared fascinated by his descriptions.

"And you added rocks to the back wall all the time?"

"I tried so hard when I was little, I once broke my arm with a big rock." Clanless patted his forearm. "The wall protects us from High winter winds. And if barbarians attack the clanhold, no one wants their home to be the place they break through the wall. A strong back wall is… it's a sign of honor, I guess." With a sudden thought, he pulled the scarf from his pocket. "Like this."

Kekeen took the scarf and spread it on the table. "Oh, how delightful! You didn't stitch this, did you?" She looked up, her eyes glittering in the flickering lamp light. "Did a girl back home send it with you to remember her by?"

"No, I, I found it in the market on our way here," he stammered. "You can have it."

"Oh." Kekeen looked back down at the scarf. For the first time since she'd approached their table, she appeared to have nothing to say.

"Charming," Bain whispered loud enough for all of them to hear.

"I'm flattered, Aldan," Kekeen said at last. She folded the scarf in precise lines down into a small enough shape to slip inside her sleeve.

He nodded, not knowing what else to say.

"What about you?" Bain asked. "Have you grown up here in Rochinbal?"

Kekeen regained her smile. "Here? No. I've grown up… everywhere." She spread her arms and almost smacked the serving girl as she arrived with the flatbread. They all filled their mouths with butter and bread, and the conversation lagged for a few minutes.

As it resumed, Kekeen shifted the topic toward the Hawk King and his eternal reign. Aldan listened quietly, knowing almost nothing about such things. Bain, however, dominated this one. He seemed to know something about each clan, their connection—or lack of one—to the Hawk King, and their place in the greater Empire.

Kekeen returned to the stage twice more to sing, and they all sat silent to listen to her father tell two more tales. By then, Tunt reluctantly pointed out they needed to go. "I don't want to clean latrines tomorrow," he reminded them. With even greater reluctance, the boys stood and told Kekeen farewell. Only two or three other tables held any customers this late.

"I hope to see you all again," Kekeen told them, but her eyes settled on Aldan.

"I hope… we see you again too," he answered.

She smiled, nodded, and turned away. She joined her father as he stood by the bar, having abandoned the stage half an hour earlier. Aldan watched her go. Tunt pulled on his sleeve. He followed the others out, his legs feeling heavier than usual for some reason.

The other three stayed in an upbeat and loud mood all the way back to the arena. Aldan remained pensive, though he took part in some of their talk and endured a fair share of teasing over his obvious infatuation.

"You must teach me in the way of love, oh master," Jik proclaimed, mock-bowing to him. "When you bought the scarf, I thought you a fool. But it turned out brilliant! She'll remember you now, even if she forgets the rest of us."

Aldan shrugged. "I'll probably never see her again."

"Stranger things have happened under the moon's gaze," Bain said.

Aldan glanced up at the ever-watchful and ever-bright moon. Maybe. But likely not. The moon had no care for him. He wondered what his blood-woman friend would have to say about all this.

((((●))))

With half an hour remaining until midnight, the boys arrived back at the arena. Nerlesen, to no one's surprise, was already asleep. Aldan muttered an excuse about the latrine and slipped away. A few days earlier, he'd discovered an unused storage room not far from their bunks. Making sure no one watched, he slipped inside.

He sat down next to a small bowl he'd left here the last time. After some consideration, he lifted his left leg over the bowl. A bad cut on the back of his calf should work. He picked at it, tearing the scab off, until blood began to drip into the bowl. He let it drip until it looked like enough, then put pressure on the wound to cut it off.

Using the Taint became easier the more he did it. It took only a moment before his eyes burned. A spark appeared above the blood, the only visible manifestation of the change he made to the blood itself. A moment later, the woman's face formed within the blood.

"You really need to find a way to get some more blood," she said. "I'd like to show more than just my face sometime."

"You can do that?"

"I can show you all of me, if there's enough blood."

"Oh." Aldan hadn't thought of that. He also didn't have any idea where he'd get that much blood.

"How was training today?" the blood-woman asked.

"We didn't train today." Aldan told about their time in the city and especially the singer, Kekeen.

The woman sighed when he'd finished. "Oh, Aldan. What do you think will happen here?"

He wrinkled his brow. "What do you mean?"

"Do you think this singer will be your wife someday?"

"I—"

"Or even a mistress? How would that work?"

Aldan didn't answer.

"You are a slave. You are going to be an arena fighter. Your life has no opportunity for relationships."

"You said I could become the greatest arena fighter ever," he countered. "Won't that mean something?"

The blood-face flickered. "Of course it will. Long before we near the top, you'll have women throwing themselves at you. You can have as many as you like." The face moved back and forth. Shaking? "But none of them will be a real relationship. You won't have time for that. And of course, you can't marry."

"Why not?"

"Slaves cannot marry without their master's permission. And why would you want to restrict a woman to your life of slavery and peril?"

"What about when I win my freedom?"

"If you are able to do such a thing, it's at least ten years in the future. Will you ask this girl to wait for you? And if you recall, the Daghilch said your brand forbids you from marriage or having children. Even should you gain your freedom, you won't be rid of that."

"I'll hide it."

"No. You can't. By that time, you'll be famous, either way. Everyone will know your status. And... you may have developed other goals by then."

Aldan didn't answer.

"Aldan... I'm sorry to be so blunt, but you must know the truth. You will likely never see this girl again. When you graduate from Kan's training, you will be sold to another arena in another city."

Aldan looked away. He knew this, of course, but for one brief evening, he'd dared to dream. He'd told Borde he didn't think marriage was for him, but after meeting Kekeen, his desires shifted. Unfortunately, some fears still remained. Did the blood-woman understand that part of him?

"You can have women, like I said." She paused. "But I suppose that might be a problem as well. At any rate, you have to focus. You must become the best, and you're not even the best of this class yet."

Aldan took a few breaths before answering. "Have you ever discovered something you didn't think possible, and then… just wanted it so much?"

"I know exactly what you mean, believe it or not. But I had to learn patience… patience that endures longer than you will even live."

He wrinkled his brow again. "I thought you were a part of me?"

"I am. But I existed before you came along. Don't ask me to explain right now. It's complicated. But trust me: I understand you better than anyone ever will." The face lifted up as much as the small amount of blood allowed. "You want companionship. You know what? You'll always have me. You can always talk with me. I'll be here."

"It's not the same," he grumbled.

"I know. But I belong to you and no other. I know all about you. This is real intimacy, Aldan. Believe me."

"I don't even know your name."

"That's easily remedied." She chuckled. "You can call me… Zektel. That works with your language. Yes, Zektel."

"Zektel. But what's your real name?"

"That is my real name, the name I've chosen to use with you."

Names had turned into much more of a fluid attribute ever since the Taint. Aldan didn't know what to think about them any more.

"You'd best get to your bunk, dear. It's only a minute or so until midnight."

Aldan's eyes widened. He left the bowl and raced out of the storage room.

STOLEN HEALING

Then

With bleary eyes, Aldan watched Kan walk down the line of boys. He'd let them sleep in a little later than normal after their night out, but all of them showed signs of fatigue. The morning's strength training, though truncated, caused most of them to drag through lunch.

"Never again," Uyan muttered at one point. Aldan wondered what the other boys had ended up doing the night before.

Nukai pushed out the rack of weapons they'd first seen weeks ago. Aldan's heart beat a little faster. Real weapons. Life was about to get much more dangerous.

"The question arises," Kan said, continuing his walk, "How can I train eight boys to fight with real weapons in nine months, ready to kill or be killed… when they'll probably all kill each other during the training?" He walked over to the rack and picked up a mace. "These are meant to break bones. And if one of you breaks a bone, it takes weeks to heal, maybe even months. Am I right?"

The boys murmured agreement. Aldan remembered his own broken arm, but also a neighbor who broke his leg in the field. He'd been unable to work for at least two months. If Aldan's father and other neighbors had not helped carry his share of the work, the family might have starved.

"I can't afford to lose any of you eight. And thanks to the goddess and her loyal servants, we have a solution!" Kan gestured toward the entrance.

A tall figure walked out onto the sand, and Aldan stiffened. At first, he thought it was the Daghilch. But no. This blood-priest wore similar robes, but a golden sash, instead of purple. A thin tail of hair hung down from his moon-shaped haircut. If anything, his facial features were even more severe than the Daghilch. Did these people ever smile?

"As you all know," Kan said, "blood is life."

"Blood is precious. Blood is power," the boys recited.

"Exactly. And everyone makes regular blood donations to the temples, even though you've been exempted from that while training."

Aldan swallowed. Was that about to end? Maybe it wouldn't be a problem. He could control the Taint now. Or at least, he thought he could.

"That blood is used for various purposes throughout the Empire," Kan went on. "You've heard, and maybe had the good fortune to even see, that the priests can perform magic with it."

Aldan took another look at the priest, this time noticing several crystal vials hanging from his belt. They looked similar to the ones they'd used in the city, but much larger. Each one must hold almost a full cup of blood.

"One of those magical uses is healing."

Several of the boys murmured in understanding.

"Etkeegh here will be our healer for the remaining part of your training." Kan looked them over, patting the mace against his hand. "Nerlesen, step forward!"

"Sir!' Nerlesen took a long step out from the line at once.

Kan approached him. "Stretch out your arm."

Nerlesen hesitated for only a moment before holding his left arm out in front of him.

With a sudden move that caught everyone by surprise, Kan lunged forward and brought the mace down on Nerlesen's forearm. Everyone heard the sickening cracks and crunch as the bones shattered under the impact. Nerlesen, to his credit, let out only one shout of anguish before falling to his knees, clutching the useless arm with his other hand.

Aldan wanted to throw up. The brutality of the strike and its result shocked him, but he knew... he would have to get used to such things to survive the arena. But to see it happen to someone he knew hurt more than he'd expected. And he didn't even know Nerlesen very well.

Kan looked down at the injured boy. "That's a bad break. One of the worst. You'd be absolutely useless to me as a fighter now, if not for him." He gestured to the priest.

Etkeegh stepped forward, removing one of the blood vials from his belt. "Only blood from clan Kurav contains the power to heal," he declared in a nasally voice. He removed a stopper from the vial and held it up toward the moon, chanting something too low to hear.

Nerlesen rocked back and forth on the ground, his mouth sealed shut, but eyes bulging.

The priest lowered the vial and knelt beside Nerlesen. He poured blood from the vial into the palm of his other hand. Aldan strained to see what happened. The priest spread the blood over Nerlesen's forearm, eliciting a short cry of pain from the stoic boy. Then he grasped the arm with both hands and screamed, "Blood is power!" Nerlesen lost his control then and screamed, an agonizing cry that made all the boys cringe. A flash of light blinded them for a moment.

The priest stood, recapping the vial. "It is done. Praise the goddess." He stepped back so they all could see.

Nerlesen released his arm, staring at it with wide eyes. He stood up and twisted the arm back and forth. It appeared completely healed. Not even a trace of the blood remained, consumed by the magic or absorbed into his flesh somehow. Nerlesen flexed his fist and experimented with a range of movements. "It's—" He swallowed. "It's as if nothing happened."

"It still hurt," Tunt muttered.

"This is how you will keep training," Kan declared. "You will be injured. Devastating injuries. You will scream and soil yourselves and cry for your mothers. But then Etkeegh will heal you. And you'll get back to work. All of you."

"Not him."

Aldan tore his gaze from Nerlesen and saw the blood-priest pointing right at him. Kan looked back and forth between them, his brow furrowing. "Why not?"

"The blood-magic is not for a clanless one."

Kan stepped toward the priest. "I train boys from every clan. Clan has no meaning in the arena."

The priest folded his arms. "Nevertheless, he is different. The magic is not for him."

"Are you going to pay me for his bloodbond then?" Kan demanded. He pointed at Aldan with the mace. "He's near the top of this class right now. I will not lose him because of some blood-cursed bias of yours!"

"It is the will of the goddess."

"If you won't do it, I'll find another healer! I will take this to the leaders of clan Shasin and Dalbai!"

"You are welcome to do whatever you like. It will not change a thing."

Kan grabbed the priest by the arm and dragged him out of hearing from the boys. They watched him rant at the priest, who stood unmoving.

"Sands," Uyan said. "What did you do, Clanless?"

Aldan didn't answer. Fear had crept over him at the priest's first words, but now resolve hardened inside. "I just won't get injured," he said aloud.

Yeltek snorted. "Of course you won't."

"You're very good with a buckler," Bain said. "But you can't block everything."

Aldan shrugged. "What choice do I have?"

Kan returned, scowling. The blood-priest remained behind, his expression unchanged.

"We'll deal with that issue later," Kan said. "Let's move on. There's one more issue I need to address." He pointed back at the priest. "The healing magic can fix almost any wound... except one." He tapped his head. "You hurt your brain? Nothing we can do. So. While you're in my training, heads are sacred. You'll each be wearing helmets in case of accidental hits, but no one—no one!—is to target someone's head or face. Eyes don't always repair well either. Do you hear me?"

"Yes, sir!" they answered.

"Once you graduate, you're free to bash as many heads as you want in the arena. But not one of these heads here." He swept his hand to include all of them. He paused. "If you disregard me, and destroy one of my future arena fighters here... I won't kill you. Because I still need to sell you at graduation. But I will make you wish I'd killed you. I will personally break every one of your bones, let Etkeegh heal you, and then break them all again." He paused. "And that's what will happen before breakfast. Every day. Am I understood?"

"Yes, sir!" Quite a few stutters were included in this response. Clanless didn't know about the others, but the threat terrified him.

One by one, the boys were called forward and equipped with helmets, bucklers, and a mace. The helmets were unadorned and solid metal, covering the top of the head as well as the sides and back. Aldan adjusted it on his head and frowned. It wouldn't provide much real protection. A solid hit would simply cave in the helmet. Only Kan's threats could truly protect their heads.

When it came his turn to take a weapon, Aldan pulled a short sword from the rack. He'd barely had time to flick his wrist around a few times before Kan noticed. "Maces for now, Clanless," he said. "I'll teach the sword later."

Aldan pointed toward the priest. "They hate me already. Why should I follow their rules of honor?"

Kan hesitated and glanced at the priest. "Maces for now," he repeated.

Aldan traded the sword for a mace and turned to see who he would be partnered with this day. It was Jik.

"Spread out!" Kan ordered. "And… begin! Let's see some action, boys!"

Jik and Aldan circled each other. "I don't want to give you an injury the priest won't heal," the shorter boy said.

"You fight your best," Aldan countered. "I want you to do everything in your power to hurt me." Prior to now, with the practice weapons, the boys had given each other bruises, some of them significant enough to cause problems for a day or two at a time. But this would be different.

"If you're sure…"

Aldan nodded. "And I apologize in advance for the pain I will cause you."

Borde's words rippled through his thoughts: "Be a kind man, Aldan. Don't change." A kind man would not survive this training. A kind man would not win an arena fight. A kind man would not win his freedom.

Aldan lunged forward, swinging the mace in what looked like a wild stroke. Jik caught it on his buckler, but the impact knocked his buckler arm down. At the same time, Aldan smashed his own buckler against Jik's right hand and weapon, knocking it wide. He brought the mace back in a swift backhand. Jik managed to twist just enough for the mace head to strike him on the shoulder instead of the chest. The crunch of broken bone was drowned out by Jik's scream.

Aldan stepped back, lowering his weapon and buckler. Kan nodded at him and beckoned to the priest. Aldan waited while the priest did his work. He knew he should feel horrible about hurting Jik like that. But he pushed those feelings down. Already, he began thinking about his next fight. The same trick would not work on an opponent stronger than him. He would have to adjust his tactics based on so many factors.

His eyes went to the vial as the priest poured out more blood. How easy it would be to use the Taint against that vial. He considered it for a moment, drawing in a deep breath to prepare himself. But it would only cause problems for the boys, not for the priest himself.

One of the other boys screamed and fell. Aldan's eyes flicked to see Duurald, writhing on the sand with his leg turned the wrong way. Nerlesen stepped toward his fallen opponent before backing away.

Kan checked things out and summoned the priest again. Then he looked at Nerlesen and Aldan. "Since you two won and did damage so fast, you can fight each other now."

Aldan's eyes darted to the priest, who smiled as he knelt beside Duurald.

Kan had referred to him as near the top of the class, but Nerlesen was the best, no question. What if he got in a good hit and the priest refused to help? The only option that made sense now was full defense. He took a firm grip on his mace and buckler and turned his eyes to Nerlesen.

The two boys circled. Nerlesen abruptly changed direction, but Aldan adapted without missing a step. Nerlesen tried the same trick again, but with equal results. Aldan continued to move, keeping pace with Nerlesen's every step. If the other boy stepped forward, Aldan stepped back. They roamed the sand, staying well away from the other boys, but still getting no closer to each other.

Nerlesen had enough and leaped forward. Aldan planted his feet in a defensive stance and let him come. He deflected the first blow easily enough. In his attack, Nerlesen left himself open for a quick counterattack, or so it appeared. Aldan resisted the temptation and backed off to circle his opponent again.

Three more times, Nerlesen attacked. And each time, he made sure to leave an opening for Aldan to attack. But Aldan never did. The openings might be real, but he doubted it. Nerlesen was good enough to offer fake openings. Even if they were real, Aldan wouldn't risk anything in this fight.

"Attack me, Clanless!" Nerlesen growled at last. "We're supposed to fighting here."

"You're too good," Aldan said, keeping his eyes fixed on Nerlesen's. "I'm not giving you the slightest chance."

"You're afraid the healer won't help you."

"I'm not afraid. I'm certain."

"Coward."

Aldan ignored the insult. They could call him whatever they wanted now. He didn't care. His thoughts were solidifying now. A kind man? No. He couldn't be a kind man now. The only way to survive this, the only way to come through on the other side, was to become something different.

A cowardly man? No. A cruel man.

Aldan watched Jik rotate his shoulder one way and then the other. "It moves normal, but… I don't know. Something still seems wrong." He sat down on his bunk and looked around at the other boys preparing for bed. "Anyone else feel that way?"

"It's your mind," Bain offered. "Your brain remembers what happened to it and expects it to need natural healing, not magic. It hasn't caught up with you yet."

"Maybe a good night's sleep will solve it," Jik grumbled.

Aldan looked down. Out of all the boys, only he hadn't required the blood-priest's magic. Nerlesen hadn't required it beyond Kan's demonstration, but all the others suffered some kind of painful, sometimes devastating injury. And then were healed.

"We still have almost seven months left of this," Uyan said. "I don't want this kind of pain every day for seven months!"

"Then don't get hit," Yeltek said with more nastiness than usual. "Be like Clanless over there."

Several of the boys muttered, but didn't say anything else out loud for a few minutes. Most of them stretched out on their bunks, grateful just to lie down.

"Kan is a sick, sick man," Duurald said from his bunk. "What kind of man enjoys watching boys getting their bones shattered over and over?"

"I hate him so much," Uyan griped. Others murmured their agreement.

"I hate him too," Yeltek said, "but… I'm going to impress him." He paused. "If it's the last thing I do."

"Isn't that weird?" Jik sat up. "I want to impress him too, even though I despise the man."

Aldan mulled it over. He had to admit he felt the same way. The things Kan put them through were agonizing and cruel. Sometimes, he seemed to delight in making them do more than they thought possible, to hurt more than they thought possible. And yet… Kan had praised him today, and it stuck with him all day. He would trade a day of pain and hardship for one sentence of affirmation from that blood-cursed man. Strange how that worked.

"Does anyone not care what Kan thinks about him?" Yeltek asked.

"I don't," Bain said.

"Liar," Duurald scoffed.

Bain waved in the air without looking at him. "I don't. I will take what I need from him, and move on. Once I graduate from this place, I'll never think about him again."

"He's right," Nerlesen said from his bunk, staring up at the ceiling. "Don't look up to Kan. He's a means to an end and nothing more."

"What end?" Tunt asked.

"Survival." Nerlesen rolled over. "Somebody turn down the lantern. We need to sleep."

Aldan lay awake in the darkness that followed. Something had changed in him today. Yesterday's Aldan wouldn't have done that to Jik. Yesterday, he still clung to who he was before: a son, a brother, a cousin, a farmer… a kind man. None of that mattered any more.

He wasn't Aldan any more. The priests claimed to have taken his name, but he'd still thought of himself that way. Kekeen was right; no one could take a name away from you.

But you could abandon it yourself.

Aldan was gone. From now on, he would answer only to Clanless.

☾ ☾ ☾ ☽ ● ☾ ☽ ☽ ☽ ☽

Kan did not have them fight each other with real weapons every day. In fact, that practice turned out to be reserved for once a week. The chaos of their first battles with each other had been another kind of lesson, one that none of them were sure they understood. From then on, when they fought, they fought one-on-one with Kan and everyone else watching. It became like real duels. Most of the boys considered it their favorite day of the week, as they could sit and watch when it wasn't their turn. Kan put a chart up near the arena entrance where the boys could track their victories and losses. It soon became evident—if it weren't already—who fought the best among the class.

Nerlesen led the pack, of course. But Clanless and Yeltek were right behind him, followed by Duurald. Bain sat in the middle, with Uyan, Jik, and Tunt at the bottom.

Yet even Tunt, the least skilled of them, now appeared far different from the soft and pleasant boy he'd been on arrival. Like the rest, he'd lost any childhood fat and developed musculature across his chest, arms, and legs. But it still wasn't enough. Tunt needed the healing magic more than any of them, and that took a toll. Unlike some of the others, he never grew accustomed to the pain.

"Blood take it all," Kan griped while watching a duel between Bain and Tunt. "Tunt's like a whipped dog, flinching at every move his opponent makes."

Clanless looked past Kan at Nerlesen, but neither said anything. They weren't sure Kan intended for his words to be overheard by the two standing closest to him. He might be talking to himself.

"Bain could be top of the class if he wanted to," Kan went on. He looked back and forth at the two boys beside him. So he did intend for them to hear! "He thinks he gains an advantage by pretending to be less than he is. Don't let him fool you."

"Understood," Nerlesen answered. Clanless nodded.

Kan soon made a habit of giving commentary on duels in the hearing of Nerlesen and Clanless. Sometimes, Yeltak was included in the conversation as well. These commentaries were quiet and specific thoughts, not like the loud observations he made to everyone. He appeared interested in teaching the best members of the class more advanced concepts, things he didn't think the others were ready to hear.

In the confines of the small group, Clanless asked a question that had been bugging him since the priest's arrival. "With healing magic, does every arena fight have to end in death?"

Kan glanced at him, but didn't dismiss the question. "Not… always," he said. "Your graduation fight is a fight to the death. What happens after that will depend on the arena owner. Most want fights to the death. But if both fighters are valuable enough, they will allow the loser to survive and be healed." He raised a finger. "But only if losing that fighter would cost him more than he's willing to pay."

High Winter came in strong, dropping the temperature as the sun surrendered to the goddess every day. The arena gave them shelter from the winter winds, at the least, but when snow fell on the sand, Kan acted as though nothing had changed. The boys ran in the snow and fought in the snow. Though he struggled at first, Clanless grew accustomed to the frigid air against his bare shoulder over time. The fireplace in the dining hall became the most popular location. The bunk room, though it lacked a fire, stayed above freezing, being so deep within the structure.

As the weeks progressed, Clanless continued to avoid major injury. Kan never commented on it, or brought up the problem with the priest.

Until the day it happened.

❨❨❨●❩❩❩

The injury happened in a fight with Bain. Clanless told himself he should have known better. Should have seen it coming. Kan had warned him about Bain's deceptions, and he'd seen it in action plenty of times. Yet none of that knowledge saved him.

Bain behaved as he often did in their duel: mediocre attacks, barely-sufficient defense, just enough to get by. Kan called him lazy at one point. And so it seemed. Yet every once in a while, Bain would show his true capabilities. Clanless hadn't expected this duel to be one of those times.

One moment, Bain was blocking his attacks with a buckler that looked ready to fall off his hand… the next, he smashed aside Clanless's own buckler, spun in close, and delivered a back-handed mace strike on the right side of his chest.

Clanless heard and felt ribs breaking. The impact alone knocked him to his knees in half-melted snow, but he kept his buckler and mace up, watching for a follow-up strike. Bain stepped back, even as Kan yelled and ran toward them.

The pain exploded up through his chest. Somehow, he didn't cry out. Seeing Bain back off, he let his defenses fall. He dropped the tools and fell forward onto his hands and knees. His breathing came in shallow gasps, each one sending stabs of agony through his chest.

"Don't move! Don't move!" Kan shouted. He slid to a stop and bent down next to the boy.

Bain looked around. "Where's the priest?"

"He's not coming." Kan put a hand on Clanless's shoulder. "I need you to lie down, Clanless. Come on."

"Hard to… breathe…"

"It's all right. Lie back. You can breathe. It just hurts. I know." He turned his head. "Bain! Find Nukai as fast as you can. Tell him what happened and that we need to do something about the pain! Go!" The other boy dropped his mace and buckler and ran.

Some of the other boys trickled closer. Clanless could hear them murmuring with each other. "Let's see if his demon helps him now." That was Yeltek's voice, the loudest.

"Listen to my voice, Clanless. I need you to concentrate." Kan's hand on his shoulder was firm. "Is all of the pain at the point of injury, or is it spreading?"

"What?"

Kan repeated the question.

Clanless shook with the shallow breaths. He longed for more air, but even the short breaths caused pain. Every attempt to draw in more sent it stabbing up through his chest. He tried to communicate this to Kan.

"Yes, yes, I understand. But is it anywhere else?" Kan pressed harder on his shoulder. "Up here at all?" Clanless shook his head. "What about in your stomach? Anything there?" Kan's other hand pressed gently on his stomach. Clanless shook his head again. So hard to keep breathing this way.

"Good, good. Duurald! Nerlesen! Over here. Hold him down, arms and legs. No, Duurald, hold both of them. Like that. Good."

Clanless tried to understand what was happening. Why would they need to hold him?

"I'm going to have to touch the wound, Clanless. Boys, don't let him thrash around." Kan words spilled out much faster than normal. "I need to find out how bad things are broken, and this is the only way. Clanless, I'm sorry. This will hurt."

Unbearable pain, greater than the impact of the mace itself, exploded in his side. Clanless screamed now, unable to hold it back and not caring what anyone else thought. He screamed again as Kan's fingers continued to probe. Unable to keep getting enough air and scream at the same time, Clanless lost consciousness.

He woke again only a few moments later. He still lay on the sand, but the other boys no longer held him down. Kan still knelt beside him. Nukai appeared in his view, still bundled up in his furs, holding a drinking cup.

"You're going to have to drink this, Clanless. Do you hear me? And that means I have to lift your head and shoulders up. It's going to hurt some more, but this is how we help with that." Kan kept talking. Maybe he had been talking all along, and Clanless had missed some of it.

Kan's powerful arm came around behind his shoulders and lifted. As his chest moved, new pain erupted, but he managed not to scream this time. Nukai brought the cup to his lips and poured. Clanless struggled to swallow the thick liquid. At least the swallowing didn't hurt as much as trying to breathe in between. The drink tasted of herbs and honey disguising something quite bitter.

"Good. That will help." Kan let him back down, then stood. "We need to carry him inside, but keep him lying flat. Nukai, find a flat surface."

Breathing continued to be a struggle between the need for air and the desire to avoid pain. Every time he gave in and took a deeper breath, the pain tore the air back from his lungs. Yet his body continued to demand it. Darkness grew around the edges of his vision again, but he didn't succumb to it. At least, he didn't think he did. Events became a little unclear after that.

They found something on which to carry him. Together, four of the boys lifted him and walked back to the bunk room. The transition to his bed didn't work well, making him scream again. But at least he could relax. Kan said something about tomorrow, but he didn't hear it all. A deep drowsiness took hold, dragging him down into the darkness.

（（（●）））

Clanless stared up at the ceiling of the bunk room. He'd been lying on his back for at least a full day. Nukai's drink, delivered every few hours, kept the pain in his side manageable. He thought he'd gotten used to the struggle for air, but it seemed to be getting worse. Several blankets kept the chill away… barely.

Kan appeared by his bed during the boys' lunch break. For a moment, fear clutched Clanless when the big man knelt next to him. But Kan only changed the bandage and examined the wound. His words were encouraging, but when he stepped outside to talk with Nukai, Clanless overheard something about "…worsening… rib stabbed something inside… temple… another priest?"

So now, staring at the ceiling, his prospects looked bleak. Something inside him wasn't improving. Part of him considered whether that might not be a good thing. If he died now, he'd never have to kill someone in the arena. Never have to fight and fight and fight until either he died anyway, or somehow won his freedom.

Freedom. He'd never have a chance for that. To forge his own life, choose his own companions and his own future. To find that girl again—Kekeen—or someone like her.

The blood-priests wanted him dead. Giving up would please them, and that's the last thing he wanted to do. The faces of the priests back home, the Daghilch, and Etkeegh danced across the ceiling in his mind, all of them with cruel smiles. No, he'd defy them, no matter what it took. And if the Taint was what caused this to happen to him, he'd defy it too. And the goddess, if that's what it took. She certainly didn't care about him.

He rolled his head to the side and noticed his old bandage lying beside the bed. Kan hadn't taken it. Was the blood staining it enough? Clanless reached out his hand and focused the Taint. His eyes burned as usual. "Zektel? Can you hear me?" he whispered.

The woman's voice answered, more faint than ever: "I can save you, if you can get some of the blood from the priest…" It faded away.

Clanless looked up again. It wasn't much of a hope, but it gave him something to do. Unfortunately, it would probably mean revealing Zektel's existence to one or more of his friends. But… it would be worth it to wipe those cruel smiles off the priests' faces.

Tunt slipped in after eating his lunch. Clanless sent him to get help, and he returned with Jik and Bain.

"I'm getting worse," he told them. "Something's damaged inside me." Each breath he took in between the words hurt more than ever.

"Sorry," Bain said. "Maybe I am the enemy, after all."

"I need you to get a vial of blood from the priest."

"He'll never give us one!" Tunt protested.

"Besides, he's the only one who can do the magic with it," Jik said.

"Someone else can," Clanless said. "But I need the blood."

"I'll get it," Bain said. "Jik, later this sun's retreat, I'm going to have an accident with one of the weapons next to you. When the priest comes to heal you, I'll steal a vial from him."

"Why do I have to get hurt?"

"I'd use Uyan, but he might see it coming and dodge. You have to let it happen."

"I'll do it," Tunt said, swallowing hard. Clanless smiled. That was a true friend.

Bain paused before answering. "Tunt, you… you're too afraid of getting hurt."

"I'll do it for Aldan."

Bain sighed. "Sands. If you flinch and don't get hurt… I can't have two accidents in one day. That would look suspicious, even for me."

"I'll do it," he repeated.

Bain looked down at Clanless. "Unfortunately, we won't be able to come back with it until tonight."

"I'll be here."

Bain nodded. "I'll do this, but if it works… you might have some explaining to do."

Clanless nodded and closed his eyes. Nukai's last dose was taking effect, putting drowsiness above his pain.

"Hang on," Tunt whispered.

When he opened his eyes again, the other boys were gone.

❨❨❨❨●❩❩❩❩

His condition worsened while the sun retreated across the sky. As he fought for each breath, he thought he heard a bubbling sound during his exhales. His chest and shoulder muscles grew sore from the constant tension of trying to pull in more air. He slept little. Over and over, the struggle to breathe woke him up within a few minutes of dozing off.

His thoughts wandered far as the hours passed. He thought of home: his parents, his sister, cousin Borde. He thought of the boys he'd played with in the fields when their labor wasn't required. Working beside his father was nothing compared to the work in the arena training. How much stronger he must be now, compared to those he left behind. Stronger even than his uncle…

He pushed those thoughts aside with the memory of the singer,

Kekeen. Why was she so different from other girls he'd known? Her voice entranced him, and not only while she sang. Zektel might be right about potential futures, but why give up on fantasies now? He might be dying.

When Tunt finally returned, Clanless had almost given up. Each breath hurt so much and took so much effort. Was it even worth it?

"If I could, I'd kill that Bain," Tunt declared. "He didn't have to hurt me that much!"

Clanless wanted to ask what happened, but didn't want to expend the effort.

Jik appeared a moment later. "Bain's on his way. He had to sneak back into the arena to get the blood from where he hid it." He sat on the bed next to Clanless. "The priest noticed the missing blood almost right away. He insisted on searching all of us. I don't know how Bain got it hidden before that."

"The priest was furious!" Tunt added. "He told Kan he'd have to pay for it. Kan told him to take out of the what the priest cost him by not healing you!"

"I thought his face was going to explode." Jik laughed, but then noticed Clanless wasn't reacting to any of their words. "Sands. Are we too late?"

"No…" Clanless whispered.

Bain charged into the room and slid to a stop, panting. "Nukai almost caught me. How can someone wearing that many clothes move so fast?"

"Did you get it?" Jik asked.

Bain pulled the vial of blood from inside his shirt, but looked toward the door. "We can't get caught with this."

"Not here," Clanless managed to say. "Help me up."

Tunt's eyes widened. "You can't get up! You'll hurt yourself worse!"

"I don't think he cares, Tunt," Bain said. "If this works, it'll heal him. If it doesn't…"

If it didn't work, Clanless would die, anyway. He started to push himself up, gritting his teeth.

"All right, but you can't scream," Jik said, taking one of his hands. "They'll come see what's wrong." Tunt took the other hand. Together, they helped Clanless first sit on the edge of the bed, then get to his feet. The darkness swirled in around the edges of his eyes, threatening to overtake him. Without the other boys' support, he would have fallen on his face.

"Where to?" From the door, Bain looked down both directions of the hall.

Clanless directed them to the empty storage room. Every step sent agony arcing up through his chest, and breathing grew even harder. Once in the room, they lowered him to the floor. Shivers wracked his body, adding to the pain and discomfort. He beckoned for the empty bowl. "Pour some blood in," he told Bain.

"All of it?"

"No. Just a little." Clanless held his fingers apart to indicate a small amount.

Jik backed up. "Uh-uh. I helped you this far, but I don't want to see whatever happens next. No thanks."

"It's just Aldan," Tunt said.

Jik moved to the door. "In case you missed it last time, he has something weird going on. The less I see, the better." He slipped out.

Just as well. Clanless didn't want anyone to know about his secrets, but he would have to trust these two if he wanted to survive. For the moment, anyway.

Bain uncorked the vial and spilled the designated blood into the bowl. "You've done something here before." He must have noticed the dried blood on the bowl's edges.

Clanless stretched a hand toward the bowl and tried to use the Taint. It proved harder than usual; his concentration kept getting broken up by his painful breathing. He accepted the agony and took a deep breath. It almost knocked him out. But he held it long enough to ignite the blood.

"Goddess," Bain whispered.

"Aldan, your eyes…" Tunt took a step back.

Clanless let out the held breath and almost choked trying to get more air. He coughed, a violent reaction that almost flipped him.

"Zektel," he gasped. "Help…"

A loud sigh came from the bowl. "This is not good, Aldan."

Tunt backpedaled and fell. Bain took a step back as well, but kept his eyes on the blood. "What is that?" he whispered.

"Only way," Clanless said.

"If it must be," she answered. "Who has the priest's blood?"

"I do." Bain regained his composure and curiosity.

"Pour a little on Aldan's injury, and stand back."

"Th-the bandage," Tunt said, pointing.

Bain rolled his eyes. He ripped the bandage off and poured some of the priest's blood on the uncovered wound. Something arced from the bowl to the wound, a moving spark or a motion of light; no one got a good look at it before light exploded outward from Clanless.

Clanless screamed, a horrific cry that tore his throat and kept going.

Tunt waved his hands and stared back and forth from the writhing boy to the door. Bain took a single step back and replaced the cork on the vial. Clanless thrashed about, barely aware of the two other boys' reactions. The searing pain was worse than the original injury. And something… something inside him moved. Broken bones moving back into place? An inner organ repairing itself? Whatever it was, he regretted the entire process. He should have given up, let himself die. It would have been better than this…

The pain eased. It subsided faster than it had come, fading down to a dull ache. Clanless gasped for air, over and over, and found he could breathe. It still hurt, but nothing like it had before.

"D-did it work?" Tunt asked. He kept looking toward the door. "Sands. Kan will have heard that. Someone must have."

"It looks… better," Bain said, cocking his head and crouching.

Clanless lifted his arm and tried to look. His side still looked horribly bruised, but… that was all. The insides were healed. "Zektel… why did it hurt so much?"

"I'm not a healer, Aldan. I did what I could. You should recover much faster, at least."

Bain nodded. "This is good. Yeah. If it were completely healed, Kan would know we did something. This way, it just looked like he's getting better on his own."

"Much better," Tunt muttered. He pointed at the bowl. "And who is talking?"

"This is Zektel," Clanless said, letting his head back down to the floor. "Zektel, this is Bain and Tunt."

"Thank you for helping him," Zektel said. "But you must never tell another soul about any of this. Especially about me."

"Who are you?" Tunt asked. "Are you a demon?"

A tinkling laughter came from the bowl. "No, dear one. I'm not a demon. I'm a part of Aldan here. He's very special."

"We should get out of here." Bain stood and put the blood vial back within his shirt. "Clanless—Aldan—can you walk?"

"I think so." He rolled over, almost colliding with the bowl, paused, then pushed himself up. The other boys helped him to his feet. He discovered he could walk, almost on his own, step by careful step. He stared at the ground, trying not to let the other boys see anything in his face. At least they hadn't heard Zektel's final words, the ones she'd whispered to him when he almost hit the bowl:

"We'll have to hope both of these boys die in the graduation."

THE PRISONER

Clanless made his way to the cells beneath the arena. Few ever visited these depths, but he knew it well enough. Hagh and Sugh brought him here a couple of times to spy out some future opponents. It didn't take long to find the correct cell: the only one with four guards standing outside it. Clanless nodded to them and stepped past, almost touching the row of iron bars. At one time, he'd wondered: why use bars like this, instead of a simple wall? But then he realized the reasoning. Bars created a cage. Cages were for animals, not people.

"Clanless?" A disheveled figure emerged from the shadows at the back of the cell. Daviland's overall appearance had not changed much since the last time Clanless had seen him, though his clothes were now stained and torn. A dirty string hung around his neck and beneath his shirt, a pale imitation of the fine necklace he'd worn before. Bruises decorated his face. Whatever struggle he'd gone through in his capture had not been gentle to him. He limped as he approached the bars. Clanless winced. Bad enough he'd have to kill this man. Did they have to make it easier? Spending the frigid nights in this cell would make him stiff and slow the next day. Combined with his injuries, it seemed an insult to keep him alive that long.

"It is you." Daviland took hold of the bars and stared at him. "They say I'm to fight you tomorrow."

"The Hawk King has so ruled." If not for the king's order, Clanless wouldn't be here now. Evaluate his opponent? Daviland knew how to fight; that much Clanless knew. But like the king's son, he wasn't a true warrior. He hadn't faced death day after day for years on end. He'd be lucky if the fight lasted longer than thirty seconds.

"It's not too late," Daviland said in a low voice, trying to keep the guards from hearing. "We can still work together, you and I." He pointed to the brand on Clanless's shoulder. "They gave you that. Why would you serve them?"

Clanless tapped the brand himself. "I am one fight away from escaping this. Your death sets me free."

"My life can set you free as well. Turn against the Hawk King tomorrow. You know who he is. You know he is evil. We've been over this."

"The Hawk King holds my bloodbond. If I turn on him, I will never be free." Clanless didn't know why he even bothered to answer. He didn't need to justify himself. He started to turn away.

"It is corrupt! All of it is corrupt!" Daviland's voice rose. "The Hawk King. The blood-priests. The arena system. All of it! Corrupt through and through. They enslave others for their own entertainment and power."

"And you would be different?"

"Yes!" Daviland gripped the bars. "You know this. I was raised in a clanhold, like you. I grew up seeing the oppression of the lower clans. I saw no hope for change either. Until…"

Clanless didn't speak. He knew part of it already, but was curious to hear Daviland tell it himself.

"Until a prophet came to my hold one day. He arrived just in time to rescue me from a barbarian raid, a raid he'd told the priests was coming… and they ignored him. Yet everything he has said has come true!"

"Did he say you would be in the Hawk King's prison?"

"No." Daviland's eyes sought his out, trying to force Clanless to focus on him. "But he said I would kill the Hawk King. Me. Daviland of clan Tokuur. I would kill the Hawk King."

Clanless looked past Daviland into the cell. "And where is this prophet now? Why is he not with you?"

"The priests killed him. They didn't like how he pointed out their corruption."

"And he didn't see that coming?"

"He did see it coming. That's the point!" Daviland pushed his face against the bars. "He knew he would die, and he kept standing up for what was right. You can do the same."

"I'm not going to die for you, Daviland."

"You don't—"

"Listen to me now," Clanless interrupted. "Tomorrow, we will step out into that arena. And I will kill you. I don't want to. I never want to. But I will, because your death buys my freedom from all of this. I will say a prayer, and then I will take your blood, the final ounces of blood I need. And then I'll be free."

"Do you really think the Hawk King will let you go?"

"I've done what I needed to do. I've collected the blood to pay for it. Why wouldn't he?"

"When has the Hawk King ever let go of something he possessed?" Daviland shook his head. "He won't do it now. You're too valuable to him. More so than you know."

Clanless fought down his anger. "Eight years I have served and fought and killed. And tomorrow it ends. Regardless of your words and your prophecies, 'Chosen One.' Tomorrow it ends."

"It will end tomorrow," Daviland said, stepping back from the bars. "But not the way you think."

"Because you're going to kill the Hawk King?"

He nodded. "And if you are in my way…" He took a deep breath. "Then I have no choice."

Clanless raised his eyebrows. "You think you can win?"

"I know I can win." The quiet confidence with which Daviland gave the statement made Clanless step back this time.

"Then you are a fool." The fighter shook his head and turned away.

"The Hawk King will fall, Clanless!" Daviland called after him. "You can still decide not to fall with him!" His voice grew louder: "She wouldn't want this, Clanless! You know that!"

Clanless paused as anger rose up within. "Thanks for reminding me why I hate you so much," he growled before stalking away.

BECOMING THE VILLAIN

Then

Kan appeared relieved at Clanless's recovery. If he had suspicions, he didn't say anything. In fact, the lack of questions bothered Clanless. Kan didn't ask questions. Tunt didn't ask questions. Bain didn't ask questions, not even with his usual "let's exchange information" method. Why not? Didn't they want to know what happened? What he'd done to the blood? Where Zektel came from?

Jik pretended nothing had happened, and he hadn't been involved. He didn't even speak to the other three for several days. Bain got back at him by pretending like Jik didn't exist, walking into him and looking around confused while ignoring Jik's complaints. The smaller boy was not amused.

In two days, Clanless returned to the arena. The wound cleared away, but left behind an odd dark scar, shaped like a starburst with thin arms. Kan took it easy on him for a couple of days, but Clanless pushed himself. By his reckoning, they'd been here for at least four months now. Almost halfway through the training period, and he didn't know half of what he needed to know. By the next day of duels, Clanless stood ready to take part. His loss to Bain pushed him below Yeltek, and he couldn't let that stand. He fought his way back with a vengeance.

Five months into their training, Kan finally allowed the use of swords. The other boys were leery of the dishonorable weapon, but Clanless took one up with delight. He couldn't help a quick glance at the scowling priest healer, Etkeegh.

"I teach you the sword because I have to," Kan said. "It is an option for arena fighters, however dishonorable it may be."

"Dishonorable and downright blasphemous," Etkeegh added behind him.

Kan turned toward him. "I do not need nor desire your input in my training, priest. If you wish to address my fighters, you can speak to them at the evening meal."

Clanless almost laughed. By the time of the evening meal, none of them were in any condition or mood to hear speeches, and the priest knew it. His scowl grew deeper somehow.

"As I said," Kan went on, "it is an option. But I've trained you best, and will continue to train you, in the use of the mace. I strongly recommend you use one in your graduation fights. There is a chance, however, that you will face someone who uses a sword, even if you never use one yourself. Because of that, you need to know all about them." He lifted a sword. "The mace is a pummeling weapon, meant for bashing, breaking bones. You know this. A sword is different. A sword is meant for spilling blood."

Several of the boys muttered. Clanless caught the word "Blasphemy."

"If you use a sword the way you use a mace, you won't be very effective. A sword is for slashing and stabbing." Kan made a few motions. "I will be teaching you various forms of each type of attack. So. Spread out! I won't have you accidentally cutting each other open."

The boys took their places. Kan demonstrated a simple slashing move and made them repeat it. By now used to the weight of a mace, Clanless found the short sword lighter and easier to move. That much was evident to all when Duurald dropped his sword on the next slash.

"Dropped weapon, dead fighter!" Kan snapped. "Pick it up. Door-to-door twice. Go!"

As Duurald ran, Clanless tightened his grip on the weapon. He hadn't dropped one since their second day with the practice weapons, and he didn't want to change that now.

The more he used the sword, the more Clanless appreciated it. A sword slash could have a follow-through, whereas a mace bash had to be pulled back after a strike. The sword allowed for faster recovery and swifter attacks.

In the evening, most of the other boys griped about the sword training. Most proclaimed how they would never use such a dishonorable weapon.

"Don't we still need to know how they're used, though?" Uyan asked hesitantly.

"Why?" Yeltek demanded. "What good does it do us? I'll take a mace against a sword any day. And win!"

"What if you're up against someone like Clanless?" The others turned their attention to Bain, who lay on his bunk. He tossed a ball made from one of his old shirts into the air and caught it.

"What difference does that make?" Yeltek asked. "I can beat Clanless."

Clanless rolled his eyes and climbed into his own bunk.

"But if you're fighting someone like him, whose skill is at least close to yours…" Bain threw the ball and caught it again. "Then doesn't it make sense to know how he's going to fight? Won't that give you an advantage?"

"Maybe…" Yeltek's slow answer indicated he suspected a trap.

"So we learn swords for that reason alone." Bain tossed the ball at Yeltek and rolled over. "Someone put out the lamp?"

The darkness descended before Clanless asked his own question: "Then none of you would even consider using a sword in the arena instead of a mace?"

A chorus of "No" answered him, though it didn't sound like everyone answered. "Why would we choose dishonor over honor?" Yeltek's voice dripped with derision.

"Why would we let the blood-priests define what is honorable?" Clanless countered.

"Just because they think you're an abomination doesn't mean the rest of us have to hate them."

Clanless froze. Abomination? What did Yeltek know?

"The blood-priests control a lot of what happens in the arenas," Nerlesen said. "It's best not to antagonize them."

"I'll do whatever they want if they keep healing me," Duurald added.

After a moment of silence, Uyan added, "And I'd rather be on the side of the goddess than against her."

Clanless almost said "there is no goddess," but bit his lip instead. Blasphemy might be a step too far. Maybe she did exist. But if so, she cared about him no more than the priests did.

"Swords are a coward's weapons," Yeltek declared.

"We'll see in our next duel," Clanless said.

Several of the boys reacted to the taunt with "oooh!"

"As long as you don't cheat, we will! Then you can run to your demon for more healing."

"I don't cheat." Clanless knew responding didn't make any difference, but he didn't want to leave the charge hanging.

"Hard to see it any other way," Duurald put in, "when you do so well without getting hurt like the rest of us."

"Maybe he's just that good," Tunt said.

"Maybe you should stop defending him, Lump!" Yeltek snapped, receiving snickers from his supporters. "When have you even won a single fight?"

Clanless sat up. "Remember what happened last time you came after me in here, Yeltek?" Silence answered him. "Leave Tunt alone, or we can go again."

Yeltek didn't answer. Clanless waited a few minutes before lying down again. That was foolish. Fighting Yeltek in the bunk room would not make him a better arena fighter. Even the verbal sparring was a waste of effort. In four months' time, he would be leaving these boys for good. Some would be dead, and the survivors would be spread across the Empire. Making enemies of them—or even friends, for that matter—was pointless.

"Thanks," Tunt whispered from the next bed.

❲❲❲●❳❳❳

Yeltek got his wish at the end of the next week. He and Clanless were designated to fight each other in one of the practice duels. The other boys gathered around Kan to watch. Etkeegh stood near, but only for Yeltek. Kan's appeals to higher authorities had thus far proven unsuccessful. The priesthood's hatred of the Taint extended all the way to the top.

Given the choice of equipment, Clanless took the buckler and short sword. Yeltek sneered as he took the mace. "Not only will you fight without honor, you'll fight with less training! Idiot."

He wasn't entirely wrong. The boys had weeks of training with the mace versus less than a fortnight's time with the sword. And yet Clanless felt confident. Enough of the mace training bled over into the sword. He might not use it to its full potential, but he didn't think it would make things harder.

"Positions!" Kan called. The boys moved into the open and walked two dozen yards apart from each other. "Begin!"

Clanless took his first steps to the right, as he almost always did. Yeltek did the same. They walked a wide circle, slowly closing the distance between them. It wasn't the only way of beginning; sometimes, one or the other would charge all the way. Sometimes, Clanless would charge halfway across the distance just to see an opponent's reaction, before he came to a stop and resumed the circling.

"No taichin tricks!" Yeltek called.

Clanless didn't answer. It would be so much easier to ignore Yeltek if the other boy wasn't also a talented fighter. Right now, the best way to defeat him would be to set aside anything personal and focus on technique.

But Yeltek didn't make it easy. He stopped and took several steps closer before shifting to a leftward circle. Clanless changed direction to match him. "Everyone hates you, Clanless." Yeltek spoke quieter now, not yelling for all to hear. "The priests want you dead. All of the other guys here can't stand you. Except lumpy Tunt, of course. And he's only your friend because he hopes you'll protect him somehow."

Only a few feet separated the boys now. "You've even scared Jik away," Yeltek went on. "He's the one who told us about your demon, you know. He's terrified of you now."

"Like you, you mean?" Clanless couldn't resist the taunt. Keeping his own emotions down was one thing, but he could try to goad Yeltek into an emotional reaction instead. At the same time, he watched his opponent's movements. Previous bouts with Yeltek had shown him certain inclinations he could exploit, if timed right.

Yeltek's right foot shifted forward in an apparent preparation to lunge, but he pulled back instead when Clanless didn't react. He liked that trick.

"Come on!" one of the other boys shouted. Kan no longer criticized them for this kind of thing. In the beginning, he'd wanted them to work on actual fighting. Now, he let them work out the mental details as well, however long it took.

Yeltek pulled his mace behind his buckler, a position that would allow him to make quick backhanded strikes and uppercuts. But the added strain of holding both weapon and buckler up made the pose a difficult one to maintain, meaning he probably meant to strike as soon as possible.

Clanless used Yeltek's own trick of shifting his foot forward for a moment. Yeltek took the bait and lunged, bringing his mace out and upward in a vicious uppercut. If challenged on the move, he would claim to be aiming for the chest, but they all knew the strike was meant to smash an opponent's face.

Prepared for the move, Clanless had only to lean to the side to avoid the strike. At the same time, he whipped his sword beneath Yeltek's strike. The blade nicked the other boy's elbow, drawing blood. The watching boys reacted with shouts.

Yeltek brought his mace back down as fast as it had gone up. Too close to back up, Clanless caught it on his buckler. The heavy blow staggered him. Yeltek followed up with his own buckler, shoving Clanless back. His foot caught on something in the sand, and he fell.

A few months earlier, Kan spent almost an entire week shoving the boys onto the sand over and over. "You have to learn how to fall!" At first, they all thought him insaneand cruel. But now, they all knew. They'd been practicing for moments like this. Clanless used the momentum of the fall to roll himself twice and regain his footing. Yeltek's mace crunched into the sand a split-second after he left it.

Back on his feet, Clanless circled. He tried to ignore the blood dripping from Yeltek's elbow. How easy it would be to use the Taint, to end this fight in a matter of seconds. But he didn't need to do that. Not yet. He could still defeat Yeltek without it. Besides, Kan watched too close. He would see. Somehow, Clanless didn't think he would approve.

His blood pounded. He breathed faster. Was this what Kan meant by the bloodrush? Yeltek did appear to move slower, but nothing else changed.

Another feint, another attack, another dodge, another block. So the battle progressed. The retreating sun, well past its dance with the moon, beat down. Sweat poured from both boys, especially beneath their helmets.

Yeltek's taunts grew fewer and farther between. He needed every breath. The boys were too evenly matched.

The mace grazed Clanless's hip. It would leave a bruise, nothing more. His sword's tip stabbed into Yeltek's thigh, but no deeper than a fingernail. As the fight wore on, they nicked and bruised each other repeatedly, neither able to land a definitive blow of any kind.

After far too long—who could measure time in the middle of a fight?—Clanless grew tired. The initial rush of energy he experienced at the start of a fight faded when nothing major happened. Perhaps his earlier injury still took a toll. Whatever the cause, eventually, he stumbled.

And Yeltek took full advantage of the mistake. He attacked with a flurry of shoves from both buckler and mace. Clanless took steps back, but didn't fall. Yeltek ducked under his counterswing, and whipped his mace down toward Clanless's legs. Unprepared, Clanless jumped over the mace swing, but couldn't make a stable landing. Yeltek kept the momentum from his lower swing in a complete circle, coming up into the air and down again. The mace struck a solid blow against Clanless's helmet, knocking him to the ground.

Convinced of his victory, Yeltek repeated the same maneuver, spinning and coming down. It was a good plan and would have shattered through anything Clanless put up in defense. Except Clanless dropped his buckler and rolled to the side, slashing upward and across. His sword cut right through Yeltek's gut. Clanless rolled to his feet, covered in blood, his eyes frozen on the injury he'd caused.

Yeltek screamed, trying to form words, but failing. Blood poured out of the gaping wound across his body, more than Clanless had ever seen at one time. And more than blood. Yeltek's insides were pushing their way out.

Kan shoved him out of the way, screaming for the priest to hurry. Clanless turned away, his head suddenly exploding with pain. The other boys stared at him. He fell to his knees and emptied the contents of his stomach onto the sand. A moment later, he fell face-forward into the mess he'd just made, and his consciousness fled away.

❨❨❨❨●❩❩❩❩

Clanless woke up in his bed again, head pounding. He tried to sit up, and his vision swam. He fell back to the pillow. "Owwww." He put a hand to his head and discovered a bandage wrapped around it. Only then did he remember the fight and its conclusion.

He turned his head, wincing at a sharper stab of pain on the left side. The bunk room was empty, except for Shool Baina. The other boy sat on his bed against the wall, playing with his ball of crumpled cloth again.

"Oh, good," Bain said without looking at him. "You're not dead yet. I can still be the great enemy of the hero."

"What happened?" Clanless swallowed after the words and licked his lips. He needed water.

"Yeltek smacked you in the head, and you ripped his guts open. You won. He lost. But he was healed, and you weren't." Bain tossed the ball in the air. "Again."

Clanless felt the tenderness on the side of his head. "Do I need healing?"

"You tell me." Bain looked at him for the first time. "Is your brain scrambled?"

"I don't—ow—think so." Clanless forced himself to sit up. Brief dizziness almost made him fall back again, but he gripped the edge of the bed and held still. "Just hurts a lot."

Bain hopped up. "I was assigned to watch until you woke up, so I'll go let Kan know." He paused. "Unless you want to consult with your other friend first."

Clanless started to shake his head. "Ow. No. I just need some water. And maybe a new head."

"I can help with one of those." Bain jogged out of the room and returned a moment later with a mug of water. Clanless thanked him and took a drink of the lukewarm liquid. How the water in this place could be consistently warm when the weather was cool baffled him, but at least it satisfied his thirst.

"I'll go report to Kan then." Bain started to leave.

"Wait." Clanless took another sip of water. "You said they healed Yeltek. Is he all right?"

Bain shrugged. "As all right as Yeltek gets, I suppose."

Clanless breathed a sigh of relief. He wanted to erase the view of Yeltek's blood from his mind. Even as he thought it, the image in his memory lost focus and faded. Still, maybe using a sword wasn't the best idea.

"Anything else?" Bain asked.

"Yeah… are the others afraid of me, Bain?"

"After that fight? They're terrified of you. Most of them. Half, at least. Nothing scares Nerl. Duurald's too stupid to be scared. And I'm not." He jogged back out of the room.

Clanless put his head back down on the pillow. How had he come to this? What would his family think if they had witnessed that fight? Borde wouldn't think him very kind after that. Kekeen wouldn't think of him as a hero either. Zektel probably approved, but he didn't know whether to listen to her any more.

Yet what could he do? He couldn't quit, unless he accepted death at graduation. At least, he could go back to using a mace. Destroying someone's body without having to see it spilling out somehow seemed less horrible.

Kan entered the room. Clanless scrambled to sit back up, but couldn't stop another exclamation of pain as he did. "Hurts, does it?" Kan asked.

"Yes, sir."

"Look at me. Focus on my hand." Kan held up a hand and moved it back and forth. Clanless followed it with his eyes. Kan lowered the hand. "You aren't showing any signs of major head damage. That's good. I've penalized Yeltek for the head shot. You've moved ahead of him on the chart."

Clanless didn't answer. None of that seemed important now.

"After your first real experience, now what do you think of the sword?" Kan folded his arms and watched him intently.

"I didn't like what it did."

"Of course you didn't. If you did, I'd be very worried about you." Kan glanced at the door. He unfolded his arms and sat down on the next bed, facing Clanless. "I don't like the emotions I'm getting from you. You're thinking about quitting, aren't you?"

Surprised, Clanless looked up. "How did you know?"

"I've trained a hundred or more arena fighters. I can tell what you're thinking." Kan put his elbows on his knees. "I said you're ahead of Yeltek on the chart, but as of now, he's on the way to becoming a real arena fighter. And you're not."

Clanless opened his mouth to answer, but Kan pushed on. "That's because he's not afraid to hurt people. You are. In an ordinary person, that's fine. It's a good thing, even. The world needs more men who don't hurt other people." He shook his head. "But not here. Not in this place.

"You're a slave, Clanless. My slave, at the moment. That means you don't get a choice for your immediate future. But… you do have a choice, in one and only one way." He held up a finger, as he so often did in his training speeches. "You can choose to give up, stop trying. First, the other boys will start beating you, and you'll be lying in here in pain all the time. And if they don't beat you, I will. And then, you'll die in your graduation fight, and some mooncalf from a different trainer advances on to the real thing."

Kan leaned forward and tapped the brand on his shoulder. Clanless flinched. "Or you can keep fighting back. They took you from your family, took away your name and your clan, and dumped you in here, hoping you would die. Do you want to make them happy?"

Clanless shook his head and winced.

"Then here's what you have to do." Kan stood up. "You have to stop seeing your opponents as people."

"What?"

"Everyone you fight, from now on. They're not your friends. They're your enemies. They're not even people. They're agents of the priesthood that put you here. You want to fight back against them, right? To pay them back for sending you here? Then live. Win."

Kan took a few steps toward the door. "I know you can do it. You have a natural talent, when you let it come out, maybe the best I've seen here in years. The bloodrush works strong in you." He pointed at him again. "But you have to be willing to hurt. And kill. Only then can you fight your way to freedom and choose your own destiny."

"But—"

"Use the sword," Kan interrupted, walking away. "It makes them hate you all the more. Use it to win." As he stepped out the door, he paused and added, "Use every single weapon you have, every ability you can muster, to win. Whatever it takes." He waved. "Rest today. Let your head recover. Tomorrow, we'll start new."

☾ ☾ ☾ ☾ ● ☽ ☽ ☽ ☽

Kan didn't give Clanless much time to think over his words. The very next day, he announced a new set of fights. "I didn't see enough yesterday. I want you all to go at it again." He looked over the boys. "Starting with Nerlesen… against… Clanless."

Several of the boys murmured. Clanless took a deep breath before heading to the weapon rack. He'd had a good night's sleep and drank a little of Nukai's painkiller, but his head still ached. Combined with his own doubts, it did not create the best condition for a fight against the undisputed best warrior in the group. He also hadn't fought against Nerlesen with real weapons since the first day, when he spent the whole time on defense.

"Do not hold back," Nerlesen said, as he picked up his mace. "I will not."

Clanless nodded, hesitated briefly over the weapons, and took the short sword again. Holding it again, seeing Yeltek's blood in his head, overwhelmed him. He knelt beside the rack and leaned on the sword, its tip in the sand.

"Praying to the goddess?" Uyan called. "She won't listen to a clanless slave!"

Thoughts whirled through Aldan's head. Nerlesen was the best. He could die here and now. The priest would not heal him. But could he strike back and hurt the other boy like he'd done with Yeltek?

He looked up. Nukai gazed back at him through the weapons rack. The hunched man licked his lips. "Every weapon," he said quietly. "Whatever it takes."

Clanless blinked. Nukai must have been listening when Kan spoke with him yesterday. Every weapon. Every ability. He nodded and stood. Time to show the rest of them who he was. A kind man. A cruel man. The hero of the story. Aldan. Clanless. A fighter. A killer. All of the above, or maybe none of them.

He took his place facing his opponent. The image of Yeltek's blood faded more. "Begin!" Kan shouted. Rather than starting with the slow circle, Clanless paced directly toward Nerlesen. The other boy narrowed his eyes and moved to his own right. Clanless did the same, but continued to advance.

"Bash him for Yeltek!" Duurald yelled.

Clanless held sword and buckler at ready. He kept his mouth shut. Nothing the other boys shouted mattered. And taunts did nothing against Nerlesen. Words were useless now. Only actions mattered.

He charged straight at the other boy. Nerlesen braced himself, but a shift of his feet gave him away. He meant to dodge left as Clanless arrived.

Something washed over him, fueling his intensity. He saw another shift of Nerlesen's feet, amazed he could perceive such a slight movement even as he ran. This must be the bloodrush Kan talked about! He grinned and charged on, calculating his upcoming moves. He held his sword at an angle high and to his side.

Nerlesen shifted to the left, as expected, bringing his mace up from a low position, hoping to catch Clanless in the stomach. Instead, Clanless dove headfirst up and over Nerlesen's swing. He kept his buckler tucked at his chest for protection. He curled his body and landed hard on his left shoulder, rolling. At the same time, he swung his sword back. Nerlesen moved fast, but the tip of the sword scored a cut across the back of his right calf.

Clanless rolled to his feet, spinning to defend against the expected counterattack. His earlier fights had all been too slow! He gave his opponents too much time to think. Full-on attacks like this would keep them off-balance, force them to adapt to him, not the other way around. Why hadn't he thought this before? Why hadn't Kan suggested it?

Because reckless attacks could fail spectacularly, of course, and wear the attacker down faster than the defender. But that wouldn't matter now. He'd cut Nerlesen. He could end the fight at any moment. But it would be better to win by ordinary means, if he could.

The larger boy's counterattack came in three swift strikes of his mace. Clanless had seen him use this exact combination multiple times and blocked or dodged all three. In response, he borrowed a trick from Bain, blocking the third mace strike and spinning to slash from an unexpected direction. Nerlesen dodged it without difficulty.

The bloodrush took hold of him more and more. All other thoughts fled away. All of his earlier concerns and worries vanished. Only the fight mattered. Only defeating this opponent. Only spilling his blood.

Over the next few minutes, they fought back and forth across the sands. Their fellow trainees yelled in support and derision with every movement. Nerlesen's mace caught Clanless on his upper left arm, hard enough to bruise, but nothing more. Clanless cut him three more times, but never deep enough to matter.

"You've changed," Nerlesen observed in a lull. "What happened?"

Clanless didn't answer. He didn't know how to answer. He considered a response for only a moment before dismissing it. It wouldn't help him win.

At last, he pushed Nerlesen to his limits. The other boy abandoned careful strategy and swung his mace over and over in downward strokes. It was pure, brute force. Clanless could block the attacks with his buckler, but not for long. Either his arm or the buckler itself would give out before Nerlesen did. The larger boy actually did have the stamina to pull off an attack like this, and Clanless could do little against it.

Except, of course, the Taint. Blood trickled from Nerlesen in at least four locations. Exposed blood. Clanless could smell it. Almost taste it. His eyes burned.

Nerlesen's sudden intake of air and pause said it all. "You cheater," he growled, staggering back.

Clanless dropped his buckler and leaped forward. "Kan told me to use every weapon I had," he snarled back. He seized Nerlesen's shaking mace arm with his free hand and drove the point of his sword into the other boy's side. He whipped it back out and watched as Nerlesen collapsed in pain, both from the Taint and the stab. The bloodrush faded as Clanless stepped away from his fallen opponent.

The healer hurried forward, pushing past Clanless on his way. Kan stepped up and took a quick look at Nerlesen. Satisfied the boy would recover, he turned to Clanless and nodded. "Well done."

"I felt it," he said, swallowing against a suddenly dry mouth. "The bloodrush."

"I could tell." Kan turned around. "Everyone back in line! Duel's over! Next up are Jik and Uyan. Let's go!"

Clanless looked at the blood dripping from his sword. Nerlesen's blood. No. He couldn't think of it that way. It was his opponent's blood. The opponent he defeated. Nothing else mattered.

"Clanless! You too. Get in line!"

（（（（●））））

Things changed after the two duels with Yeltek and Nerlesen. None of the others had seen what he'd done against Nerlesen, and the other boy didn't tell. Over the next few weeks, Clanless took his place at the top of the class. He didn't use the Taint against anyone else for a long time. His fighting skills, improving on a weekly basis, were sufficient to defeat any-one other than Nerlesen—and maybe Yeltek or Bain.

The other boys spoke less and less to him. Even Yeltek's mockery all but disappeared. Sometimes, it bothered him. But Zektel continued to encourage him to be even tougher with his fighting, and not worry about their opinions. And she was right; he'd always known he couldn't fully trust them. Not for long.

After supper on a rest day, Clanless returned to the bunk room alone. He relaxed for a few moments on his bed and closed his eyes. He heard someone else enter the room, but didn't react.

"Do you remember our first week here?" Tunt's question hung in the air as he sat on his own bed.

"Of course I do," Clanless answered without opening his eyes.

"No one knew what to make of anyone else. But we all knew one thing: that big guy on the end, Nerlesen… he was strange. He didn't talk to us much, and spent his extra time exercising, even when Kan didn't tell us to. So strange."

Clanless didn't answer.

"You've become Nerlesen, Aldan. You never talk with us any more."

"I'm not Aldan any more."

"Why not? Nobody can take your name, remember?"

"They didn't take it. I'm changing it." He opened his eyes and looked up at the ceiling. "I can do that. It's my name, and it's what everyone calls me, anyway."

"I don't. The girl in the city didn't."

"I'll never see her again, anyway, so it doesn't matter what she calls me."

"What's happened to you?"

Clanless didn't answer or look at him.

"You don't care about anything but the fighting now."

Clanless sat up. "Of course I don't!" He looked at Tunt. "Don't you get it? The only way out of this place is to become good enough to win. Every. Time. And then the only way to survive after that is to become the absolute best."

"The best killer?" Tunt asked in a low voice.

"Yes, the best killer. It's the only way, Tunt. I decided I would survive, and I'll do whatever it takes to get there." He waved toward the arena. "And one day, I'll buy my freedom and escape all of it. Maybe then I can have a name again."

Tunt shook his head and slumped. "She was wrong." He got to his feet.

"Who was wrong?"

Tunt headed for the door. "The girl in the city. The storyteller's daughter. She called you the hero." He paused at the doorway. "You're not the hero. You're the villain now."

Clanless sat alone. "Kekeen," he said a minute later. "Her name was Kekeen."

12

GRADUATION

"It's time to start thinking beyond graduation," Kan announced to the boys at the start of a new day's training well into High Spring. "We only have a few weeks until then."

The boys glanced at each other. It was hard to believe they'd been together for over seven months now.

"It's not enough to win an arena fight," Kan went on. "If I train you right, you'll win. But you have to think about more than your opponent. Who else matters?"

"The audience," Yeltek said at once.

Kan nodded. "That's right. The audience. The crowd." He looked up toward the empty seats and turned in a circle, arms outstretched. "They came to see a show. They did not come to see you walk into the sand, knock somebody on the head, and walk back out."

He stopped his turn and pointed at them. "Fight, yes. Fight to win, yes. But also… fight with style. Fight to entertain."

"What difference does it make if we keep winning?" Nerlesen asked.

"Let me put it this way." Kan walked to the weapons rack and leaned against it. "Let's say I'm one of the eight rich elites of clan Dalbai, and I'm in charge of my own arena. People pay to see the fights in my arena. Now I've got two good fighters in my stock. One is good. So very good. He never loses a fight. But his fights last all of 30 seconds at most. Boring. The other fighter knows how to put on a show. His fights can last five, ten, even fifteen minutes on a good day. He's not as good as the first guy, though. He could lose if he gets a tough opponent. So as I'm planning the fights… what do I do?"

"You give the showy fighter the best fight times," Bain said. "And you make sure he always fights people less skilled than him."

"Exactly. And what do I do with the other one?"

Bain shrugged. "I don't know."

"I don't care about him. I give him a fight when I need another one on the schedule, but then I try to find a way to sell him to another arena, or trade him for someone who knows how to entertain."

"Why does this matter?" Uyan asked. "Do we want more fights?"

"Yes, you want more fights! As many fights as you can! Who can tell me why you want that?"

"More fights means more fame," Bain said. "It means more privileges."

Kan pointed at him. "You're getting it. Arena owners want fighters who draw a crowd, and they will reward those who perform well."

"It means freedom," Clanless said. "Eventually."

"Possibly," Kan said. "But for now, keep in mind that you're still slaves. And in order to be treated well by your masters, you have to do what they want. For the arena owners, that means entertain the crowds. For me… it means become the best. And none of you are the best yet." He paused, his eyes darting over each of them. "I will teach you about entertaining the crowd. But I also have to finish teaching you how to survive."

"Will this make a difference to our graduation fights?" Duurald asked.

"For the graduation fight, you want to win, by any means necessary. The performance is not as important." He hesitated. "But… if you realize at the start of the fight that you're much better than your opponent, and you know you're going to win… put on a performance. You'll impress your next master that way."

Clanless hadn't considered the details beyond graduation, except in a vague sense. They would all have new masters, then. Kan would hand over their bloodbonds to someone else. And that someone else would control their future.

"So we should let our opponents look like they're winning? Before we actually win?" Uyan asked.

"Something like that." Kan pointed to the seats again. "The crowd wants to see a show. A story. They want heroes and villains."

"Which one are we." Bain didn't make it sound like a question.

"You can be either one. Or both at the same time." Kan pushed off the weapons rack and walked over to them. He stopped in front of Jik. "They like to see the smaller guy triumph over a foe much bigger than himself." He moved on down the line, past Nerlesen. "They like to see someone triumph over and over and over again, building a reputation." He stopped at the end, near Clanless. "They like to see the villain they love to hate keep winning, even while they're rooting against him."

"That doesn't make sense," Yeltek complained.

Kan turned back. "No? Then you don't truly understand people, Yeltek." He pointed at the stands again, pretending to single out a specific seat. "The merchant up there has never thrown a punch in his entire life. But he likes to imagine he could, especially against that rival across the street." He pointed to a different chair. "The guy visiting from another town wishes he could be strong enough to overthrow the corrupt politician who's stealing his income." He spread his arms to indicate the sands. "So they come to watch a despicable villain destroy people… because they wish they could do it. People are dark, boys. Haven't you figured that out yet? You all came here as soft children, but I've turned you into killers. And it wasn't even hard." He lowered his hands and nodded. "People want to see the villains, because deep down… they want to be one."

((((●))))

The boys debated Kan's opinions late into the night. Yeltek and Tunt, surprisingly, were on the same side this time, insisting people wanted to be heroes, not villains. Bain, to no one's surprise, argued on Kan's side, supported by Uyan and Nerlesen, though neither said much. Duurald backed Yeltek, and Jik vacillated between the two sides.

Clanless kept his thoughts to himself. He could understand the points made by both sides. But Kan's words, bolstered by Bain's arguments, made more sense. Hadn't he seen it enough times in his short life? The priests and their guards, the Daghilch, Kan himself, the other boys… and even before that, he'd seen it. Oh, he'd seen it. People were evil. The thought process bothered him, though. Something was missing. He almost remembered it, but it slipped away, along with his consciousness.

The next day, Kan decided to spend some time explaining graduation to them. At breakfast, he wrote eight names on the dining room wall. "These are the men—and one woman—who will be watching you on graduation day. Each of them run the biggest arenas in the Empire, in each of our largest cities, except the capital. You won't get to that arena without making a serious name for yourself first."

Kan pointed at each one in turn. "They're all clan Dalbai, because our clan runs all of the major arenas. I've written them here in order of prestige, more or less."

"The third one is a woman?" Duurald asked, incredulity in his voice.

"Yes. Orgina is not someone you want to mock. She's probably the most independently-minded of all this list, and the most likely to pass on all of you. She's only going to choose someone if she's very impressed, and since she's third, it means she has to be very impressed with someone the first two don't want." Kan shrugged. "I've never fully understood her myself."

"Are there minor arenas?" Uyan asked.

Kan nodded. "Yes. And if you win your graduation fight, but none of these men are impressed enough to purchase your bond, that's where you'll end up. The minor arenas…" He hesitated. "They're not a place you want to be. Trust me on that."

Yeltek pointed to the top of the list. "So that man, Baduhan. He's the one we should be trying to impress the most?"

"He has the best-run arena outside the capital," Kan said. "But any of the top four are almost equal in that regard. The other four still do a good job, but their cities are smaller."

Kan proceeded to list the names of the cities and their locations. Clanless leaned over next to Bain and whispered, "Who runs the capital arena?"

"It's a partnership," Bain answered, "between clan Dalbai and clan Torov, who owns most of the city outright. Why do you ask?"

"So I know who I need to impress."

Bain nodded without looking at him.

"After the graduation fights," Kan explained, "when there are eight fighters still standing, from this class or… that other trainer, these eight will make their choices." He pointed to the name at the top again. "Baduhan will decide whether he sees anyone from this group who is worthy of his arena. If so, he'll purchase that bloodbond. If not, he'll go home without anyone new."

"But… don't they always need new fighters?" Duurald asked. "Some of them keep dying, right?"

"You'd think so," Kan answered. "But they have ways of keeping their favorites around. Healing magic helps, of course. And they don't always fight against other arena fighters. Sometimes, they fight criminals. Sometimes, they'll have challengers from outside come in, hoping to make a name for themselves without proper arena training. Sometimes… they'll have more exotic battles."

"Like wild animals," Yeltek said.

Kan nodded. "It happens, though not as often as you might think. Wild animals of that sort are not so easily procured."

"How do we fight those?" Nerlesen asked. "It has to involve different attacks, different defenses. You haven't taught us that."

"As I said, they're not so easily procured." Kan shook his head with a wry smile. "I can't very well send Nukai out there in a lion skin and have him crawl around on all fours. Some things you have to learn on your own."

"Why not?" Yeltek snorted. "He already wears animal skins."

"A sword would be a better weapon then," Bain observed. "You want to weaken the beast through loss of blood. And since it's a beast, the blood itself won't matter."

"Yes, but we'll discuss this more later," Kan said. "For now, let's stick to the men you should be trying to impress. Once Baduhan makes his decision, Chuluun will make his, Orgina will make hers, and so on down the line. After all eight have had a choice, they will be asked again if they wish to purchase a second fighter. If there are any fighters left afterwards, they go to the minor arenas, as I said.

"And then you'll begin your new careers as arena fighters. That career will look somewhat different for each arena, but your training will never end."

Some of the boys groaned.

"If you want to stay alive, that's what it takes," Kan snapped. "You'll train hard, work hard, several days a week, at least. And then you'll fight. Most of the arenas hold weekly events, except during parts of High Winter. During some parts of the year, it may decrease to every other week. How often you fight in those events comes down to how much the crowd loves you, remember? Then there are the feast events, the holy days." He shook his head. "For the greatest holy days, there will be several days in a row of events. You may be called upon to fight many times… again, if the crowds like you.

"With that fame, however, comes privilege. You will still be slaves. Make no mistake of that! But you may become popular enough to be treated well, given your own place, even an income for your own expenses outside the arena."

"Can't we use that income to buy our freedom?" Clanless asked.

"It doesn't work that way. Freedom depends not just on how much you can earn, but how many fights you survive. I've told you it almost never happens. Better to accept your lot and do the best you can with it. Enjoy what time you have."

Enjoy? When you would be asked to kill someone almost every week? What kind of life was that? For a moment, the idea of quitting pushed its way up into Clanless's mind again. He shoved it back down. No. He wouldn't give up. Everything might be against him, but he wouldn't give up.

He looked at the name at the top of the list. "Baduhan," Kan had said. "That one," Clanless whispered. "He's the one who will take me."

((((●))))

Graduation came faster than Clanless expected. One day, he trained hard; the next… it was almost over.

"I've taught you almost everything I know, in the time we've had," Kan said to the gathered boys in the dining room. "Tomorrow, it all comes to an end. By this time tomorrow, everyone in this room will either be dead… or have killed someone and moved on to their new life."

Clanless looked around at the others and saw them doing the same. No one wanted to think about who would die, but it pushed its way into their thoughts, regardless.

"How does this work?" Nerlesen asked. "How do you decide who fights?"

"The other trainer, Dimur, and I have each given a list to the organizer of tomorrow's event. We ranked our students in order of ability. The organizer will put the lists together. We have no say in the matter." Kan shifted his stance. Was he uncomfortable with this? "I don't know who each of you will be fighting. I don't know if it will be fair. Whatever happens is in the hands of the organizer. And the goddess." He glanced toward Etkeegh, who'd been lurking behind him.

The priest stepped forward. "Tonight, before you return to your beds, I will be available in the arena's shrine. If you wish to pray for tomorrow's fights, you may come to me there."

A few of the boys nodded.

"There's one thing I haven't taught you," Kan said. He pulled out a chair and put one foot on it. He leaned on his knee. "And it's not something I can teach you, really. I've taught you the skills to kill another man. All of you—all of you, I can say—now possess those skills. But having the skill to kill someone doesn't mean you will kill someone."

Kan let those words sink in before continuing: "It's one thing to talk about killing someone. It's quite another thing to actually do it. You all have the skills. You all have the strength. Tomorrow, we find out if you have the one thing you need the most: the will." He pointed at all of them. "You have to be willing to kill. And some of you, right now… aren't. That has to change by tomorrow, if you want to live.

"Your opponents are already here." At that, everyone stirred and glanced around. "They arrived a few hours ago. They're sleeping tonight in a bunk room on the other side of the arena. You won't see them until you step out on the sands to face them tomorrow. This is important, because you can't think of them as anything other than your opponent."

Clanless had heard this part before. As Kan went on about how to think about the other fighters, his thoughts wandered. Two things mattered tomorrow: winning his fight, and impressing Baduhan. Should he use the Taint or not? If he did, should he make it obvious? He'd tried to ask Kan about it several times since the trainer had told him to use "every ability." But Kan wouldn't speak of it directly. He wouldn't actually acknowledge—out loud—that Clanless possessed a special ability. Only that he should use everything he had to win.

But what if the arena master was a very religious man? What if he believed, like the priests, that the Taint was something horrible and evil? Or maybe he knew nothing of the Taint, but feared taichin or sorcerers or something like that? Using a special power in a fight might just doom him. Considering how much the Taint had already ruined his life, it seemed more than likely.

"…so it all comes down to whether you have the will," Kan said. "Some of you may fight through it and not even realize what's happening until it's done. Some of you may freeze up at the crucial moment. And that's why I've drilled you over and over on specific moves, so that your body knows what it's supposed to do, even when your will falters. I can only hope that it saves your lives tomorrow."

Kan took his foot off the chair and looked down at his feet. For a long time, he stood there. The boys looked at each other. Yeltek opened his mouth to ask a question, but shut it when Kan looked up again.

"This will be my last group of boys to train," he said. He glanced back at the priest, and then his eyes flickered toward Clanless. "I'm getting old, and I've done this for many years now. It's time I let someone younger take over."

"We, uh, we appreciate everything you've done for us," Yeltek said.

"No, you don't. You hated me. You wanted to kill me."

No one said anything.

Kan broke into a smile. "And that's all right. I expected you to. The only way I could forge you into the weapons you needed to be was to drive you hard, so hard you would hate me. I did what I had to do to you, in order to give you the best chance you have at surviving tomorrow."

Clanless swallowed. A lump rose in his throat for some reason. He had hated Kan, many times. But he respected him as well. He'd never come across as "old." Why couldn't he keep training?

"So make me proud tomorrow," Kan finished. "Feel the bloodrush. Win your fights." He paused, and an odd look came over his face before he smiled again and looked at each one of them in turn. "Live," he said, before turning and leaving the room.

No one said anything else for a few minutes. A few whispers began, and some of the boys got to their feet, presumably to go to the shrine. Clanless sat alone with his thoughts until everyone else left. At last, he got up and made his way to the bunk room. There, he found Bain and Nerlesen. A few minutes later, the other boys trickled in. Everyone prepared for bed.

"I have something to say," Nerlesen announced when the last of the group had arrived.

"So say it, Nerl," Yeltek said.

Nerlesen gave him a look, but went on: "We arrived here nine months ago as complete strangers to each other. And I'll admit: I didn't care about any of you one way or the other. I only wanted to be the best."

"We could tell," Duurald offered.

"That's changed," Nerlesen said. "We've gotten to know each other, and, uh, I just want to say… I hope you all win tomorrow. It would be a shame for any of you to die." He sat down on his bunk.

"Yeah," Uyan agreed. "I don't… I mean, I would hate for any of you to die tomorrow. Even Clanless."

Clanless snorted. "Thanks for that."

"Seriously," Uyan said. "I don't like you, but I don't want you dead."

"Whether we live or die, tomorrow will be the last time we see each other," Jik pointed out.

"Until some big celebration, where champions from different arenas fight each other," Bain suggested. "Or we end up in the capital, on the Hawk King's Dohor."

"I'll be there next year," Yeltek said with an airy wave. "I'll try to wait for the rest of you."

Duurald shoved Yeltek out of his bunk. "You won't last two years in the arena."

"Sure he will," Uyan said. "He's too mean to die any sooner."

The others laughed, and the banter continued, including ridiculous boasts, veiled threats, and absurd promises. Clanless glanced at Tunt. He'd been strangely quiet throughout the conversation. Even when mocked for it, Tunt usually shared his opinion. "You all right?" Clanless asked.

Tunt jerked. "How can you ask that? It's my last night before I face the goddess. Of course I'm not all right."

The room fell quiet. Tunt had spoken loud enough for all to hear.

"You don't have to die, Tunt," Jik said.

"He's right," Uyan agreed. "You beat me once. You can beat... whoever you meet on the sands tomorrow."

Tunt shook his head. "I said at the beginning that I was going to die. Nothing has happened to change my mind. I'm just not good enough."

Nerlesen walked to the center of the room. "Kan said we all had the skills to win tomorrow." He stared at Tunt. "All of us, Tunt. You can do it."

"Besides," Yeltek added, "those other guys can't possibly have been trained as hard as we have! There can't be another Kan in this world. The goddess isn't that cruel!"

"Look at you," Clanless said, sitting up and facing Tunt. "You look nothing like you did nine months ago. You're a fighter now, Tunt."

Jik pointed his thumbs at Clanless and Nerlesen. "See? The two best fighters in here say you can do it. Kan said you can do it. What more do you need?"

Tunt smiled a little. "Thank you. All of you. Maybe I'll do all right. I don't know. When it comes down to it, I just don't know if I can kill someone else."

"None of us knows," Bain said from the other side of the room. "Until we face that exact moment, we don't know for sure."

Most of the boys nodded. "I guess we'll find out tomorrow." Clanless wasn't even sure who'd said it, but everyone returned to their beds, preparing to sleep.

He waited until the lantern had been turned down, then rolled out of his bed and slipped out. Once in the storage room, he drained blood from a cut on his calf into the bowl and ignited it with the Taint. Zektel appeared, only a face this time.

"We fight to the death tomorrow," Clanless said. "Some of my... friends are going to die." Were they his friends? He didn't know any more.

"It's sad, but there's nothing you can do," Zektel said. "You have to focus on yourself. After tomorrow, you start a new stage of your life. They won't be a part of it, any more than your old family is a part of your life right now."

"I still think about my family, though." He'd been thinking about them a lot in the past couple of weeks. Nine months since he'd seen them. His mother would have given birth by now. He had another little brother or sister, whom he'd never know.

Zektel's eyes closed briefly. "Of course you do. You learned things from them. Just as you've learned things from these other boys. So it is in life. You take what you can from others, and then you move on. They can help you or hurt you, but you decide which it is."

"I can't decide whether people hurt me."

"Yes, you can, now that you're older. When you were a small child, you couldn't, of course. But now… you simply don't let them get too close to you. In the arena tomorrow, if you keep your opponent away from you, he can't hurt you, right? The same is true with friends and family. If you don't let them get too close, then they can't hurt you. You know what I mean."

He hated it, but he did. And he'd known all along. Some people should not be allowed to get too close. But how could you tell? If he listened to Zektel, he'd never let anyone close, anyone at all. Not even someone like Kekeen.

"You have me, Aldan. I'm always here. I won't leave you."

"Of course she won't. She needs you," another voice intruded.

Clanless scrambled to his feet and spun around. Bain stood at the door, arms crossed. "What do you mean?"

Bain took a few steps into the room. "I've tried to tell you when we're spinning tales, Clanless, but you don't listen." He pointed at the bowl of blood. "She's a blood-wraith."

Clanless wrinkled his brow. "You… don't know that." Of course he remembered Bain's stories. The blood-wraiths were evil creatures who devoured souls. "Zektel is nothing like your stories."

"You listen to her, and not to us, don't you? She tells you to ignore other people, doesn't she?"

Clanless didn't answer.

Zektel laughed. "Do you see what he's done, dearest? If I tell you not to listen to him now, it proves his point. Clever, clever Shool Baina."

Bain snorted, shaking his head. "She's pushed you away from your friends, Aldan. You abandoned Tunt, especially. If you had stuck by him through all of this, encouraging him, maybe he'd have a better chance tomorrow."

"I didn't see you doing any of that."

"Heh. No, I didn't. But I never portrayed myself as a nice guy." His eyes narrowed. "I also didn't switch my attentions to a blood-wraith."

"She's not a blood-wraith!" Clanless took a step toward Bain.

"My people have been called that over the centuries," Zektel admitted. "I don't mind the title. But it doesn't mean we're anything like the scary stories little Bain's nurse used to tell him."

Clanless blinked. "Nurse?"

"Oh, didn't he tell you?" Zektel's tinkling laugh came from the bowl. "Dear Shool Baina here grew up as part of clan Ghutalta, second most-powerful clan in the whole Empire. Makes you wonder what he could have done to end up here, doesn't it?"

Bain shook his head, mouth agape. "I never told that to anyone here. How does she know these kind of things, Aldan? It's supernatural."

"She's been here for me every day," Clanless said. "No one else has done that, least of all you."

"I never wanted to. Still don't." Bain pulled out the vial he'd taken from the priest. "I only wanted to warn you, and I've done that now." He tossed the vial to Clanless. "Here. You need this more than I do."

Clanless caught the vial. It was still at least half full. He turned it over in his hands, considering its crystalline structure.

"Moon's stability to you tomorrow, Clanless," Bain said, making the name sound almost like an insult. "If I don't see you again in the arena…" He paused, then shrugged. "It's been interesting." With that, he left the room.

"It's certainly been that," Zektel said. "I find him the most fascinating of your little companions, except for—"

"Why did you do that?" Clanless interrupted, dropping to his knees to stare at her face. "Why antagonize him? We could have worked things out. He wouldn't… I wouldn't…"

"What difference does it make, dearest? As you both have pointed out, you're not likely to see each other ever again after tomorrow. Let him go. Focus on what you need to do." Zektel's face shimmered in the bowl. "His gift there, now… you could take me with you in the arena."

"What do you mean?"

"If you wear that vial and activate it before the fight, I could be there with you, advising you."

Clanless considered it. "I don't know. You might distract me too much… but I guess hearing a female voice in the middle of the fight would throw off my opponent too."

"Oh, I don't have to speak aloud, you know." Clanless suddenly heard her voice inside his head: "I can speak to your mind, like I did at the very beginning, the first time you heard me."

He frowned. "No, I think that would be even more distracting. Kan's trained me well. My body knows what to do. And in an emergency, I'll use the Taint."

"Of course. Whatever you think best." The blood bubbled. "I'm losing my hold here. Good luck, darling. Tell me all about it when it's over."

The face faded away, leaving only blood behind. Clanless sat watching it for several minutes, pondering all of the day's events and revelations. Unable to come to any solid conclusions, he got to his feet and went back to bed.

☾☾☾☾●☽☽☽☽

On graduation day, Clanless stood before the arena entrance he'd entered hundreds of times over the past nine months. This time, a portcullis had been lowered to block passage. Once it opened, his life would never be the same again. Or his life would be over.

Also this time, something else caught his attention: the noise of many voices combining together, some yelling, some cheering, some just talking to each other. A crowd waited for him out there, a crowd of hundreds who'd come to see games of death. Remembering his one evening in the city of Rochinbal, Clanless wondered how many of the people he'd encountered that night were in the stands today. How many of the merchants on the road, or the customers who listened and cheered for the storyteller and his daughter? Were those two here? Would Kekeen come, wondering if the boys she'd met would live or die?

He doubted it. Whether he ever met her again or not, he'd learned enough about her that one night. She was a good person, too good to show up here. Kan said the people who watched did so because they wanted to be the villain themselves. Not her. She would always want to be the hero. Some people were like that.

Aldan had been like that. But he wasn't Aldan any more. He was Clanless, and today he would make his first kill.

Nukai stood hunched beside the weapon rack. Kan would be sitting with the arena masters, no doubt extolling his students to them. After all, he would be making money today when he sold their bloodbonds. Sometimes, that detail got overlooked.

The boys had been separated after breakfast, each led to a different room. He had no idea now whether any of the others had fought yet, or whether they survived. He'd been waiting long enough for several other fights, or at least so it seemed.

Clanless took a buckler, then hesitated over the weaponry. Should he use the mace instead? A sword might offend some of the arena masters. "Don't change now," Nukai said. He took a short sword out and handed it to Clanless. One of his furs fell off in the process.

Clanless chuckled. "Don't you change either, Nukai." He took the sword. "Are you leaving with Kan also?"

Nukai picked up the fallen fur. "Maybe. May be." He studied Clanless for a moment. "May I suggest something?"

"Why not? Everyone else is."

Nukai moved behind him and threw the fur over his shoulder. Clanless gasped. "Nukai. I can't wear this. It's—"

"Honor me, Aldan." Nukai moved around him and fastened the fur in the front, careful to leave the shoulder brand exposed. He stepped back and nodded. "Now you look fearsome."

Clanless rotated his shoulder and swung the sword a few times. The fur did not appear to restrict his movements in any way. It was much lighter than he'd anticipated. "I… thank you. I don't know what to say."

The hunched man nodded. He appeared about to say something else when a loud clang reverberated. The portcullis rose in fits and starts, catching on hidden deformities in the recessed opening. It would have been far less nerve-wracking if it rose smoothly. Or maybe not. The slow rise gave Clanless more time to think about what he might do, to remember his training… to live.

With a final thunk, the portcullis stopped, not quite retracted. "It's time. Go. Fight," Nukai said.

Clanless ducked under the protruding points and took his first steps out on to the sand. The smell of blood and sweat struck his nostrils, coppery and stale. Maybe more than blood. Other fights had taken place already, then. He continued walking forward, his bare feet sinking into the coarse sand, crunching with each step. The warm air and sun of High Spring heated the sand outside the shaded areas. His feet had long since callused over to the point he barely felt any change in temperature.

The noise of the crowd grew much louder, but he couldn't make out any words. Better to ignore them, anyway. He didn't lift his eyes. Instead, his vision focused on the figure walking toward him from the opposite door, that door he'd run to so many times.

When only fifty yards separated them, his opponent stepped to the right and began his circle. Clanless did the same, evaluating the other boy. He had a height advantage, but not by much. Looked to be in the same weight range. He carried his mace with a firm grip, angled outward and a little down. He held his buckler at the proper height, poised to move in any direction for blocking. Here was an opponent who'd paid attention to his trainer. Of course, Clanless had expected no less. He was the best fighter of Kan's group, so he would likely be paired against the best fighter from the other group.

Clanless tried to ignore any other details about his opponent: hair, eyes, facial features… anything that would make him more human. This was not another boy with a name and a family. He was an arena opponent. Nothing more.

"I am sorry," the opponent called.

"What?"

"I am sorry you have to die for me to live."

In that instant, Clanless knew he would win the fight, yet it puzzled him. The opponent's words showed compassion, not a trait for a trained fighter. Nerlesen wouldn't make a statement like that. Or Yelnek, Duurald, Bain… This was the best the other group had to offer? Something felt off, but he pushed those thoughts aside.

A light breeze swept down through the arena, lifting Nukai's fur from his shoulder. In response, Clanless lifted his sword into the air, daring his opponent to charge. The crowd noise grew louder at the gesture.

The opponent charged forward several yards, but slowed as Clanless lowered his sword. Though he still couldn't make out individual sounds, Clanless could tell the crowd noise grew disappointed. Time to give them a show then.

He lowered his sword and buckler to his sides and strode forward, straight at his opponent. The other boy stopped and took a step backward, unsure about this tactic. He recovered quickly enough, dropping into a standard defensive stance.

Clanless didn't care. He'd realized, somewhere along the way, that all he had to do was inflict a single cut on an opponent, and he'd be able to win. The Taint guaranteed his victory, as long as he didn't die first. His strategy then came down to two things: inflict a cut, and put on a show for the arena masters.

He broke into a run and charged full speed at his opponent. At the last minute, he twisted his buckler to catch a mace swing, then spun completely around on his left foot, sword extended. The blade caught a bit of flesh right above his opponent's belt. In the moment, Clanless could taste the blood. He'd won already, as long as he kept things safe from here on.

The crowd roared its approval of his reckless attack and spin. They roared again as his opponent, furious, attacked him in return, swinging his mace left and right. Clanless quickly spotted a routine in the swings. His opponent was using the basic mace attacks Kan taught them months ago, and using them in a specific pattern. Maybe that worked in practice fights, but out here, it made him too predictable.

Clanless sidestepped to dodge one of the swings, then slipped inside to stab. This time, his sword penetrated the opponent's right thigh, spilling blood once more. It wasn't much of an injury, but more blood couldn't hurt… and the crowd liked it.

A backhanded mace swing came from out of nowhere and almost took off his head. It caught the edge of his helmet and twisted it. Clanless cursed himself for forgetting. For the past two weeks, Kan had made them use practice weapons again, specifically to prepare for using and blocking head shots. Yet the moment he picked up real weapons again, he'd let himself think his head was safe.

Clanless tore off his twisted helmet and shouted at his opponent, surprising him just enough to keep him from following up the head strike with something else. A narrow escape. Enough of this.

Clanless swung his sword out to the right, leaving an opening to tempt his opponent, Bain's favorite tactic. The other boy took the bait and lunged forward, bringing his mace upward. Clanless smashed it down with his buckler as he pivoted forward on his left foot. He thrust his sword straight ahead, piercing his opponent's chest right through the left breast. The sword slid in much further and easier than he'd expected.

His opponent gasped. He lifted his eyes and locked in with Clanless's gaze. "I… thought… I…"

The sword suddenly felt so much heavier. The opponent's knees gave way, and he slumped down, pulling the sword and Clanless with him. Clanless held tight to his sword, not knowing what else to do. As the body fell back, the sword pulled free. Blood erupted from the wound, more than when he'd cut open Yeltek. Much more.

He stared as the body shook. The young man coughed, thrashed in the sand a few times, and then went limp. His head rolled to the side, pulling his eyes away at last.

Blood continued to pour out, creating a new stain on the sand, spreading outward from the body.

Hearing the noise of the crowd, Clanless looked up for the first time. Several hundred people were on their feet, cheering and clapping for him. He lifted his sword and buckler into the air and turned in a circle, acknowledging them. His eyes drifted over a sheltered seating area. Those inside weren't cheering. Kan and the arena masters, no doubt. He bowed to them.

As he turned, he noticed two blood-priests hurrying across the sand. He stepped out of their way and let them reach the body. They glared at him as they passed, either for his status, or for spilling so much blood. For a moment, he thought of using the Taint on the fallen boy's blood, in order to spite the priests. But the roar of the crowd distracted him.

He'd won. He'd survived. He'd… killed someone.

Clanless didn't wait any longer. He turned and jogged back toward the entrance with its raised portcullis. Had it shut during the fight? He hadn't noticed at all.

Nukai greeted him with a grunt. Clanless handed him the sword and buckler, then turned, collapsed to his knees, and emptied the remains of his breakfast onto the floor.

Part Two

GHOYOR

ZEKTEL

Now

Perturbed by his visit with Daviland, Clanless made his way to his personal quarters. Upon arrival, he first checked his belongings for tampering. His moonblade had been cleaned and hung on the wall by an attendant. His bed looked untouched. Most importantly, his blood stores remained sealed. He'd added the blood he'd drawn from today's combatant himself.

Clanless used the Siphon to draw a few ounces of blood and squirted it on to a metal plate on his small table. He snapped his fingers over the plate. A spark erupted over the blood. A moment later, the blood started moving. It drew together and formed the shape of a young woman who stretched as if just waking up.

"It's about time," she said. "How did today's fight go?"

"Easy victory." Clanless dropped onto the bed and stretched out, putting his hands behind his head. He knew from experience that she already knew the answers, but enjoyed the conversation.

"You know we've done what we said we would do. You are now the greatest arena fighter the Empire has ever known."

Clanless grunted. The fame didn't matter. Mostly. Freedom mattered. "One fight left. The Hawk King wants me to fight Daviland." He described his meetings with the two men.

"You can beat him, can't you?"

"Of course I can beat him. He's not an arena fighter. He doesn't stand a chance." And yet Daviland had seemed so confident. Unnerving.

"Tell me more about this Daviland."

"You know everything I know," Clanless griped. "He made a name for himself saving some clanhold and then started a movement against the Hawk King. After that, he saved a city or something. And now he's got a huge following."

"Does he believe in this movement? Does he believe in himself?"

"I think he does." Clanless rolled to his side to look at the blood-woman. "He's about to die, and he still believes he'll prevail, Zektel. He's insane."

She knelt on the plate and ran her hands back through the semblance of long hair. "Such men are very dangerous, Aldan. You must take me with you to this fight."

"You're always with me."

"You know what I mean. Bring the blood. Let me speak with you."

Clanless rolled to his back again. "You're a distraction when you do that. I won't have any problems with him."

"Please. I need to be there for this one. It's the fulfillment of everything we've worked toward. I've been with you all these years. Don't leave me behind now."

"I'll think about it."

"Do you think Daviland has assembled a large group of followers?"

"I'm guessing so. At least, it seems like they're everywhere." He tried not to think about the ones he knew best.

"This is what should happen then: you kill this man, as everyone expects. Then you buy your freedom." Zektel stood up and pointed at him. "And then you go to these followers and tell them you're joining them."

"What? Why would I do that?"

"You already know some of them. They will welcome you."

"Not after I kill their leader!"

"You tell them how the Hawk King forced you to do it. You describe how you've been misused all these years. Maybe even throw in a heartfelt plea from the dying man that changed your mind. They will take to you. And as famous as you are, you can bring far more people to their cause... which will become your cause."

Clanless shook his head. "I don't want a cause. I want to be free."

"And what about all the other slaves in this world? What about your friend at Pasque House? You could free them all."

"How? By overthrowing the Hawk King?"

"And taking his place! They'll back you, Aldan. They will follow the clanless one anywhere.”

“I don't see it. And I don't want to rule everything.”

“You won't have to. Not for long. Just enough to set things right. And then turn over the rule to a council or something.”

“I think that's what Davil wants to do.”

“You see? We just take his plan and use it for ourselves.”

Clanless considered. “There's one other thing. The Daghilch is back.”

“What do you mean?”

“The man who took me from my family, who turned me into a slave. He's here. He's worked his way up to the top of the religion.”

“He's the Ghamba Lam now?”

“Yes. And he remembers me.”

Zektel didn't answer. Clanless sat up on the edge of the bed. “Did you hear me? I don't know how, but he's going to stop me. He made me a slave, and he's going to make sure I stay one.”

“How? Tomorrow, you win your freedom by the laws of the Empire.” Zektel stood and pointed at him. “This religious man can not stop that, no matter what he does.”

“They'll never let someone free with the Taint. I'm too dangerous to their systems. And the Hawk King is above the laws. If he decides I'm still a slave after tomorrow, there's nothing I can do about it.” Clanless almost winced. Daviland had said much the same thing… and he was right.

“Then you should kill him. The priest, I mean. Not the king.”

Clanless blinked. He hadn't expected that.

Zektel shrugged. When she did, the shrug moved down her entire “body,” a flowing ripple of blood. “If this Ghamba Lam is the only thing standing in your way after your last fight, you should kill him before he ruins everything.”

“I wanted to today,” he admitted. “I thought about it. Right in front of the Hawk King.”

“That would have been foolish. You should seek him out privately. Do it in a way no one will know it was you. Remember when you taught a lesson to the nobleman?”

“I've never killed anyone outside the arena.”

She cocked her head. “We both know that isn't true.”

“It's not the same thing.” Clanless rubbed his face with his hands. Had he killed outside the arena? He didn't remember killing anyone, but his memory had been troubling him lately.

“Freedom is everything, right? Don't you still want it?”

“Of course I do.”

"Then by the goddess, be a man! Take what you are owed, and don't let anyone stand in your way!"

Clanless nodded but did not reply.

Zektel shrank, some of her blood form pooling below her. She sighed. "You need a break to clear your head. Go see your girlfriend."

"She's not my girlfriend."

"But you talk to her. Go on. Have some fun." Zektel shrank smaller still.

"Maybe you're right."

"Just… don't do anything to jeopardize tomorrow, Aldan. Have fun, but be careful." With that, the blood form collapsed onto the plate with a plop. Gone again.

Clanless sighed. Zektel was right, of course. She'd been with him for all these years, ever since his training. She knew everything about him, and still she stayed around. He couldn't say that about anyone else. Of course, he'd never told anyone else everything.

Maybe… maybe someday he should change that.

ORGINA

Nukai escorted Clanless back to the same waiting room after his fight. For the next several hours, he sat alone with his thoughts. Down here, the noise of the crowd didn't penetrate much, but he heard an occasional muted roar. The fights continued.

He wished he could watch, but didn't want to see, either. How were the others doing? Despite his attempts to detach himself from them, he found that he did care… a lot. He didn't want any of them to die. He should have said more the night before, joined Nerlesen in telling them he cared. At least he'd encouraged Tunt. Some.

He could still smell and taste his own vomit, even though he'd drank plenty of water since then. He reproached himself for the weakness, but hated himself for killing someone. Everything was a contradiction right now.

He looked down at his shaking hands. Blood spatters decorated his right one in an almost regular pattern that extended all the way to his elbow. He rubbed at it with his other hand, trying to get it off.

His mind continued to replay the fight. In the end, he hadn't even needed the Taint. His own skills won the fight. Had he put on enough of a show? Were the arena masters impressed? He'd tried to be dramatic. Nukai's last-minute gift of a fur gave him a different look, at least. He wondered how much that kind of thing influenced the crowd.

Nukai insisted he keep the fur after the fight. Clanless pulled it off his shoulder and took a closer look. A couple of white streaks broke up varying shades of gray. He didn't know what kind of animal possessed those colors. Some type of wolf, perhaps? A single cord connected two corners of the fur, allowing it to drape over one shoulder. Funny how Nukai dropped it; hadn't he fastened it on himself?

He tried not to think of the body of his opponent, bleeding out in the sand. "I wish I could forget that part," he muttered.

The door opened. Clanless jumped to his feet to face Kan, who stood watching him for a moment, his eyes wandering over the fur. "It's over," he said at last. "The masters have made their decisions. You will be leaving in a few minutes."

"Where am I going?" Clanless asked, then caught himself. "I mean, who am I going with? Baduhan?"

"No. He took the fighter who defeated Nerlesen."

For a moment, the statement didn't make sense. Then: "Nerlesen... lost?"

Kan nodded. "That was a shocking and brutal fight. However, your bloodbond has been purchased by Orgina. Once the crowds have dispersed, you'll be escorted to her carriage."

Orgina. The third arena master. The woman. Which meant he was the third choice, not the first.

"I think it's the best fit for you," Kan went on. "Orgina is known for doing things... different. She defies the traditional power structures quite often. It makes sense that she would choose someone like you."

Clanless struggled with the revelation about Nerlesen. The biggest, strongest of them all... was dead. And if he hadn't succeeded...

"Who else lost?"

Kan shook his head. "We keep you all separated at this time for a reason. It's best to make a clean break, to just move on, and—"

"Who else?" Clanless demanded. He clenched his fists and took a step forward. He didn't intend to attack Kan, but his desperation spilled out.

Kan sighed. "You were an exceptional class. Seven of you are moving on to fight in the Empire's arenas."

Two others then. "Tunt?"

Kan nodded slowly. "And Uyan. I'll write their names with the others I've lost, on the wall of my office—" He broke off with a wry chuckle. "I guess it won't be my office much longer now. The next trainer will probably have it painted. But I'll remember." He paused. "I'll remember."

"Did... did Tunt fight well?"

"He made me proud." Something caught in Kan's voice. He reached out and ran his fingers across the fur. "Fascinating," he murmured so low Clanless almost didn't hear it.

"Do you have any other belongings in the bunk room?" Kan asked. When Clanless shook his head, Kan turned to go. "I'll be back for you in a few minutes."

"Wait."

Kan paused, but didn't turn around.

"Thank you." Clanless swallowed. "Thank you for teaching me how to survive."

"My training got you through this fight, maybe." Kan gripped the doorframe. "The next ones will be up to you." He looked back over his shoulder. "Now you're a man, Clanless. I'm… proud."

He left in a rush and closed the door behind him. Clanless waited alone with his thoughts again.

⟨⟨⟨⟨●⟩⟩⟩⟩

Kan led Clanless out of the arena for only the second time since the day he arrived with the Daghilch, nine months earlier. Several carriages of various types waited on the road outside. Off in the distance, a crowd of people hunched against the wind as they walked toward Rochinbal. High Spring faded into Low Winter. The winds would increase over the next few weeks, but never reach the height of High Winter's. Clanless wondered if crowds came to the arena during harder weather.

"This one," Kan said, pointing to a carriage. Much finer than the wagon he'd ridden with the Daghilch, this device had four wheels and a larger enclosed box. Bands of metal reinforced the hardwood sides to resist the harshest of winter weather. Horses pulled it instead of an ox. The ride would be faster, at least.

Clanless started to climb up next to the driver, but a voice came from inside: "You ride inside this time, boy." Clanless glanced at Kan, who only gestured with his chin at the carriage.

Clanless opened the door on the carriage and stepped up. Inside, a woman sat on a cushioned seat facing front. She pointed at another seat across from her. He climbed in and closed the door behind him. The carriage started moving at once.

Orgina studied him, so he returned her gaze. He had little experience estimating the ages of adults, but she had to be older than his parents, at least. The gray streaks in her dark hair stood out, even pinned up as she wore it. Her face had a wide nose and cheeks, though she herself didn't appear overly heavy. She wore a heavily-patterned blue and gold dress and a round hat with a red tail hanging over her shoulder.

"Your skills in the arena were adequate," she said abruptly. "For someone your age, they were almost impressive. You also have a flair for the dramatic, which I appreciate."

"Thank you." He didn't know what else to say.

"But that's not why I chose you. Not completely, anyway."

Clanless waited for her to continue. The carriage swayed as it moved from the dirt path of the arena onto a more solid road leading beyond Rochinbal.

"No matter what some of the other arena masters think, people do not come to our arenas to see two muscular idiots pound each other into the sand."

Clanless considered bringing up what Kan had to say about the people in the stands, but decided to wait and hear Orgina's opinions.

"They come for personalities." Orgina picked up a cloth bag from the seat and pulled it open. She reached inside, took out a pair of nuts—or so Clanless assumed—and tossed them into her mouth. Once she'd chewed a bit, she went on: "My arena fighters have to be personalities. They have to have character, something that sets them apart from the other fighters. It could be as simple as a fighter who always wears red. And then a rumor spreads that he wears red to hide the blood, or something like that. So people show up to see the red warrior, over and over, because they're curious. They've established a connection with this character they see every week, and want to see what happens to him." She swallowed. "And maybe they're waiting to see if the red really does hide the blood."

"I think I understand," Clanless said.

Orgina pointed at him. "It won't be hard with you at all. You've already got something started here. We don't even have to make up a name or title for you. You've already got one."

"Clanless."

"Exactly. People hear that and see your brand there, and they want to know: why is this guy branded? What did he do? What clan did he originally come from?" She chuckled. "We can start the most outrageous rumors about you that we want, and people will believe them. They'll delight in debating each other. Did Clanless really kill the Hawk King's cousin? Did he betray an entire clanhold to barbarians?"

"That's horrible!" Clanless's eyes widened.

Orgina shrugged. "People will believe almost anything. And then they show up to the arena. Why? They've become fascinated with this warrior they've heard stories about. They want to see him fight. They want to see if he's really tough enough to have done some of the things they've heard. And as long as he keeps fighting, they'll keep coming." She tossed another handful of nuts into her mouth.

Clanless didn't know what to think. On the one hand, he hated the idea of people believing those kind of stories about him. On the other... he had to admit: the fame of it all did hold appeal.

"We build the personality as we go," Orgina went on. "The outfit, for example, becomes an integral part of it." She nodded toward his fur. "You've already got a start on that as well. The fur is a nice touch."

"It was given to me."

She nodded. "Regardless, it caused a stir in Kan's run-down arena when you stepped out wearing it. Some of the older audience members no doubt remember a great arena fighter known as the Wolf, who wore furs like that. Not only did you look different from every other fighter today, you made a connection between yourself and someone they used to watch. Good job."

Clanless pulled at the fur. Could Nukai be this Wolf? How did that make any sense? He would have left the arena, but still alive...

"We might add to that over time," Orgina went on, cocking her head. "Maybe a special helmet or something. And then there are weapons."

"I like the sword."

"And that's good. Even that in itself is a little unusual. Most people consider that a dishonorable way of fighting. See? Personality."

Clanless hesitated. "You don't consider it dishonorable?"

Orgina snorted. "Honor and dishonor don't matter to the arena. What matters is bringing people in. Blood matters. Nothing else. I'm talking about weapons here. If you succeed the way I hope you will, then we'll have a special weapon made for you. Some kind of sword, I'm sure. And then that adds to the personality, and the stories spread some more. That's what I do. I take a fighter and turn him into a legend."

Clanless nodded. It all made sense. Still... "I don't know how much you know," he began, "but the priests... they don't like me."

"They don't much care for me either." Orgina ate a couple more nuts. "Even though I provide them with more blood than just about anyone else."

"They won't even heal me if I'm wounded. That's not going to work very well to create this personality you want."

Orgina smirked. "The priests like to think they control the healing magic. They don't. I have my own healer. Don't worry about that." She shifted and leaned forward a little. "But let's talk about that, shall we? Why don't the priests like you?"

Clanless's heart sank. He'd allowed himself to feel positive about the future for a few brief moments. "Did Kan tell you?"

"Let's assume for the moment that he didn't."

Clanless took a deep breath. "It's called the Taint. I can do something to blood, something the priests don't like." He looked up and met Orgina's eyes. "And it guarantees that I'll never lose a fight in the arena."

She raised an eyebrow. "Bold claim. Did you use it in today's fight?"

"No. I didn't need to."

"I didn't think so. It looked like a clean kill. How obvious is it when you use this… Taint?"

"My eyes glow. Or so they tell me. Otherwise, nothing else happens. My opponent collapses in pain."

"Hmm. For now, we won't say anything about it. Don't use it unless you have to. I'll have to think about how to introduce it, if we need to."

Clanless blinked as Orgina sat back. "Did you already know?"

"It's my business to know everything before I purchase a new slave."

Somehow, Clanless suspected Orgina didn't need to think about how to introduce his power. She probably already had a plan for it mapped out in her head.

"I will get my blood's worth out of you, clanless one," she said. "Whatever it takes, you're going to be a big hit with the crowds." She shrugged. "Or, you'll die at next week's fight, and I'll make a legend out of the man who kills you." She tapped the wall behind her. "Driver! Pick up the pace a little, please. I'd like to spend as little time on the road back as possible."

((((●))))

It took three days of travel to reach Ghoyor, the location of Orgina's arena, which Clanless would now call home. To his surprise, the arena lay within the city walls—built right into the wall, in fact. From the top of the stands, you could look out over the countryside or the city itself. They couldn't enter the arena from outside, of course. Instead, the carriage entered by the main gate and made its way through the streets.

Clanless stared at all of it. He'd only seen one city, Rochinbal, in his life, and thought it enormous. But Ghoyor made Rochinbal look like a small town. Almost all of the buildings were multi-level, and many boasted roofs with upturned corners. Some had more than one roof, a concept Clanless found baffling. The light of the retreating sun reflected from glass windows in almost every building.

"I can't wait to sleep in my own bed again," Orgina griped, stretching.

Clanless didn't know what she was complaining about. The past two nights, they had slept at roadside inns. The concept had been new to Clanless, but the beds, from his perspective, had been excellent. Much nicer than the flat bunk he'd been sleeping on for the past nine months.

The carriage drove right into the arena grounds, passing beneath an overhang and right up to an enormous entrance. Clanless waited for Orgina to exit the carriage first, before climbing out himself. He looked around, fascinated by the opulence. This area had clearly been designed for rich patrons of the arena to arrive and enter, away from the masses. The overhang was an extension of a secondary roof topped with green tiles. Multiple arches held up by decorative pillars surrounded the entrance.

"Gogeku, our new fighter is here!" Orgina tapped her foot. "Where is that man? I need to get home and wash this road dust off. I'd sell someone's bloodbond for a bath right now." She yelled again: "Geku!"

A few moments later, one of the large ornamented doors swung open. The most bizarre man appeared, hurrying as fast as his overweight frame would allow and wiping sweat from his bald forehead even in the cool air. Only a thin half-ring of stringy hair decorated the back of his head. As he pulled the sweat-cloth aside, he revealed narrow eyes and the sharpest nose Clanless had ever seen. His clothes, finer than any Clanless knew—except Orgina—seemed on the edge of bursting from his weight.

"My lady!" he exclaimed in a nasally voice which fit perfectly with his appearance, "I did not expect you back so soon!"

"Clearly." Orgina gestured toward Clanless. "Here is our new fighter. Get him settled in and acquainted with everything he needs to know. Then put him on the schedule for the end of the week."

Clanless blinked. "So soon?" He hadn't meant to say it out loud.

"I need to be sure your first fight wasn't an accident. And you need to kill again, to be sure you can keep doing it." She brushed dust from the front of her skirts. "Geku, he's yours now. I'm going home." She turned to get back in the carriage.

"Thank you, my lady," Clanless said. "I won't let you down."

She paused and looked over her shoulder at him. "I should hope not." She pulled herself into the carriage and tapped the wall. The driver flicked the reins, starting the horses moving before the door fully closed. Clanless watched her go, contemplating all that she'd told him over the past three days. He had a lot of work to do.

"Yes, well, let's get you settled, shall we?" the short man said. "What do we call you?"

"Clanless."

"Ohhh, very nice. The crowds will like that." He patted his hands together in not-quite-a-clap. "We have so many fighters show up saying their names are something simple like Ghan or Durken, and then we have to make something up for them." He shook his head. "Fighters generally aren't overly creative folk. But you—already with the title… and this look!" He reached out and fingered the fur pelt. "Crude, but effective. Could do with a washing."

"And the lady called you… Geku?"

"Gogeku of clan Torov, but she says she doesn't like longer names." He gave an exaggerated sigh. "Which is patently ridiculous, because it's no longer than her own. You may call me either. I've grown used to it. Now come along, come along. We must get you where you belong." He waved repeatedly while hurrying back toward the door. "So much to do," he muttered.

Clanless followed him into an ornate hallway, no doubt leading to the best seats of the arena. Gogeku opened a side door and left the main hallway right away. At once, they descended a stairway well below the ground.

"Are all of the rooms underground?" Clanless asked.

"What's that? Oh, no. Not at all. However, you will probably appreciate the quarters down here." He rolled his entire head with his eyes. "The earth provides protection from the winds and some degree of warmth. It gets so beastly cold this time of year, don't you think?"

Clanless shrugged. "I grew up under the moon. It doesn't bother me all that much."

"Well, that explains a few things, doesn't it? Now. Here we have the quarters for the fighters. You'll be lodging with our other latest arrival. Oh, what's the common name he gave?" Gogeku fanned himself with his hand. "Zaluu, I think it was. Right. Yes. Here we are."

The short man pushed open a door and led the way into a room at least the size of the bunk room from Kan's arena. However, it held only two beds, one on either side of the room. A wooden chest sat beside each bed. A table and four chairs sat in the center, while a short bookshelf with a handful of tomes decorated the back wall. Another door led off to the right.

A young man, certainly not much older than Clanless, got up from one of the beds as they entered. He wore only a loincloth; his bare muscles appeared similar to what Clanless had seen develop in all of the other boys being trained over the past nine months. He pulled back a surprising amount of very long, black hair as he got up.

"Zaluu, this is Clanless," Gogeku said, gesturing at both of them before wiping his head again. "Newest fighter. You two will share this room. Please do us a favor and explain to him how things work around here, where to find food… and the baths." He sniffed loudly. "I do have so very much to do, oh." He nodded to Clanless. "A pleasure to meet you. May you survive long enough to actually enjoy this job. Zaluu will tell you everything, but do feel free to ask me any other questions you may have. Goodbye!" He whirled and trotted out of the room, closing the door behind him.

Zaluu sat back on the bed and laughed. "That Geku. He's quite a character, isn't he?"

Clanless sat down on the other bed and found it nicer than he'd expected. "He's a… personality."

"Oh ho. Did the old woman give you that whole speech?" Zaluu laughed. "She says I need to figure out something else for mine. My hair's not enough." He pointed. "But you! You've already got a head start on me! Look at you! I bet she loves you!"

Clanless shrugged.

"Right. So… I'm Zaluu. I'm from clan Zavi. Zaluu from Zavi. Ridiculous, I know. Not sure if my parents thought they were being funny or not."

"I… wouldn't know." Clanless hated his ignorance, but he did remember one other person from clan Zavi: Jik.

"Where are you from? I mean, Geku called you Clanless, but obviously you came from somewhere originally."

"I grew up in a clanhold a, uh, long way from here."

"Wilderness boy, huh? First time in a big city?"

"I got to visit the one where we trained…"

"Not a total innocent then. We might have some fun together out there."

Clanless took off Nukai's fur and spread it on the bed. "They let us go into the city?"

"When Orgina's happy with us. I've only been here two months, but we got two nights out so far."

Orgina gave more freedom than Kan, it appeared. But it made sense, Clanless supposed. If you kept the fighters happy, it might help with their motivation. Even so, Clanless wasn't sure what he would do in the city, especially if it slowed down his pursuit of actual freedom.

"Two months… how many fights have you had?"

"Six." Zaluu patted his left knee. "This one got smashed in my last bout. Kept me out last week. Even after healing, it's taking me time to get my speed back. So you've only had the one fight so far, right? Only killed one other guy?"

Clanless nodded. Did everyone here talk this much?

Zaluu hopped to his feet. "Come on then. I'll show you around. Are you hungry?"

"Yes." Now that he thought about it, Clanless felt ravenous. He hadn't eaten since noon.

Zaluu opened the door and led the way down the hall. "We can go just about anywhere within the arena grounds," he explained, "except on Arena Nights. Then we're restricted down below except when it's our turn."

One of the other side doors opened, and one of the tallest men Clanless had ever seen stepped out. He stifled a yawn before noticing the two boys. "Ho, Zaluu. Got someone fresher than you now, eh?"

"This is Clanless." Zaluu thumbed over his shoulder. "Clanless, this is Allaka of clan Shasin. He's been here at least a decade, I'm thinking."

"Hardly. Six years." Allaka's grin was split by an ugly scar on his upper lip. "Three hundred and four kills."

"I don't think I'll be keeping count after that long," Zaluu said, shaking his head.

"Then what's the point?" Allaka looked back into his room. "Patch! Ya want to meet the new blood?"

"No! Get your loud voices out! I'm trying to sleep here!"

Allaka chuckled as he shut the door. "He's in a bad mood today."

"We call him Patch because he wears an eyepatch in the arena," Zaluu explained. "But his eyes are fine. It's just the personality Orgina created for him. The patch is actually full of holes he can see through, but it looks solid from the seats."

"How many fighters live here?" Clanless asked.

"With you now, it makes twelve. Again. It was thirteen last week." Zaluu gestured on. "Let's get some food. Coming, Allaka?"

"Nah. I'm off to the practice grounds." He nodded to Clanless. "Hope you survive a while." The tall man moved past them and disappeared down the hall, his head narrowly missing the ceiling with each step.

Clanless caught up to Zaluu, who'd kept moving. "Are the practice grounds different from the arena itself?"

"Oh, sure. But they're only big enough for two or three people to use at a time. When we do full training, we use the arena." Zaluu kept walking while he talked. "Speaking of which, I guess you need to know the routine. Eh, I'll walk you through it tomorrow. None of it is really required, necessarily. Orgina doesn't check on us every day. Geku will pester you if you miss anything, though. It gets annoying. And Badaar—he's the trainer—gets grumpy if you don't show up. But if we don't train like we're supposed to, I guess the odds are greater we'll lose a fight at week's end." He shrugged. "You do your best, and you live."

Clanless couldn't imagine any reason for missing daily training time, since one's life depended on it.

The hallway led to a set of stairs going back up. Right before the stairs, they passed a heavy, locked door on the right. An unpleasant odor came from within. "What's that?" Clanless asked.

"There are cages back there," Zaluu said. "For wild animals, when they have any. I don't think they have any right now."

"Have you fought an animal?"

"No, not yet. I'm kind of excited to, but terrified at the same time. It's got to be so different from fighting a person."

They made their way up the stairs to the ground floor. Clanless gave a sigh of relief at seeing the sunshine coming in again through the windows. Sleeping underground might be cooler, but he disliked not being able to see the sun or even the moon. It seemed unnatural.

"Here's one of the main entrances to the arena itself." Zaluu gestured to the left. "But we can look at that later. With all this talk, I'm getting hungry now."

He led the way to a dining hall much bigger and nicer than the one at Kan's training grounds. Throughout the walk, and while they filled their plates from an array of available meals, Zaluu never stopped talking. He expounded on Orgina's management system, her design of personalities, some of the other fighters' odd habits, life in a harbor city versus this one, the latest rumors about the Hawk King, and a rumor of war with a neighboring country Clanless had never heard about. He couldn't keep up and hoped Zaluu didn't ask him to repeat anything he'd said.

The choice in foods was extensive, and Zaluu assured him they could take as much as they wanted. "Orgina wants us well fed," he pointed out. "But if you gain too much weight, Geku will notice and throw a fit about it. Isn't that funny? He's fatter than most of the nobles that come to watch us!" Several breads were available, but no flatbread. Clanless determined his primary purpose when going into the city would be to find a place that served flatbread. What other luxury could he want?

（（（●））））

Clanless woke the next morning to the sound of Zaluu praying. "… And should it flow, let it flow for you as well. Bless our work and our growth. Blood is life. Blood is precious. Blood is power."

Clanless swung his legs over the side of the bed and blinked a few times.

"You get used to waking up at the right time," Zaluu said. "It becomes part of the routine."

"I haven't heard that prayer in nine months," Clanless said. It reminded him of home, and too much more.

"Training is over. Time to get back to life, Clanless. Morning prayers. Routine."

"Not sure I see the point." Clanless stood and stretched.

Zaluu feigned shock. "No point in praying to the goddess? How can you say such a thing? She cares for us!"

Clanless couldn't tell whether he was being serious or not. He wanted to ask, "then why did she give me the Taint?" Instead, he settled on a grunt as he looked for his clothes. He'd tossed them on the floor beside his bed, but they seemed to have vanished.

"Geku left some new clothes for you in your chest," Zaluu said, combing out his hair.

Clanless opened the wooden chest beside his bed to discover it packed with clothing. He pulled some of the pieces out to look them over. Of course, he found plenty of underclothes and leggings for wearing in the arena. Some of the others, however, were far too fine for that purpose: colorful leggings with wide belts and embroidered shirts—all of which left his branded shoulder bare, of course. Nukai's fur hung neatly on the end of the bed.

"This is…"

"A lot?" Zaluu finished. "Yeah, Geku goes a little overboard. The nicer clothes are for when you go into town, or if Orgina wants to show you off to her noble friends."

Clanless pulled on one of the shirts. To his surprise, it fit perfectly. He fingered the carefully stitched seam that curved to expose his brand. "This was made for me," he realized. "Just for me. How could he do that overnight? And get it so right?"

Zaluu shrugged. "That's one of the reasons he has his job, I guess. We do have to give him credit for that." He slapped the table. "Let's get moving. Finish up, and we can get some breakfast. After that… training time!"

Clanless finished getting dressed and picked up the fur pelt. Gogeku had replaced the old cord holding it together with a chain, fastened by a clasp. It would hold together in the arena much better. The strange little man thought of everything.

When they arrived at the arena, Clanless got more of an idea of how things would be different. For starters, the fighters weren't all working together. Everyone appeared to be doing their own thing, scattered across the arena grounds. The arena itself appeared a bit larger than Kan's. Running door-to-door in this one would be a more difficult task. Zaluu introduced Clanless to the trainer, Badaar of clan Dalbai, then scampered off to do his own thing.

Clanless found Badaar both like and unlike Kan. He was shorter and broader, but maybe even more muscular. His graying hair was cut short against his scalp. He scowled as he looked Clanless over. "I've heard you prefer the sword."

Clanless nodded.

"Slashing or stabbing?"

He blinked. "What do you mean, sir?"

"Do you generally prefer to use it for slashing or stabbing? It's a simple question."

"Slashing, I suppose. But I've done both."

Badaar nodded. "I'll observe you in practice some more, then. Try to get a feel for your style. Once I understand it, I can design the proper improvement plan for you."

"A plan just for me?"

"You're one of Kan's, aren't you?" Badaar chuckled. "Great man. Great trainer, at least to get you started. But here… I help you take the next step, if you apply yourself." He pointed at some of the other fighters working at various tasks around them. "I've designed a personal plan for each one you see here. You're now beyond the point where a basic plan for everyone works. If you're going to continue with the sword, for example, we need to drill you on that daily. Kan probably had you going back and forth with the mace, didn't he?"

Clanless nodded again.

"And it was right for that point in your training. But now… you're in the real arena world now. You need to be prepared for anything and everything. And you need to be constantly improving. Follow my plan, and that'll happen. Don't follow it…" He shrugged. "And you're dead before long. Zaluu!" he yelled. "Work that knee out and do some more running! You've let it rest long enough!" He turned back to Clanless. "All right. Let's see what you've got."

Between breakfast and lunch, Clanless worked with Badaar, learning the ins and outs of the training possibilities. By the time they broke up to eat, Badaar said he understood enough to work on a personal plan. "Come back tomorrow during the sun's pursuit, and we'll get you started. We need to work fast too. Your first fight here is the day after that."

"Already?" Clanless knew fights were at the end of the week, but he'd lost track of the days.

"Like I said: you're in the real arena world now. Speaking of which…" He walked over to a crude desk and picked up an odd-shaped conglomeration of objects. "I don't suppose anyone has explained this to you yet?"

"What is it?"

"Of course they haven't." Badaar wiped sweat from his brow. "This is called a Siphon. It's part of how you get paid. Save up enough, and you can have a better life."

"Or buy my freedom?"

He paused. "Yeah. Sure. Anyway, this is what happens. When you kill someone in the arena, you're allowed to take some of their blood. The Siphon lets you do that." He held up a straw-shaped object with a pointed end. "This is the punch tube. You stick this in their body, preferably an open wound. The heart is even better. When you do that, blood runs up through it into this hose"—he moved his hands along the device—"and then into this bladder here."

"And you get to keep that?"

"Sort of. The priests will take a tithe of whatever you get, and then it gets a little more complicated. We'll give you some crystal containers for the blood. To convert it into actual blood currency that you can use, you have to take those containers to the shrine connected to the arena. After that, you can do what you want with it."

"How much does it take to purchase my freedom?"

Badaar didn't answer for a moment. "I don't know how to answer that. I mean, there is an answer, but it's such a staggering amount that no one's ever gotten close. However…" He paused again for a long time. "Your owner, Orgina, will keep track of the number of fights you win. For each victory, the purchase price for freedom goes down." He sighed. "I'm telling you all of this because you asked, but I want to be honest with you: no one does it. First, you'd have to save your blood, not spending it on yourself."

"I can do that." Clanless had grown tired of being told no one ever made it far enough.

"Maybe you could. But the more you accumulate, the harder it's going to be to keep it safe." He twirled his finger in a circle. "You see these guys? Are you going to trust them not to… siphon a little of your savings away for themselves if they find out you've got a lot?"

Clanless frowned. "That's not right."

"Of course it's not. Welcome to the real world. So even if you do manage to keep saving up all this blood, then… you have to keep winning. You have to survive." He paused again. "And you have to do it for years and years."

"How long?"

Badaar shook his head. "You're stubborn now, but we'll see how it goes. I'd guess a decade or longer. And believe me… nobody survives a decade in the arenas."

"Allaka said he's been here six years."

"Allaka spends all of his income every week." Badaar snorted. "Even if he were offered his freedom, I don't think he would take it. He's become… addicted to the arena."

Clanless wrinkled his brow. "What do you mean?"

Badaar turned and toyed with one of the swords on the weapons rack. "How can I put this? Killing is part of the job here. You know that now. Some fighters hate it, especially when they begin, like you. Over time, that changes. Most become numb, where the killing doesn't even mean anything any more. And then there are those like Allaka, who… begin to enjoy it."

Clanless opened his mouth but didn't say anything.

"Allaka likes killing now. He looks forward to it." Badaar turned back to him. "The arena changes everyone. You'll see."

❨❨❨❨●❩❩❩❩

Clanless soon learned all the differences between Kan's training world and Orgina's arena world. Though he was still a slave, everyone treated him now as if he were an adult. If he'd never left home, he would have been considered an adult for the past nine months, of course. But after all this time of Kan calling him and treating him like a boy, it was a welcome change.

Training, once Badaar devised a plan, turned out to be more intense than Kan's workouts, but still using fewer hours in the day. Meals became much more luxurious, both in the content and in the length of time available. He spent most of these times with Zaluu, as the only other fighter around his age. Apparently, Orgina hadn't purchased any new fighters in several years. She and Badaar took good care of their investments, scheduling their fights with purpose: not creating too much risk, while still giving the people a good show.

On the second day, Badaar offered Clanless a variety of sword options.

In addition to the short sword he'd learned from Kan, he had choices of sizes and lengths ranging all the way up to an enormous two-handed blade almost as long as he was tall. He settled on a weapon a couple of inches longer than the short sword. Perhaps in time, he might try a longer weapon, but keeping something near the weight he'd trained on seemed the wisest course for now. But he couldn't resist getting a little more reach to his strokes.

One by one, Clanless met the other fighters. Most had been at this arena two or three years. Allaka held the record for the longest, but a couple of others weren't far behind. Clanless didn't know what to make of most of them during the first three days. None of them seemed especially interested in getting to know him yet.

He faced the most difficult adjustment in the baths. Being able to soak your entire body in warm water after a hard sweat was certainly a luxury. But he wondered if he'd ever get used to sharing the baths with the other fighters at the same time. Public nudity wasn't something he'd experienced in the clanhold, or even at Kan's arena. Here, it was a daily occurrence.

Those first three days went by in a blur, leading to the time of his first public fight in this arena. Rather than being sequestered in a room by himself, he stood waiting at the arena entrance with Badaar and Zaluu, watching the previous fight wrap up.

Allaka jogged in from his battle, covered in blood and grinning. "Did you see his head explode? Priests aren't going to like that one!" He laughed, shaking blood from his enormous flanged mace, a one-of-a-kind weapon. "Time to see what you can do, Clanless."

"Who is my opponent?" he asked Badaar, testing the balance on his sword for the tenth or eleventh time.

"A criminal." Badaar helped adjust the fur on his shoulder. "One of the worst sort. This is his one chance to escape justice for his crimes. If he beats you, he goes free." Badaar pulled him around and looked him in the face. "And that would be a travesty. Bring him justice, Clanless. Death is what he deserves."

Clanless nodded and swallowed. His nerves were on edge even more than before his first fight. There, he'd been fighting for survival, and to impress a new boss. Here, it mattered what the crowd thought of him as well. His future in this arena depended on pleasing them.

No slow-moving portcullis here. Two attendants swung open the barred doors and motioned for Clanless to enter. He took a firm grip on his buckler and sword and stepped out onto the sands.

"Noble people of Ghoyor, here he is! The latest sensation to join our arena fighters! The mysterious young man known only as… Clanless!"

The voice, loud enough to be heard over the roar of the crowd, echoed across the entire arena. The others had explained to him about the presenter and how his voice was amplified by blood-magic. But it still caught him by surprise. It puzzled him how blood could power such different types of magic. Zaluu said every clan's blood worked differently with the priests' magic, creating all sorts of effects.

The presenter's next words were garbled, but Clanless understood enough: his opponent was coming. Gates opened on the other side of the arena, and a medium-sized man rushed out. Spotting Clanless, he slowed and approached with caution, mace and buckler at ready.

"Born on the very edges of the Empire, Clanless committed a crime so unspeakable, he was branded and forever cast out from his home! Refusing to bow to the rules of the society that made him an outcast, he chooses to fight with a sword, spilling the precious blood of his opponents onto the sand, denying the priests their rightful claim!"

It made him sound more like a villain than a hero… and didn't that fit right in with what Kan said about the people in the stands? Making sure his enemy was still far away, Clanless lifted his sword and turned in a circle for them. The crowd noise filled the air, equal parts cheering and derision. On inspiration, Clanless pointed the tip of his sword at his own brand as he turned, taunting the crowd with it.

He turned back toward his opponent, surprised to see he hadn't come much closer. The man looked fierce enough: wild hair hanging out beneath his helmet, a prominent scar on his bare chest, and an angry glare strong enough to curdle goat's milk. But he hadn't been trained for this. Neither his buckler nor mace were held in their optimum positions. Even Tunt had understood that much.

His confidence bolstered, Clanless strode across the sands. He picked up his pace, moving from walking to jogging. He lifted his sword with a roar as he charged the criminal. The crowd loved it, shouting their approval. The presenter said something else, but Clanless didn't hear it. The bloodrush seized him. His own pulse pounded in his ears. He leaped the last few feet, bringing his sword down in a reckless stroke.

The criminal blocked the attack with his buckler, but couldn't manage a counterattack swift enough. His mace swung through the spot where Clanless had been, but Clanless used the momentum from his charge to spin around to the right. The criminal pivoted quick enough, preventing a fast end to the fight.

The crowd's noise, far louder than during his first fight, competed with the bloodrush pulsing in his ears. Clanless re-evaluated his opponent yet again, surprised at how well he moved. Both combatants attempted several attacks, but neither succeeded.

A spin and a slash managed to connect, ever so slightly, with the criminal's left forearm behind his buckler. Blood dripped from the gash, its smell and taste filling Clanless's senses. An odd sensation pulled at him. The Taint? He felt a sudden, strong desire to use it, right away. His body craved the feeling it gave him. He'd never experienced it in this fashion.

The criminal took advantage of his momentary confusion. He swung his mace hard enough to push Clanless's buckler to the side. It didn't seem like much, since his mace had swung the wrong direction for a swift return strike. But then the criminal lunged forward and kicked Clanless in the chest. The kick didn't hurt much, but the force of it was enough to push him back a step. He instinctively threw both arms out to maintain his balance. In that moment of opportunity, the criminal brought the mace upward. Clanless flung his head back, barely keeping the mace from taking off his head, but it scraped against his upper chest.

"There's a surprise for Clanless!" the presenter boomed. "Feet can be weapons too, people!"

Angered, Clanless had enough. He stepped back, remembering his training, and delivered a series of slashes and stabs that drove his opponent back and back. Unrelenting, he kept up the attacks, watching the sweat pour down the criminal's face. At last, he paused, as if tiring. The criminal, thinking he saw an opening, stepped forward himself to deliver a counter-attack. Clanless threw his buckler upward, knocking the mace aside. At the same time, he ducked in and slashed across the criminal's chest. His blade cut deep.

The mace and buckler fell from shaking hands. The criminal dropped to his knees. Clanless spun in a complete circle and stabbed his sword into the open chest wound, plunging it all the way through. He ripped it back out and let the other man fall to the sand.

Clanless turned to the crowd and lifted his bloody sword. "Clanless victorious!" the presenter shouted over the roars. He turned in a slow circle, making sure he faced the most expensive seats longer. The crowd continued to cheer. The bloodrush, so strong a moment ago, faded.

Movement caught his attention. Clanless turned to see a blood-priest and two attendants approaching the fallen criminal. Remembering the Siphon, he stabbed his sword into the sand and fumbled to remove the strange device from his belt. He got it loose as the attendants reached down to pick up the fallen man.

"Wait! I haven't used this yet!"

The blood-priest laughed at him. "You'll need to be faster than that, boy. He belongs to us now."

"I made the kill. Some of his blood is mine!"

"Only if you get to it before we do." The priest smiled. "It is the way of things."

Enraged, Clanless dropped his buckler and clenched his fist, activating the Taint. His eye burned. "Then the blood is all yours now," he growled. "You're welcome to it."

Without waiting to see if the priest realized what had happened, he picked up his buckler and sword and turned away. He jogged back toward the door, waving to the crowd for their final cheers.

Back inside, he caught his breath and looked to Badaar, who was helping Patch gear up for the next fight. "There's a time limit on using the Siphon?" he demanded.

"Eh, I should have been more specific about that, I suppose," Badaar admitted. "You have to get it in before they get there. And they'll come as fast as they can when it's a bleeding wound. Save your crowd performance until after you get the blood."

"I lost that blood!"

"It's your first fight." Badaar lifted his hands, palms out. "You're learning. Next time, you'll do better."

Clanless tried to calm himself, breathing in through his nose. Badaar was right, but it stung. As did his chest where the mace had scraped him. He rubbed it, wincing. "I need to learn that kick."

◖◖◖◖●◗◗◗◗

As Patch headed out for his fight, the blood-priest charged into the waiting room. He leveled a shaking finger at Clanless. "You used the Taint! You corrupted the blood!"

"What are you babbling about?" Badaar asked.

The priest trembled with rage. "They told me a clanless fighter possessed the Taint, but I didn't believe it. Now I've seen it myself!"

Badaar looked at Clanless. "Do you know what he's talking about?"

Clanless didn't answer.

"Did he violate any rules of the arena?" Badaar asked the priest.

"He ruined the blood. It's useless to us now!"

"So he didn't violate the rules."

"He must be punished! If you won't deal with this, I'll go to Orgina!"

"You can file a complaint with Gogeku." Badaar folded his arms. "It's not my business."

The priest appeared about to rant some more, but instead spun on his heel and stalked away. Clanless let out a breath he hadn't realized he'd held.

"Whatever this is… it will make its way to Orgina," Badaar said. "I hope you know what that will mean, if anything."

Clanless licked his lips. Orgina knew, but she'd told him not to use it unless he had to. Irritating the priests probably didn't fall under "had to." He took another deep breath. "It's complicated," he said at last. "But it won't happen again. At least, not for a while."

Badaar nodded. "Fine. I've seen a lot of strange things in this arena, and I know when I shouldn't know anything more. Go get cleaned up. You're done here for tonight."

Clanless made his way back to the room he shared with Zaluu. His roommate wasn't there and likely wouldn't be for a while. The fighters often celebrated together after a day's fights. Clanless didn't feel like celebrating.

He took out the stolen vial of blood Bain had given him. For a moment, he considered its value. How much was this worth? Did a vial of blood's value change depending on its power? On which clan it came from? There was so much he still needed to learn about the way all of this worked. The way the Empire worked.

He poured a small bit of the blood onto the floor near the bookcase and ignited it with the Taint. Zektel's face appeared almost immediately. "Learning things, aren't we?" she asked.

"Not enough. I lost blood tonight because I didn't know enough. I need to know everything." Clanless paused. "About everything."

"That's an awfully big goal, dearheart. Where will you start?"

"You can't tell me?"

"I know my own story, and I know yours, Aldan. I am ignorant of the ways of your Empire. All these clans. All the blood. There's a lot to understand."

"I guess I'll have to start asking people everything I can think of." Clanless snorted. "Everyone here seems to like to talk, anyway."

"Yes. Start with your hairy roommate. But don't trust everything he says. I think he talks more to hear his own voice than to give out real information."

Clanless almost laughed, but the stress of the day was taking its toll. The bloodrush was long gone. Sleep pulled at his mind, beckoning him back toward the bed.

Zektel's face shifted. "You might also want to take a look at these books. They're full of information too, you know."

Clanless looked up at the bookshelf. "I suppose you're right… but I don't know how to read."

"Hmm. That is something we need to correct. You'll have to find someone to teach you."

"You can't?"

Zektel's tinkling laughter filled the room. "I'm a face in a pool of blood, Aldan. How can I give lessons? How can I point to letters and words?"

"I don't know. I don't know what's involved."

"You need a teacher. Someone who knows how to read and won't mind explaining it to you. I'd make that a top priority."

"All right." His eyes sagged. So sleepy.

"You need rest, my dear. We can talk more later. I'm always with you, you know."

He nodded and pushed himself off the floor. He staggered over to the bed and fell into it, asleep almost before he hit the pillow.

ZALUU THE MAGNIFICENT

Then

Clanless woke in the darkness, feeling like he hadn't slept for long. A shadow loomed over his bed, reaching down toward him.

Fear seized him, and he lunged upward. His head narrowly missed the figure, who dodged backward. Clanless tried to punch at him, only to catch his fist in the fur pelt tangled around his arm and shoulder.

"Hey, hey, hey! It's Zaluu! You're in bed, not the arena!"

Clanless untangled himself as Zaluu lit a lantern and set it on the table. His heart continued to beat so fast he wondered if the bloodrush had overtaken him. He took deep breaths, trying to calm himself.

"Did you come straight here after your fight?" Zaluu asked. "I guess you did, judging by your clothes and your smell. Hit the baths first next time, partner! Whoo." He waved his hand in front of his nose.

"What-what time is it?" Clanless took a few deep breaths.

"Around midnight now." Zaluu cocked his head, his loose hair swinging. "Remind me never to wake you again. You might have knocked my head off!"

"Sorry. I don't… I don't wake up well."

"Whatever you say." Zaluu held up both hands. "Lesson learned. So. You won your first fight. I saw it. Not bad. Not bad at all. You finished a little too fast, but otherwise, it looked good."

"Yeah?" Clanless ran a hand through his hair. "How was your first fight here?"

"Ha!" Zaluu sat in one of the chairs. "I won, but they almost had to carry me off the arena floor. Geku griped about how much my healing cost." He shrugged. "I got better."

Clanless unhooked the fur and hung it over the back of the other chair. He regretted falling asleep in his clothes. Zaluu was right about the smell.

"Hey, what's that?" Zaluu got up, carrying the lantern. He looked at the blood on the floor. "Are you injured? Should I call the healer?"

"No, no. I'm all right. That was… an accident."

"Accident," Zaluu repeated. "Be sure to clean it up tomorrow. There's no rule about it, really, but Geku gripes at us if the room is messy."

Clanless pointed past him at the shelves. "Have you… read all of those?"

"Who, me?" Zaluu set the lantern back on the table. "Nah, I never saw much point in reading that much. I mean, I can read. Who can't? I'm just not interested in reading something that long. Help yourself any-time, though. I think they were left here by the previous residents of this room. Either that, or Geku put them there for us, hoping we'd improve our minds or something."

Clanless nodded and stretched. "I'm going back to sleep. I'll clean up in the morning."

"Sure, sure." Zaluu moved around the room a little longer, talking to himself. Clanless couldn't tell what he was doing and didn't care. Eventual-ly, his roommate put out the light and went to bed himself.

Despite his weariness, Clanless lay awake for a while. The rush of fear and action still permeated his blood. His body needed time to relax again.

He couldn't ask Zaluu to teach him to read. He needed someone else. Someone whose company he wouldn't mind so much. He fell asleep think-ing about going into the city.

❨❨❨❨●❩❩❩❩

Two voices talking over each other woke Clanless the next morning. He shook his head and sat up. Gogeku stood on one of the chairs, adjust-ing a bright purple cape on Zaluu's shoulders. The little man's outfit gave the cape competition in its gaudiness.

"The sleeper awakens!" Zaluu proclaimed. "See, I told you he wasn't dead, Geku. You should trust me more."

"The smell said otherwise." Gogeku sniffed. He flipped the cape over Zaluu's left shoulder and cocked his head to examine the effect.

"That won't work," Zaluu protested. "It will restrict my buckler arm. Really, the whole thing is too much. Tell Orgina thanks for me, but I'll stick with my regular outfit."

"You'll do no such thing." Geku re-adjusted the cape. "We told you from the beginning that you needed more of a personality. Long hair is not enough."

"But now you'll be hiding my hair!"

"Nonsense." Geku patted him on the shoulder. "Your hair stands out nicely. It's why we chose this magnificent color."

"Zaluu the Magnificent," Clanless said.

"Yes!" Geku pointed at him. "The dead man speaks wisdom! Zaluu the Magnificent it shall be. I'll inform the presenter." He jumped down from the chair and ran around to look at Zaluu from the front. "We'll add some bright yellow leather bracers. They won't restrict your movement and will actually add some protection. We can also paint your buckler. Maybe even some boots…"

"Absolutely not!" Zaluu flexed his shoulders, watching the movement of the cape. "No boots. That would definitely cause problems fighting. I have to move fast, you know. If any of this weighs me down, it makes it harder to win, no matter how good it looks." He paused and looked toward Geku. "But, uh, a custom weapon now… that would be nice, you know. When can I design my own mace?"

Geku wagged a finger at him. "You don't get to design anything, thank the goddess. If you want expensive custom weapons, you have to prove you're worth it. And that means making the crowd want to see you again and again. And to do that, you need…"

"Personality," Zaluu said in unison with him. "I get it." He whipped the cape around. "I guess the cape's not too bad."

"How very relieved I am to hear it," Geku said drily. He picked up a bag from the chair, took a step toward the door and paused. Turning to Clanless, he sighed before speaking: "Mistress Orgina is aware of everything that took place with your fight yesterday. She wished me to inform you that while she understands what you did at the end, you are not to do it again, unless you have no other choice. Is that understood?"

"It won't happen again," Clanless said.

"We will inform her of your acquiescence. As it turns out, the audience did respond favorably to your first appearance. This bodes well." Geku sniffed again. "Zaluu, you did show this one where the baths are located, did you not?"

"I'll head there right now." Clanless got to his feet.

Geku stepped back to the chair and picked up the fur pelt. "We'll see this gets washed as well, and returned to you. I don't know how Kan ran things, young man, but here in Ghoyor, we pride ourselves on cleanliness. You would do well to remember that."

"Yes, sir."

Geku brightened visibly and hurried out of the room.

"You just made his day," Zaluu observed, removing the cape. "Calling him 'sir.' I don't think I've ever seen him that pleased."

"He speaks for Orgina," Clanless pointed out. "I don't want to get on his bad side."

Zaluu shrugged. "He's not worth the effort. If I want something from Orgina, I'll ask her myself. I don't need a fat clothing designer between us."

"I think I'll stick with my plan and try not to antagonize him." Clanless headed toward the door. "I don't need him thinking up ways to make me more magnificent."

Zaluu balled up the cape and threw it at him as he ducked out of the room.

((((●))))

By the time of his second fight a week later, Clanless understood much more about the way things worked. He didn't ask where this opponent came from, nor did he want to know. He reminded himself of what Kan said. His opponents weren't people. They were agents of the priesthood that put him here. With that in mind, he destroyed his second opponent without hesitation. He had to force himself to drag the fight out, for the sake of the crowd. When it ended, he immediately knelt and took as much blood with the Siphon as he could, before the priest showed up to force him away.

Another priest showed up as soon as he left, demanding the "tithe." Clanless watched, fighting anger again, as the priest took a portion from what he'd siphoned. It was supposed to be ten percent, but neither of them had a method for measuring it. The priest took what he wanted.

Geku gave him a large crystal container in which to store the blood. When it filled, he could take it to the priests and receive either sealed vials of blood or a paper documenting his ownership of the blood. Either one could be used as currency—or to save for his freedom. Before paying him, the priests would test the blood for impurities. If they found any, they would pay less. Blood directly from the heart was considered the purest. Clanless made a mental note to extract as much as possible from his opponents' chests instead of other areas, a simpler task since he used a blade weapon instead of a mace.

He didn't fight the next week. Badaar couldn't give him a reason. "Sometimes, it's just the way the schedule goes," he said. "Either they had enough fights already, or it's all part of the plan to build your audience. Take what you can."

The weekly fights were known as Arena Night, even though they weren't held at night. Most fights took place in the mid-afternoon, under the sun after it retreated from the moon's power. Even so, the name persisted, mostly because of the celebrations and parties that often followed the fights well into the evening. Arena Nights happened almost every week throughout the year, save for an eight-week period of the coldest days of the year. During High Winter or the Sun's Surrender, the arena fighters enjoyed a two-month break from their labors. Unfortunately, most of them had no idea what to do with this time and often got into more trouble than they should.

Clanless worked hard at his training. He followed every bit of Badaar's plan, exceeding it and adding even more than suggested. The plan involved continued physical training to keep himself strong and fast combined with constant weapons training to improve his skills. Zaluu called him obsessed, but only because Zaluu didn't want to work as hard. Clanless noted that older fighters, like Allaka, worked hard on their training as well. He determined to equal or best them.

Only one other fighter at this arena used a sword: a young man named Darghan. He'd been at Orgina's arena for three years, after being traded from another arena where he'd fought for two more years. He took Clanless under his wing and worked with him once a day on flashy sword techniques.

"None of these are necessarily the best moves for a real fight," Darghan cautioned. "But when you already know you've won, these can make the ending more dramatic. You know, the stuff the crowd likes to see."

Darghan wielded a broadsword thicker and wider than anything Clanless had used. The blade appeared red at all times, having been forged with some process neither of them understood. "Darghan the Red Sword," the presenter called him at its first appearance, an name the crowds loved.

Clanless experimented with the various sized swords. Most intriguing were the even larger weapons, those requiring two hands to wield effectively. To use one, he'd have to give up his buckler.

"If you're good enough, that's the way to go," Darghan said. "You won't get as many hits on your target, but the ones you do get will be devastating."

In response, Clanless added another hour of workout to his routine: two-handed weapon training. He didn't know whether he'd ever feel comfortable enough to switch to the larger blade, but the added training could only benefit him.

Badaar also gave him some training and pointers on more advanced arena concepts. "What happens if you have to fight two opponents at once?" he asked one day.

"Does that happen?" Clanless wondered.

"You haven't watched many fights, have you?" Zaluu sat nearby, eating a pear while he watched. "It's a regular thing."

"It's only for the most advanced and skillful fighters," Badaar clarified. "Once you've proven you can take down any one opponent, the crowd may start to get bored. That's when it gets interesting. Two opponents is one possibility. Animals are another. Sometimes there may be team fighting: say, you and Zaluu versus two others."

"We would destroy them," Zaluu said.

"The best way to win against two opponents is not to let them attack you at once," Badaar explained. "Split them up. Charge one of them and take him down fast, before the other can get to you. That kind of thing."

Clanless nodded. He'd thought Kan had taught him everything he needed to know, but it seemed every day brought new knowledge. And that only applied to the arena. He needed to be learning more about the rest of the world, but to do that, he still needed to learn to read.

At the end of the fourth week, Clanless fought his third battle. This time, the crowd knew him and roared as he entered the sands. Maybe the week off had built anticipation. The presenter continued to play up his outcast status, and his quest to strike back against those who'd branded him… which wasn't too far from the truth. The crowd ate it up.

His opponent turned out to be a much larger man this time, standing at least a foot taller than Clanless. His sheer strength made up for a lack of skill. By the end of the fight, Clanless's buckler arm needed healing from the severe bruising it had endured. He'd been tempted to use the Taint throughout the fight, unsure about his victory at several points. But given enough time, he turned the momentum to his own advantage and killed another opponent, nearly beheading him in the process. The crowd loved the drawn-out fight and went crazy over the conclusion.

Soaking in the baths that evening, Clanless considered his progress. Everything seemed to be going in the right direction. Zaluu entered and splashed down into the water as well. "I've got good news for you!" he announced.

"Go ahead." Clanless lay back with his eyes closed.

"Tomorrow evening, we get a night in the city."

His eyes flew open. "Really?"

"Word just came down." Zaluu sank into the water as well. "Goddess! This water is too cold."

Clanless's mind whirled. He hadn't been out in public since that one night with the other boys. How many months had it been?

"Got any ideas what you want to look for out there?" Zaluu asked. "It's your first time in this city. Anything goes!"

"Flatbread," Clanless said. "Flatbread and… a storyteller."

((((●))))

Five months passed, and Clanless accepted his role in Orgina's arena system. He usually fought three out of every four weeks. The crowd liked watching him and cheered his victories with abandon. In time, he became the most popular of the younger fighters. Zaluu declared he would have been jealous if he cared about such things, which he didn't.

The quality of his opponents began to change as well. He didn't ask where they came from, but they no longer fought like criminals. These fighters had training; not on the same level as his, but significant nonetheless. The fights grew more difficult and lasted longer. For some of them, Badaar told him not to fight to the death, only to incapacitation. Sometimes Clanless appreciated not having to make the extra effort to kill an opponent once he hit the sand. Sometimes, it made the battle more difficult. It also made using the Siphon a bit more awkward.

He built up a significant supply of blood, taking the large crystal to the priests twice. He collected a bag full of the currency vials, though he soon realized he couldn't keep doing that. He'd have to settle for the paper statements. He took special care to spend as little of the blood as possible.

Clanless struggled to understand the other fighters. Almost all of them spent every bit of their blood within days of earning it. The city of Ghoyor was happy to take it from them, in exchange for all forms of entertainment and commerce. The fighters were regulars at the brothels and almost all of the eating establishments, despite the excellent food they received at the arena. As Darghan and Patch explained, it wasn't about the food; it was about the company… usually feminine company.

In the eyes of the culture and his peers, Clanless was a man. But at fourteen, he didn't feel like one. Surely there was more to manhood than this. He stayed away from the brothels and continued to spend almost nothing anywhere else. His reluctance to spend time with women added to his mystique. New rumors spread about a lost love, perhaps the very reason he'd been branded in the first place. Clanless had no doubts that Orgina—or Gogeku, come to think of it—was behind the stories.

In their time in the city, the fighters were expected to maintain their "personalities." For most of them, that didn't mean much more than taking care to wear clothing reminiscent of their arena garb. Clanless kept his shoulder bare to show his brand, as always, and wore Nukai's fur everywhere he went. The only one inconvenienced by this policy was Patch: he had to wear an actual eye patch in the city, restricting his vision.

Clanless eventually found an eating establishment that served flatbread the way he liked it. Called Dugh's End, it also featured singers and storytellers on a regular basis. It seems that storytellers traveled from city to city, never staying in one place for very long. In this way, they accumulated more stories to tell in the next town. Clanless spoke with several of them in person. He considered asking one of them to teach him to read, but they were so transitory. None of them would have the time it would take. At least, Clanless thought it would take a long time; he had no idea.

One evening, the day after the week's fights, he persuaded Darghan and Zaluu to join him. Both were interested in more exciting entertainment, but agreed to his eating establishment as a first stop. Clanless turned to face them as they entered, promising them the best flatbread they'd ever tasted. Behind him, he heard a suddenly familiar voice say:

"My name is Koland of clan Dendsu, and I will be your storyteller this evening."

FRIENDS

Now

Clanless pulled on the clothes he wore when leaving the arena. The loose-fitting pants always felt odd after all his time in the arena leggings that held tight to every muscle. As he had for eight long years, he kept his left shoulder bare to expose the brand, throwing his well-worn fur pelt over the opposite shoulder. Whatever else changed with his position, his fame, or his location, the wolf fur had remained with him.

He stepped out of his room and met Hagh and Sugh coming down the hall. Sugh's eyes brightened at the sight of him. "Ah, you had the same idea! Let us celebrate your last night in the Dohor!" He slapped Clanless on the back.

"Careful," Hagh warned. "You wouldn't want to injure the poor boy before such an important fight." He coughed. "On second thought, maybe he should just lie in bed. You know, to keep him safe until then."

"Oh, no. There's another bed I think he would rather lie in." Sugh laughed. "Am I right?"

Clanless smiled. These two were the closest friends he'd had since… since the barbarian fight. "You know me well. Shall we make that our first stop?"

"Food first," Hagh countered. "You need to keep up your strength, boy."

Sugh rolled his eyes. "Sands! We can eat first, old man. Wouldn't want you to pass out from hunger in a whore's arms. She might be offended."

"Can't have that," Clanless agreed.

"Should we check with any of the others?" Hagh wondered.

"Not tonight," Sugh said. "We three have survived together the longest. Let's go!"

The three fighters left the arena and stepped out onto the streets of Et-Baylak, capital of the Sar Empire. To the casual observer, they were three (powerfully-built) men wandering freely through the city, celebrating some special occasion, like so many other groups. But of course, they would be recognized. The Hawk King's arena fighters, his Dohor, were well known to the residents of the city. Almost everyone who lived here had seen them fight many times. They were the elite of the elite, in some ways more popular than the Hawk King himself.

A cold wind swept down the street, bringing with it a feeling of High Winter. The official beginning of the season would be tomorrow when the sun fully surrendered. But tonight, everyone would be celebrating before the cold and winds grew too strong. And if Hagh were right, they were in for the worst winter in decades.

Yesun the arena attendant burst out of the door behind them. "Wait, wait!"

"What is it, little man?" Sugh asked, turning back.

"Clanless! There is someone to see you. It's very important. Waiting in your room!" The words spilled out of the boy's mouth in a torrent.

"Horrible timing!" Hagh complained.

"It's very important," Yesun repeated.

"All right, all right. I'm coming." Clanless followed the boy back inside.

"We'll wait for you!" Sugh called.

THE WEAVING OF WORDS

Clanless spun around and stared at the stage. Koland sat there, strumming his instrument exactly as he had in the eating establishment in Rochinbal a year before. He hadn't changed a bit.

"Arena fighters!" someone shouted. The crowd cheered, some shouting out their names. Zaluu waved with a grin. Darghan nodded to them all, but didn't say anything.

"Let's get close to the stage," Clanless said, moving on. He found space at a long table. The other occupants gladly shifted to make room for the three warriors.

A server hurried over to take their requests. While Zaluu and Darghan spoke with her, Clanless kept his eyes on the stage. Koland strummed his instrument, looking down at it, waiting for the commotion to die down. Kekeen was nowhere to be seen.

"And you, clanless one?" the server asked.

"The usual," he told her. "Flatbread and a meat pastry." She nodded with a shy smile and hurried away.

"Tonight, a story for you all," Koland announced. "From the far borders of the Empire, near the high hills and the home of the beastmen."

"Where do they find these fablers?" Zaluu asked.

"Quiet," Clanless said. "I like this one."

Zaluu chuckled. "This is where you wanted to come, so we'll play along. I just don't see—"

"He said quiet," Darghan said, putting a hand on Zaluu's shoulder. "You don't interrupt a storyteller."

Koland ignored the exchange and began his story, the tale of a poor farmer's son whose family were captured by beastmen. The farmer's son, with the help of a tame wolf, tracked the beastmen and freed his family, but not before befriending one of the beastmen who'd been injured and left behind by his own people. Clanless sat fascinated through it all. He'd heard half a dozen other storytellers over the past few months, but none of them could captivate an audience like Koland. By the climax of the story, even Zaluu hung on every word. Koland knew just when to alter the tone of his voice, raising and lowering it when needed, adapting for the voices of different characters and the pace of the action scenes. When he completed the tale, the room erupted in praise.

"He's more popular than we are," Zaluu observed.

"And well earned," Darghan said. "The weaving of words is a greater skill than the strength of a sword."

Koland made several rapid strums of music. "How about a song?" he called. The crowd cheered their approval.

And then she was there. Clanless hadn't seen her approach, even though he'd been watching for her. Kekeen stood on the stage, a few steps in front of her father, a gentle smile on her face. In the one year since he'd seen her, Kekeen had blossomed into womanhood. Her face had grown slimmer, and her pale brown hair a shade darker (and no longer in braids). The curves of her body were much more evident beneath a dark red dress and open blue vest. But her voice captivated Clanless even more than it had the first time. Over the months, her voice had strengthened, mellowing into a richer tone. Her vocal range had broadened as well, reaching new heights as well as lows in tonality. Clanless had listened to a number of singers and songs in Ghoyor's establishments, but none compared to the melody that filled the room now.

Zaluu leaned close. "Now there's a reason to be here. Think she likes arena heroes?"

Clanless gave him a quick glare. "Stay. Away."

Zaluu's eyes widened as he leaned back with an enormous grin. "Oh-ho! Darghan! We've found a woman that finally captures our young friend's interest!"

Clanless ignored him and stayed focused until the end of the song. When the crowd applauded, he leaped to his feet in his enthusiasm. He caught Kekeen's eyes for a brief moment before others of the audience also got to their feet to clap. In the ensuing confusion, he lost sight of her.

As the applause died, Koland announced, "We'll take a break now, friends, but there will be more to come. Enjoy your food and drink! There's more where it came from!"

Clanless sat, but kept watching toward the stage. Zaluu nudged him. "I never thought I'd see it. You're smitten with that girl, aren't you?"

"I met her a year ago," Clanless answered without looking at him. "During training."

"Tell us all about it," Zaluu insisted, tearing off a piece of flatbread.

Clanless didn't answer. The events of that day seemed like a lost part of his childhood in some ways, a final moment of innocence before he became a killer.

"Did the death worm steal your tongue?" asked a familiar voice behind him.

Clanless jumped to his feet again and spun around. Kekeen stood there smiling, a twinkle in her eyes. His mouth fell open, but no words came out.

"It is Aldan, isn't it?" she asked. "We met… months ago."

"A y-year," he said.

"My friend seems to be struggling with the use of his voice," Zaluu put in. "Please, join us, and perhaps he'll regain it in time."

Kekeen slid in across from Clanless. "This seems familiar, but your friends are different this time."

Zaluu stood and bowed. "I am Zaluu the Magnificent," he declared. "Perhaps you've heard of my arena escapades. Beside me is Dargahn the Red Sword. You apparently already know our Clanless friend here."

"We met," Clanless repeated.

"Arena names. So what's yours?" Kekeen asked him.

"Just Clanless," he said. "That's who I am now."

She frowned. "You gave up your name, after all? I liked it. Clanless isn't a name; it's a title."

"You can still call me Aldan." As he said it, he realized it was the first time his own name had left his lips since the last time they met.

"So obviously, you graduated into a full arena fighter. What about the others? Your three friends?"

Dargahn stood up. "Pardon me, my lady. Zaluu, let us allow these old friends to get reacquainted without our prying ears."

"What? But I—"

"We have some other places to visit, remember?"

Zaluu brightened. "Of course we do. Clanless, enjoy this young woman's company, while we seek out—"

Dargahn smacked him on the back of the head. "Enough. Let's go."

"What was that for?" Zaluu complained, getting up to follow him out.

Kekeen watched them go with a bemused smile. "Not like the innocent boys from a year ago, are they?"

"No, not at all." Clanless tried not to stare at her. He swallowed. Her nearness gave him odd feelings. His nervousness was greater than any of the times he'd entered the arena.

"So… the others?"

"Tunt… died at graduation. Jik and Bain survived. They were taken to other arenas. I don't know how they're doing by now." It was the first time he'd said their names since graduation as well.

Sadness came over Kekeen's face, and Clanless wished he could wipe it away forever.

"The Empire is a horrible place," she said quietly. "Boys sold into slavery and killed so easily. Or they survive, like you, and are forced to kill themselves. Have you… killed a lot of people now?"

"Some. I have to. Like you said, I'm a slave."

She ran both hands through her hair, pulling it back from the sides of her head. "So I'm told. But you arena fighters: you have a lot of freedom, right? I mean, you're here. You get to carouse through the city when you're not fighting."

"Hardly." He frowned. "They let us out sometimes, if we're doing well. If the people like us."

Kekeen glanced at a nearby table, where a young couple were whispering to each other while staring at Clanless. "They seem to like you well enough."

"I'm starting to make a name."

"And all the girls like you?" She reached across the table and squeezed his bicep. "The big, tough arena fighter. I'm sure you meet new ones every time you're out and about."

"I… try to avoid that. This is the only place I usually come." He pointed at the almost-empty platter. "They have the flatbread. And good storytellers."

She raised one eyebrow, almost smirking now. "Really? That's not the behavior I hear about for arena fighters. They're famous for their… carousing."

"Not me. I'm trying to save as much blood as I can. To buy my freedom."

"Is that so? I didn't know it was possible."

"It takes many years. Or so they tell me." Clanless clenched his fist under the table. "But I will do it. No matter how long it takes."

Kekeen's expression softened. "Are you—?" she began.

"Kekeen!" Koland's voice boomed across the room. "It's time for another song and story!"

"Can you stay?" she asked quickly.

Clanless nodded. "All night, if I have to."

"It won't be that long, silly." She jumped to her feet and ran to the stage.

Clanless sat enthralled through another pair of stories and songs. He noticed that the characters in Koland's story generally matched up with the group of people in the closest table to the stage, not unlike what he'd done a year ago. While Clanless enjoyed the story, Kekeen's singing left him awestruck with each song.

Halfway through the story, two young women approached his table. "Aren't you Clanless from the arena?" one asked.

"Yes," he answered. This kind of thing happened often, but he still didn't know how to handle it.

"I love to watch you fight!" the other girl gushed. "It's so sad about what the barbarians did to your family! You were so right to get revenge, even if it got you branded!"

He'd lost track of the stories spread about his background. That was a new one.

The first girl started to sit down. "May we join you?"

Clanless pointed to the stage. "Actually, I'm waiting on her to come back."

The girls behaved as if they'd been insulted, though he couldn't understand why. They stalked away, grumbling.

When Koland next announced a break, he came to the table with Kekeen. Clanless stood up, trying to keep his eyes from going too wide.

"Sit down, son," Koland said. "I'm not the Hawk King."

"You'd make a better king than he does!" Kekeen answered, taking her seat across from Clanless again.

"Not so loud, my girl. You never know when a crowd is safe for that kind of talk." Koland sat beside her. Clanless finally sat as well.

Kekeen gestured. "Remember him, Father? From Rochibal. He had other boys with him, all training to be arena fighters."

"I rarely remember audience members. You know that." Koland tapped his beard. "But I do recall something… you talked about them for days, I think."

Clanless swallowed. Kekeen had talked about them for days?

She rolled her eyes. "I thought it was sad! How they were being forced into this life, and some of them might—did—die!"

"It's a horrible system," Koland agreed. He eyed Clanless. "You look like you're doing well enough, son. How many fights have you had?"

"Fifteen, sir. Ah, fifteen here. One more back in Rochinbal, when I finished the training."

Koland nodded. "So you've survived that many attempts to kill you, making you quite the killer yourself."

"I suppose." Clanless expected images of his dead opponents to flash before his eyes, but nothing came. Odd. Had he forgotten them already?

"And you're… what? Only fifteen years old?"

Clanless nodded, not seeing the need to clarify. He'd be fifteen soon. In a number of months. A moderately-sized number.

The server brought food and drink for the two performers. Clanless politely joined them in eating a little more flatbread. Koland kept the conversation going even while he ate. "I'm guessing you weren't raised in a city. Would I be right?"

"Yes, sir. I grew up in a clanhold, far from here."

"Clanholds." Koland nodded and took a drink. "Been a lot of them attacked to the west lately. The barbarians are getting bolder. If something isn't done, they may end up striking a city someday, maybe even this one. It's probably the first major one they'd come to."

"That's a horrible thought!" Kekeen exclaimed.

"Ah, but stories come from such things." Koland swallowed a bite and kept talking. "For example, I'm hearing hints of rumors about a boy who was saved from one barbarian raid by a prophet, and then saved his whole clanhold from the next raid. Have you heard anything about that, Aldan?"

"No, sir. I haven't." A moment later, he realized Koland had called him by name. He was pretty sure it hadn't been mentioned earlier in the conversation. So Kekeen had talked about him, and Koland did remember. He smiled.

"I hope to find that boy sometime," Koland went on. "I'm always searching for new stories. Can't keep telling the same ones over and over, you know."

"As if you do," Kekeen said. "You change them up everywhere we go."

"Tell me more of the rest of the Empire," Clanless said. "I know so little. I barely know anything of the Hawk King, or, or, barbarians or anything."

"Raised in a clanhold and then taken to the arenas." Koland nodded.

"I would understand why you've had little time to learn. I can tell you some; though perhaps it might be simpler for you to read the Empire's histories."

Clanless's shoulders drooped. "How long—" He glanced at Kekeen. "How long will you be here? I mean, in Ghoyor?"

"I'm not altogether certain. We travel from city to city as the whim takes us."

"When he gets tired of one place, he means," Kekeen put in.

"Perhaps so." Koland chuckled. "But I don't know. We should be here a few weeks, at the least. As I said, I'll be looking for more stories."

"I don't know how to read," Clanless said suddenly. "I need someone to teach me. Could you do it?"

Koland's eyes widened only a little. "There's a request I've never heard before. But I understand it well. The power to read stories for oneself is a vast treasure for those who recognize it."

"Then… you'll do it?"

Koland hesitated. "I would like to help you, lad. Truly, I would. But I work in these places"—he gestured about—"until very late at night, then sleep in until the sun practically finishes its pursuit. After that, I have other business I must be about, before preparing again for another night's tales."

"I can pay you," Clanless said recklessly.

"I thought you were saving for your freedom!" Kekeen exclaimed.

"What kind of a free man would I be if I cannot read?"

"An ignorant one," Koland said. "And I suppose we can't have that. But I meant what I said, son. I can't take the time to teach you."

"But—"

"But Kekeen can," Koland interrupted. "She has much more free time, and it sometimes gets her into trouble."

Clanless's heart skipped a beat. This couldn't be true. And it shouldn't be. He didn't deserve it. It almost killed him to say what he knew he should: "Thank you, sir. But… it wouldn't be right. You said it yourself. I'm a killer. You shouldn't trust your daughter with me."

Koland leaned back from the table. "I've been mildly surprised at several points tonight at this table, Aldan." He shook his head. "But now you've shocked me. I wouldn't have expected that kind of honor. The very fact that you say it means I can trust you." He leaned back in. "So don't betray that trust."

"No, sir." He glanced at Kekeen. Her eyes sparkled. He still didn't deserve it, but… he wouldn't object.

"A few weeks will not give you enough time to learn everything you need to know about reading," Koland cautioned. "But it should get you through the basics. I'm assuming you can't leave the arena every day?"

"No… but if I talk to Badaar—he's the trainer—I might be able to work something out, more than just once a week."

"You do that." Koland tapped his beard again. "And you can get in touch with us here. We're staying upstairs." He pushed himself up from the table. "But now I need to earn this food I've just eaten. Daughter?"

"Yes, Father." Kekeen got to her feet as well, tugging at her sleeve. Before she turned to follow Koland, she leaned toward Clanless and showed him: the edge of a sand-colored scarf tucked inside the sleeve. "I kept it," she whispered.

(((●)))

Clanless stayed until the proprietor asked him to leave, sometime far after midnight. He bid farewell to Koland and Kekeen and made his way through the dark streets back to the arena. The rules allowed him to stay out all night, but he'd never bothered to stay out this late. He'd never had a reason.

Zaluu hadn't returned when he got to his room, which was a relief. Clanless wouldn't have to deal with his questions. He got into bed, wondering at his good fortune. The prospect of seeing Kekeen on a regular basis for a while, however short it might be, was the greatest thing that had ever happened to him. Zektel would probably warn him about it again, but he didn't care. The blood-wraith didn't know—or understand—everything.

When the sun began its pursuit, he skipped breakfast and went straight to find Badaar. He explained to the trainer that he'd hired someone to teach him reading and needed time to meet with them. "I'm not asking for nights out," he said. "It would work better during the day, actually."

Badaar looked skeptical. "You'd be taking time away from your training."

"To train my mind," Clanless pointed out. "If I'm to keep improving my skills, I need more knowledge. And I can't get that without reading." He gestured back toward the door. "There's a whole shelf of books in my room left behind by older fighters. I'd like to read them."

"I'll bring it up with Orgina when the sun retreats," Badaar finally agreed. "I don't know what she'll say. It doesn't really match with your… personality."

"I need this," Clanless pleaded. "I'm tired of being ignorant about things. I don't know anything about anything outside these sands. Why is the Hawk King called the Hawk King? Why a hawk? I have no idea."

Badaar cocked his head. "You know… I don't remember myself." He laughed. "You've made your point. I'll talk to her."

Orgina apparently didn't need a lot of persuasion. She gave tentative permission for Clanless to meet with his tutor three times a week after the noon meal but warned that if Badaar noticed any decline in his martial abilities, the permission would be revoked. As a trade-off, he couldn't go out with the other fighters on the night after the arena fight. He didn't mind at all.

The next day, he hurried to Dugh's End at the designated time. Upon entering the door, he stopped, staring.

Kekeen, clad in a simple blue dress, twirled back and forth on the stage alone. She hummed a tune as she danced at a leisurely pace, swishing her skirt to either side as she moved. Most of her motions were graceful, but she faltered now and then, stutter-stepping. She spun one last time and spotted him at the door. A delighted smile spread across her face. "Aldan!" She hopped down and started toward him.

He hurried across the room, barely noticing the house's proprietor working on the other side. "That was… that was beautiful," he said, gesturing at the stage.

"Did you like it? My father doesn't think I should dance, but I think if I sing at the same time, it will draw larger crowds. Nothing too crazy, of course. But something soft and slow like that." She spun in a circle.

"You're building a personality!" Clanless realized.

"What?" Kekeen blinked, tilting her head with a curious smile.

"It's something Orgina, the arena mistress, does." The awkwardness of standing still while talking struck him. What should he do with his hands? He reached up and toyed with the clasp on the fur. "That's why you'll hear all sorts of stories about me and the other fighters if you listen to the people around here. She spreads those stories to create our personalities and, uh, draw larger crowds."

A single laugh escaped Kekeen's mouth. "I guess we're both in the same kind of business, in some ways."

"Except you don't have to kill people." Clanless regretted the words as soon as he'd said them.

Kekeen grimaced. "Let's not talk about that part." She shifted to a smile. "But you're here! Does this mean we can start the reading lessons?"

"Yes!" He explained the arrangement, which she agreed to without reservation.

She led him to a table in the corner where a single book lay open. "My father has his doubts," she said. "He doesn't think I can teach you enough in the time we have."

"But he doesn't even know how long that will be."

"It's never very long." For a moment, as she slid into the chair, Kekeen looked somewhat... sad. Clanless didn't like that expression on her face and wished he could make sure it never appeared again.

"Then we'd better get started, I guess." He sat down next to her and stiffened when she pulled her chair closer to his.

"Of course." She opened the book to the first page. "I've never done anything like this before. I'm nervous."

"You'll be great," he assured her. "If anything goes wrong, it will be my fault. I'm far too stupid."

"You are not!" She rolled her eyes and shook her head. "I've learned a number of things about you in our conversations, and 'stupid' is absolutely not one of them!"

He wanted to ask what she'd learned about him but pointed at the book instead. "Just treat me like a child, then. What do I need to know first?"

"Your letters," she said. "Letters build words. Words build sentences. Sentences build stories." She gestured at the open pages. "Do you recognize anything here?"

Clanless peered at it and pointed at a word. "That looks like my name. Um, we had a list during training. I only know what my name looks like because the others told me where I was on the ranking."

Kekeen tilted her head. "Were you the best?"

"Not at first." He shrugged. "I got there eventually."

"All right, let's look at this. We call this script Usek. You don't really need to know that. I don't even know why they call it that. Anyway, this word is similar to 'Clanless,' I guess, but not much. I'll show you the difference..."

For the next hour, they worked together, bending over the book and writing crude letters on a scrap of paper. Clanless found the whole thing more daunting than the physical training at the arena, but he kept at it. By the end of their time, he'd grasped a few small details. He was relieved to learn that the thirty-four shapes—letters—used to form words were consistent and knowable. Storytelling, the weaving of words as Darghan called it, might be an art form, but reading appeared to be a straightforward skill.

"So you'll be back in two days?" Kekeen asked, closing the book.

He nodded. "Thank you. I'm sorry I'm such a poor student."

"It's your first time at this. And my first time teaching! I think we're doing well for our first attempt."

He nodded again, reluctant to leave.

"You said you had books in your room?"

"Oh. Yes. I don't know what they are, of course."

"It doesn't matter. Right now, you just need to work on recognizing the letters. Spend some time with one of the books tomorrow. Practice. It'll help you prepare for the next day." She stood up, and he followed her example.

"Thank you, Kekeen. I'll.. see you the day after tomorrow."

Her smile grew, as it so often did. "You're very welcome, Aldan."

He liked the sound of his name in her voice.

((((●))))

Zaluu finally cornered Clanless that evening in their room. For two days, Clanless had managed to avoid talking much with him, but he couldn't escape this time.

"Tell me everything!" Zaluu demanded, plopping down at their room table across from him.

Clanless looked up from the book he was studying. "Everything?"

"About the singer! What was it she called you? Alban? Aldan? You do have a name, after all!"

"The priests took it from me."

"But she gets to use it, doesn't she?" Zaluu emphasized "she" both times.

"I told you: I met her a year ago, while I was still training." Clanless closed the book.

"And now you're 'meeting' her on a regular basis. How'd you manage that with the old woman?"

Clanless scowled. "It's not like that. She's... teaching me."

"A girl at the brothel taught me some things last week too." Zaluu's grin grew wider. "Come to. You're not fooling anyone."

Clanless slapped the book. "She's teaching me to read!"

Zaluu's grin disappeared. "You're serious? You don't know how to read?"

Clanless glared at him, trying to control his breathing.

"I'm sorry." Zaluu held up his palms. "I didn't mean to... that is, I thought... huh."

"Are you satisfied?" Clanless clenched one of his fists under the table. "You found out the ignorant clanhold boy's secret. Are you going to tell everyone else so they can laugh too?"

"I'm not laughing."

Clanless didn't answer.

Zaluu took a deep breath. "Listen, I'm sorry. I won't tell any of the others. I guess… I guess it's easy to forget how big the Empire is, and how people are raised different in different parts of it." He shrugged. "But we're all the same, even so."

Clanless begrudgingly nodded.

"But…" Zaluu's grin returned. "You can't tell me that your reaction when you first saw her the other night was because you were hoping she'd teach you to read!"

Clanless rolled his eyes and got up.

"You can't tell me that! So it's not just about reading, is it? Come to. Tell me. She's special, isn't she?"

Clanless threw up his hands. "How can I tell you anything? You talk to everyone all the time!"

Zaluu stood and swept his cape around himself, putting one arm across his chest. "May I never win another arena fight if I betray your trust in me," he declared solemnly.

Clanless stared at him. "I have no idea whether you're serious."

"We share a room. We fight together. One of these days, we really will, when the old lady puts us together on a team. If I get you mad at me, I'll end up dead one way or another. I'm not stupid."

"All right." Clanless sat down on his bed. "Yes, I like the girl. But I know there can never be anything real between us."

"Guys like us? We don't get real." Zaluu took his cape off and looked at it. "We get fake personalities and fake lives. Fake love too." He shrugged. "That doesn't mean you can't enjoy it while you've got it."

Clanless shook his head. "She's good. I mean, really good. I'm not going to hurt her."

Zaluu wrinkled his brow. "Then why bother? You'll only hurt yourself."

"Maybe." Clanless stared down at his own feet. "But maybe… maybe I just want to be close to something that good and that real… for even a little while. I'll… enjoy that while I've got it."

Zaluu tossed the cape on the table. "I get it. Sort of." He sat down on his bed too. "Like I said: I'll keep your secrets. Just be careful who else finds out. Some of these guys around here like to talk a lot, for some reason."

Clanless looked up at him. Zaluu met his gaze with a flat stare. He held it for at least ten seconds before his grin erupted again. "Idiot," Clanless muttered, throwing a pillow at him.

Clanless worked hard on the reading, as often as he could spare the time. After two weeks, he could recognize all the letters, and even understood how they formed a few small words.

"Here's my name," Kekeen said, writing on her much-used single sheet of paper. Clanless understood the letter-shapes, but not how they formed the sounds of her name. Even so, he focused on it, memorizing the shape of her name, at the very least. Even if he never grasped another word in these lessons, he would get that one. "And here's yours." She wrote "Aldan," not "Clanless."

"I know we're not working on teaching you writing just yet, but I want you to copy these two." Kekeen handed the quill to him. "And you never know. You might have to write your name sometime."

"Then I should learn how to write Clanless, shouldn't I?"

Her smile faded a little. "We'll do that one too. For now, copy these."

Clanless obeyed her, scratching out horribly awkward-looking letters. Kekeen praised him anyway and moved back to sounding out some words. She wrote a few more specific words on the edges of the paper for him to work on. Clanless pointed to a second, blank sheet of paper nearby. "Why aren't we using that one? This one is so full, the words are almost overlapping."

"Paper is expensive! My father only gave me these two sheets because of how much you paid him."

"But we haven't even started to use that one."

Kekeen hesitated. "I'm saving that sheet for later. Now stop stalling. What's this word?"

"Um… chair?"

Kekeen giggled. "No, it's 'sword,' like you use all the time. Sorry, I shouldn't laugh." She wrote next to it. "This is 'chair.'"

"They look exactly the same!" Clanless protested.

Kekeen used the quill to point to a specific shape. "This letter is different. See?"

Clanless sighed and peered closer. He thought he'd been doing so well. What kind of idiot couldn't tell the difference between "chair" and "sword"?

As their session wrapped up, he finally asked the question he'd been wondering all along. He knew of no way to lead up to it, so he burst out with: "Why did you keep the scarf?"

Kekeen reached into her sleeve and pulled it out. She spread the scarf on the table. "I'm not entirely sure," she admitted. "I liked the story behind it, about your home. And I wanted to remember."

"Remember what?"

She ducked her head a little lower. "You, of course. And your friends. I just… I hate what happened to you. Every time I saw the scarf, I said a little prayer to the goddess for you."

"Oh."

"So, I'll see you again in two days?"

"Um, three days this time. It's three times a week, remember? And I have to fight tomorrow."

"Oh." She looked up. "Then… I guess there's a chance I won't see you again at all."

"I'll be all right. I can defeat anything they throw at me." He paused. "I don't mean to sound arrogant, but… it's actually true."

"It does sound arrogant." She giggled. "But I suppose you've gotten this far." She picked up the scarf and folded it. "Do you… want me to come see your fight?"

"No!" His answer came out harsher than he meant it. "That is… I don't think you would enjoy that kind of thing."

She got to her feet. "You're right. I was only asking in case it was something you wanted."

"You would go if I asked you to?"

Kekeen smiled and shook her head. "You know, you called yourself ignorant two weeks ago. I'm starting to believe it now."

Clanless wrinkled his brow and stood up. "What do you mean?"

Koland walked in through the front door. Kekeen stuffed the folded scarf into her sleeve again. "Never mind. I'll see you in three days."

Clanless moved around the table. "I wish it were tomorrow."

Her smile widened. "Maybe you aren't so ignorant after all."

"How is the reading coming?" Koland asked as he approached.

"He's making progress," Kekeen said. "But now he has to go kill someone again."

"It's not that I want to," Clanless protested.

"We know, lad." Koland hesitated. "Do you feel confident about this one?"

"Apparently, he feels confident about every fight," Kekeen answered for him. "He says they can't defeat him."

Koland frowned. "That's not a very healthy attitude, Aldan. The prideful often fall when they think they're standing."

"It's not… it's not pride." Clanless hesitated. He didn't want to tell them about the Taint, especially after spending so much time with Kekeen.

"I… just know. Right now, I can defeat any of the opponents they give me."

Koland tapped his beard. "Forgive me, son, but that still sounds like pride."

"I know, I know. I can't really explain it. But there's a… reason why I'm a slave, and that reason is why I can't be beat."

Koland's eyebrows went up. "Now that sounds like the beginning of a story!"

Clanless stepped toward the side. "I can't tell it. Not now, anyway."

"Some other time then." He nodded. "We'll see you later."

Clanless said goodbye and headed back to the arena. Should he tell them about the Taint? He knew what Zektel would have to say about that, although he hadn't spoken with her since he started learning to read. Koland would almost certainly have heard of the Taint; he probably had some stories about it! But would it make them hate him? He'd terrified the other boys back at Kan's arena. Yet Kan had known. And Orgina knew. Neither of them hated him; although in their case, it didn't matter. He was their property. If the Taint brought them income, then they wouldn't care. It certainly never brought him anything good.

No, best to keep it to himself for now. He had a limited time with Kekeen. He couldn't risk ruining it now.

BEING SEEN

A week later, Badaar informed Clanless that Orgina wanted to see him in her office at once. After getting directions, he left his lunch half-eaten and hurried to the office. He hoped this meeting wouldn't cut into his time with Kekeen.

To his surprise, Orgina's office looked more like a meeting room. A large table dominated, with six chairs scattered around it. Orgina sat at its head. She gestured for him to have a seat while she poured herself a glass of wine.

"I need you to go visit a brothel," she announced.

Clanless blinked. "What?"

"You need to visit a brothel. Tomorrow night, after the fights. Zaluu can take you, if you don't know where to find one."

"I don't understand."

Orgina took a sip of wine and set the cup down. "It's very simple. You've been here five months now, correct?"

He nodded.

"You're doing well. Undefeated. The crowds like you. We're making a nice profit on side bets. We've built up a very solid personality for you. In a few more months, we may even accelerate things. Take the next step. Work on making you even more popular. If it goes well, you could end up as our biggest draw."

"All right." He didn't know where this was going.

"But…" She leveled a finger at him. "Word is getting around that you have a girl. That you've spent hours and hours with her alone."

"Sh-she's teaching me to read," Clanless stammered. "You said I could."

"That's not the problem. The problem is your personality."

"I don't understand."

Orgina took out her little bag and popped some nuts into her mouth. She kept talking while chewing: "The people believe that you're a rebel, a man who did something horrible in the past, and you're fighting back against the injust system that punished you. There are variations on the story, of course." She swallowed. "Most of them believe that whatever you did, it couldn't have been that bad. Surely, you're a hero, not a villain. Some, however, believe you really deserve what happened to you, and they despise you… but they still want to see you fight. Either way, it's good for business."

He nodded. He understood that much, even if he didn't always like it.

"But a single girl—a mistress or whatever—doesn't fit well with your story. In fact, it's in your best interest to build a reputation for liking many girls."

"Why?"

She chomped another nut. "It reinforces the rebel idea, but it does much more than that. It means all the girls will think they have a chance with you."

He tried to understand. "We want them to… think they can be my… woman, even though we want to build the idea that I can't have a woman?"

"Exactly."

He shook his head. "I still don't understand at all."

"It's the allure of the rebel," she explained. "Every woman knows he's had many other women and has never settled down, but they think they can be the one to do that. To be the one who captures your heart."

"But I'm only fifteen years old!" Almost.

"What difference does that make? You're old enough to start a family. Not that I want you to do that, of course. That would totally destroy the personality."

Clanless didn't know what to say. Orgina studied him for a moment, eating some more nuts. She snorted. "So. The mighty Clanless, angry young arena fighter, is scared to spend a night with a woman."

He didn't answer, afraid of what might slip out of his mouth.

Orgina waited a bit longer, and then sighed. "Sands. I never would have believed it. Either you're really into this girl with the reading, or something's wrong with you." She looked away. "Very well. I won't force you, but you need to be seen with some other girls. Go out with Zaluu tomorrow night. Celebrate your victories at some disreputable location. Let some girls get near you, at least. Pretend you're having a good time. Can you do that much?"

"I… yes."

"Good. Get out of here. Next time we talk, it'll be about something more pleasant, I hope." She picked up her wine glass. "Most young men would think this was a pleasant topic."

Clanless got to his feet.

"One last thing."

He stopped.

Orgina met his eyes. "If this doesn't work, and I keep hearing stories about you and this singer, you'll be banned from seeing her. I won't risk the reward I can gain from you for the sake of adolescent romance. Do you understand?"

He swallowed. "Yes. I do."

((((●))))

Clanless won the next fight, as usual. He worried they were becoming too easy for him. So far, he hadn't even been tempted to use the Taint. But as he grew in fame, he knew Orgina would have to find better opponents for him. The crowd would demand it. Already, he'd heard some grumbling in town that his fights had all been straightforward, against a single human opponent. He couldn't let himself grow complacent.

Zaluu found him while he cleaned up. To his relief, Orgina had only told the other fighter to take him out somewhere. She hadn't given him any other details.

"Why am I getting orders to take you out to carouse?" Zaluu asked as they left the arena. "I don't mind, of course, but it's not the normal kind of orders the old woman gives out."

"She says I need to be seen with more girls," Clanless answered. "A personality thing."

"Ohhh! I get it." He slapped Clanless on the back. "I know just where to take you then!"

"Somewhere public!" Clanless warned him. "We want people to see me."

"That will not be a problem!"

Zaluu led the way to a different part of the city. Clanless had only visited it once, the first time he'd gone out with Zaluu. They wouldn't find any storytellers out here, and the only singing would be of the vulgar sort.

In an astonishingly short time, they ended up at a back table in a much more boisterous eating house. Smoke curled up to the dark ceiling from a dozen or more thin pipes. The smell mingled with the odors of the fermented milk, honey wine, and the zokin Clanless preferred.

They were recognized when they entered, of course: Zaluu with his bright colors and cape, Clanless with his fur and exposed shoulder brand. A group of young admirers gathered around their table. Before Clanless even knew what was happening, Zaluu made sure to position two of the girls on either side of him.

"You're having fun, remember?" Zaluu said in a loud whisper before sitting down.

"You think you're funny!" Clanless answered much louder.

"He is a little funny," said the girl on his left, a short girl with jet-black hair. "Who calls themselves 'Magnificent,' after all?"

"I do!" Zaluu said, lifting his face in a lofty sneer. "Because I deserve it. Who else fights with such style and poise in the arena?"

"Clanless here has a style," said the girl on the right. She moved closer to him, letting her long pale hair fall over his bare shoulder. He tried not to flinch. "I think he's magnificent."

"Hear that, Zaluu? I may take your title!" Clanless had to admit he enjoyed the teasing sometimes, as long as things didn't go too far.

"You already have a title!" Zaluu threw his arm around another girl and pulled her closer.

"That's right!" exclaimed the dark-haired girl. "Clanless is a title. They took your name away! Do you even remember it?"

"I don't tell it to anyone," he said. "That's not who I am any more."

"What if we guess it?" asked the pale girl. "What will you give me if I guess it?"

"Is it Dimur? Or Ezen?" the other said quickly.

"I'm not telling you, even if you guess it," Clanless protested.

A young man leaned across the table. "Did you really kill the Hawk King's cousin?"

So Orgina had spread that story. "I've killed a lot of people. How would I know if one of them was the king's cousin?"

"He means because of the brand," the girl on his right said. She traced the mark on his shoulder with her finger. This time he did flinch. "Is that why they gave you this?"

"No, that is my own dark secret to bear." Clanless used one of three answers Gogeku had given him before his first visit to the city.

"That's soooo romantic," the dark-haired girl gushed. "I heard the Hawk King killed your true love, and you vowed revenge."

Clanless laughed. "Don't believe all that you hear, please. There are many rumors out there."

The girl on his right moved her fingers down to wrap around his bicep. She leaned in close to his ear to whisper: "I'll be happy to pretend to be your true love for tonight." She squeezed his arm.

Clanless swallowed. Things had gone much further than he considered comfortable, but he had to create the right impression. If he tried to get out of this now, Orgina would hear about it, and he'd be barred from seeing Kekeen. He turned to the girl and gave her his best smile. "We'll see where the moon leads us tonight, shall we?"

As the evening wore on, Clanless grew more and more uncomfortable with the part he had to play. Their table drew many other young people, seeking to be near the famous duo, but the two girls next to him never left. A third girl managed to squeeze into a seat directly across from him and stared at him unashamedly for the next hour or so.

Trying to avoid another proposition from the girl on his right, Clanless grabbed for his drink. Until he poured it in his mouth, he didn't realize someone had replaced his juice with the fermented milk. It had an acidic tang to it, but wasn't unpleasant. He took another swallow.

Zaluu, of course, enjoyed himself throughout the process. He took equal delight in attracting attention to himself and directing it to Clanless. He demanded the proprietor give them fancy ceramic mugs instead of common wooden ones. He even danced on the table, threatening those same mugs. Clanless barely grabbed his out of the way in time.

As he leaned back with his mug, he thought he caught a glimpse of a face watching him across the room. The smoke and low light obscured his view. A lot of people had been watching him throughout the night, of course, but his one look at that face troubled him for some reason. Was it someone he knew?

"Maybe all three of us could find a room," the dark-haired girl suggested, looking across at the other one. "You could lie back and relax, and we could—"

"Why wait?" The girl on his right pushed the table out a few inches, eliciting exclamations from those seated on the other side. Zaluu teetered and almost fell. In one swift moment, the girl twisted around and straddled Clanless, sitting in his lap, looking down at his face.

This was too much. He wanted it to continue, but it terrified him at the same time. He almost panicked.

In that moment, the smoke cleared enough for him to see the eyes watching him. And he recognized them at once. Koland stood up, shaking his head.

"No!" Clanless grabbed the girl and removed her, pushing her none-too-gently back onto the bench. "Ow!" she gasped.

As he jumped to his feet, five young men appeared at their table, blocking the way. "So you two are supposed to be these great arena fighters, are you?" one demanded.

"Why yes, we are!" Zaluu exclaimed. "What can we do for you, my man?"

Clanless pushed past the dark-haired girl and tried to get around the table.

"Everyone knows all that arena fighting is fake," another man said. "You couldn't survive a real fight."

Zaluu flexed his arm. "Do these muscles look fake?"

Clanless caught a glimpse of Koland moving out the door. He tried to shove past the group to chase after him. Two of them caught him by the arms. "Are you trying to start something?" one asked.

"We're not," Zaluu said, still on top of the table. "But we can finish it if you start it."

"Let's find out!" A third man punched Clanless in the stomach. Since he'd been watching the front door, it caught him by surprise more than anything else. He doubled over, even though it hadn't hurt much. Two of the girls shrieked.

"Oh, you have started it!" Zaluu kicked one of the men in the face.

Clanless spun, shaking both of his captors free. He snarled and punched the left one. The young man fell back against two others. Zaluu shouted and dove off the table into two more, carrying them to the floor amidst a roar from the crowd.

As Clanless turned around, he met another man who'd grabbed one of the mugs from the table. "Not the mug!" Zaluu yelled from the floor. But he was too late. The man smashed the mug across the top of Clanless's head, shattering the ceramic into multiple pieces.

Blood trickled down his face. The smell and taste of it filled his senses.

Zaluu elbowed one of his opponents and scrambled to his feet. "Oh, you shouldn't have done that!"

Clanless caught the man's arm and twisted it. He'd had enough. He hadn't wanted to be here, it had been incredibly awkward and uncomfortable all evening, and now Koland had seen him. He'd tell Kekeen and ruin everything. Clanless reached his breaking point.

His opponent yelled and dropped the broken mug. Clanless caught it. In one smooth motion, he spun it back, cutting a gash across the young man's lower arm.

"Orgina wants rumors? I'll give her rumors!" he snarled, activating the Taint.

Eyes burning, he turned to the next opponent, slashing at him with the broken mug. Zaluu fought beside him in a more traditional way, but Clanless would not stop. The smell of the blood overwhelmed his nostrils. Even as the gang assaulted him from every direction, he kept cutting with the broken mug. Once four or five of them were bleeding, he unleashed the Taint on all of them. Screams filled the room. At least one of the girls shouted something about his eyes. Around him, five—no, six—men collapsed to the floor, writhing in agony.

"What are you doing?" Zaluu shouted.

"Building my personality!" Clanless whirled left and right, the bloody mug at ready. No opponents remained. They'd all fallen or fled. In fact, most of the room had emptied out. Those remaining stared wide-eyed at the two arena fighters in fear or awe. Behind them, the remaining girls screamed and ran for the doors.

"This might cause some problems," Zaluu admitted.

❨❨❨❨●❩❩❩❩

The next morning, Clanless didn't wait for a summons from Orgina. After breakfast, he skipped training and headed into the city. He couldn't get into more trouble than he already was, or so he thought.

Along the way, he rehearsed what he would say, how he would explain himself, both to Koland and Kekeen. But when he entered Dugh's End, he saw neither.

"They're gone." The proprietor of the house emerged from the kitchen.

"Gone? Where?" Clanless hurried across the room.

The proprietor shrugged. "They travel, here and there. I'm fortunate when they're here." He let out a deep sigh. "I'd expected them to stay a few more weeks, at least. But Koland showed up late last night and told me they'd be leaving this morning."

Clanless's heart sank further with each word. It was all his fault. "Morning? Then they just left?" For a wild moment, he considered chasing after them. Maybe Orgina wouldn't notice soon enough. Maybe the bloodbond would let him go, at least far enough to catch them…

The proprietor shook his head. "Left before the sun started its chase."
Clanless turned and slammed a fist against a table.

"Here now, don't get carried away! She left you something."

He spun around. The proprietor held out a folded piece of paper.

With a trembling hand, Clanless took it. Even without a careful examination, he knew: it was the second piece of paper, the one Kekeen had kept empty. He pulled out a chair and sat, not trusting his legs. He unfolded the note and breathed a sigh of relief at the sight of Kekeen's careful Usek script. He swallowed and read, struggling with a few of the words, though she appeared to have avoided anything too complicated.

My dear Aldan,

Father woke me early this morn, saying we had to leave at once. He has learned where to find the young man who saved his clanhold. He wants his story.

I am sad that we will not be able to finish our reading lessons. I am more sad that I don't get to see you again.

We will return to Ghoyor one day. I hope you will still be here. I will miss you if you are not.

I will keep the scarf close.

Kekeen

(Be careful with your chair!)

Clanless leaned back, overwhelmed relief. Koland hadn't told her. Or at least, he hadn't told her before they left. And she'd cared enough to leave this note. He smiled at the joke at the end; he knew which word she'd used this time. He let out a deep breath and got to his feet.

He turned back to the proprietor. "I don't suppose you know when they might return?"

"I never know." The proprietor's face grew longer as he shook his head. "It could be a few months. Or it might be a few years."

Clanless nodded. "Let's hope for months. But when they do come back, whenever that may be, will you have word sent to me at the arena?" He set a small vial of blood on the table. "I will pay again then."

The proprietor gave him an understanding smile. "Of course, son. But don't... don't expect too much." He waved toward the stage. "These storytellers and singers: they're flighty. They come and go. Whatever she says there"—he pointed to the note—"she may not even remember you by the time they come back through here."

"Even so," Clanless insisted. The proprietor nodded and took the vial.

Clanless folded the note and slid it into his shirt. Returning to the arena, he stored it in his personal chest with his blood supply. Aside from clothes, he didn't own anything else.

Before returning to training, he turned to the only other person he could talk with, even though he knew what she would say.

"How did you think it would end, Aldan?" Zektel asked after he told her what happened.

"I'd hoped… for a little more time. And to say goodbye in person, at least."

Zektel, in almost full form, thanks to the amount of blood he'd used, shook her head. A droplet of blood shook loose, fell to her feet, and merged back into her form. "You know I will tell you the truth, however much it hurts you. The father will tell her everything once they are well on their way. He just didn't want to upset her before they left. She would have demanded to see you in person, and they would have fought over it. This way, he tells her after it's too late."

He knew she was probably right, but it still hurt to hear it.

"She's a distraction, Aldan. You need to focus. Become the best. Win your freedom. I'm glad she taught you some reading, but you need to get back to work. There's no time for romance. Enjoy a moment or two, as your friend Zaluu does, and move on."

"If I am to win my freedom, shouldn't I have a plan for afterwards?"

"Once we get closer, those plans will develop. And they might be something far greater than you can imagine right now. Besides, you know what kind of person you have to become to get there. Your singer friend would not want to be around such a person." Zektel sighed. "I'm sorry, again, to be so blunt. But you have to accept these facts, Aldan."

He didn't answer.

"You're still young. You'll have time for such things. Even if it takes another ten years to win your freedom, you can start over then. Find someone who will accept you for who you've become by then."

"Who will I become?" Clanless asked quietly.

"The greatest arena fighter this Empire has ever seen. Maybe even this world."

To his surprise, Clanless did not receive a call to Orgina's office again. In fact, for several days, he wondered if she even knew about the fight in town. No visit from Gogeku. No reprimand from Badaar. Zaluu did have questions, but Clanless put him off for now, promising to tell everything later.

Meanwhile, his own anger grew. If he believed Zektel—and he had no reason not to—he would never have a normal life until he won his freedom. He'd known this, of course, but the departure of Kekeen made it real. He brooded over it, letting his rage spill over into his training times. Badaar made no complaints when he destroyed several practice dummies.

On the following Arena Night, Clanless decided it to make a big change. He arrived at the arena entrance bearing one of the largest swords the arena possessed. Badaar frowned. "You're going to miss that buckler tonight," he warned.

"My personality is changing." Clanless set the sword aside and adjusted the fur on his shoulder. As usual, he wore only his short fighting trousers and the fur pelt. He'd added a pair of bracers on his forearms; they wouldn't replace a buckler, but they might provide a brief moment of protection. Outside, he heard the presenter shouting something about Allaka.

"Not the best day for that." Badaar looked out onto the sands. "There's also been a change in the schedule. You're fighting two opponents today."

Clanless paused. "Two fights? Or two at the same time?"

"Same time," Badaar confirmed.

"I haven't trained for that! I—" Realization dawned on him. "Orgina is mad at me, isn't she?"

"I wouldn't know. I only got the change a few minutes ago." Badaar picked up the sword for him. "I would have said I'm confident you can handle it. But that was before I saw this."

Clanless took the sword. "I'm confident I can win, but... there may be consequences."

Badaar's eyes narrowed. "What does that mean?"

"You remember my first fight?" Clanless looked down at the sword. "The priests might not be happy again."

"I don't care about them. Will Orgina be unhappy?"

"I won't know until it happens."

An enormous roar from the crowd outside drew their attention.

"That doesn't sound good," Badaar said, hurrying to the door. In their discussion, they'd been ignoring the current fight.

"It seems we have a new champion, everyone!" the presenter shouted over the roar.

Badaar and Clanless stared out over the sands. Someone they didn't know stood holding Allaka's flanged mace high, covered in blood. Allaka lay on the arena floor, unmoving.

"Goddess!" Badaar exclaimed. "I was starting to think he'd never fall."

They watched as the attendants ran out with the priest and retrieved

Allaka's body. "I guess Orgina won't be happy about this either," Clanless said. He turned away from seeing the body. Allaka had been an unusual man, but one of the team. They'd sparred together during training on numerous occasions. Six years of survival in the arena had ended in one moment.

Badaar wiped sweat from his brow. "That's putting it mildly. If I were you, I wouldn't add to her displeasure."

The door attendant gestured to Clanless. "It's time."

Clanless took a deep breath and stepped out onto the sands. Had he trained enough with this large sword? He'd find out soon enough.

"Oh, look at this, citizens! Clanless has made a change. Look at the size of that sword!" The presenter's voice echoed across the arena. "But without any other protection, how will he do against… two opponents at the same time?"

The crowd cheered the unexpected alterations. Clanless could almost hear new bets being placed. A young fighter using a new weapon for the first time? And fighting two opponents for the first time? He would either go down in expected defeat, or build his own legend in a stunning victory. He knew which way he'd bet, if he were allowed.

Across the arena, two men approached him, each carrying mace and buckler. They separated from one another as they came, moving further and further apart. They intended to come at him from either side, an appropriate strategy, but one he couldn't allow to succeed.

The presenter babbled on about these two, saying something about the "far reaches" of some region of the Empire. Likely as not, it wasn't even true. Clanless knew by now to ignore most of what was said; more than half of it would be completely made up anyway.

Clanless stalked a straight path, splitting the gap between them. If he moved too soon toward either opponent, the other would start to close the gap. Every so often, he took one quick step to the left or right. To his satisfaction, this caused the two fighters to widen the gap even more.

A smooth and fast transition: that's what he would need when he switched from walking to running. He had to catch them by surprise. He shifted his grip, tightening both hands on the sword's large hilt.

"There's a rumor that Clanless is more than he appears to be." The presenter's voice broke into his concentration. "Some say he has hidden powers he has yet to expose in this arena."

What? What did that mean? Did Orgina want him to use the Taint? He growled to himself. If she wanted it, she should tell him directly. He hated all these hints.

The moment arrived. These men would be expecting him to make a move at some point. They knew him to be a well-trained arena fighter, undefeated in his short career. But they didn't know one thing: under Kan's daily insistence, Clanless learned to run across sand faster than anyone else. At the right moment, he pivoted and transitioned from walking into a full-on sprint, straight at the man to his left.

Both opponents yelled something to each other, but the roar of the crowd and the shouts of the presenter drowned it out. The bloodrush exploded in Clanless's ears, pushing all those extraneous sounds out of the way. He held the massive sword out to his right side, running with his left shoulder forward. He roared his own shout of rage at the enemy.

To his credit, the opponent charged to meet him. Doing so would cut the gap, giving his ally time to catch up to them. But that would only help him if the ally arrived in time.

Clanless knew exactly what moves the enemy would make. He would lift his left-hand buckler, hoping to deflect the downward swing of the great sword. And then he would pivot inward, hoping to strike with the mace when Clanless left his own left side unshielded.

For a year and a half, Clanless had worked his body to a strength level far beyond what he would have considered possible before leaving home—and he hadn't been weak then! He'd chosen the left enemy as the smaller of the two. In this first exchange, it didn't matter how well the buckler was positioned. Clanless brought the great sword down with both hands with every ounce of force he possessed. The sword powered through, shoving the buckler down. It cut deep into the opponent's shoulder and head. The impact threw him to the ground.

Clanless didn't take time to see whether he was dead. He spun to meet the charging attack of the next opponent. The man's momentum wouldn't give him time to slow. Clanless dropped to his knees at the last moment, ducking under the swinging mace. He swung the great sword in an arc only a few inches from the surface of the sand. The opponent saw it coming and tried to jump over it. One foot made it, but the other didn't. The blade struck him where the foot met the ankle.

The opponent stumbled, trying to stay upright, but his left foot was useless. As Clanless spun back around, the enemy fell. He had enough presence of mind to roll with the fall, bringing both mace and buckler up to meet Clanless's next attack. It did him little good. Clanless stabbed down at him. The enemy managed to deflect the stab with his buckler, but not far enough. The sword pierced through the left edge of his chest instead of his heart.

Clanless yanked his sword free and ran past the fallen foe before spinning back around. He couldn't take the chance the first enemy might get upright enough to attack him from behind. Now he faced both of them… and both remained on the ground, bleeding and moaning.

Badaar hadn't given him reason to leave them alive. He advanced, keeping a wary eye on both. The nearest foe started to struggle back to his feet. Clanless took him back down with a brutal slash. He wouldn't be getting back up.

The second man, with the head injury, didn't get up. He moaned, showing no indication that he even saw his death coming. Clanless stabbed down, pinning him into the sand and putting him out of his misery.

"Looks like Clanless doesn't need any hidden powers, does he?" the presenter questioned over the roar of the crowd. "Two opponents, and he made it look easy!"

Clanless ignored him and used his Siphon on the body beside him. The attendants rushed to the second body, as expected, but that gave him more time with the first. He harvested more blood than normal. As the priest and two more attendants arrived, he got back to his feet.

Now he acknowledged the crowd, lifting the great sword high. Today, he reveled in their adulation. He'd surprised himself with how quickly he'd taken down two opponents. He hadn't been able to do any crowd-pleasing moves, but they didn't seem to mind this time. Seeing him win so decisively and quickly appeared to have been exciting enough.

He wondered what Orgina would think of it.

((((●))))

Zaluu found him relaxing in the baths afterwards. "Looks like you're moving up in this system." He sat on the tiles next to the water. "I had a suspicion after your first fight that you'd surpass me before long."

"Is that what's happening?" Clanless didn't look at him.

"You haven't seen me fighting two opponents, have you?"

Clanless grunted. "I thought it was a punishment."

"For the fight in the city? That doesn't make sense. Orgina wants you to be worth your blood. She won't get that if you're dead." Zaluu idly flicked water with his fingertips. "She wants you famous, doing more and more outrageous things in the arena. Especially now that Allaka is dead."

"She didn't know he'd be dead before she gave me that fight," Clanless argued.

"Doesn't matter." Zaluu shrugged. "It's still her motivation. She knows we're all going to die sooner or later. She needs the next big attraction, for however long that attraction lasts. Right now, you're on your way to becoming that. I think Patch and the Red Sword are still the top draws, but that's only because they've been here longer."

Clanless considered all of it. "The presenter said some weird things. I don't know what Orgina wants me to do any more."

"Oh, the part about the 'hidden power'?" Zaluu got to his feet. "You haven't even told me what that's about. I don't know what you did to those idiot thugs in the eating house, but I've never seen you do it in the arena. Am I right?"

"I don't need it."

"But you have it… whatever it is." Zaluu shook his head. "Sands, I hope I never have to fight you."

Clanless allowed a small smile to reach his face. "Yeah, you wouldn't be magnificent any more."

Zaluu snorted. "You coming out tonight?"

"No. I think I've had enough of the city for a while."

"Heh. When you're done mourning, you're welcome with me any time." He gave Clanless a jaunty wave and left.

When Clanless returned to the room alone a few minutes later, he almost regretted not going with Zaluu. As much as he didn't want to spend more of his earnings, at least a night in the city would give him something to do.

And then his eyes found the bookshelf. Of course. He took the largest book from the shelf and opened it to the title page. *A History of the Sar Empire and the Reign of the Hawk King,* he read (though he struggled with a couple of words). He didn't even bother to look at the other books, but took this one to the table and set it down beside the lamp.

The first line of the book raised more questions: "In the year 157 of the Goddess, the Sar Empire was founded." How long ago was that? What year was it now? What happened 157 years before the founding? Why did that matter? He had a lot to learn.

And so he worked his way through the pages, struggling with many words, and sometimes forced to skip over parts he didn't understand. In this way, he began to grasp a basic understanding of the Empire and its people. Twelve clans made up the Sar Empire. He'd had a vague knowledge of the clans, but might not have remembered the exact number if asked. Some clans were rich and powerful; others were not. The book only hinted at what he already knew: each clan's blood worked a different magic. That belonged to the realm of religion, which this book ostensibly didn't cover… and yet references to the goddess and her involvement in the Empire's operations seemed to appear almost every other page.

Clanless kept reading until Zaluu staggered in, hours after midnight. He looked up from the book as his roommate collapsed on the bed. "Did you know why the Hawk King is named after a hawk? It's because his earliest warriors described his tactics as swooping in on enemies like a bird of prey."

"All this time, I thought it was because he had a big nose," Zaluu muttered.

"Why is he a king and not an emperor? That's the part I don't understand."

"That's easy." Zaluu's words slurred.

"Why then?"

Zaluu waved a finger in the air without opening his eyes. "Because, student, an emperor conquers his land. A king owns it by divine right."

"He wants people to believe the goddess gave it to him," Clanless mused. "What year is it?"

"What?" Zaluu threw his arm over his eyes to shield them from the light.

"The year. The number. What is it?"

"Oh, it's, uh… 792, I think. Can you put the lamp out now?"

"792?" Clanless paused. "Then the Hawk King has been in power for over three hundred years? How is that possible?"

"Blood-magic, I suppose. Can we please go to sleep now?"

"Sure." Clanless turned down the lantern and crawled into bed himself. His mind, full of facts and confusing stories, took a long time to calm itself and find sleep.

THE MOONBLADE

Then

The days and weeks began to bleed into each other. Clanless read his books, fought hard, and trained harder. He rarely took the opportunities to go into the city, except when the craving for flatbread struck him. On those occasions, he would visit Dugh's End and listen to whatever storyteller or singer happened to be there. None of them matched up to Koland and Kekeen. Each time, the proprietor assured him they hadn't returned.

Zektel became more and more of a confidant. When Zaluu grew bored with his questions about the Empire, Clanless would find time with the blood-wraith instead. She asked as many questions as he did, and sometimes knew answers he didn't expect.

Having made the decision to use the great sword, Clanless stuck with it. His next two fights were his narrowest victories. He blamed himself for thinking too hard about the changes, instead of using his instincts. In both fights, he needed help leaving the arena; his injuries prevented him from walking out alone. Orgina's healer took care of him without a priest's bias, but the aches persisted for several days. Now he understood Zaluu's knee problem from their first meeting. He wondered if healing magic done by a priest was inherently more effective, or if there was another element he didn't understand.

He didn't sleep well. Darghan claimed to have seen him sleepwalking through the hallways. "Almost didn't recognize you at first, without that wolf fur."

Allaka's death troubled him the more he thought about it. Patch got revenge on the man who'd killed him in a fight a week later, but it didn't help. It was a stark reminder that any of them could die any week. He thought of Tunt and Nerlesen for the first time in months. It made him think of the others of his class. How were they doing in their arenas? Had any more of them died? These thoughts, together with Kekeen's departure, dragged him down into a gloom from which he didn't easily recover. The other fighters noticed it and did their best to cheer him up, but their words meant little. He found his thoughts drifting even further back: to the clanhold and his family. Father and Mother. Little Ot. Borde… and Uncle Sejikdi. These thoughts took him even deeper into the gloom, until Orgina summoned him to her office again.

"If something doesn't change, you're dead within a month!" she warned him. "I've seen it before. I don't know what's bothering you, but you've got to get out of it. What will it take? Another girl, maybe?" That seemed to be her standard answer… since most of the other fighters saw it as the answer to everything.

"You're asking what I want?" Clanless snorted. "I'm your slave. You can do whatever you like with me."

Orgina rolled her eyes. "Of course you're my slave, but you're also how I make a profit here. Do you know how much it costs me to keep you men fed and trained? To pay all the non-slaves who work here? Your performances in the arena pay for all of that. And the better you perform, the better things get around here. You want a new bed in your room? New clothes? Fight harder."

"New books." Clanless blurted it as soon as he realized it. "I want new books."

Orgina blinked and sat back. "Ah… I've never had that request before. Hmp. Books are expensive, you know. The only reason that stack is in your room is because the previous fighter spent all of his blood on them. And I forgot to sell them after he died. I suppose… I could probably trade some of the existing books for different ones. That might not cost as much." She wagged a finger at him. "But if I do this, and can find some different books for you, you've got to get back into the right mindset. You're bringing everyone down here."

Clanless took a deep breath. "I'll do better," he promised.

And he did. He turned his focus back to the training and the reading, especially once Orgina fulfilled her word. Gogeku took three of his books away and brought four new volumes to his room a few days later. He talked endlessly about how pleased he was that one of the brutes sought greater enlightenment. One of the books was a religious tome, a paean of sorts to the goddess. Clanless didn't finish that one. He grasped some of it, but the rest didn't seem to resemble facts in any way.

He didn't know what he thought of the goddess any more. The moon remained as steady in the sky as it had been his entire life; he couldn't deny that. He also couldn't deny the blood-magic, which was inextricably linked to the worship of the goddess, or at least so it appeared. But did a powerful deity exist within the moon and create the blood-magic? That part he couldn't decide. The priests gave the goddess credit for everything, so why would she create the Taint? Why would he have it and be cursed by the priesthood for something over which he had no control?

Such were the thoughts he pondered alone in his room. Zektel gave him no guidance on religious issues. He didn't understand why. In fact, the more he studied things, the more he didn't understand Zektel. She claimed to be a part of him yet to have existed for ages. She'd also said he brought her into this world; he hadn't forgotten that statement. Where would he find information on blood-wraiths? They hadn't appeared in any of the books he'd looked at so far. Neither had the Taint, for that matter.

He needed more information. For these particular topics, he could think of only one place to go.

ᨀ ᨀ ᨀ ᨀ ● ᨆ ᨆ ᨆ ᨆ

"Your jar is full, I suppose?" The blood-priest met Clanless inside the entrance to the shrine. During his stay at this arena, the jar had been his only reason for visiting this place.

"Not today," Clanless answered. "Today, I seek… guidance, if one such as I can obtain it." He ducked his head in a deferential bow.

The priest blinked and almost took a step backward. Clanless had waited to make his visit until this particular priest was on duty; he was the only one who'd never sneered at or verbally abused him in his time here. "I… see. What type of guidance?"

"I assume you are familiar with my condition." Clanless kept his head bowed.

The priest snorted. "If you mean the Taint, then of course I am. If you have another condition beyond that, I am not aware nor interested."

"I am seeking to understand. I was told the Taint was a curse on, on my former clan, because of shedding too much blood. Is that accurate?"

"So the tales tell us," the priest answered cautiously.

"Why?"

"Why what?"

"Why would the goddess curse the clan's children for the actions of their fathers so very long ago? Why curse me?"

"She is the goddess. It is her right to visit the sins of the fathers upon the children, if she so desires." The priest folded his arms, clearly not interested in continuing the conversation.

But Clanless pressed on: "But the Taint has a specific outcome. It makes blood worthless for the goddess. So why would she create something that would damage her own sacrifices?"

"As you well know, it is a curse. Of course it is a bad thing."

"But it's bad for her, not for those cursed with it, save for how I am treated. It does not harm me, but harms her sacrifices. Please. I am only seeking to understand."

"She is the goddess. We are to serve her, not question her ways."

Clanless resisted the urge to scream. "Very well. Is there any way to remove the Taint?"

The priest paused. "I… have not heard of such a thing, no."

"Then I am cursed for nothing I did, with a punishment that I cannot remove, with no hope of salvation?"

"I cannot say." The priest hesitated again. "I have not considered your particular condition very deeply. I am sorry."

"Is there anywhere I can learn more of this, perhaps learn more of the goddess herself?"

The priest frowned. "You must have gone through a child's class in your home temple. Before the Taint, that is."

"I did." Clanless recalled almost nothing of the class, which took place when he was only seven or eight years old. "But I need to know more."

"The search for knowledge can be a dangerous thing." A third voice intruded into their conversation from behind Clanless.

The priest's eyes widened, and he ducked his own head. "Daghilch, sir."

Clanless turned, his eyes narrowing. The tall, thin man standing in the doorway was all too familiar. "You."

The Daghilch moved past without looking at him. "We came to check on your progress, Clanless." He put special emphasis on the last word.

"Here I am." Clanless kept his head up now. No use pretending any more.

"Indeed." The Daghilch nodded to the priest. "You may leave us now."

As the priest scampered out of the shrine, Clanless folded his own arms across his chest. Rage churned in his stomach, threatening to boil over, at the sight of this man. "Why do you wish to keep me from learning?" he demanded.

"I did not say that. I only said that the search for knowledge can be dangerous, as it is for all." The Daghilch turned at last to face him. "In this case, knowledge would do you no good whatsoever."

"Why do you add to my troubles? Isn't it enough?" Clanless uncrossed his arms and spread them out. "Isn't it enough that I'm banished? That you took everything from me? That I may not live another week?"

"We are not here to add to your troubles, Clanless. In fact, I wish to spare you further difficulty, if I can."

"How?"

The Daghilch raised a finger, like Kan always did, and began to pace. "Your continued existence is an affront to the Empire. Most of my colleagues expected you to be dead by now. The fact that you aren't has led some to consider whether we should… pay to make sure that happens."

Clanless's blood run cold. He'd never considered that possibility. The priests could buy his bloodbond from Orgina. Or at least pay her enough to ensure his death. It would be an easy thing for them, since they effectively controlled all the wealth of the Empire.

"I will fight you," he said, though he had no idea how.

"No need," the Daghilch replied. "I've talked them out of that particular strategy. Most of them, anyway."

"Why would you do that?"

"The Sar Empire is beset with foes round about. In your recent studies, I assume you've learned some of this?"

Clanless nodded. "The barbarians."

"Yes, on the west side of our borders. Their attacks grow ever more bold. One day they'll reach as far as one of the cities. We all know this. Yet the Hawk King does nothing."

The Daghilch waited for Clanless to comment, but he kept silent. This was a confusing turn to the conversation.

"The reason he does nothing is to the north, the Melkute Kingdom. Tensions are very high with them right now." The Daghilch looked up through the shrine's moon window. "They envy our land, where we have the most direct view of the moon. And so, the Hawk King needs his army at the ready in case of invasion. He cannot spare significant forces to deal with the barbarians. And there are other threats, such as the beastmen in the high hills or the cult of Suirel. All these things weigh heavily on the Hawk King's mind, and those of his advisors. The Empire stands at a crossroads."

Clanless shook his head. "Why are you telling me all of this?"

"Have you heard any more… voices, perhaps?"

"No." Clanless answered at once. If he were ever to confide in anyone else about Zektel, it would certainly not be this man.

The Daghilch smiled at him. "Ah, well. I wondered. At any rate… The questions you were asking, before I entered the room. They have answers, you know."

Clanless wrinkled his brow, trying to keep up with the shifts in topic.

"The goddess never does anything without reason." The Daghilch moved toward the door again. "You see, Clanless, I have an… unorthodox belief." He paused. "I believe that someday, you may be of great use to the Empire. I don't quite know when, and definitely not how. But I have faith." He stepped through the doorway. "Farewell again. We will continue to watch your career with curiosity. Curiosity… and faith."

((((●))))

On the one-year anniversary of his arrival in Ghoyor, Clanless received a summons to the arena floor before breakfast. He hurried to obey and found Orgina herself waiting, along with Badaar and a short, thin man with a balding head. The stranger wore the roughest clothes Clanless had ever seen, nothing at all like the rich people Orgina usually entertained.

"Here he is," Badaar stated the obvious.

"Clanless." Orgina pulled her red coat tighter. "You've done well for a year now. It's time to move on to the next stage."

"You're sending me to another arena?"

"What? Goddess, no! That's not—Ugh. Never mind." She took a breath and started again. "It's time to reward you and advance your personality a step further. Badaar, will you explain? I can't believe it's this cold already. I don't know how you men stand it." She blew on her hands and hugged herself.

Badaar held out a hand toward the stranger. "This is Kandulka of clan Berge, the smith we hire for jobs such as this."

Clanless took a sharp intake of breath. Did that mean what he thought it meant?

"I've watched some of your fights." Kandulka's gravelly voice almost made Clanless flinch. It sounded painful. "I assume you wish to continue with a large blade?"

"Yes. I've alternated between two lengths." Clanless walked to the weapons rack and pointed them out. "Something in between this would be perfect."

"Remember what we discussed, smith," Orgina called. "Will that concept still work?"

"I believe so. Yes." Kandulka nodded. "In fact, a longer weapon is better."

"What concept?" Clanless asked.

"You'll find out when I want you to know," Orgina said. "What else do you need, smith?"

Kandulka took out a cord. "Measurements." He stepped next to Clanless. "Lift your arms straight out from your sides, please."

Clanless obeyed. "Why measure me?"

"I am designing a blade for you and only you. As such, I need to make sure it will balance correctly with your weight and reach. And other details. Pick up that larger sword, will you?"

He continued to make measurements of Clanless's arm length, muscle width, height, and more. He stepped back and cocked his head. "You're still growing, aren't you?"

"He's only fifteen years old," Badaar said.

"Gogeku complains on a regular basis about having to fashion larger clothes for him, since he keeps outgrowing them," Orgina said. Clanless didn't know why Geku bothered; he wore the fancy clothes on so few occasions.

Kandulka scratched the top of his head. "That makes it a bit more difficult, but not unsurpassable. I can make estimates based on expected growth."

None of it made much sense to Clanless, but the excitement of getting a custom weapon kept him from asking more questions. Except one: "How long will this take?"

Kandulka shook his head and didn't answer.

"He doesn't like to be rushed," Badaar said. "It's going to take a while." He leaned in close and whispered: "I'd expect several weeks, if not months."

The excitement faded a bit.

"Excellent." Orgina clapped her hands. "Smith, I look forward to seeing this beauty. Now I'm getting out of this cold." She headed for the door, grumbling.

Kandulka took the great sword and held it up, muttering to himself.

Badaar pulled Clanless after Orgina. "She would never tell you this, but I saw what she asked of Kandulka," he said in a low voice. "I don't think it's overstating things to say this is going to be the most expensive weapon he's ever made for us."

"Because of the size?" Clanless asked.

"No." Badaar shook his head. "Because she believes in you."

☾ ☾ ☾ ☾ ● ☽ ☽ ☽ ☽

When Clanless returned to the room, he found Zaluu throwing a pair of daggers against the wall. A dozen small holes decorated the once-empty surface.

"When did you start throwing blades?" he asked.

Zaluu walked to the wall and pulled the daggers free. "When I found these for sale in the market last week. I think I'm doing remarkably well with them." He walked back to the middle of the room and threw one of the blades. It thunked into the wall in the same area as the other holes. Only then did Clanless notice a crude circle Zaluu must have carved into the plaster. The latest throw was inside the circle, but not by much.

"You thinking of using them in the arena?"

Zaluu threw the second dagger. It hit at an angle and didn't stick into the wall. It made a clanging sound as it bounced on the floor. "Not especially. It doesn't match my personality very well. But it's fun." He retrieved the fallen dagger. "It would probably work better with your tricks. You're the one who sheds all the blood."

"I've never been all that good with throwing things." Even back home at the clanhold, he'd usually been last among the boys when it came to rock-throwing competitions.

Zaluu shrugged. "I don't regret buying them. I might go back and get the other two he had available. Maybe someday I can work it in." He tried to balance one of the blades on his finger, but it fell almost at once. "Thrown weapons in general don't play very big, except in larger scale fights. Think about it: if I walked out there and threw one of these right in my opponent's eye before he ever got near me... the fight would be over without a show. Orgina would hate it."

Clanless agreed. "Did you get breakfast? I haven't been yet."

"Nah, I was waiting for you. What did the boss want, anyway?"

"Looks like I'm getting a custom weapon."

"What? That's fantastic! What is it?"

Clanless headed for the door. "Some kind of sword. I guess I'll find out when it's done."

Zaluu tossed the daggers onto the table and hurried after him. "I told you! I told you she liked you!" He clapped Clanless on the back and sighed. "It's such a burden being so right all the time."

"And yet here you are."

When Kandulka returned six weeks later, Clanless had almost given up hope. Gogeku informed him of the smith's arrival, walking into the room while he and Zaluu were getting dressed.

"He has the weapon?" Clanless exclaimed.

"That is what I am telling you." Gogeku sniffed. "Your presence is requested out on the… sands." He said the last word as if it were a horrible place, worthy of being avoided at all costs.

"Let's go!" Zaluu exclaimed. "I want to see this too!"

"Why not?" Clanless led the way. Out on the arena sands, they found the smith standing beside a temporary table with a large weapon case closed on top of it. Badaar and Orgina were present, the latter wrapped in what looked like two heavy coats. She frowned at Zaluu, but didn't say anything.

"I have completed my work," Kandulka announced once they drew near. He put a hand on the case. "This is my masterpiece, the greatest weapon I have ever forged." He turned pointedly to look at Orgina.

"Yes." She rolled her eyes. "You'll get your bonus, assuming it's all you've claimed it to be."

The smith put his other hand on the case. "I will make no other weapon after this. It would be an insult to even attempt to replicate the greatness of this one. The goddess's own hands guided me."

"Get on with it," Orgina growled. "You're worse than my presenter."

Kandulka gave an exaggerated sigh. He undid two clasps, flipped open the case, and stepped away. The other four moved closer to see. Clanless leaned in, nudging Zaluu to the side. What he saw took his breath away.

An exquisite two-handed sword lay resting on red velvet. The blade was shaped like a crescent moon—not a tiny crescent, but a strong one-third-of-the-moon crescent, not unlike the moon's shield on a bright day in High Spring. Craters of various sizes, so exquisitely formed that everyone looked up at the real moon to compare them, decorated the surface of the blade itself. The handle, formed of a wood Clanless didn't recognize, was steel-banded and attached to the blade a few inches above the bottom tip. A round pommel of engraved brass completed the weapon.

All four of them exclaimed over the beauty, pointing to various aspects, before Kandulka stepped back to the table. He lifted the weapon with one hand on the handle and the other at the back of the blade's curve. "Behold the moonblade! The blade itself is single-edged for the lower half of its surface," he explained, "meaning it could be used somewhat like an axe. However"—he ran his hand closer to the top point—"the top half is double-edged, allowing for slashing in both directions. But if you wish a direct stab, it will require a specific angle."

Clanless didn't care. He would adapt his style in any way necessary for the privilege of wielding this incredible sword.

"The handle is terebinth," Kandulka went on. "An odd choice, I know, but I was inspired. The steel band and pins, forged with the same care I give to all my projects, ensure it will stay strong for longer than you yourself will live, I am sure." He turned the blade to reveal the bottom of the brass pommel. "And should there be any doubt as to its wielder..." Clanless pushed against a lump in his throat when he saw the engraving: an exact duplicate of his clanless brand.

Kandulka looked to Orgina. "Are you satisfied, my patron?"

"It is beautiful, Kandulka. But beauty is one thing. Is it functional, and, more importantly, does it fit with my fighter's personality?"

The smith turned to Clanless and offered the moonblade to him with a slight bow, turning it so that the hilt faced him. Clanless took hold of the grip with both hands before lifting it from the smith's. He held it vertically, staring in awe. Up close, the detail work was even more incredible. He let go with his left hand and moved it up and down with just his right, finding it surprisingly light. The length was a little bit shorter than the great sword he'd been using.

Kandulka tilted his head, hands clasped together. "The circles there upon the blade"—he pointed as if no one had noticed them yet—"act as unconventional fullers, reducing the weight without reducing the blade's strength."

Clanless stepped further away from the others and made a few practice swings. He found the balance perfect, pulling the blade forward just enough, while not making it difficult to retract. "The blade wants to move!" he exclaimed.

"Indeed. She is almost a living thing," the smith agreed. "My child. My final offspring."

Orgina grunted. "You have outdone yourself, smith. It is... amazing."

"Amazing?" Badaar cried. "It's more than that. This is the blade of a king, not an arena fighter!"

"Nonsense," Orgina said. "It's what I asked for, and a bit more. Kandulka, you have earned everything you asked for, and a bit more. When you leave, Gogeku will pay you as instructed. I look forward to seeing how you top yourself next time."

Kandulka shook his head. "No. I will forge no more, I tell you. This is my last piece, my masterpiece. I can do no better, though I spend a thousand hours with my hammers in the heat of my forge. This is my all."

"You exaggerate, I'm sure," Orgina said with a dismissive wave. "We'll talk later."

Kandulka shook his head and started to turn away.

"Wait!" Clanless hurried to catch him. "I have never seen its like, master smith." He gave a deep bow, clumsy though it might be. "I have never owned, nor so much as held something so exquisite."

"You still don't own it," Orgina said from behind him. "Everything here is mine, remember? It belongs to you only so long as you serve me."

Clanless kept his eyes on Kandulka. "It will be an honor to fight with this blade," he whispered.

The smith nodded and turned away again. He straightened his back and strode from the arena.

"Do some testing," Orgina instructed Badaar. "Make sure it's everything he says it is. And get the boy familiar with it at once. I want everyone to see him using it next Arena Night. I have a story half-prepared already and—"

"No," Clanless interrupted, still staring at the blade. "I know the story."

Orgina raised her eyebrows. "This should be good. Proceed."

"Furious with the priesthood for taking away his name and his heritage, the clanless one vowed revenge. In defiance of their wishes, he forged for himself a mighty blade in honor of the very goddess from whom they tried to cut him off." Clanless lifted the sword to the moon itself, turning its blade to match the angle.

"Hmp. Needs work, but shows promise. I'll see what the presenter thinks." Orgina nodded to Badaar and headed toward the exit.

Clanless looked at Zaluu. "You haven't said anything. That's not like you."

Zaluu shook his head. "Friend, if I were to say anything, it would come across as nothing but sheer jealousy."

Badaar chuckled. "That goes for the both of us." He reached toward the sword. "May I?"

Clanless let him take the moonblade and stepped back to watch the trainer at work. Badaar went through a practice form he'd taught Clanless for the two-handed sword. Every movement was precise and sharp with smooth transitions.

"Ever wonder why he doesn't fight?" Zaluu asked. "He'd be incredible out there."

"He's not a slave," Clanless pointed out.

Zaluu grunted. "There's that, of course."

Badaar returned, wiping sweat from his brow. "Clanless, I have worked this arena for many years." He set the moonblade into its box with care. "In that time, I've seen many weapons created for individual fighters, those who reached the next level of fame. Orgina pays well to have them made, because it's an investment well worth it." He left a palm atop the blade and shook his head. "But I've never seen one like this. This... I completely believe what the smith said. He'll never top this sword."

"I need to be better," Clanless said. "I need to be worthy of this sword."

"We will step up your training." Badaar took his hand away from the sword. "You will need to make some changes."

"I'll do whatever it takes." Clanless gazed at the sword. Maybe the goddess did care about him, after all.

GHAMBA LAM

Now

Clanless threw open the door to his room. The Ghamba Lam sat at his table, examining the metal plate he used to summon Zektel. A blood-priest stood beside the open chest. He lifted a bag of blood vials and opened it to peer inside.

"Put that down!" Clanless snapped. "It's mine!"

"A slave does not own anything," the Ghamba Lam said placidly. "All that you have belongs to your master, the Hawk King. And he has given me authority over anything."

Clanless lowered his eyebrows and glared at the religious leader. "You've tormented me enough. Why show up on my last day before freedom?"

The Ghamba Lam set the metal plate down and ran a finger across its surface. He examined the flakes of dried blood that clung to his fingertip. "I've told you before, you know. I believe the goddess has a purpose for you, even for the Taint. I'm not inclined to allow you to run where I can't find you. Not when I haven't discovered that purpose yet."

"You tried to have me killed."

The Ghamba Lam looked up. "No, I haven't. I told you that others were behind that. The cult of Suirel, to be precise."

Clanless didn't know whether to believe him or not. He moved across the room and stood beside the moonblade on the wall. "I have worked too many years to let you steal this from me now."

"And what will you do? Kill me? That would not get you what you want."

"If you take away my freedom on the night before I earn it, then I will have nothing left to live for." Clanless put his hand next to the moonblade's handle. "I will no longer care."

The Ghamba Lam shook his head. "Such theatrics. I am not here to take your freedom away." He snapped his fingers at the priest. The priest responded by taking one blood vial from the bag and handing it to his leader. The Ghamba Lam held it up, letting the light from the window shine through. "V-blood from clan Shukan. Very valuable indeed. Would you kill me if I only took this one?"

"It would set me back weeks," Clanless said, not moving his hand.

The religious leader tapped the vial on the plate. "And if I dumped it out here. What would happen then?"

"It would be a waste. And have the same result as you taking it."

"Indeed." The Ghamba Lam watched him without speaking for a while. Clanless didn't move. If this were some kind of contest to see who would blink first, it would not be him.

At last, the Ghamba Lam sighed. He glanced back at the other priest. "Leave us." The priest nodded, returned the bag of vials to the chest, and left the room.

"Now we can speak clearly." The Ghamba Lam twirled the blood vial in his hand. "As a child, you spoke of hearing a voice, a voice you thought to be the goddess. I need not ask if you have continued to hear that voice." He waited, but Clanless did not respond.

With another sigh, the Ghamba Lam set the vial down on the plate and took his hand away from it. "You are not the only one to hear voices, you know."

Clanless took his own hand away from the moonblade. "Are you telling me you suffer from voices inside your head, Ghamba Lam?"

The religious leader snorted. "No. I am not so burdened. I am speaking of... others. Near me. In positions of... great power."

Clanless didn't answer. He had no idea what this meant.

The Ghamba Lam folded his hands together with the index fingers pointed upward. He rested the fingertips against his chin. "I am... concerned about those who listen to these voices. I do not believe they have the Empire's best interests in mind. Do you understand me?"

"I have no idea under the moon's gaze what you are talking about."

The Ghamba Lam chuckled without humor. "Perhaps you don't. I've tried to tell you, and you don't listen." He leaned forward. "There is a...

faction within the priesthood that worships Suirel instead of the goddess. They're the ones who've tried to kill you, and I'm afraid their influence has grown too much in the past few years."

"What does that have to do with me?"

The Ghamba Lam took an empty crystal vial from a pouch at his belt and held it up. "I would like you to fill this for me, please."

"Now you want my help in stealing from me?"

The priest set the vial on the table. "You misunderstand. I want your blood, your own."

"Why?" Clanless furrowed his brow. "Clan Tokuur blood isn't worth much."

"Call it scientific curiosity." The Ghamba Lam held his empty palm toward the vial. "Do this for me, and I'll leave you alone. I can fetch a knife, if necessary—"

Clanless threw his hand up and sliced the side of his wrist on his moon-blade. He held it over the table and squeezed his fist, letting the precious blood trickle into the vial. "Enough for you?"

"Enough for now." The Ghamba Lam snatched the vial. He got to his feet with a swift movement and headed toward the door. As his hand rested on the handle, he paused.

"The coming of Suirel is seen as a time of great danger." He looked over his shoulder. "I see it as a time of great change. Some change is for the better, you know. Later tonight, Clanless… I suspect you will be asked to do a great task involving the Taint. I would appreciate it if you would accept that task." With that, he opened the door and disappeared.

Clanless picked up the vial and returned it to his stores. He shook his head. Trying to make sense of the priests had always been a fool's errand. If he hurried, he could catch up to Hagh and Sugh.

ANIMALS

"You need to learn how to fight animals," Badaar said.

Clanless nodded, resting the moonblade on his shoulder. Over the past five weeks, he'd used it to spectacular effect in his fights. The crowd loved the new weapon and cheered all the louder. "Is that likely to happen soon?" he asked.

"We have some coming, or so I'm told." The trainer wiped sweat from his brow. The sun had only begun its pursuit of the moon, so soon after breakfast. Low Winter transitioned into Low Spring. After weeks of cold, the milder temperatures almost felt stifling. "And since you're the current popular draw, it's almost certain that you'll be facing some. Unless, of course, I inform Orgina that you're totally unprepared and might die. But I doubt you want me to do that."

Clanless snorted. "What kind of animal?"

"That I can't tell you. I don't know at this point, and it's supposed to be a surprise to the fighter. But if you think about what might be most appropriate for your story, it shouldn't be too hard to guess." He gave a quick look at the fur pelt Clanless had set aside for now due to the heat.

"All right." Clanless nodded. "What do I need to know?"

"I'm guessing you may have read some stuff in all those books you've been consuming?"

"A little."

"Forget all of it. Animals in the wild behave a certain way. But here in the arena, things will be different." Badaar led Clanless to the shade near the arena wall. "First of all, they'll enter the sands desperately hungry. The handlers will not feed them for several days before the fight. Sometimes, they may give them some kind of stimulants in their water to further agitate them."

"That seems cruel."

"Of course it's cruel." Badaar snorted. "These animals have been captured and brought here for the express purpose of being killed or brutally tearing a man apart. How they're treated before that moment doesn't seem to matter much in light of that."

"I suppose." The only experience Clanless had with animals before the arena came from the goats his family raised in the clanhold. They hardly seemed like the type of creature that would put up much of a fight. He had read some, as Badaar surmised, about the various animals that lived within the Sar Empire, as well as the rumors about more exotic creatures that existed beyond their borders. And from what he'd heard of other arena fights, feline predators or wolves were most common.

"When you combine how they've been treated with the confusion they encounter upon entering this place, their behavior is highly unpredictable," Badaar went on, gesturing toward the stands. "Some will freeze up at the noise, while others will charge madly across the sand. But eventually, they'll all realize they're free out here… with one target waiting for them. Then they'll come for you."

"If they're so crazed and confused, what makes them dangerous?"

"That's part of it right there: if any opponent is unpredictable, you've got problems. You should know that by now." Badaar held up both hands as if they were claws. "They also have more than one simple weapon. How many sets of claws can hit you?"

"Two?"

"Wrong. Four. They've got four legs, remember? And each one of them has claws, to various degrees. Some of them are long enough to tear out your guts." He pointed to his mouth. "And then they have teeth. Don't forget that part. With some creatures, that's easily the most dangerous part."

"But they don't carry shields," Clanless argued. "They're vulnerable to just about any weapon strike."

"That much is true, if you can hit them. But where do you hit them? Most of them time, they're going to be guarding their underbelly. You won't be able to go for the heart or guts."

"Head and neck should be most obvious targets then."

"Of course they are. But here are two factors you need to consider." Badaar held up two fingers. "First, you don't carry a shield either, and there might be more than one of them. They'll be faster than your human opponents too. While you're striking one, another will be coming after you. Second, there's the skin."

"The skin?"

Badaar patted his own bare chest. "We humans have pathetic skin. You can cut through it with a long fingernail. Most animals aren't like that. They have thicker skin, complete with fur. What that means for you is that a glancing blow isn't going to accomplish much. You have to cut deep. It also means your blade is going to be harder to pull free."

"Giving the other animals more time to attack me."

Badaar nodded. "Now you're getting it."

Clanless swung the moonblade down from his shoulder. "Then let's train for it. How do I begin?"

True to Badaar's prediction, word came down that Clanless would fight wild animals at the next Arena Night. Except it wouldn't be a night but a special daytime event, coinciding with the day the sun fully emerged from the moon's dominance and submitted to her height. During the first day of full light, a series of special arena battles would take place. Zaluu and Darghan would be fighting as a team against a trio of captured barbarian warriors. Patch would be fighting against an exotic swordsman from a land across the sea. And Clanless would be fighting… something with teeth and claws.

Zektel seemed especially curious about this fight. "Will they take the blood of the beasts?" she asked.

"No. The priests have no use for blood that is not from humans," Clanless answered. "In fact, I don't think they'll even take the blood of the barbarians."

Clanless had obtained a second large crystal container, ostensibly to store more blood before turning it in to the shrine. Instead, he used it to store blood for summoning Zektel. Together, they'd discovered that as long as a single drop of his own blood was included, she could appear using any other blood. It made things so much easier. And now, he could use enough to allow her to create larger forms for herself. This time, she'd created an entire head, her upper torso, and two dripping arms. Clanless pointedly avoided commenting on the voluptuous shape of the torso.

"Do they believe the barbarian blood has no power?" Zektel asked.

"Each clan's blood provides a different power." Clanless polished the moonblade while he spoke. "I suppose, since the barbarians don't belong to one of our clans, their blood isn't the same. Or at least, that's how the priesthood would say it."

"That doesn't make much sense." Zektel adjusted her appearance, giving herself longer and puffier sleeves. Blood dripped down only to be absorbed and flow back up to reinforce the image. "First of all, why would only the people of this particular empire have empowered blood?"

"The priests would say we're chosen of the goddess."

"And second, your people and the barbarian tribes have intermingled their blood many times in the past, sometimes forcibly, alas. So some of them will possess the same type of blood as you do, or some of the other clans."

Clanless rested the moonblade on his knees. "I hadn't thought of that."

"And what of all the other people groups scattered about this world? What of the Melkute Kingdom? Is their blood useless?"

"I don't know. But here's another thing I don't quite understand: where does all the blood go?" Clanless had been thinking about this for some time. "If every temple and shrine in every clanhold and city is accepting blood sacrifices on an almost daily basis, where is it going? They're not putting all of it into crystals for people to spend. What do they do with all of it? Is all of it used for magic?"

"Do you see a lot of magic taking place?"

Clanless thought for a moment. "Aside from the presenter's voice and the healing, I don't see any magic happening at all."

"A curious conundrum then."

"What's a conundrum?"

"A confusing problem."

"Oh." Clanless thought he'd gotten beyond feeling ignorant, now that he could read, but every once in a while, something would remind him how much he still needed to learn.

"I can understand the difference between human and animal blood," Zektel said, turning the conversation back on topic, "but not between differing humans. If your goddess exists, would she really choose one special people group and give them this power?"

Clanless shrugged. "I don't understand the religious stuff. I've tried, but the priests don't want to give me any more to read, thanks to the Daghilch's visit."

"Religion seems to be an intrinsic part of your society, dearheart. The priesthood controls both magic and the economy, as well as most of the common people through their teachings."

"I've noticed. But none of this helps me deal with the animals in the arena." He got to his feet. "I need to go practice some more."

"Hasn't the sun already retreated? Will you practice in the dark?"

Clanless swung the moonblade over his shoulder and started toward the door. "Until I'm free, I can't practice too much."

((((●))))

As the special day's events began, Clanless watched Zaluu and Darghan head out onto the sands. He'd been surprised to hear his fight would be second. He'd expected to follow after Patch. Surely the animals provided a bigger spectacle than whatever this other warrior brought. He didn't know if he'd ever understand Orgina and her scheduling.

"Did you tell her I might have trouble with the animals?" he asked Badaar as they watched the others begin their fight.

"No, I told her I wasn't the least bit worried about you." Badaar shot him a quick glance. "Was I wrong?"

Clanless shook his head, watching Darghan do a spin move to separate two of his opponents. "Those barbarians are big men."

"That they are. Not as big as beastmen, mind you. But still impressive."

"You've seen beastmen?"

Badaar nodded. "Oh, come on, Zaluu! You can do better than that!" He rolled his eyes. "That boy makes me tear my hair out."

"You don't have much hair."

"And that's why! Argh. Darghan is pulling all the weight here. Zaluu will be lucky to survive this one."

Clanless agreed. Zaluu had grown increasingly reckless since the reveal of the moonblade. He'd admitted jealousy of Clanless. Was he trying to prove himself or destroy himself in response?

"That's done it," Badaar declared a minute later. "Idiot. If he'd been alone against even one of them, he might not have made it."

"He's limping." Clanless moved to help open the door.

"Don't worry about him. It's your turn." Badaar reached over and straightened Clanless's fur pelt. "We can both chew Zaluu out later."

Clanless smiled at Badaar's confidence in him. He walked out into the arena as the crowd erupted in cheers. He blinked at the bright sunlight, so different from the half-light he'd grown used to. He hoped it didn't affect his vision too much. Was there a blood-magic that helped vision? That would be interesting.

"Clanless is here, citizens!" the presenter boomed. "He's carved a deadly swath through some of the best we've had to throw at him ever since he forged that moonblade! But today's challenge is something he's never faced before!"

The crowd's usual roar became more organized. It took Clanless a moment to realize they were chanting his title! It was just as Zektel had predicted, almost two years earlier.

"Behold!" The presenter's voice erupted even louder than usual, and the crowd quieted in response. The doors on the far side of the arena swung open.

Clanless had fully expected the creatures that burst out, but he still couldn't help reacting with a knowing smile. "Wolves." The crowd, upon realizing the connection, erupted again. He lifted his moonblade high to encourage them, but kept his eyes on the animals as they approached.

He counted four—no, five—of the creatures. The fifth one cowed at the noise of the crowd, and shrunk down near the wall. Clanless lost sight of it in the shadows. The other four advanced at various speeds across the sand. They saw him almost immediately and came, far faster than his human opponents.

The wolves, mangy and starving, were a blend of brown, black, and white. None of them matched the colors of his pelt. A curious fact, but one he couldn't waste time considering. They were already almost within striking range. Clanless held his moonblade in front with both hands, trying to watch all four of them at once.

Though they'd charged at first, the wolves slowed as they approached, perhaps realizing this man showed no fear. They moved as one, circling him. He waited, turning with them. At last, one grew bold enough to lunge forward, jaws snapping. Clanless swung a quick twist of the blade, catching the beast on its chin and tossing it aside with a yelp. He couldn't tell if he'd killed it or not, as the other three moved closer.

With one of them bleeding out on the sands, these three would not be so reckless. They tried to advance on him from all sides. Clanless backed away, making it harder. The presenter's voice was going on and on above the noise of the crowd, but Clanless tuned it out, as he always did. The bloodrush pounding in his ears made it easy.

One of the wolves leaped closer, snarling. Clanless swung the moonblade to meet it, but the wolf stopped short. At the same moment, the other two charged. But Clanless had anticipated that. He continued the motion of his swing at the first wolf over his own head and down into the skull of the next one leaping at him. The third managed to claw at his side before getting knocked aside by the body of its companion.

Clanless yanked the moonblade free with an effort. Badaar had been right about the thick skin. Two wolves were dead or dying, leaving only two more…

A sudden pressure on his left ankle alerted him too late to the danger. The fifth wolf had found its courage and joined the fray, sneaking in behind him. Its jaws clamped down on the back of his ankle with a horrifying crunch. Clanless shouted in pain and swept the moonblade back with only his right hand. It connected, tearing the wolf free from his leg.

His ankle would no longer hold his weight. Clanless fell to one knee. The other two wolves charged. With a roar, he slashed across both of them in mid-leap. Eyes burning, he activated the Taint for good measure.

One of the leaping wolves still slammed into him, knocking him to the ground. He shoved it off with the moonblade and pulled himself back up. The wolves lay about him, bleeding. Three were clearly dead. The other two still lived, evidenced by flinching legs, but they would not be getting back up.

The crowd noise erupted louder than ever. Clanless leaned on his knee, but lifted the moonblade with his right hand, acknowledging the cheers. He didn't even feel the scratches on his side. But waves of pain cascaded up his leg from his destroyed ankle. The healer would have to work hard on that one.

No attendants and priests rushed out to retrieve these bodies, of course. Clanless waited, trying to calm his breath, until a hand touched his shoulder. "On your feet," said a voice.

"I can't." Clanless turned his head and tried to focus on the man standing beside him. "Patch?"

"There's been a change of plans," the other fighter said rapidly. "You're fighting with me. It turns out my opponent brought a pet of some kind with him, and Badaar said it would take two of us."

"My foot is ruined. I can't even stand."

"Then we've got a big problem. Here. Lean on me." Patch set his buckler aside and put an arm around Clanless's shoulder. They stood together, on three feet. Clanless held his moonblade with his right hand, and Patch held his mace with his left.

"This isn't going to work," Clanless gasped.

"From across the sea," the presenter shouted, "comes an opponent the likes of which neither of these fighters have ever seen! A mystical warrior from the island nation of Aral, he fights with the most exotic creature you've ever seen… and the most terrifying! Behold!"

From the opposite door, an immensely tall man appeared, wearing only a loincloth but covered in strange tattoos. He carried some kind of spiked weapon connected to a chain wrapped around his own body. He held up one end of the chain and the spiked piece dropped down, hanging from his hand. He bellowed what sounded like a war cry, though not in a language Clanless understood. From behind him, a creature bounded out onto the sand.

"Goddess preserve us," Patch muttered.

The creature looked like some kind of enormous lizard, though it stood much more upright on its four legs. From its head filled with sharp teeth to the tip of its long tail, it must have been at least seven feet long. Atop its back were a series of tall spines with a kind of webbing between each of them arching to a man's height before descending to the tail. Clanless had never seen anything like it, not even in book illustrations.

The enemy warrior shouted something else, pointing at the two arena fighters. The creature screamed, a piercing sound that hit one high note before trailing off multiple times in a row. It pawed the sand before charging straight at them. Behind it, the enemy warrior started forward as well, swinging his chain weapon.

"When it gets close, swing me at it," Clanless said hoarsely. "I'll keep it occupied while you go after the man."

"You want me to throw you to that thing? It'll eat you alive!"

"I can deal with it," Clanless insisted. He twisted his left arm off Patch's shoulder and gripped his moonblade with both hands.

The half-light over the arena grew a little brighter. Clanless risked a quick glance up to see the sun beginning to emerge from behind the moon.

The creature was almost upon them. "It was nice knowing you!" Patch heaved Clanless forward into the beast's path.

Seeing his prey coming at him, the creature hissed and tried to twist out of the way. Clanless slammed into it. His moonblade carved into the spines on its back, but didn't reach the creature's actual body. His left foot hit the ground momentarily, eliciting a scream from his lips as it collapsed under him again. Clanless rolled against the creature's tail. This close, it smelled of decay and mold. Its flesh appeared to be made up of many tiny scales, but larger armored scutes decorated the underside of its belly and tail.

Before Clanless could do anything else, the tail smacked him back the other direction. His vision blurred for an instant. He struggled to regain his concentration and scrambled to his knees. The creature rushed at him again, mouth wide, horrible teeth dripping saliva as they prepared to descend.

With no other options, Clanless stabbed the moonblade straight forward into the creature's maw. The large blade kept the teeth from getting to him, but the monster's front claws scratched at his arms and chest. It started to pull back. Clanless yanked the blade free, twisting it as he did. The tip tore through the creature's lower jaw, almost severing it completely. The sounds coming from it now weren't so intimidating. It took a few steps back.

His eyes burned as Clanless activated the Taint again.

Except the creature didn't react. It turned back to him and hissed.

The crowd roared at something behind him, but Clanless couldn't take time to see how Patch fared. This creature was still dangerous; he had to put it all the way down. He mentally tried to prepare himself for the approaching pain.

Clanless planted his right foot and lunged forward. He lifted the moonblade high before bringing it down as far as he could reach without help from his left foot. The top curve of the blade slammed down into the beast's head, penetrating into its brain.

With his knees scraped and bleeding, Clanless fought to free his blade from the dying creature. It thrashed around for a moment, dragging him with it. When at last he jerked the weapon loose, the monster gave one final spasm and lay still. Leaning on the moonblade, Clanless turned to see the other fight. His heart sank.

The tall warrior stood a couple dozen yards away, holding Patch in the air with one hand. The spikes at the end of the chain were embedded in Patch's back. The warrior jerked the chain with his other hand, and the spikes came loose with a spurt of blood. He tossed Patch to the side and turned to face Clanless.

Clanless groaned. From the looks of it, Patch hadn't gotten a single hit on his opponent. Clanless couldn't detect any blood at any rate. If the warrior bled, there was a chance. But Clanless couldn't get to him, and with the range of his chain weapon, he had no reason to come close.

Indeed, the warrior smiled, spreading apart a pair of star tattoos around his mouth. He advanced with precise steps, swinging the chain over his head.

Clanless's body didn't want to move. Between the torn ankle and the scratches everywhere, he must have lost a lot of blood already. This fight had lasted longer than any previous arena encounter. And regardless of anything else, his bleeding body created a timer for fighting that could not be exceeded.

"Come closer," he murmured. He pulled himself a few inches forward, dragging his left knee.

"Having fought his way through an entire pack of wolves and a ferocious beast from afar, Clanless now faces against the mystical warrior that already defeated his comrade! Can our badly-wounded hero survive one more fight?" The presenter's voice penetrated his thoughts for once. Clanless gritted his teeth. The crowd was getting quite a show today.

The enemy stopped at least a dozen feet away. His smile grew even larger, if possible. He brought his chain around one more time before launching it forward. To Clanless's confusion, he threw it at his own shoulder height. It had no chance of hitting its target.

And then the enemy spoke, a single-syllable cry from his strange language. The spikes at the end of the chain stopped in mid-air, levitating right above Clanless. A split-second later, he realized his peril and dove to the right. The spikes impaled the sand where he'd been kneeling. The enemy yanked his weapon back and began swinging it again.

Magic! The presenter kept calling this a "mystical" warrior, and he hadn't been exaggerating. The enemy used magic to control his weapon. What other capabilities did it have? How could Clanless defend against it?

Again, the chain shot forward, this time a little lower. Again, the enemy stopped it in mid-air with a shout. Clanless lunged to the side again as it fell. This time, one of the spikes connected with his left calf, piercing deep into the muscle. He couldn't hold back another cry of pain when the warrior jerked the weapon loose.

His two dodges had taken him a couple of feet closer to the enemy warrior, but it wasn't enough. If he got any closer, his opponent had only to take a few steps backward. He had no way of getting to him. Maybe if he caught the chain when it fell again, he could pull the enemy toward him… but he'd have to drop his sword to do that.

Only one other thought came to his mind, an insane thought. If it worked, he had a chance. If it didn't work, he'd be dead. And if this kept up the same way, he'd be dead anyway.

More sunlight bathed the arena as the moon relinquished its hold on the sun.

Once more, he succeeded in dodging the chain weapon. As the blood-rush filled him with a last-ditch burst of energy, Clanless rolled across the sand. He lifted himself as high as he could, using the momentum from his roll to hurl the moonblade at his opponent.

Since Zaluu had purchased the throwing daggers, both he and Clanless had worked on their throwing skill. For Clanless, it meant moving from no skill to at least hitting a target more often than not. But throwing the moonblade? Completely different.

The sword spun through the air. The enemy's eyes widened. He tried to dodge. The moonblade's tip caught his left thigh, cutting a single gash, barely deep enough for him to even feel it. Clanless fell onto his palms.

The enemy warrior laughed. He drew the chain back to him. He took a step closer to Clanless and swung the chain again, still laughing.

Clanless lifted his head, his eyes glowing. "Burn," he growled.

The enemy's laughter stopped. "Aiyoi!" he yelled, reaching for his leg. Then his whole body jerked, muscles twisting in various directions. The chain fell from his hands. He collapsed in the sand, writhing.

Clanless didn't know how long the Taint would keep his opponent down. It hadn't even worked against the monster. He scrambled forward on hands and knees. He seized the moonblade and turned around. The enemy warrior, his fists clenched, started to pull himself up.

Clanless screamed and brought the moonblade down on the warrior's exposed neck. The head and body fell separately back onto the sand.

The crowd screamed louder than ever, followed by a renewed chant of his name. The presenter tried to speak over them, but for once, couldn't get loud enough.

Clanless leaned on his moonblade until even that became too much. Then he too collapsed onto the cool sand.

ᵔ ᵔ ᵔ ᵔ ● ᵔ ᵔ ᵔ ᵔ

"What was that about?" Clanless demanded.

"Hold still!" the healer barked, pouring some of the special blood onto his ravaged ankle.

Clanless ignored him and glared up at Orgina and Badaar. He'd regained consciousness as the attendants helped carry him off the sands. The mistress of the arena had been there waiting and watching with Badaar, Zaluu, and Darghan.

"That was spectacular," Orgina declared. "One of the most legendary fights this arena has ever seen."

Clanless threw his head back and screamed as the healing magic began its work. Every time, he somehow forgot how much the process hurt.

"He had to reveal his power," Badaar said. "Everyone saw it. The crowds will expect it now. And we'll never get away with having him fight anything simple again."

"Exactly." Orgina rubbed her hands together. "Every one of his fights will be an event now. No one would dare miss any of them."

The pain faded enough for Clanless to turn and glare at her. "Patch is dead! How does that help your finances?"

Orgina sighed and waved off the healer. "Bandage the scratches and let them heal normally," she said. "He needs a few more scars." She started toward the hallway but paused halfway there. "Patch was getting too old for this. As cynical as this may sound to you, he was going to end his career sometime soon, regardless of what I did. This way, at least he died as part of a story everyone will be telling for years to come." She continued on, leaving the others to stare after her.

"She has no heart," Darghan muttered.

Clanless let his head fall back onto the stretcher. More than anything, he wanted to let himself fall asleep. But one other fact still troubled him. "What was that magic he used?"

"I've never seen it before," Zaluu said. "He could control his weapon in the air!"

Badaar shook his head. "He wasn't controlling the weapon."

Darghan pointed out at the arena. "He stopped it in the air and made it fall where he wanted!"

"He didn't do that against Patch," Badaar pointed out.

"So?"

"Because he couldn't." Badaar looked out toward the arena. The workers would be removing all the animal bodies by now. "He controlled it after he killed Patch with it… because it had Patch's blood on it." He turned back to face them. "He wasn't controlling the weapon. He was controlling the blood on the weapon."

With his eyes closing, Clanless managed to ask one more question: "Is that… is that one of the clan's blood magics?"

His consciousness faded, but he did hear Badaar's answer: "No. No, it's not."

THIS CAN'T BE TRUE

Then

Orgina was right, of course. The story of how Clanless fought an entire pack of wolves and a lizard monster and a foreign sorcerer spread quickly and did not fade away. Nor did the part of how he had used some form of magic himself. As the story was told and re-told in the weeks to come, the details became less… factual. In every telling, it seemed Clanless's injuries grew worse, and still he fought on. His mysterious power grew in the telling as well. In some versions, fire erupted from his eyes to consume the sorcerer who'd killed his friend. In others, his moonblade glowed with the fire of the sun as it severed the sorcerer's head. Those who had been there and watched the fight tried to explain what they'd actually seen, but many seemed to prefer the exaggerated versions over the facts.

When Clanless returned to the sands three weeks later, the stands were packed. He faced off against three barbarians this time. The battle lasted a good six or seven minutes, but the outcome was never in doubt. Free to use the Taint, Clanless didn't need as much effort to succeed. In fact, he found it freed him up to perform more crowd-pleasing stunts he ordinarily wouldn't risk doing. Between the Taint's guarantee of winning (assuming he could make the enemies bleed), and the skill of the arena's healer to restore any wounds he did suffer, Clanless made every battle a spectator's delight from then on. He never failed to entertain the crowd, though some of them griped that he needed better opponents to truly display his skills.

That became the hardest part for Orgina. She searched farther and wider to find deserving enemies. Every so often, they employed magic in their fighting. Some used healing in the middle of a fight; others used blood that magnified their speed or strength. The strong ones didn't add much to the challenge, but the speedy ones proved more difficult. None ever used the power the foreign sorcerer had employed. Clanless found it curious that none of them combined multiple magics. He never fought anyone with both speed and strength magnified. Yet the Hawk King used many magics, or so the stories told.

As Orgina expected and predicted, Clanless at once became the arena's primary crowd draw. If he wasn't fighting, people wanted to know why. People even tried to demand refunds for their entry fees when they discovered he wouldn't be fighting on a particular Arena Night.

In this way, time passed. Clanless fought hard and kept mostly to himself in between battles. He ventured into the city maybe once every month or two. When he did, he hated the attention his fame brought him. Every so often, some tough guy would challenge him on the street. It never ended well for the challenger.

Orgina purchased new fighters to replace Patch and Allaka. Clanless and Zaluu found themselves in the unfamiliar role of mentors to these younger warriors. Clanless did his part to teach them everything he could, hoping to keep these two alive as long as possible.

He couldn't protect the other arena fighters unless they fought with him. Over time, others died. Each one hurt, even if he didn't know them very well. Clanless spent less and less time with anyone outside of training, except for Zaluu who he couldn't avoid. When he felt the need for conversation, he spoke with Zektel.

Two full years passed, faster than Clanless anticipated. One day, as Low Spring dawned, he realized he would soon be seventeen years old. He'd killed over two hundred men in that time. Like Allaka, he started to keep track, even though he told himself it was pointless. But the numbers stuck in his head.

At the same time, he seemed almost no closer to purchasing his freedom. He saved as much blood as he possibly could, but when he compared it to how much was needed… he despaired.

With all of these realizations filling his head, he went into the city with Zaluu and allowed himself to get thoroughly drunk. The hangover the next morning convinced him not to try that again. Or so he promised himself, anyway.

The arena fights became almost routine. Nothing mattered in his life any more.

He chafed at the approach of High Winter. While he appreciated the break it gave him, he didn't get any closer to freedom when he couldn't fight.

And then, as Low Spring faded, Orgina announced a surprise event, something that had never been done before.

((((●))))

Badaar gathered the arena fighters to explain the news.

"We're going to have a special event before the sun surrenders and High Winter begins. Orgina has pulled off something I don't think has ever been done before in arena history," he announced. "We're going to have visiting fighters from a different arena. The one in Mantukhai."

"To fight against us or with us?" one of the younger fighters asked.

"Both." Badaar shook his head. "This is an enormous risk, but Orgina and the other owner are counting on collecting a lot of blood this time."

"They'll lose a lot too," Zaluu pointed out. "We're going to lose some fighters. Or the other arena will. Or both. Won't that cost more than they'll make on this?"

"They're hoping to make this a regular occasion every year or two, if it works out. Next time, we would go to Mantukhai."

Clanless shook his head. "I don't like it. It's one thing to fight the barbarians and criminals and such. But to fight other arena fighters?"

"I'm pretty sure the fights will be to defeat, not death." Badaar sighed. "But we all know that doesn't guarantee everyone lives."

Zaluu slapped Clanless on the back. "Think of it as being back at training!"

"I hated training." Clanless noticed Zaluu shaking his hand a little; the slap must have hurt his palm. Clanless smiled to himself. Over the past three years, he'd worked his body into solid muscle, even as he shot up several inches. Though still younger than many of the other fighters, he'd grown larger than most.

"Will we know these fighters?" someone else asked.

"Unless you keep track of arena fighting in the rest of the Empire, I wouldn't know," Badaar answered. "I have a hard enough time keeping track of you men."

"What do we need to do to prepare?" asked Durken, the newest and youngest fighter.

"Not much different than what you already do." Badaar held out an open palm to him. "You're probably better prepared than most, having left training the most recently. The rest of these idiots haven't fought against equally-trained opponents in years."

Durken sat back, grinning. Clanless chuckled. Was it so long ago he'd been that fresh from Kan's oversight? How could he be less than eighteen years old and yet feel so ancient?

A young boy hurried up to Badaar, making Clanless feel even older. One of the boys who delivered messages and ran errands around the arena, he whispered something to the trainer and handed him a note. The other fighters had stopped paying attention and talked amongst themselves. Badaar looked over toward him. "Clanless? It's for you." He held out the note.

Clanless got to his feet and approached. He couldn't remember the last time a note had come for him... from Orgina or anywhere else. Gogeku sometimes got a kick out of delivering messages from women asking to marry him, something that happened with all the fighters, but that wouldn't involve a hand-delivered note.

He took the paper and unfolded it. The note came from the proprietor at Dugh's End. At first, his mind didn't grasp the words. It had been so long. And then the impact of it burst into his mind:

"Koland will be returning next week."

((((●))))

Clanless wasn't sure what to think. It had been over two years since Koland left, taking Kekeen with him. Alone in his room, he took out Kekeen's farewell note and re-read it. Had she kept true to these words? Or had her father told her about the other girls? Did she miss him or hate him? He'd been waiting so long for this moment, but now he feared it.

He didn't speak with Zektel about it. He knew what she'd say. Even though she might be right, he didn't want to hear it.

The upcoming sun's surrender event made things more complicated. The fighters from Mantukhai would be arriving any day. Clanless made the decision to visit Dugh's End two days before the event. With his level of fame, he could get away with a mid-week visit. He so rarely went into town, the arena owed him. He took Zaluu and Durken along, both of whom were quite happy to head out for a night, even one as tame as Clanless suggested.

"I can't remember the last time we came here," Zaluu said as they approached the eating house. "It's been months, at least."

"Two years," Clanless answered automatically. He was having second thoughts about this. Maybe he should have come alone. Maybe he shouldn't have come at all. They could still turn around and leave.

"What's so special about this place?" Durken asked. He reached for the door handle.

"If I remember right, Clanless likes the stories and songs," Zaluu said, "and he—oh, right! This was where that one singer was! The one you—"

"Shut your mouth," Clanless said. He caught Durken's arm. "This was a stupid idea. Let's go back."

"What? Why?" Durken sniffed. "The food smells good. And listen!"

Zaluu's smile grew. "It's her, isn't it?" He reached past Durken and pushed the door open.

Someone inside was singing. And Clanless knew the voice. And the song.

"Touching a story,
Grasping a cloud..."

Zaluu shook his head. "You dog. But why bring us? Last time, you kicked me out so you could be alone with her."

"Stupid, stupid, stupid," Clanless muttered.

"Clanless has a girl?" Durken asked. "This I have to see!" He pulled free from Clanless's grasp and entered, followed by Zaluu. Clanless hesitated a moment, called himself "Stupid!" again, and joined them.

"Goddess above!" Durken whispered. "Now I understand."

Clanless ignored him, staring at the stage. Koland sat there, strumming his instrument, looking the same as he always did, except perhaps a few more gray hairs. Kekeen stood beside him, swaying and lifting her hand as she sang. Two years had passed, and she... if anything, she looked more beautiful than ever. While she'd clearly grown older, she still held on to a girlish look in her features. Caught up in her song, she kept her eyes closed. She wore a much more colorful outfit than the last time she'd been here: an outer robe of maroon and blue, with a simple inner dress of maroon. Both were trimmed in gold.

"What a voice," Zaluu whispered. "You sure you want us here, friend?"

"Let's sit down." Clanless threaded his way through the dining hall, eliciting muted comments from the audience. They were surprised or thrilled to see him but didn't want to interrupt the song. He found an open table not too far from the stage. Only one other table separated them; several large men sat there with their backs to Clanless.

"I mean, she's pretty," Durken said in a low voice, "not gorgeous, mind you, but pretty. Still, that voice..."

"Quiet."

The song ended, and Kekeen took a step back, opening her eyes and smiling at the crowd. Clanless leaped to his feet, applauding. Kekeen's eyes widened at the sight of him. She glanced at Koland, who hadn't looked up yet.

"Another!" the crowd chanted.

Koland strummed in response and Kekeen launched into a song everyone else in the house seemed to know. Soon they were all joining her:

"On the day the sun surrendered
I met my love around the bend
In the shadow of the goddess
We pledged our love would never end…" *

Clanless knew he'd heard it before but didn't remember the words. Zaluu sang along beside him, so he moved his mouth, pretending to join in. His eyes remained fixed on Kekeen. He saw hers flicker toward him a few times through the song, thrilling him with each glance.

When at last it ended and the audience applauded again, Kekeen bowed repeatedly until Koland finally stood and waved to everyone. "Friends, friends! Let my daughter rest her voice for a while! Have a seat and enjoy your food. I'll have a new story for you very shortly."

Kekeen made her way past the first table, patting one of the men on the shoulder as she passed. At last, she stood in front of Clanless, who hadn't sat down since the end of her first song.

"You're alive," she said breathlessly. "I'm so glad."

"You came back," he answered.

"You two have such amazing conversations," Zaluu put in. "I'll contribute: the roof is tall. The floor is under our feet. You're both still standing."

Clanless gave him a shove. Kekeen laughed and slid into her seat across from Clanless, who also sat, almost in slow motion. "We just got in earlier today. We were actually on the road with some other arena fighters, from Mantukhai."

"That's right," said a tall man at the first table. "She came with me." Clanless took a sharp intake of breath. He knew that voice.

The man stood and turned around, revealing a narrow face with dark hair and a goatee. That last bit was new, but there could be no doubt. Clanless leapt back to his feet.

"Bain!" He stared at the smiling face in absolute shock. "Shool Baina. I don't… I can't—"

---

* For the musical notation of *On the Day the Sun Surrendered*, see page 439

Bain laughed. "Clanless! You never were one for eloquent speech, were you?"

Clanless pushed his way out, ran past Kekeen, and embraced Bain. His old friend had gotten much taller and broader, as had he. They gripped each other tightly to laughter and murmurs from the crowd.

Bain pulled loose first. "Look at you! Still wearing that old fur, I see!"

"Yes, but you… you're one of the fighters from Mantukhai?"

"I am. And I take it you've been here all this time?"

"Since we graduated. I'm… I do all right. I've survived."

"So I see."

"You two know each other?" Kekeen asked from her seat, bemused.

Clanless turned to her. "Do you remember the first time we met? Years ago? This is Bain, one of my friends from that meeting! We haven't seen each other in, in over three years!"

Kekeen cocked her head. "I remember your friends, a little bit. Which one were you?"

"I was the villain," Bain answered, joining her on the bench, across from Zaluu.

Clanless rolled his eyes. "You were never a villain. And what did you mean that she came here with you?"

Bain shrugged, a light smile still on his face. "We traveled with the same caravan. I was just trying to get a reaction from you."

"Can we be a part of this conversation?" Zaluu asked. "I've only known you for three years, Clanless. Is that enough to be included?"

"Of course, of course. Kekeen, you may remember him—"

"I never forget a cape," she said.

"Bain, this is Zaluu, one of the other fighters here, and that's Durken at the end." The younger one waved.

"Sands," Bain said, looking at Durken. "Were we that young?"

Durken lifted his mug. "Moon's stability to you, old man."

The entire table laughed.

Clanless didn't know what to say or do next. He'd been scared and thrilled to see Kekeen, but to now see Bain as well… his emotions fought in an arena of their own.

Bain apparently recognized the discomfort. "You and I can catch up later at the arena," he promised. "You shouldn't waste time talking with me when she's here." He tilted his head toward Kekeen.

"You don't have to leave on my account," she protested.

Bain got to his feet. "No, no. He and I will have our time together. You should have this." He nodded to the other fighters. "Men. Clanless." He stepped over the bench and rejoined his own comrades.

Kekeen turned back to Clanless. "That was unexpected, I take it."

"Completely." Clanless shook his head. "I never thought I'd see him again… or anyone else from those days."

They stared at each other a moment.

"So."

"So."

"Are you two going to be this eloquent all night?" Zaluu asked. "Am I going to have to carry the entire conversation? Durken, listen. Clanless knows this girl from way back, and I've never seen him—"

"Enough, you." Kekeen wagged a finger at him. "When two people only see each other every year or two, it's awkward at first. You'd know that if you had more friends."

"Owww!" Durken exclaimed. "Can you handle that blow, magnificent one?"

Zaluu laughed. "I'm sure I'll survive, somehow."

Clanless ignored him and leaned across the table. "I'm so sorry about last time. I never got to say goodbye."

"We left all of a sudden," Kekeen answered. "As we usually do." She glanced over her shoulder toward her father.

"I kept your note. And I paid the proprietor to let me know when you came back." To his right, Clanless heard Zaluu go on explaining his life story—with many inaccuracies—to Durken. It melded into the rest of the crowd noise.

"Oh. That's… nice." Kekeen looked down at her hands on the table.

Clanless stared at the top of her head. A narrow braid formed a sort of crown around it, decorated with a series of silver-colored rings. "Um… so… where have you been traveling the past two years? I know a bit more about the rest of the Empire now, thanks to the books I've read."

She looked up with a smile. "So you kept reading?"

"Yes." Clanless nodded. "I've been careful with the chair too."

Kekeen stared at him a moment before it hit her. She threw a hand over her mouth to stifle the explosive laugh. Zaluu paused his story to eye her with raised eyebrows.

Clanless laughed as well, relieved to move past some of the awkwardness. "I've tried to find new books," he added, "but they're hard to come by."

"Try finding some when you're always on the road." She snorted. "We've been just about everywhere, it seems. I told you we just came from Mantukhai, but before that, we went way out to—" She gasped and looked around before leaning closer across the table. "We met the most amazing person! You need to know about him, but I can't tell you right now."

Clanless wrinkled his brow. "What?"

"I'll let my father tell you after the show. He'll do a better job of it, anyway."

"I don't understand."

Koland played a loud string of notes at that moment. "Friends! Allow me to regale you with another story!"

"We'll talk more later," Kekeen promised.

Clanless opened his mouth, but Zaluu leaned in. "Lovers, please. I want to hear the story."

Kekeen giggled and spun to look toward her father. "I'm going to strangle you with your own cape," Clanless promised.

Zaluu mocked horror. "And ruin another good cape? Geku hates how many I go through as it is!"

As Koland began his story, Clanless contented himself with watching Kekeen's back. Just being in her presence again was… he didn't know how to describe it, even to himself. It felt right. So right.

His eyes wandered past her to the next table. Bain. Of all people. He'd survived this long. He'd thrived, in fact, if he'd been selected for this special event. What did he do with his blood? Did he save it for his freedom, or did he spend it all like Zaluu? With Bain, Clanless couldn't guess. He'd always been confusing. Clanless couldn't wait to talk with him more.

But first… Kekeen.

((((●))))

Koland's story lasted longer than usual, or so it seemed to Clanless. Afterward, he called Kekeen up for another song. So it went for the next couple of hours. Clanless couldn't help wondering if Koland were deliberately dragging things out to keep her away from him.

At last, the crowd diminished. Surprisingly, Zaluu and Durken both claimed to be enjoying themselves and wanted to stick around. A few arena followers came and went from the table throughout the evening. After one final story, in which Kekeen assisted her father with some voices, the storyteller proclaimed an end for the evening. A few minutes later, both he and Kekeen joined Clanless at the table. Zaluu moved down a little bit, but stayed well within listening range.

"Aldan. Good to see you're still surviving the arena," Koland greeted him.

"Aldan?" Durken muttered.

"Surviving?" Zaluu put in. "He's the number one fighter in our arena! Everyone loves him!"

"Is this true?" Kekeen asked. Behind her, Bain glanced over his shoulder, clearly interested.

Clanless shrugged. "The arena mistress likes the way I fight. She tries to find new challenges all the time."

"Because you've got power!" Zaluu insisted. "If I hadn't seen it for myself, I'd never have believed it. You—"

"That's enough," Clanless cut him off. "They're not interested in the details of our fights."

"Oh, I don't know," Kekeen said. "I might be."

At once, Zaluu launched into an exaggerated version of Clanless's fight with the foreign magician and his monster. Clanless tried to protest, but Koland shushed him, saying: "You know that I, of all people, enjoy a good story!"

"…Bleeding and near death, Clanless crawled across the sand," Zaluu finally finished, "gathering just enough strength to lift the moonblade one… last… time… and cut off the vile magician's head!"

Koland applauded. "Not bad. If you ever get out of the arena, you might have a new career as a storyteller. You have the flair."

"I do?" Zaluu's eyes and grin widened.

"You shouldn't have told him that." Clanless groaned. "I already have to listen to him too much as it is. Now he'll never stop."

Durken laughed. "As if he'll ever get out of the arena. No one does!"

The table quieted. Kekeen shot a look at her father. "Should we?"

"Not yet. So, Aldan. Still reading?"

The conversation drifted on, moving from his reading to wider events in the Empire itself.

"The barbarians grow ever bolder." Koland shook his head. "It's one of the reasons we traveled back this way. The further we are from them, the better." He glanced around. "Even so, it may not be far enough."

"The Hawk King still worries about Melkute?" Clanless asked.

Koland nodded. "I see you have been paying attention. Yes, he won't send enough soldiers to deal with the barbarians. He's too afraid."

"That's a strong word to use for the Hawk King," Durken put in, eyes narrowed.

"Perhaps you're right," Koland said. He shifted the conversation to food and drink for a few minutes. He regaled them all with descriptions of unusual foods he'd encountered during his travels. Clanless admitted surprise at how much variety could be found without leaving the borders of the Empire.

"The Sar Empire is far more diverse than most people realize." Koland swirled the liquid in his mug. "We are, after all, twelve different clans of people united mostly by the land and its view of the moon."

"View of the moon?" Durken asked. "It's always in the same place!"

"Ah, but it's a different place depending on where you travel," Koland told him. "Here, not too far from the Empire's center, the home of the goddess is directly overhead. But if you travel far enough, it's a little off to the right or left."

Durken wrinkled his brow. "How is that possible? The moon's stability is unchanged throughout time."

Koland held his hand in a fist above the table and rested the other beneath it on the table itself. "Imagine my fist is the moon. You're down here on the table, looking up at it. Now, if you travel this direction…" He moved his other hand a foot away, keeping the fist in the same place. "The moon hasn't moved, but you have. And your view of it is different."

Durken scratched his head. "I still don't get it. When I came here from another city, the moon didn't change."

"You didn't travel very far. It may have seemed far to you, of course, but when you consider the size of this world, it's not much."

"The world is a big place," Zaluu said. "Or so they say."

"If you follow the old stories back far enough, to before the Sar Empire existed," Koland continued, "you'll hear tales of a time when the moon moved much as the sun does, before the first coming of the chaos moon."

"The chaos moon?" Clanless asked. "What's that?"

"You've never heard of Suirel?" Kekeen cocked her head. "The other moon that appears once every thirty years?"

Clanless shook his head.

"My mother used to warn me that Suirel would come for me one day," Zaluu said. "She called him the enemy of the goddess." He paused, then added quietly: "I haven't thought about her in years…"

Clanless had a vague memory of his father saying something about another moon, but even as he thought of it, the memory faded away.

"There are many stranger tales if one ventures far enough back into the past," Koland said.

Durken looked down at his own drink. "I think I've had enough for tonight."

Zaluu got to his feet and stretched. "Come to. I believe it's time to return to our beds, youngster."

Clanless looked around, surprised to discover the rest of the room was empty. He hadn't even noticed when Bain and his companions had left.

Zaluu and Durken made their farewells and departed. Koland took a long drought from his mug and chuckled. "Kekeen, would you mind taking my instrument up to our room? I want to have a few words with Aldan."

Kekeen rolled her eyes. "Be nice," she warned as she got up to do as he asked.

Clanless watched her go for a moment before turning back to Koland, suddenly nervous.

"She won't take very long," Koland said, "so I'll be fast and blunt." He leaned across the table, staring Clanless in the eyes. "I want you to know that I do not object to my daughter's interest in you."

"Oh."

"Despite what happened when we left last time—"

"That was a mistake!" Clanless interrupted. "I didn't—"

Koland held up a hand. "I know what I need to know. I've heard from others what your life is normally like. Here's the thing: some of that doesn't even matter all that much." He looked down and traced a circle on the table with his finger. "If Kekeen weren't thinking about you as much as she does, she would be more susceptible to the advances of other men in every town we visit… and there are a lot of those men." He looked back up. "I would much rather she yearn after you than chase after all those others, especially since"—He glanced up the stairs, seeing Kekeen already coming back—"to be honest, there's so little chance of anything ever coming from it all."

Clanless nodded. "I think I understand. But my one purpose is to win my freedom someday. If that happens…"

"We can all talk about that," Koland said as Kekeen sat back down. "Now that your young and idealistic friend is gone, we can get more serious."

"You're going to tell him about Daviland?" Kekeen's eyes sparkled.

"Why don't you start?"

"Do you remember the story of the boy who saved his clanhold from barbarians?" Kekeen put her hands in front of her on the table while she spoke.

"I don't think so…" But as he thought about it, Clanless could recall them mentioning something about it.

"First, a prophet saved him from a different raid, and then he came back and helped save everyone else!"

Clanless wasn't sure of the point of this. "Makes for a good story for you, doesn't it?" he asked Koland.

"Much more than that, though I will do my part to spread the story. The young man we're talking about is named Daviland—Davil to those close to him—and you, of all people, should pay attention to that name."

"Why?"

"Because the prophet told him something else," Kekeen said. She lowered her voice. "He said Daviland would kill the Hawk King!"

"That would be… something."

"Isn't it exciting?"

"I… don't know. Is it?"

Kekeen reached out and punched at his arm with her fist. It was such a cute gesture. "If he overthrows the Hawk King, everything will change! Slavery, the arena system, all of it!"

"Oh." Clanless hadn't thought about it that way. "I don't… I don't see how that's possible."

"Why not?"

Clanless pointed to the brand on his shoulder. "The priesthood. They have the real power. They control everything, and they support the Hawk King. Killing him won't make a bit of difference. They'll just put someone else in his place."

"It's all connected. You're right about that," Koland agreed. "But killing the Hawk King is only part of it. Daviland wants to tear down the whole corrupt system. That means the priesthood too."

"How would he do that? They control everything. Everything!"

"He can't do it alone, of course. That's one of the reasons to spread his story. He'll have to create a movement, an uprising, a rebellion."

Clanless frowned. "I'd like to believe that, but… I just don't see it. Why would people join such a thing? Fighting back against the priesthood and the Hawk King doesn't end well. I've seen their power."

"Exactly! You're one who knows first-hand their corruption, and what they do to people. In your own way, you're preaching out against them." Koland chuckled. "Isn't that what your arena 'personality' is all about?"

"I guess so. I just never thought other people would take it seriously." He shrugged. "It's a great dream, but…"

"But that's how you can be free!" Kekeen exclaimed. "Without having to fight for years to earn it!"

"What you're talking about will take years, though! To build an army and change the Empire? By the time all that happens, I'll have already bought my freedom."

"But if people like you fight for it now, it could happen sooner."

Kekeen's earnest expression made him hesitate, but he couldn't deny reality. "Kekeen… I'm a slave. I can't fight for anything. Orgina holds my bloodbond. If I step outside what she wants for me in any way, my blood will stop me."

"Will it, though?" Koland asked softly.

Clanless gave him an odd look. "I've seen it happen to others."

"Maybe you'll change your mind if you meet him," Kekeen suggested. "If you could hear how he speaks, instead of me…"

Clanless shook his head. "I don't want to argue with you. But I don't see how I could have any part in this… at least not until I'm free."

"How long do you think that will take?" Koland asked. "At your current progress?"

Clanless knew the answer to that one. "Eight years, if I stay here and keep saving as I have been. Sooner if I somehow can get to the capital."

"And join the Hawk King's fighters?" Koland tapped his beard. "I'm sure it's a way to earn more, but it's also more dangerous, if that's possible. The arena in Et-Baylak is the deadliest in the Empire."

"I can handle it." Clanless paused. "I know that sounds arrogant, but I'm not trying to be. It's almost impossible to defeat me."

"Anyone can be defeated, and you've said this before." Koland smiled. "But I understand your confidence. Your friend earlier certainly portrayed you as unstoppable."

"What is this strange power he talked about?" Kekeen leaned closer. "Do you have magic powers?"

"It's… complicated."

Kekeen's eyes widened even more. "You can trust us, you know."

"If you can't trust an itinerant storyteller and his flighty daughter, who can you trust?" Koland asked. Kekeen slapped his arm.

Clanless sighed. "No one else knows this… except the priests, of course. And Bain knows… some of it." He pulled a platter in front of him and glanced around to make sure no one else had wandered back in. Under his left forearm, he tore off a scab and held it over the platter.

"Ew." Kekeen wrinkled her nose.

"I need blood to show you." Clanless glanced up at her before returning his focus to the platter. He squeezed his forearm to elicit a few more drops of blood. Once he had enough, he pushed the platter across the table between the other two. "Watch the blood," he instructed, licking his lips. Once they both leaned over it, he activated the Taint.

Kekeen gasped when the blood bubbled. She looked up and almost fell off the bench. "Your eyes!"

"Yeah. They glow. I know." Clanless closed them against the burn. Once it faded, he opened them and pointed to the platter. "When I do that to someone else who's bleeding, it runs through their whole body. The pain knocks them out." He shrugged. "So all I really need to do to win a fight is to make someone bleed."

"And that's not very difficult in the arena," Koland said. "I've never seen anything like it."

"It's called the Taint." Clanless couldn't keep the bitterness out of his voice. "It's why they branded me and made me a slave."

"Because you can do this?" Kekeen asked. She reached a finger toward the blood on the platter but pulled it back.

"It makes the blood useless for their sacrifices. They don't like that."

Koland picked up the platter and examined the blood. "I've heard the term 'Taint' before. In some parts of the Empire, it's even used as a curse word. But I've never known what it actually meant." He looked back at Clanless. "I can see why they wouldn't like you."

Clanless looked back and forth between them. "You're not... disgusted?"

"Why would we be?" Kekeen asked. "It's strange, but it's not your fault. Is it?"

"No. It just happened to me. They said it shows up in our clan every so often. It's apparently a punishment from the goddess."

"That doesn't make much sense," Koland observed.

"That's what I said! Why punish someone with something that damages her own sacrifices?"

"And when you use this in the arena, doesn't that make the priests angry as well?"

Clanless nodded. "I try not to use it, unless I have to. I'm... pretty good without it. And nigh unstoppable with it."

Koland tapped his beard again. "Keep this up, and I do believe you will make it to the capital." He stood and stretched. "But this is enough for me. We older people need our sleep, you know. I have stories to tell tomorrow."

"Good night, Father," Kekeen said with a little wave.

Koland chuckled. "All right. You can stay here." He pointed at Clanless. "But don't take her out of this room."

"Yes, sir."

Koland waved to them both and headed up the stairs. Clanless watched him go. When he turned to face Kekeen, he found her smiling at him. "What now?"

She glanced around. "This bench isn't the most comfortable place. Let's go sit on the stage."

"All right." Clanless followed her, unsure of himself now. This reunion had gone better than he'd expected in many ways, but even so, being alone with Kekeen was… He didn't know how to describe it. Thrilling, yes, but also frightening, if he was honest with himself.

She sat on the edge of the stage and indicated for him to sit beside her. As he settled in, she touched his bicep. "I don't think I've ever seen anyone our age with muscles this big."

"I, uh, spend most of my time training."

She wrapped both her hands around it. Her touch was surprisingly cool… and gentle.

"You lead such a sad life. Always training. Fighting. Killing."

"It's not so sad. Every once in a while, some light shines in." He put his own hand over hers. She pushed it free and entwined her fingers with his.

"Such a sweet thing to say."

He tried to smile. "When I'm with you, I… somehow things just come out of my mouth, and I don't know where they came from."

Kekeen slid her left hand over to his chest, pushing aside the fur pelt, and patted over his heart. "From here, of course."

Clanless swallowed. He opened his mouth, but this time, the words didn't come out.

Kekeen took her hand away from his chest, but continued to hold his other hand. "Why do you wear that fur, anyway? I'm sure it helps during winter, but doesn't it get warm in the spring?"

"It was given to me by an older… fighter. Back when I finished my training."

She ran her hand along the fur. "It's so soft. Do you keep it to remember him?"

"I guess. He was kind to me when I didn't expect it." Clanless thought back to Nukai. "And I wonder about who he really was."

Kekeen let go of his hand and reached for her sleeve. She pulled out the familiar scarf Clanless had given her almost four years earlier. "Then it's somewhat like why I keep this thing."

The edges were frayed and discolored, but the embroidered image remained as clear—and poorly done—as ever. A pang erupted in his chest at the memory of carrying rocks for the back wall.

"I can't believe you kept it," he said. "Do you… do you still pray for me?"

"Every time I see it."

"Maybe it helps. I mean, things really changed for me when I got the moonblade. Maybe there's a connection." Clanless leaned back with both hands on the stage behind him.

"Maybe the goddess does care about you."

"Or maybe she just cares about you and listens to what you ask."

Kekeen tried to give him a shove, but it didn't work. Their weight difference was too great. "Stop demeaning yourself!"

"I'm a slave, Kekeen. No god or goddess cares about me, and very few people do."

"You're becoming famous, though! People do care!"

He shrugged. "Only until my next fight. If I ever lose one, my popularity will go down dramatically. People only care because they like the story, or the 'personality,' as Orgina calls it."

"And what about me?"

"You? I… I don't really understand why you care, to be honest. I assumed it's because you feel sorry for me."

Kekeen's mouth dropped. Clanless regretted what he said immediately. "I'm sorry. Those words shouldn't have come out. I don't… I mean…"

Kekeen caught hold of the fur pelt and leaned across him. Before he could stammer anything else, she planted her lips on his. He didn't know how to respond, but… it felt good. He tried to open his lips a little wider as she pressed against him. As pleasant as it was, a twinge of fear swept over him as well.

Kekeen pulled loose. "Was that your first kiss?"

"I… yes."

She giggled. "I could tell."

"Not your first, then?"

"I kissed a boy some years back, but it didn't really count. I—"

Clanless caught hold of her and leaned in to kiss her himself. From this angle, under his control, all fears vanished. He pressed harder, and she responded, letting herself go almost limp in his arms, letting him control the closeness of her body. She reached both hands up around his neck, running fingers up through his hair.

When they broke apart this time, Clanless sat back, gasping for air. "I'm… that was amazing!"

"Does it seem like I'm just feeling sorry for you?" Her eyes twinkled.

Clanless snorted and lowered his head with a smile. No. No, it didn't. "You're different."

"Different how?"

He waved toward the front door. "Out there, on the streets, girls will throw themselves at me if I let them."

Her eyebrows went up.

"But I don't let them!" he added hastily. "My point is: they only like me for my arena personality. It's a twist on my real life, but it's still fake. And that's what they like."

Kekeen squeezed his bicep again. "I don't think that's all they like."

Clanless ran a hand through his hair. "But you... you haven't even seen me fight. And you know more about me, the real me. And you still... um..."

"Like you?"

He nodded.

"I like you for who you are, Aldan. I liked you before you got this... big. Remember?"

Clanless laughed.

"So I guess the only question left is: do you like me?"

He stared at her in astonishment. "How could I not like you? You're amazing!"

"Amazing. That's a good start. Keep going." She put her hands around his arm again, holding it this time.

"You're kind and loving and beautiful and, and your voice... I don't have the right words." He paused. "If there is a goddess, I'm sure her voice can't be any sweeter than yours."

Kekeen leaned in and kissed him again. "Those were the right kind of words. You did just fine."

Even as he reveled in her nearness, Clanless felt doubts creeping in. "But..."

She cocked her head. "But what?"

He sighed and looked down. "This can't be. I'm a slave. Worse than that, I'm a clanless slave. You... you can't like me. It isn't right."

"Isn't that my choice?" Her voice grew firmer.

"It's just... I know I said I can win any fight, but... anything can happen in the arena. I might die this week. And, and even if I keep going, it's going to be years before I'm free. Many years. I can't ask you to wait that long for me."

"Maybe I want to wait." Her eyebrows narrowed and she let go of his arm.

Clanless groaned. "The priests said I can never marry or have children, even if I do get free."

"All the more reason for you to support Daviland!" Kekeen exclaimed, straightening up. "He'll change all of that!"

Clanless stared at her. "You're willing to… wait years and years for me, on the slim hope that things will be different by then?"

She folded her arms. "I'm stubborn."

He wanted to say more, to tell her other reasons why she shouldn't like him or wait for him. But staring into her face, it all melted away. "This is crazy," was the only thing he could manage to say. Wild hopes leaped up inside of him. Maybe it was possible. Maybe Zektel was wrong. Maybe he and Kekeen could be together someday. "What if we ran away? Away from the priests, away from the whole Sar Empire!"

"Now?" Her eyebrows went up again.

"No, the bloodbond would stop me now. But when I'm free. I mean," he stammered, "if this Daviland isn't ready yet or something happens to him. Maybe we could go somewhere else, where it doesn't matter what clan anyone is from." He paused. "I don't even know what clan you come from."

"Does it matter?"

"No." He jumped to his feet and pulled her up with him. "But somewhere else! Like Melkute, maybe. Or some island somewhere."

"Anything is possible with love!" Kekeen exclaimed.

Clanless stared into her eyes. "Love?"

Her eyes darted away a moment. "I guess… I guess we didn't use that word yet, did we?"

He opened his mouth, about to use the word himself, but Kekeen rushed on: "Let's pretend for a moment. If you'd met me back where you grew up"—she displayed the scarf—"in the clanhold, what would you do?"

"I would… make an arrangement with your father. And, and then I'd build us a house next to my own father's place. Once it was done, we could be married."

"You'd have to build a whole house?"

"Not a whole house. It's kind of an attachment."

Kekeen giggled. "Maybe you can still build me a house someday." She patted his arms. "I think you're strong enough. Just make sure it has a good back wall, right?"

"The strongest." Clanless smiled. He pulled her to him, and they kissed again.

"Go find a room or something!" a voice called.

They both turned to see the proprietor holding a lantern. He waved them away. "You can find a better place for this. Go on."

Clanless laughed. "I should get back to the arena before sunrise." He glanced at the darkness outside. "It can't be far now."

"When will you come back?" Kekeen asked.

He considered for a moment. "It's two days until Arena Night. I should be able to come after that."

"I'll be here."

He kissed her one last time. "I think I'm getting better at this."

Kekeen touched his lips with a finger. "You're not bad at all, hero."

"Good night… or morning, I suppose." He pulled himself away from her reluctantly and headed to the door. He paused and glanced back. Kekeen stood on the stage, smiling, hands clasped in front of her. He wished he could keep that image in his mind forever.

Clanless stepped outside and looked up at the constant moon. "Maybe you aren't so bad after all," he murmured.

CLEVER, CLEVER

Then

Clanless climbed into his bed, still thinking of Kekeen standing on the stage, and their thoughts for the future. Zektel would disapprove. She'd tell him he was distracted, but that made no sense. The other fighters spent time with women—many women!—and they could still fight. Why couldn't he spend a little time with one particular woman and still be a great arena fighter?

"Don't you even think of going to sleep yet!" Zaluu's voice was punctuated by the sudden unveiling of a lantern.

Clanless blinked and lifted his hand to block the light. "What are you doing?"

"You just now got back? Something happened." Zaluu set the lantern on their table. "Tell me all about it. All about her. And don't try to tell me she was teaching you more about reading." He rubbed his hands together. "Come to. I want details."

For the briefest of moments, Clanless considered making up something to satisfy Zaluu's prurient interest. It wouldn't be hard; Zaluu gave plenty of descriptions himself of some of his weekly escapades with women. But he immediately rejected the idea. It wouldn't be right to do that, not to Kekeen.

"We… talked."

"You talked?" Zaluu rolled his eyes. "And then?"

"We kissed."

"Now we're getting somewhere. And then?"

Clanless shrugged. "And then I came back."

Zaluu put his hand over his face and shook his head. "No, no, no, no, no. You can't tell me that. You can't say you were out alone with this woman you adore for hours and all you did was talk and kiss. I can't believe it."

"Believe what you want." Clanless closed his eyes. "It doesn't change what happened."

Zaluu gave out the most exaggerated sigh he'd ever heard. "Clanless, my friend, you are quite possibly the only virgin arena fighter in the entire Sar Empire. Something is not right here. You've avoided all the other girls for this one, and all you've done so far is kiss her?"

"I'm a slave, Zaluu."

"So am I! What difference does that make?"

"Kekeen is special. I'm not going to... to put a child inside her while I'm stuck here for years to come."

"There are ways to avoid that, you know."

"She's special," Clanless repeated, opening his eyes. "She's... worth waiting for."

Zaluu bounced off his own bed and paced across the room. "Are you saying you're going to wait until you've won your freedom?"

"Maybe. She'll wait for me."

Zaluu shook his head, hair flying. "Oh no, no, no. She says that now, but... two years from now? Three years? That girl? As pretty as she is? As she gets older and the men keep coming after her?" He pulled one of the chairs away from the table and sat backwards in it, facing Clanless and his bed. "Our lives don't work that way, my friend."

Clanless rolled over to face Zaluu. "Stop. Just stop. I had a wonderful night, and I won't let you ruin it."

Zaluu held up his hands. "All right. Whatever you say. Just keep my words in the back of your head there, because you'll remember them someday." He got up. "You'll say to yourself, 'You know, that Zaluu was not only magnificent, he was right about everything.' And then you'll smile because I left such a great impression on your life."

Clanless threw his pillow. Zaluu caught it and tossed it back. "You'll see." He walked to the lamp but paused before turning it out. "By the way, Badaar wants to see us all right after breakfast to talk about the visiting fighters. So you've got maybe two hours to sleep. If you skip breakfast."

Clanless groaned.

((((●))))

Badaar waited until all of Orgina's fighters were assembled in the entrance to the arena. Clanless rolled his eyes when Zaluu showed up last.

"You may have noticed the guests at breakfast a few minutes ago," Badaar began. Clanless, true to Zaluu's suggestion, had skipped breakfast. "Our visiting fighters are here. They're staying on the other side of the arena."

"You mean where we keep the other animals?" one fighter asked.

"Very funny. But it gets to my point: these are our guests." Badaar didn't normally address all of them at once, and it showed. He shifted his weight repeatedly. "I don't want any fighting until you're actually in the arena facing each other. Got it?"

The fighters murmured their agreement along with some grumbling. Clanless didn't understand those who didn't like the rule. Why bother fighting with each other outside the arena?

"They'll be doing some training at the same time we do," Badaar went on. "And eating in the same place, obviously. So try to behave like civilized men. That's all I ask."

Shool Baina was here in the arena now. Clanless considered going to look for him but decided they'd run into each other soon enough.

He wasn't wrong. An hour later, while working out on the sands, a voice came from behind: "So that's the famous moonblade, is it?"

Clanless smiled and turned to see Bain. His old friend stood at ease, wearing a leather vest and holding a pair of spiked maces. "How have you heard about my weapon all the way in Mantukhai?"

"I make it my point to know about things." Bain set his maces aside and held out his hands. "May I?"

Clanless turned the moonblade and extended the hilt to him. Bain took it and examined the weapon. His eyes ran over its entire length. "I've never seen a finer sword. Orgina must have spent a fortune in blood on this."

"I have no idea."

"Of course you don't." Bain took a few swings with the blade. "It's extraordinary. Not only is it exquisitely designed, but the weight and balance are amazing. And considering how many fights you've already won with it, we know it's durable as well."

Clanless walked over and picked up one of Bain's maces. "These are fine as well." He touched one of the spikes with his forefinger. "Do the priests complain about bloodshed from these?"

Bain shrugged. "They grumble. But I give them so much as it is, they don't make too much fuss over it."

"You've done well then? I know nothing about the arenas outside of this one."

Bain appeared to be testing the edge of the moonblade against a corner of his leather vest. "I do well enough," he answered. "The crowds enjoy my work."

"You already know about me." Clanless set the mace down. "Have you heard anything about any of the others? Jik maybe?"

"No." Bain lifted the moonblade and stared down its edge. He smiled before returning it to Clanless. "Don't let me deceive you. I only know about you here because of this event. Our arena master told us all about you and the others here so we could prepare."

"Then you have an advantage. We haven't been told anything about you."

"Different styles of leadership. My master is all about knowledge and preparation. Yours is all about personality and showmanship. Guess who draws the largest crowds?"

"Ha!" Clanless swung the moonblade onto his shoulder. "It's... so good to see you, Bain."

Bain touched his own forehead with a finger and pointed it back at him. "You as well. In our... circumstances, we don't get opportunities like this very often, do we?"

"No." Clanless looked around the arena, noting some of the other visitors practicing. He didn't see any of them interacting with his people. "I guess it's pretty rare."

Bain cocked his head. "Why are you still wearing that fur, by the way? I know High Winter is almost here, but surely Orgina can afford something new for you."

"Nukai gave it to me just before the graduation fight. He said I honored him, somehow. I didn't really understand it." Clanless ran his own hand through the fur. "But it's... comforting, I guess, to remember him with it." Hadn't he just had this conversation with Kekeen?

"You still don't know who Nukai was, do you?"

"Orgina suggested he used to be a big arena fighter himself, called the Wolf?"

"Something like that." Bain shook his head. "Ah, Clanless. You're always so ignorant of the people around you." He gestured toward the doors. "Did you even know you have a former Hero of the Empire here?"

Clanless looked in the direction of his gesture. "What?"

"Never mind." Bain picked up his maces again. "Speaking of old friends, you've reconnected with that singer, have you? Is it serious?"

Clanless couldn't stop the smile that spread across his face. "We're... close. She was here—in town—once before, a couple years ago. We got to spend some time together then."

"I see." Bain gave him a knowing nod. "Congratulations to you. Relationships are not something arena fighters are known to specialize in."

"Someday, I'll be free, and things will be different."

Bain nodded and looked around. He took a step closer. "And your... other friend? The red one?"

Clanless narrowed his eyebrows. "I still talk with her."

"Of course you do." Bain scratched his head. "I've heard you've done a lot of reading lately. Have you read anything about the blood-wraiths?"

Clanless frowned. Why would his reading be a part of the report about his arena career? "No, I haven't seen anything about... that subject."

"If I survive tomorrow night, I'll see if I can find a book for you."

"Survive? Are you that worried about this fight?"

"I am now."

"What do you mean?"

Bain gestured with his chin. Clanless turned to see Badaar approach them. "Ho, Clanless. Getting to know your opponent for tomorrow?"

"My opponent?"

"I'm the champion fighter of Mantukhai," Bain said. "We'll be fighting each other in the main event."

⟨⟨⟨⟨●⟩⟩⟩⟩

"I can't kill Bain!"

Clanless paced his bedroom, thankful that Zaluu was elsewhere this hour. He'd summoned Zektel as soon as he'd been able to find a spare moment.

"Is the fight to the death?" the blood-wraith asked.

"Maybe. Maybe not." Clanless waved a hand as he paced. "They don't always tell us until the last minute."

"You can easily defeat him without killing him, as you've proven many times," she said soothingly. "You're worrying for nothing."

"I wasn't supposed to ever fight anyone I know! I don't... I don't know if I can do it. Not now, anyway."

"Why not now?" Zektel's face shifted in the blood. "What's different about now?"

"Never mind." Clanless hadn't told her about Kekeen and didn't intend to. She claimed to be with him always. If so, she already knew, and there was no need. But if not… maybe she wasn't completely honest with him after all. Maybe Bain had a point about her.

"Clever, clever Shool Baina." Zektel chuckled. "He's cast more doubt in your mind about me, hasn't he? And in doing so, he's given you more thoughts to distract you from the actual fight. He's fighting you already, you know."

Clanless paused. "You're saying he doesn't have a problem fighting me."

"Not like you do, no. Dearheart, why do you think he wanted to see your weapon? He was evaluating its capabilities. And he's been evaluating yours ever since he arrived. He's planning a way to beat you."

"He can't beat me… can he?"

"You're not invincible, no matter what your record may show."

Clanless resumed pacing. "He knows about the Taint. I'm pretty sure he knows how it works. He even knows about you!"

"Since he knows about all of your advantages, there's no reason not to use them all. Let me be with you in the fight."

"You've mentioned that before. How would that work?"

"Remember the vial Shool Baina stole from the priest? It's larger than your currency vials. Fill it with blood and wear it around your neck. Use your power before you enter the arena. Then I can speak to you during the fight. I'm always with you, but I can't speak without your help."

Clanless hesitated. He'd resisted the suggestion before, thinking Zektel's voice in his head would be too much of a distraction. But in this particular case, it might be what he needed to sharpen his focus. Left to his own thoughts, he might hesitate to strike down Bain at a key moment.

He crossed the room to his personal chest and searched until he found the blood vial. Attaching a chain to wear around his neck would be easy enough. "All right," he said. "We'll do it. I still won't kill him, but maybe we won't have to."

"Let's hope not. Then you'd have to explain it to your girlfriend. She might not like you as much."

Clanless shot a look at the blood-wraith. She arched her eyebrows and pretended not to be watching him. So she did know about Kekeen.

"In your greatest moments and your darkest hours, dear Aldan… I will be there."

The blood image collapsed in itself and faded away, a moment before the door opened to admit Zaluu.

Clanless struggled with the concept of fighting Bain for the rest of the day and into the next. But when the time came, he arrived at the arena door, geared up and ready.

"Not to death, unless you have no choice," Badaar told him. Clanless nodded, casting a quick glance at the graying trainer. Was Badaar the Hero of the Empire Bain had mentioned? He couldn't think of any other candidate that made sense.

Durken limped out of the arena, bloodied and battered. His fight with one of the lower-ranked visitors had gone longer than anyone expected, leaving both of them in dire straits. But Durken had managed to stay on his feet the longest.

Badaar hastened to get him to the healer while Clanless stepped up to the door. Somewhere across those sands, his former classmate waited. It wasn't as though Bain had been a good friend; he even denied wanting to be such a thing. But he was as close to a long-term friend as Clanless might ever meet over time, someone who'd known him before and knew him now. Aside from Kekeen, not many others fell into that category.

He grasped the vial with his free hand and activated the Taint. Almost immediately, he heard Zektel's voice in his head: "Here we go. You can do this."

"I beat him during training," Clanless murmured.

"Yes, dear, but remember what Kan said: Shool Baina could have been the top of the class if he wanted to."

He was also the only one to give Clanless a serious wound during training. Before he could obsess over that, the signal came for him to enter the arena.

"And now it's time for the main event," the presenter boomed, "the biggest fight ever seen in this arena! The champion of Ghoyor, the greatest fighter we've seen here in ages, the incomparable bearer of the mighty moonblade... Clanless!"

He lifted the weapon as he walked across the sands. The crowd roared their approval of the favorite. He turned in a circle, letting their praise wash over him. He gave only a quick glance at the moon. The sun would surrender almost completely to it in an hour or two, heralding the coming of High Winter.

"He's deceptive," Zektel warned. "He'll try to appear one way, but be something different, remember?"

"All I have to do is cut him."

The presenter's voice echoed again: "And facing him today is none other than the champion of Mantukhai, the fighter you can never count out, the undefeated and unique… Bain!"

From the far side, Bain emerged, lifting one of his spiked maces into the air. A not-insignificant part of the crowd cheered for him as well, evidence both of visitors from elsewhere and locals who were gambling against Clanless yet again, hoping to beat the odds.

"What is he wearing?" Zektel asked.

Clanless squinted against the sunlight as Bain approached. His former comrade appeared to be clad entirely in leather armor, like the vest he'd worn the day before. The outfit had been designed to allow him free range of movement, not restricting his joints, but to also hide every bit of his body. Only his eyes showed through a narrow gap in a leather-wrapped helmet obscuring everything else.

"Clever!" Clanless called to him as they drew close enough to begin circling.

"Is that your word or hers?" Bain shouted back. "I seem to recall your blood-wraith calling me that."

"My words are my own!"

"Careful," Zektel said. "He's trying to agitate you. If you're angry, you're more likely to make mistakes."

"It is clever," Clanless muttered. The leather would make it impossible to score a quick and easy scratch. It wouldn't protect Bain from a serious blow of the moonblade, but it meant Clanless would have to get in close to deliver such a blow. In that kind of fight, Bain had an advantage with his twin weapons and long arms.

"Skills, Aldan. You have the skills. You've fought worse than this. You can do it." Zektel kept encouraging him as the fighters drew closer to each other.

The presenter babbled on far above their heads, but Clanless ignored him as usual. The roar of the crowd grew dim as well. None of it mattered right now. Nothing mattered but beating that man over there. His identity no longer mattered.

"I lied yesterday," Bain said as he spun his two maces. "I did find out about Jik. Do you want to know?"

Clanless didn't answer. He kept his circling pace steady, moving ever closer.

"He only made it a couple of months past graduation. He's dead, Aldan."

"Ignore him," Zektel said. "The only words he'll speak are designed to distract or anger you. You can't trust any of them."

"You know the sad part of it all?" Bain went on. "He didn't even die in the arena. He got sick. He died in bed. Isn't that the most pathetic thing you've ever heard?"

Clanless gritted his teeth. He wouldn't believe it. And it didn't matter if he did. Only the fight mattered.

The crowd grew restless, as they often did when combatants took their time. A few jeers trickled down.

"Give them time, citizens," the presenter said. "These two are the best of the best. Neither is going down easy."

Bain ran forward a few feet before skidding to a stop at an angle. His foot threw sand in the air. Clanless squinted to protect his eyes and picked up his own pace. They were only a few feet away from each other now.

"You know who is doing well? Amazingly so?" Bain kept talking. "Yeltek. He's undefeated. Can you believe it? There's some talk that his arena master might sell him to a more prestigious spot. Maybe he'll turn up here."

Clanless made a short feint with the moonblade, if only to get Bain to shut his mouth and react. His opponent sidestepped, but didn't overreact. He made a swift backhand swing with his left mace. Clanless stepped to his left to avoid the blow, but kept his eyes on the second mace, expecting a follow-up. Bain didn't disappoint, swinging the right mace with a backhand stroke as well. Clanless swung the moonblade up into the stroke, hoping to damage the mace's handle. The blade clanked harmlessly off some of the spikes instead. Bain had pulled it back too fast.

"He does move well," Zektel observed. "If he's trying to be deceptive about his capabilities here, then they must be very impressive."

Clanless thought the same. Back at Kan's, Bain would usually start a fight with lazy footwork and movements, designed to draw his opponent into a false sense of superiority. Today, he showed none of that. Either Zektel was right, or he'd decided such a tactic wouldn't be effective this time.

Clanless dodged another blow. He ducked low and swept the moonblade out at knee-level, letting one hand go to get a longer reach with the full blade. Bain skipped over it like a child with a jumping rope.

"You don't fight at all like you used to," Bain said.

"Nor do you," Clanless answered.

"Makes sense, of course. We're not the same people we were then." Bain swept a blow upward to force Clanless a step back. He spun with a leap and brought the other mace straight down. Clanless caught that one with the side of the moonblade. The crowd roared. "That one played well with the common people," Bain added.

"How can he keep talking so much while he fights?" Zektel wondered.

"He's always been good at that," Clanless muttered.

"You're talking to her, aren't you?" Bain exclaimed. "You're talking to the blood-wraith!"

Clanless responded with one of his own fastest moves, feinting one way and spinning the moonblade in the other. This time, he connected with Bain's hip. But the blade failed to cut all the way through the leather armor.

Bain grunted. "Good one. You've probably taken out any number of fighters with that move." He responded with a whirling series of attacks that put Clanless on the defensive. He dodged and parried as fast as he could, but Bain got one blow past him. One of the mace's spikes carved a gash across Clanless's left shoulder.

"There's some blood!" Bain danced back almost in a rhythm with the crowd noise. "Now you can... oh, wait. It has to be my blood, doesn't it?"

Clanless growled. The bloodrush pounded in his ears. He went on his own offensive whirlwind, determined to show Bain exactly why he'd become this arena's champion, regardless of the Taint. Bain put his own maces to effective use parrying most of the attacks. Once again, Clanless got through, but once again the blade only cut a short gash in the leather armor.

"It's called the Taint, isn't it?" Bain asked. "I talked with a priest about it. It turns out they know all about it. What a fascinating story that makes. They're terrified of you, you know."

Bain swept both maces in unison around and down in a dual attack. It would have smashed Clanless to the ground, had he not held the moonblade sideways to catch both maces above his head. He glared at Bain's eyes through the leather helmet.

"I don't think you understand just how much they want you dead," Bain said. "We're not supposed to kill each other here, but..." He jerked the maces back. Clanless stumbled forward ever so slightly. But it was enough for Bain to take advantage. He thrust one mace forward, under the moonblade. The top spike stabbed into Clanless's chest on the right near his lowest rib. Clanless roared and yanked himself free, blood spurting.

"They offered me my freedom if I kill you."

The words penetrated into his mind like no others so far. Here he'd been working so hard, training so hard, every day of his life for years now. And the priests offered his greatest desire—freedom—to Bain? For killing him? Rage and bitterness erupted inside.

"Careful," Zektel said. "Remember: he's a liar."

But the words rang true. Of course they still wanted him dead. They hated him. He knew they were watching; the visit from the Daghilch two years ago had shown that. How frustrating it must be to them that he wouldn't die!

"I'm sorry," Clanless said aloud. "As much as I would love to purchase your freedom, my death is too high a price."

"I almost believe you," Bain answered.

The stab in his chest hurt, but didn't seem too dangerous. The two combatants exchanged several more blows, none of which connected.

"You have to do something about that armor," Zektel said.

"I'm trying," Clanless growled.

"You can't cut through it without multiple blows in the same place. Unless you can do that, I'd suggest looking for somewhere you can tear a piece off."

Clanless knew exactly where to do it. Only one spot had enough leather hanging free where he could get his blade beneath and tear it loose: Bain's helmet. But to get to it would take significant risk.

He waited for Bain to make the first move. He needed to keep ready for either mace; Bain wielded the right and left equally. Clanless knew he'd been right-handed back during their training. He must have worked very hard over the past three years to dual-wield as he did. This time, the left mace came first, swinging in an upward arc. Clanless spun into it, shoving the left arm away. He pivoted and dropped to his knees. He swung the moonblade straight up with both hands, keeping it horizontal to the ground. It caught the lower edges of Bain's leather helmet and tore it from his head.

But at the same time, Bain swung his right mace down. The impact of the moonblade slowed his strike, but it still connected with Clanless's left thigh. The bone didn't break all the way through, but the pain told him it at least cracked. Two of the spikes tore into his skin. As Bain staggered back, they ripped new holes in the leg.

"He's vulnerable now!" Zektel cried. "Go for the head!"

Clanless struggled to get back to his feet. His left leg threatened to buckle on him at any moment. Blood poured from his thigh, his chest, and his shoulder. Soon, he'd start feeling the effects of its loss.

"Heads are sacred"—Kan's words from their training resounded through his mind as he stared at Bain's face. He'd fought against this man dozens of times during training. They'd never gone for each other's head then. Could he do it now?

"Well done," Bain said, spitting to the side. "I'm almost starting to believe what they say about you in the taverns and eating houses around here."

Clanless stepped to the left to show that his leg injury wasn't impeding him. He barely kept the pain from his face. He would not be able to make many more steps like that.

"The reach," Zektel said. "Use your long reach!"

Clanless feinted left and right three or four times, and pretended to lose his grip in the last movement. As expected, Bain took a step closer. Clanless swung the moonblade out at its full length, holding it only by the very end of the handle. The swing was intended to come up and catch Bain on the chin. But as he stepped forward for his own attack, Bain leaned too far. He tried to turn at the last moment. The tip of the moonblade gouged into his right cheek and across his eye.

The shouts from the crowd drowned out the presenter's screaming voice.

Bain staggered back, blood pouring from his face and his ruined eye. He held the back of his wrist against the eye. "Finish it!" he snarled.

"The Taint!" Zektel cried. "Use the Taint!"

Clanless stared in horror at his former friend. For a moment, he couldn't move. Couldn't think. Couldn't react.

"The Taint!"

Clanless took a step forward, forgetting everything else. His left thigh gave out on him and he stumbled.

"Nyaarghh!" Bain leaped forward in what would have been a suicidal attack in any other circumstance. He swung both maces over his head, bringing them down at Clanless as he fell to his knees.

Clanless threw his moonblade up to try to block the attacks. In the same instant, his eyes burned as the Taint activated—without any conscious thought of his own! Bain screamed anew as his maces came down.

One mace struck his hand wrapped around the moonblade's handle, shattering all the bones in his fingers. The other hit the moonblade itself, driving it down. The edge cut deep across his forehead, tearing a strip of skin and hair free.

With a final burst of energy, Clanless threw Bain to the right. He rolled, shaking with the pain of the Taint igniting the blood throughout his body. "Cheat... to beat... me..." he managed to snarl. The maces fell from his hands and he lay still.

Clanless used the moonblade to pull himself up on his right leg. Blood cascaded into both his eyes, obscuring his view of the crowd. But the sound told him all. He'd won. He'd crippled his friend. But he'd won.

It would be within his rights to take some of Bain's blood with the Siphon. But even if he could have managed it, he didn't want to. He would not feel proud about this fight at all.

To her credit, Zektel said nothing more.

As the bloodrush faded, the pain of his injuries rushed in. He wavered and almost fell, just before one of the attendants arrived to support him.

Clanless limped from the arena, victorious but heartsick.

SALKHI

Now

Salkhi rolled over on the bed. "How long have we been doing this, Clanless?"

Clanless stirred out of his reverie. He'd been thinking about the Ghamba Lam's visit. He shifted in the padded chair he'd sat in almost as much as the chairs in his own room. "Two years, give or take," he answered.

"That means you've come to Pasque House almost a hundred times," she mused. "And every time, this is what happens."

He smiled and leaned forward. "We've had a good arrangement, a good relationship."

"Relationship? Is that what you call it?" Salkhi laughed.

Clanless wrinkled his brow. "We're friends, aren't we?"

Salkhi shrugged. "I guess so. I do enjoy your visits. I just never thought of it as a relationship. I would think a relationship involves more than… this."

"I do think of you as my friend. And I hope you'll still be my friend after tomorrow."

"Will you still come to see me?"

Clanless got up and walked over to the bed. Salkhi got up on her knees to face him. "If I could buy your freedom tomorrow also, I would," he said. He took her hand and squeezed it.

Her smile only reached half her face. "You probably would, wouldn't you?" She shook her head. "It's not for me, Clanless. I'm stuck here until no one wants me any more, or one of the clients kills me." He opened his mouth to answer, but she held her other hand up and went on: "And you're avoiding my question. Will you still come to see me after tomorrow?"

"I… I don't know. I don't think I will. But not because of you!" He wanted to look away, but her wide eyes kept him there. "I don't want to stay in this city, Salkhi. I want to be truly free, away from all of this, away from the Hawk King."

Her gaze dropped. "And you'll find your singer and run away with her, I suppose."

"I don't know. I don't know if, if she still wants that."

She released his hand and sat back on the bed, still looking down. "I always had this hope that… no, I shouldn't say it."

Clanless sat on the edge of the bed. "Say what?"

Salkhi shook her head.

"Tell me," he said. "It might be the last time I see you."

She looked up again. Clanless was shocked to see a tear trickling down her face. "I held out hope that if something ever happened—not that I wanted it to!—between you and her, that you'd finally see me as, as an alternative." She sucked in a deep breath. "There. I said it. Stupid, stupid, stupid. But I said it."

"Salkhi…" Clanless reached out and wiped the tear away. Before he could react, she threw herself at him and kissed him. He almost jerked away, but stopped himself. He wrapped his arms around her and returned the kiss. He was gentle; she was passionate. At last, he pulled free. "You haven't done that in a long time," he said with a chuckle.

She wiped her mouth with the back of her hand. "I've wanted to."

An ache formed inside Clanless's chest. "I don't know what to say. I care about you, Salkhi, but…"

"But you don't love me. I know." She leaned back on the pile of pillows at the end of the bed. "It's not too late to really enjoy your last time here."

"We've talked about this… I can't." He straightened up. "I should probably go."

"Not yet. Please." She hugged herself. "I'm sorry. I'm sorry for pressing you. You really are my friend, you know. One of the only real friends I have." She snorted. "Definitely the only male friend, at any rate."

"You'll have friends once you get out of this place." He glanced around the opulent room. "Have you saved the blood I've given you? Your freedom can't possibly cost as much as mine does."

"Why? Because I'm just a whore and not a champion arena fighter?"

"Arena fighters do cost more…"

She threw a pillow at him. "I'm teasing. You'd think you'd have figured that much out after two years!"

He picked the pillow up from the floor. "I've never been good at understanding women."

"Ah, so you're an ordinary male. Right."

"Ha. But now you're the one avoiding the question." Clanless tossed the pillow back onto the bed.

She shrugged. "I've saved as much as I can, what I can keep hidden. It's nowhere near enough."

"Keep trying. I'll send more when I can." He took a deep breath. "I won't forget you, Salkhi."

"I want to say that I know you won't," she said, sliding off the bed. "But I don't know that. You may run away, like you said, and forget all about me, despite your intentions. And if you're trying to get away from the Hawk King, you'll be too far away to send me anything."

Clanless found himself at a loss for words. He had no real experience in saying goodbye to anyone. He'd been taken from his home without warning, taken from training without seeing the other boys. The less he thought about Ghoyor, the better, though he'd been taken from there as well. Here at last, he was leaving somewhere of his own free will… and there were consequences.

"I don't know how to do this," he said as he realized it himself.

"What do you mean?" Salkhi stepped close to him.

"I don't know how to say goodbye. I've never done it before. I've never… been allowed to."

"You say goodbye to me every time you leave this room."

"But this is different. You're right. I may never see you again. I probably won't." His face twisted in consternation. He'd said goodbye to Kekeen twice, but… not quite the same. She'd left him. Now he was the one doing the leaving.

Salkhi placed her palm against his chest. He tried not to flinch. "That's life, Clanless. We meet other people, and they become part of our lives. And then things happen, and they're gone. Or we are. That doesn't mean they're not still a part of us, that they didn't leave an impact on our lives." She looked into his eyes. "We do. You've made a difference in my life, and that will always be true."

"You've… left an impact on me too," he whispered.

She smiled. "That's all I can hope for, I guess." She stood on her tiptoes and gave him one more quick kiss. "That's another way to say goodbye, you know."

He swallowed. "Goodbye, Salkhi."

"Goodbye, Clanless."

He turned away, almost in slow motion. Salkhi's hand slid down his chest and fell loose. He opened the door and walked out. In the hall, he paused and looked back. She stood where he'd left her, looking more vulnerable and sad than he'd ever seen. He almost went back in.

"There you are!" Sugh called from down the hall. "Let's go, Clanless! The night is still young!"

He tore his eyes from Salkhi and hurried to join his friends. He wiped a tear from his own eye as he arrived in the lobby. If they saw, Hagh and Sugh pretended not to notice.

THE RESCUE

Then

"I need to know!" Clanless insisted.

"Why?" Zaluu asked. "You beat him. What else matters?"

"He was my friend." Clanless fell back on his bed. The healer had worked hard to restore all of his injuries, but that didn't mean everything didn't hurt. He'd rarely suffered so much in a fight. Even with the healing, he'd be limping for a week, at least. And his left hand would need even longer before he could wield the moonblade effectively.

"I'll check around, see if anyone knows," Zaluu said. "But it looked pretty bad." He shook his head. "The healing magic doesn't always work so well with eyes."

He got up and headed for the door. "Orgina is thrilled, by the way. She sent Geku down to praise you, but you were screaming your head off at the healer."

"I don't care." Clanless closed his eyes. The door thumped as Zaluu left.

Clanless ran his fingers across the top of his forehead. While the healing magic had restored his torn skin, it couldn't regrow his hair. He'd look very odd until it grew back on its own. He should probably shave it all off to be consistent.

"Why?" he muttered. "Why did he force me into that? It could have been simple. We could have made a big show of it, scored a few minor wounds on each other, and then I'd finish him off with the Taint."

He knew the answer, of course. Shool Baina, despite Kan's assessment of his motivations, didn't lose unless he could gain from it. In this case, he'd been fighting for his own freedom. Clanless couldn't fault him for that.

What happened if they had to fight again? If another event like this took place? What if Orgina worked something out with a different city, and he had to fight Jik? Bain said he was dead, but… Bain said a lot of things. Suddenly, the prospect of fighting until he won his freedom didn't seem as easy as it had a week before.

He slammed his fist down on the bed beneath him. No. No need to get this frustrated. Some parts of his life were still good. Or at least one part: Kekeen. He could see her again tomorrow, once he'd fully recovered. He should send her a message to let her know… but surely his fight would be the talk of the city. She'd know already.

After about an hour, Zaluu returned with news that the other fighters had already departed. "Besides your fight, we beat them in almost every match," he said. "Their master wasn't at all happy and headed out as soon as he could. Can't blame him, really. We took them apart. I hear Orgina is absolutely beside herself with joy. Not to mention all the people who wagered on us."

Clanless groaned. "What would it take to send a message to someone in Mantukhai?" he wondered.

"It's possible." Zaluu plopped down on his own bed. "But it'll cost you. A lot."

"How much is a lot?"

"You know how you don't want to spend all your earnings on nights out, like I do? Think of about three of my nights out, and you might cover it."

Clanless thought about it for a while. Was it worth delaying his freedom by three weeks' worth earnings just to send an apology to Bain? He wavered over competing desires for several minutes. "No," he said at last. "He knows. He knows me."

"Whatever you say," Zaluu said. "But think about this: your friend showed everyone a possible way to beat you. I'll be surprised if you ever fight another opponent who's not wearing armor."

Clanless grimaced. He hadn't thought of that.

Zaluu woke him late, with the sun's pursuit well begun. Clanless roused himself, groaning at the soreness from his various wounds. His left hand, especially, didn't want to do anything.

"How late is it?" he asked.

"You already missed breakfast." Zaluu changed into his training gear while he spoke. "But I would have let you sleep on, except for the disturbance."

"What disturbance?"

"Oh, there's a girl at the gates, asking for you. The guards haven't been able to get her to leave. Different from the usual, you know. I mean, there's always girls showing up, hoping to snag one of us."

Clanless jumped to his feet. "Is it Kekeen?"

Zaluu paused in adjusting his shirt. "How should I know her name?"

"The singer! From the eating house!"

"Oh, her!" Zaluu shrugged. "I haven't been to the gates myself, so I don't know."

Clanless growled a bunch of unconnected syllables and raced out of the room. It took only a couple of minutes to make his way to the front gates of the arena. Pushing past the guard on duty, he saw Kekeen pacing back and forth outside. He rushed to meet her.

Seeing him, she gasped and threw herself into his arms. While he welcomed the embrace, he couldn't help noticing her red eyes and disheveled appearance. "What is it? What's wrong?" he demanded.

Kekeen's breath came in halting gasps as she tried to speak. "They-they took him! They took my father!"

"Who? Who took him? Why?"

Clanless glanced at the guard before guiding Kekeen out of earshot. Between her sobs and attempts to recover her composure, she managed to tell him the basics: a group of men had stormed into their room during the night and seized Koland. They told Kekeen he owed them a large debt. If she wanted to see him again, she'd bring payment this evening to an address on the other side of the city. Otherwise, they'd sell her father into slavery.

"But it's a lie!" she insisted. "He doesn't have any debts here! He would have told me about it, if he did."

Clanless didn't answer that. He knew all too well how family members could keep secrets from each other. Maybe Koland had debts, and maybe he didn't. Either way, there appeared to be only one conclusion.

"I'm guessing you don't have the payment yourself."

Kekeen shook her head. "N-no. We rarely have much of anything. The eating house hasn't paid us yet for the past week."

Clanless tried to think. He could see only one solution, and he didn't like it.

"What was the debt amount again?"

"Forty-seven vials."

He winced. He had more than enough, of course, but it would set him back months on his quest for freedom. He swallowed, still conscious of Kekeen holding on to him. He couldn't let her down.

"I—" He stammered and started over: "I can bring the payment tonight. I'll do it."

Kekeen looked up at him, hope in her eyes. "But, but that's for your freedom."

"It'll still be for freedom, just... just not mine. I'll take care of everything."

"No. No, I'm going with you!" Kekeen pushed against his chest. He winced when she hit the sore spot from yesterday's fight.

"I can't put you in danger." He looked around. "I'd take you inside right now, if I could. But women aren't allowed in our rooms."

Kekeen managed a chuckle. "For good reason."

"Do you have somewhere else you can go? Somewhere safe?"

She hugged herself. "I don't know. I can go back to Dugh's End. I don't think they would come after me in front of everyone there... would they?"

Clanless looked back at the guard watching them. "I can't leave without special permission. We're already allowed to go out tonight..." He wavered. "I hate to send you back alone, but if I come with you now and get in trouble, I won't be able to come tonight. Argh." He ran his hand along the hairless spot on the top of his head.

Kekeen noticed it at last. "What happened there?" She reached up to touch the bare spot.

"I was injured in the fight yesterday. The healing magic doesn't bring back hair." He took a step toward the guard, then stepped back. "I don't... I don't know what to do."

Kekeen took a deep breath. "I think... now that you're here and I've calmed down some... I think I'll be safe. They want their payment, right? Coming after me before the deadline tonight won't get it for them. It wouldn't make sense."

"You're probably right. Still..."

She embraced him again and kissed his cheek. "Go back inside, Aldan. Thank you. Knowing I can count on you makes everything better." She pulled away. "I'll see you tonight?"

He nodded. "I'll come find you first."

((((●))))

Clanless fretted throughout the rest of the day. Multiple times, he considered paying one of the arena attendants to go to Dugh's End and watch over Kekeen. His training was sloppy, earning grumbling from Badaar and derision from some of the other fighters.

When the sun approached the end of its daily retreat, he changed clothes and pulled out a bag full of blood vials. He sorted through it quickly, making sure he had enough to pay for Koland's release. It would be a setback for his freedom, but he couldn't worry about that now.

Zaluu entered the room and paused. "What are you doing with all of that? Counting your savings?"

"I need it," Clanless said. He closed his chest and stood up, slinging the bag over his shoulder.

"For what? You begrudge spending a single vial on your favorite flatbread."

"It's… it's a situation. I have to help." Clanless started for the door.

Zaluu put a hand on his chest. "Wait. If there's a problem, tell me. I'm your friend, Clanless. One of the only ones you've got. Let me help."

He hesitated.

"You've been upset all day. People noticed. Whatever it is, brother, let me be a part of it. You don't have to do this alone."

Clanless didn't know what to say. "I… I'm not used to anyone helping me."

Zaluu smiled. "Hey, it's in my best interests. If I ever get into trouble, there's no one I'd want watching my back more than the champion arena fighter of Ghoyor! Now tell me: what's going on?"

Clanless sank into one of their chairs and lowered the bag. In a few sentences, he outlined the problem. Zaluu listened, but his frown grew throughout the story.

"You barely know these people," he pointed out. "And you're willing to give up that much for them?"

"Kekeen means everything to me. I can't stand by while she or her father are in trouble."

"Right, right." Zaluu picked up his cape and swept it over his shoulders. "Then I guess we have our work cut out for us tonight. I've got an idea."

Five minutes later, Clanless hurried alone to Dugh's End. Kekeen was watching for him through the front window and rushed out to meet him. She threw herself into his arms. "This was the longest day in history!"

"I know. I know." He patted her back. At any other time, he would have been thrilled with the embrace. Worry put an unfortunate damper on the moment. Pulling apart, he shook the bag. "I've got the payment. Let's go."

Together, they walked the streets. Kekeen knew as much, if not more, about the city's layout than Clanless did. His few excursions had not taken him far, especially not into the area they ventured into this night. There were no eating houses of any kind in the region. Most of the buildings were ramshackle or shoddily built or both.

"Why do people live like this?" Clanless wondered.

"They can't afford anything better," Kekeen said, glancing at him. "I guess you don't know much about life outside the arena."

"Except the clanhold." He eyed another building that looked as though it might fall over at any moment. "But if this area is so poor, why would the lenders want to meet here? If they're in the business of loaning money to people, I would think they would be living somewhere nicer."

"I… I don't know."

Even the street itself suffered, Clanless noted. If wagons came through here, they'd have a hard time not breaking a wheel on the uneven rocks. Why even have a street if it wasn't maintained?

The sun had almost completed its retreat, and light glowed from only a handful of windows. Kekeen shrank a little closer. Clanless kept his head high and eyes alert. Even here, people should recognize him, shouldn't they? He wished he'd been allowed to bring the moonblade along. Weapons couldn't leave the arena. Custom-made weapons doubly so.

The address they'd been given looked no different from any of the other decrepit houses around it. Clanless kept Kekeen behind him while he knocked on the door.

Almost immediately, someone unfastened a latch, and the door opened. A scruffy, thin man with a ragged beard looked out at them. He held a dim lantern in one hand and a mace in the other. "Who are you?"

"We're here for my father," Kekeen answered. "We have the payment for his debt."

Clanless shook the bag again, letting the crystal vials clink together. The man's eyes darted to it, but then back at Clanless. He considered for a moment, then stepped back. "Right. Come in then."

Clanless took a single step then paused. "Why do we need to come in? I have the payment. Why not bring Koland out to us?"

"I'm not in charge. You want to pay the bard's price? You gotta come in."

Clanless narrowed his eyes. He took a quick look in all directions. He saw only one other person sauntering down the street, a few houses away. With a nod at Kekeen, Clanless ducked his head and entered the house.

The fetid air inside took his breath away, and a noxious odor assaulted his nose. The street outside hadn't been pleasant to smell, but this was something else. Clanless tightened his grip on the bag.

The man who'd opened the door walked past them and set the lantern down on a crude table. Another man sat behind it, chair leaned back against the wall. In the dim light, Clanless couldn't make out much of anything about him save for some rough facial hair.

"What's all this, girlie? Do you have my payment?" His voice sounded strained, as if he'd suffered a throat injury and could barely get the words out.

"I have it," Clanless answered, again shaking the bag. "Where's Koland?"

The man behind the table knocked on the wall behind him. A door opened and two more men entered, dragging a third between them. The first man held up the lantern so Clanless and Kekeen could see the prisoner's identity. Dark bruises covered most of Koland's face, but he smiled broadly on seeing his daughter. "Kekeen!"

"Father!" She started forward, but Clanless put out a hand to stop her. Four men now, all of them in front of him. He didn't want Kekeen getting between them if anything happened.

"Let's see the blood," said the man at the table, apparently the leader

Clanless stepped up and dumped the contents of his bag on the table. Sealed crystal vials containing precious blood cascaded across the rough surface. The leader looked it over and sorted through a few. "It's not enough," he declared.

Clanless leaned on the table and picked up one of the vials. "Look closer. It's all there. The exact amount you asked for."

"That was last night's price. Tonight's is higher."

"It's not about—" Koland tried to say before one of his captors punched him in the stomach.

Clanless narrowed his eyes. "You would be wise to accept this payment and let us go. Do you know who I am?"

"We know exactly who you are!" The man got to his feet, pushing the chair aside. He put his hands on the table as well and faced Clanless. "You don't have your fancy moonblade here to help you out now."

The door flew open with a bang. Zaluu stood in the opening, adjusting his cape. "Why would he need the moonblade when he has me?"

"What?" asked one of the other men.

Clanless slammed the crystal vial down on the leader's hand. The sharp edges cut into his own palm, mingling his blood with the vial and that of the leader.

At the same moment, Zaluu whipped out his throwing knives and let both of them fly across the room at Koland's captors. The one on the right struck deep into the captor's shoulder. The one on the left barely grazed his forearm.

"Eh, close enough," Zaluu said. "Clanless, do your thing!"

"You threaten my friends, and this is what happens!" Clanless snarled. He activated the Taint. The leader and both of Koland's captors screamed and collapsed, flailing about as their blood burned.

"Aldan!" Kekeen shouted.

He spun around to find the fourth enemy, the one who'd let them in. He'd grabbed Kekeen and held a knife against her neck. "All this time, I thought that was fake." He laughed. "Guess you really do have some magic going on."

"Let her go." Clanless took a step toward them.

"Or what? You hadn't cut me!" he growled.

Kekeen's eyes met Clanless's. She slowly lifted her free hand, fingers curled. He smiled.

"The payment's on the table, friend. I suggest you let us go."

Koland stepped over his fallen captors. "They don't want your payment, Aldan."

"What do they want?"

"We want you!" the enemy said. He pointed the knife at Clanless for a moment. "You give yourself up, and your girl here can go free!"

Kekeen's hand darted up. Her fingernails scratched across her captor's cheek.

"Oh, look," Clanless said. "You're bleeding."

The enemy's eyes widened a split second before Clanless's eyes glowed. He fell with his comrades, almost dragging Kekeen down with him. Zaluu caught her arm and pulled her free. She tore loose from him and ran to her father.

"Let's get out of here," Clanless said. "I don't like this neighborhood."

"Might want to gather up your blood there," Zaluu suggested, pointing at the table. "I'll get my knives."

Clanless scooped the crystal vials back into the bag and followed the others out. He paused a moment at the doorway. It would be easy to pick up the fallen dagger and cut the throats of these men. They deserved it for what they'd done. But killing here instead of the arena would be a different thing. He had a feeling the bloodbond would know if he did something like that. He growled and slammed the door behind him.

"I think we can all agree that I'm the hero tonight," Zaluu announced from the middle of the street.

Clanless grabbed his cape and pulled him close. "Zaluu. Thank you," he said, embracing his friend.

"All right, all right. No need to get all emotional about it." Zaluu pulled loose and bowed to Kekeen. "Of course, you're welcome to get emotional, my lady. In fact, I insist upon it."

Kekeen giggled and gave him a quick hug before returning to her father's side.

Clanless turned to Koland. "Are you all right?"

"What, this?" Koland gestured at his face. "I've had worse. They didn't hurt my throat or fingers, and that's all I need."

"We should go," Clanless said, glancing back. "They won't stay down."

"We could make sure they do," Zaluu said.

"No. Let's go."

Together, the four of them hurried down the street. Once they returned to the more populated area of the city, Zaluu bid them all goodnight. "I have other diversions to seek out this night," he declared with a bow. "I'll be sure to spread the story of how I single-handedly saved three people from slavers this night. Not that I'll name any names, mind you. But a good story of my own heroism always does well with the company I seek."

"Thank you again," Clanless said. "If you ever need—"

Zaluu waved him off. "I'm sure you'd do the same for me. See you back home, brother." He swept his cape around him and sauntered away, humming a bit of The Day the Sun Surrendered.

A few minutes later, they reached Dugh's End. Koland led the way around to the rear entrance to avoid the current crowd indoors. "Let's gather our things," he said to his daughter as they entered. "We can't stay here tonight."

Kekeen turned to Clanless. "I'll send word when we've found a new place," she promised.

"No." Koland shook his head. "We can't. We'll be leaving this city tomorrow morning."

A sudden tightness grew in his chest. He opened his mouth to answer, but Kekeen beat him to it: "What? No, Father! We can't leave just because of those men! If—"

"Didn't you hear them?" Koland interrupted. "They weren't after money, Kekeen. I don't have any debts, least of all to men like that." He pointed at Clanless. "They were after him. It was all a trap for him."

Kekeen put her hand over her mouth. "But… but why?"

"The priests." Clanless spit out the words. "They hate me. They want me dead. They offered Bain his freedom to kill me. And now this."

Koland chuckled. "If the entire priesthood were out to kill you, you would not be standing here now."

"I don't understand."

Koland pointed at the bag of crystal vials Clanless held. "The priesthood controls the economy of the Empire, Aldan. A single man, especially a slave, would not live another day if they wanted him dead. Not all of them. Now, it's possible that some want to kill you, a radical group that hates the Taint—or is terrified of it! But it's not all of the priests."

Clanless supposed that made sense. It matched with what the Daghilch had said, though he didn't trust the man.

"All the more reason not to leave!" Kekeen exclaimed. "If they're after him, maybe they won't bother us any more."

"We can't be sure of that. We've made them very angry tonight, without question. They may want revenge."

"No!" Kekeen caught hold of Clanless's arm. "I don't want to go!"

Clanless closed his eyes. The tightness in his chest grew stronger, turning into actual pain. He knew what he should do, but he didn't want to. Everything inside screamed at him to keep his mouth shut. He sucked in a deep breath and opened his eyes. He took Kekeen's hand from his arm and held it. "Your father's right." The words almost destroyed him.

Kekeen looked up into his face. "No…" she pleaded. "We were just… just starting."

"I know. Sands, I know." He closed his eyes again to avoid hers. "I don't want you to go. But I don't want you hurt either. And I'd do anything to keep you safe."

"Look at me!" she insisted. He opened his eyes and let her search his with her own. Those deep brown eyes, now welling up with moisture… he'd never forget them. "I love you," she whispered.

"And I you. That's why you have to go." He glanced at Koland. "I can't protect you outside of the arena, and you can't come in. So you're not safe. And, and I want you safe. And alive." He touched her face with his other hand. "And beautiful."

Kekeen finally closed her own eyes, squeezing two tears free. "I'll wait for you."

"You don't have to. You shouldn't."

She opened her eyes and glared at him. "Don't you say that now! I said I'd wait for you, and I will!"

"I, I don't want you to. I want you to be with someone you can love without danger. Without having to wait for years and years. I want you to be happy now."

She stared into his eyes again. "Liar," she whispered.

"We should go," Koland put in. "As you said, those men won't stay down."

Kekeen pulled herself against Clanless. "We'll go back to Daviland!" she said fiercely. "We'll find a way to help him overthrow the Hawk King and the priests! Then you'll be free!"

He tried to smile for her. "You're free, Kekeen. Freer than I'll ever be. Enjoy your life. Don't… don't ruin it for me."

She wrenched free of his grasp, grabbed his head and kissed him. This kiss was harder and fiercer than the ones they'd exchanged only a couple of days earlier. When she broke free, she hissed into his ear: "It is my life, and I'll spend it however I want! Loving whoever I want! And I want you!"

Kekeen whirled and ran up the stairs. A part of Aldan's heart ripped free and ran with her.

Koland put out his hand. Clanless took it without words. "You're a good man, Aldan."

Clanless watched Kekeen's feet disappear up the stairs. "But am I a kind man? I don't think that was very kind."

Koland hesitated. "It was kind in the long run. I don't know if I'll ever see you again, but…" He shrugged. "Only the goddess knows." He turned to follow his daughter.

Clanless shuffled out into the dining area, loud and busy with the evening crowd. The proprietor emerged from the kitchen, carrying a tray of food. Clanless reached into his bag, withdrew two vials, and handed them to the man.

"The storyteller is leaving again. Same arrangement as before, please."

Clanless pushed past the crowds into the street, in no mood for the adoring and curious populace. He needed something to hit. Hard.

BARBARIANS

Clanless fought invisible enemies on the darkened sands under the cold moon. He imagined the shadowy faces of the men who'd taken Koland, the men who'd destroyed the only good thing in his life. He ripped them apart with the moonblade time and time again. The imagery became so vivid, he almost believed he'd actually killed one of them. He pushed himself harder, leaping and swinging his sword in enormous arcs, falling to a crouch and stabbing down into the sand, returning to his full height with an upward slash…

"I thought I'd find you here."

Clanless stopped, his chest heaving with heavy breaths. He wiped the sweat from his brow and turned to face the voice. "Zaluu. I didn't expect to see you again tonight." Something was different; it took him a moment to realize: "Where's your cape?"

"I took it off when I went back. I needed more stealth for the second time."

"You went back?" Clanless wrinkled his brow. "Why?"

"Come with me." Zaluu beckoned and set out across the sand. Clanless slung the moonblade onto his shoulder and followed. To his surprise, Zaluu led the way not to the usual exit, but across the arena to the opposite side.

"I don't know if I've ever been over here," Clanless observed.

"There's usually no reason for us." Zaluu's answers were much more subdued than usual, nothing like his usual boisterousness. He opened the door and gestured for Clanless to precede him.

The entry tunnel had been cleaned up for the visiting fighters, but it still held evidence of previous neglect. Unidentifiable stains dotted the floor and even the walls in places. Some might be blood, but animals also came through here. Clanless wrinkled his nose; an unpleasant smell lingered.

Zaluu led the way further down the passage, ignoring multiple doors leading aside. The further they went, the more decrepit their surroundings. They'd entered a part of the arena rarely used, from the looks of it, and thus rarely cleaned or repaired. At last, Zaluu stopped and opened a black door that let out an enormous creak. Clanless looked past him at a set of narrow steps, leading down. Zaluu took a torch from the wall and lit it before starting his descent. Clanless glanced around and followed.

"When I got back to that garbage place, those fools were just recovering from your attack," Zaluu said as they descended. "It wasn't hard at all to do what I wanted."

"What was that?"

"Here." Zaluu lifted the torch higher as they reached the bottom of the stairs. They entered a small room where another torch already blazed on the far wall. A man hung by his hands from the ceiling in the middle of the room, his feet dangling a few inches from the floor. A shorter man who stood before him turned as they entered.

"Badaar?" Clanless exclaimed. "Did you tell him?"

The trainer pointed at the man hanging from the ceiling. "Zaluu brought this one to me. A plot against one of my fighters is my business, Clanless."

Clanless looked past him to the hanging man. This was one of the men who'd taken Koland? He didn't look familiar, but the room had been very dark. And this man had been beaten even more than Koland; a combination of bruises covered his entire face. Blood trickled from the remains of his nose. Clanless could taste it.

"You heard them," Zaluu said. "They weren't after your storyteller friend. They were after you." He looked at Badaar. "Has he said anything yet?"

"Very little," Badaar answered. "Mostly just cursing us."

Clanless swung the moonblade down and took a step closer. He'd been imagining cutting these men apart, and now one of them hung helpless before him. Part of him was ready to end this one now. "Why have you brought him here?" he asked.

"To get answers," Badaar said. He turned back to the prisoner. "All right, you. Talk to us now. Why were you after Clanless?"

The prisoner spat at him. "Mooncalf!"

"Looks like he needs more persuading," Zaluu said.

Clanless stepped closer. "I'll do it." He reached up and wiped blood from the prisoner's nose. He held up his finger with the blood in front of his eyes. "Remember what happened back at your place?" His eyes glowed.

The prisoner screamed as the Taint raced through his body. Badaar took a step back, having never seen Clanless's power up close. The prisoner's head slumped, unconscious.

"How's he supposed to talk now?" Zaluu asked.

Clanless slapped the prisoner across the cheek. "We wake him back up. And if he doesn't answer, I'll burn him again."

Badaar picked up a bucket of dirty water and threw it in the prisoner's face. He coughed and spluttered and blinked a few times. "You want that again?" Badaar asked him. "Tell me why you're after Clanless, or I'll let him use his magic again."

"Suirel will destroy you all!"

Clanless took a step back. "Suirel?"

"The chaos moon," Badaar answered. He wiped sweat from his brow. "No idea what that has to do with anything."

Clanless activated the Taint again.

"Wait until we ask another question at least!" Zaluu gave him a shove.

"I'm in no hurry." Clanless watched the prisoner shake.

"We're not here for you to enjoy yourself," Badaar said. "We're here to get information." He woke the prisoner again. "Talk to me, son. Clanless can do this all day."

"We-we were hired to-to kill him," the prisoner managed to stammer. Repeated exposure to the Taint appeared to have affected his tongue. Had he bit it?

"Kill him? Not capture him? Why? Who hired you?"

Clanless pushed Badaar aside. He put the top edge of the moonblade against the prisoner's neck. "You will tell me who wants me dead, or your body will be hanging here without a head."

"Dag… Daghilch."

Clanless staggered back. The Daghilch? Again? Why? It made no sense. He'd said he wanted Clanless to survive, to do something for the goddess someday. Why would he hire killers, when he said he'd persuaded the other priests not to do it?

"This complicates things," Badaar said in a low voice. "Even if we knew which Daghilch ordered this, we couldn't move against him. The priesthood would never allow it. We'd all be cursed."

"I know which one it is," Clanless said. "I've met him." Assuming he was right; it could be a different one. Maybe.

Badaar shook his head. "How do we guard against the most powerful group in the Empire?"

"They have no power over me," Clanless answered. "Not any more. I can handle it."

Zaluu pointed at the prisoner. "What do we do with him now? Cut his throat?"

"I told you the truth!" the prisoner protested. "Let me go!"

"We're always in need of new opponents for our regular fighters," Badaar said to him. "You win a fight against one of them, and you're free."

"That's... I'll never survive!"

"He's giving you a chance," Zaluu said. "Your fate is in your own hands now." He glanced at Clanless. "As long as you aren't fighting him, of course."

"Let's go." Clanless headed for the stairs. As he took the first step, he activated the Taint one more time. The prisoner's screams followed him up the passage.

⊂⊂⊂⊂●⊃⊃⊃⊃

Badaar made discreet enquiries into the movements of any Daghilchs or other upper level priests, but discovered nothing of consequence. Clanless returned to his usual practice of rarely leaving the arena. He didn't fear the priests, but neither did he want to endanger anyone else. He focused on winning fights, earning his blood, and trying to learn about the rest of the Empire.

Months passed. Getting news of the outside world within the arena was a haphazard thing. Clanless pestered Zaluu, Badaar, and anyone else he could find about events in the greater Empire. He had little hope of seeing Kekeen again unless something amazing happened... such as the overthrow of the Hawk King.

But such a prospect did not seem at all likely. Rumors of the heroism of Daviland did continue to trickle down to Ghoyor, but little more. One story claimed he'd fled to the hills with a band of followers, planning to build an army and return. Variations of this one had him joining up with a barbarian tribe or even the legendary beastmen.

Barbarian incursions did continue to be a real thing. No one questioned that the barbarians were growing bolder, unchecked by the Hawk King's army. No one knew how many clanholds had been attacked, but everyone knew it must be a lot. And then refugees began showing up at Ghoyor, claiming the barbarians had attacked and actually sacked one of the Empire's smaller cities! The Hawk King could not sit silent now; he dispatched a large military force into the hills to punish the barbarians for their effrontery. No one could say how well the excursion worked, but the barbarian raids did seem to stop for a time.

Throughout the months, Clanless heard nothing from Kekeen and Koland. They did not return to Ghoyor. And he had no way of reaching out to them, even if he'd known what to say.

Yet somehow, the time flew. Looking back, he remembered very few details of this time period. Everything blurred together in pain and waiting.

He continued to win fight after fight, remaining Orgina's champion and number one crowd pleaser. His battles may not have always been challenging, but he adapted and learned how to make them appear more difficult than they were. He only made one request during this time: a team-up with Zaluu.

The schedule pitted them against a band of six brigands at once. Zaluu finally got to use his throwing knives in the arena. The two of them made short work of the brigands, much to the crowd's delight. Seeing this, Orgina made sure they were allowed to fight together at least once every month or two.

Clanless took Zektel into the arena with him on numerous occasions: when he wanted her advice with a particularly strange opponent, or when he simply wanted more time to talk with her. His friendship with Zaluu had become the strongest he'd ever known, and he got along well enough with the other fighters and Badaar. But only Zektel truly knew him. He felt safe talking with her.

In this way, three more years passed. Three long years filled with fights, wounds, rest, and boredom (especially during the High Winter breaks). Clanless grew tired of it all, despairing of ever reaching his goal. It still seemed years away.

And then the barbarians returned.

It began with the repair work. During the High Winter break, Orgina begrudgingly authorized long-overdue repairs to the far side of the arena. It was the only time of the year when such repairs could be made, when fights weren't happening, but workers demanded higher pay during the cold days of the Sun's Surrender. It was an expensive task, one put off far too long.

Almost the entire area had to be completely torn out. Clanless and the other fighters, during their shortened daily training times, often stopped to watch the work. Their view from the sands now extended beyond the arena, through the area below the stands, all the way to the exterior wall. Until he saw dim sunlight coming through a hole large enough to climb through, Clanless hadn't remembered that the arena's exterior wall on that side was also part of the city's main wall. The winter wind pushed itself in, discouraging even limited training time.

A few days into the repair work, Clanless and Zaluu were returning from the evening meal when Gogeku pushed past them in a mad dash down the hallway. Zaluu caught hold of the back of his shirt. "Whoa there, Geku. What's the rush?"

"Let go of me, brute!" The little man tore free and kept moving. "Barbarians!" he called back. "Barbarians are at the gates of the city!"

"Here?" Zaluu scratched his head. "We're too far from their territory. Why would they come here?"

"Maybe because no one would expect it," Clanless suggested. "They're not idiots, you know. Their tactics have shown great intelligence over the past few years. Ever since they had to fight and run from the Hawk King's forces, they've gotten even more—"

"Yes, yes, you're well-read," Zaluu interrupted. "Fine. If the barbarians truly are here, what would they do? This city is huge! Nothing like what they've attacked in the past."

"If they're at the gates, it's probably not to attack there," Clanless mused as they resumed walking. "It's the traditional place to attack a city, but for that very reason, it's often the most well fortified. They've probably shown up there just for show, as a distraction or intimidation."

"Distract from what?"

"From their real attack, at a weaker or more accessible place in the wall…"

They both stopped and stared at each other. "Here," Clanless said. "They're coming here."

"Goddess preserve us."

"Find an attendant! Send him to the captain of the guard! He needs to know!" Clanless sprinted down the hall.

"Where are you going?"

"To build a back wall!"

As he ran through the sleeping quarters, Clanless banged on every door, yelling at the fighters to follow him. Most poured out of their rooms full of questions, but chased after him anyway. He led them out to the arena, stopping only to break open the weapons vault. "Grab everything you need!" he told the others. "The barbarians are coming!"

Carrying the moonblade, Clanless sprinted across the sand to the construction area. He slowed to a walk as he drew near, peering into the dark area hidden from the moon's light. He thought he could see the hole in the wall. A few steps closer and he became certain: the flicker of flame played on the edges. Shadowy figures moved on the other side.

At that moment, someone leaped at him from the darkness. Spinning, Clanless caught the attacker in mid-air with a sweep of the moonblade. He fell to the sand at Clanless's feet. "They're here!" Clanless shouted, even as three more figures emerged from the shadows. He turned and raced back to join up with the other fighters. As he did, a loud impact came from behind him. The barbarians were hitting the damaged wall with something—a battering ram, perhaps?—to enlarge the hole.

"That wall won't hold!" Durken exclaimed.

"Then we'll be the wall!" Clanless looked around. Minus Zaluu, who'd gone to send for help, they were eleven men, well-trained fighting men, to be sure, but only eleven. Would it be enough? How many barbarians were there? To his shock, Clanless realized he was one of the oldest and most experienced fighters here. The others were looking to him for leadership.

"Form a line!" he shouted. "Leave room to swing your weapons, but stay close to each other! Until the soldiers can get here, we have to hold these barbarians off. Are you with me?"

Several of them, including Durken, yelled their agreement. The others murmured, some of them still unsure.

Clanless took a quick glance back. The three barbarians hadn't come after him, returning to the shadows to help with the wall, no doubt. Another loud crash emphasized the situation.

"Listen to me! I grew up on a clanhold. Every home was part of the wall. If barbarians broke through your back wall, it was the highest dishonor a home could ever have!" He paced toward some of the hesitant fighters. "I will not allow this arena to suffer that dishonor!" He slammed his fist against his chest. "We are the back wall! If we fall, this city falls, and its people die! I won't let that happen."

"You're moonbent!" shouted one of the newest fighters. "I'm a slave. I'm not sacrificing myself to save those people!" He turned to run, along with two others. They met Zaluu as he swept out of the entrance.

"Turn around!" he snapped. "You idiots think it'll be safer anywhere else if this place falls? What's better? Running and hiding with women and children, or standing firm with your brothers at your side?"

Two of the fighters were swayed by Zaluu's words and turned back. The third kept going, rushing past him. Eleven, then.

Clanless turned back toward the barbarians. "We are the back wall!" he yelled.

"We are the wall!" Zaluu and the others shouted in answer.

The arena wall crumbled with another impact, and barbarians poured in to the fight.

Clanless had been prepared to charge to meet them if the invaders paused or showed any signs of using ranged weapons. But the swarm of barbarians rushed forward in confidence. Or insanity. In the moon's light, it was impossible to count them as they entered the sands, but the arena fighters found themselves severely outnumbered in seconds.

The enemy raised their own battle cries as they slammed into the wall of fighters, screaming in a language Clanless had never heard. He shouted back, swinging his moonblade in a wide arc. The barbarians wore outfits not dissimilar from the arena fighters' own gear; although many more of them sported some kind of animal pelts over their shoulders. Clanless was surprised to see how many of them wielded bladed weapons, but of course they would. From what he'd heard, the barbarian tribes held none of the reverence for blood that his own people possessed.

"Burn them, Clanless!" Zaluu called from his right. "Just like when we fought the cultists!" Clanless caught a glimpse of one of his friend's throwing knives striking one of the invaders. He activated the Taint, but struggled to contain it to the barbarians in front of him. He shut it off at once, afraid of hurting his allies. He could already sense some of them getting cut by the swords of the enemy. The smell and taste of blood filled his senses more than ever before. The bloodrush pounded in his ears, enhancing his senses and speeding his attacks. What did Zaluu mean by cultists? The brigands who'd taken Koland? The thought barely registered in the midst of the chaos.

The barbarians climbed over the bodies of their dead comrades to get to him. Clanless took a couple of steps back. From the sides, he could see the other fighters being forced back as well. And then one of them went down. Several barbarians leaped through the gap in the line, circling to get behind the other fighters.

"Close the gap! Close the gap!" he yelled. But it didn't matter. Enough barbarians were pouring into the arena that the fighters' "wall" couldn't contain them all. They swept around from either side, surrounding all of the arena fighters. Two more fighters were cut down in moments.

"On me, fighters!" a powerful voice roared above the fray. Clanless glanced to his left and saw Badaar charge into the battle, wielding a massive mace in one hand and an oversized buckler in the other. He'd dressed in a type of scale armor from his shoulders to his thighs, and a heavy helmet covered his head. Clanless had never seen any of that gear before.

"Hold them, boys! Help is on the way!" Badaar swung his mace like a madman, smashing through the barbarians left and right.

"This is insane!" Zektel's voice suddenly filled his head. "You need to get out of here, Aldan!"

He ignored her and kept fighting. The moonblade scythed through enemy after enemy. He followed it up with short bursts of the Taint, always limited to one or two foes.

The barbarians kept coming. Several dozen lay dead or incapacitated on the sand, but twice as many still stood. And more climbed in through the broken wall. Surely the city guard would know. Surely they would come soon.

Yet Clanless knew time could be deceiving in the middle of a fight like this. No circling the enemy. No stunts performed for an audience. Only kill or be killed. Though it seemed to have taken a long time, Zaluu's messenger might not have even reached the captain of the guard yet.

He swung the moonblade again and again. So many foes surrounded him, he lost track of anyone else. Badaar? Zaluu? He had no clue and couldn't spare the breath to call for them. At any moment, the wave of barbarians threatened to overwhelm him. The sense of blood grew enormous, saturating his nose, his mouth, and his mind. A red stain spread across his vision, even in the moon-lit night.

"You're unbelievable, Aldan," Zektel said, her voice barely perceptible in his blood-drenched mind. "But even you can't do this forever. You need to—oh! What's that?"

"What?" Clanless gasped. As if he needed something else to distract him.

Zektel didn't answer.

Badaar burst into view on his left. "Back to back, Clanless!" he snapped. The two of them swung to opposite sides, with the other behind. For a brief moment, Clanless appreciated not having to watch his own back.

"We're the only ones left," Badaar shouted. "Feel free to use that power of yours as much as you can!"

The only ones? Clanless's eyes darted around. Zaluu? Where was he?

"If I use it too much, I can't control it!" he yelled back at Badaar. "I might hurt you too!"

"Not much can stop that now, son." Badaar's voice was barely audible over the shouts and cries of the barbarians. "It's our last stand… soon to be just your last stand…"

"Nyaaarrrrgghhhh!" Clanless screamed as he activated the Taint and let it go in every direction. All around him, barbarians cried out and fell. Many on the ground thrashed where they lay.

For a moment, the attack stopped, along with the battle cries. Moans filled the air from the wounded, dying, and Tainted. The barbarians stayed out of his reach, watching him with mixed curiosity and wariness. Clanless risked a quick look behind and saw Badaar still standing but wavering.

A barbarian directly facing Clanless said something in a loud voice to those around him. He pointed at Clanless. A murmur swept through the others. Clanless stared the barbarian down while he regained his breath. This standoff would help buy time, as long as… No! Some of the barbarians were moving past him, heading into the rest of the arena! He screamed and charged the nearest foes, trying to draw all their attention to himself.

The moonblade cut a massive arc, wounding at least three of the barbarians. Clanless activated the Taint while turning and rushing at another pair. He couldn't give them a moment's peace. They needed to fear him, fear leaving him behind while they moved on. "Fight me, you cowards!"

He had no idea how many injuries he'd taken himself. Weapons had struck him on all sides, but he felt none of them. So possessed by the bloodrush was he, he didn't feel much of anything outside the grip of his hands on his sword.

Clanless and the moonblade had been together for over four years now. Almost every day for four years, he'd swung this weapon until it became a part of him. But never had he fought so long against so many enemies. Again and again, he attacked. Again and again, his eyes burned with the Taint.

Did Badaar still stand? He hadn't seen him for a while and couldn't spare the time to look. Only the next opponent mattered.

His peripheral vision caught bright colors unlike the dull browns of the barbarians' clothing. Zaluu's cape fluttered where he lay on the ground, unmoving. A fury more than any other overtook Clanless at that sight. He rushed into the largest crowd of barbarians he could see, spinning in circles, moonblade outstretched. The ancient mantra, prayed by Zaluu every morning, came to his lips: "Blood is life. Blood is precious. Blood is power!"

One of the barbarians, a leader perhaps, shouted something above all the others, pointing frantically at Clanless. As one, every barbarian in sight charged at him. So they'd decided to overwhelm him with their numbers all at once. If they'd done that at the beginning, things might have gone far worse for him.

"I'm back, dear. Sorry to disappear on you like that," Zektel's voice spoke in his head. "You wouldn't believe what just happened. At any rate, you need to burn them. Burn them all!"

"I'm trying!" His eyes burned until he thought they would melt. Barbarian after barbarian fell, but a dozen and more charged at him, leaping on him, bearing him down. He slashed and tore at them, even as they piled atop him in a massive heap of humanity. Blades pierced and cut him in a dozen or more places.

"Listen to me, Aldan!" Zektel insisted. "Use the Taint, and don't stop using it! Let it go, completely!"

Unable to do much of anything else, Clanless obeyed. His eyes blazed. Always in the past, he'd shut the Taint off after using it, or at least that's how he remembered it. This time, he kept it going. His perception of the blood around him exploded outward. Not only could he smell and taste the blood flowing from the wounds of all those in the immediate vicinity, he could feel the blood pumping through their bodies… even those who hadn't been wounded! His own blood began to burn, but not in the same way. Blood called to blood, and the Taint erupted through everyone he could sense.

One by one, the bodies piled atop him thrashed about and went limp. Cries were cut off, moans faded away. Even the pounding of the bloodrush in his ears diminished to almost nothing.

Eyes still burning, Clanless pushed and pushed upward. He threw off body after body, freeing himself from the scrum. He rolled over the final pair of bodies and dropped the moonblade in the process. He pushed himself up on his hands, finally letting the Taint cease. Every muscle in his body shook with exhaustion. He lifted his head up and looked around.

No one remained on their feet in the entire arena. Dozens and dozens of barbarians lay on the sands. Here and there, his own comrades could be seen as well. No one moved.

"You did it," Zektel whispered. "I knew you could."

He couldn't understand it. How had he affected so many? What had he done?

Pains started to blossom across his body. In the distance, at the arena entrance, he saw figures moving, coming out on to the sand. But his eyes grew dim. Blackness overtook the red tint, and he slumped down.

As his head hit the sand, he could have sworn he heard a second voice in his head saying, "He got lucky."

THE HAWK KING

Then

Clanless didn't want to wake up. The smell of blood from the healing magic overwhelmed his nostrils. They must have virtually drowned him in the liquid to cover all of the injuries he'd sustained. He didn't even want to think about that, about how much he'd needed to survive. Somehow, he'd lived when so many others had died. He wanted to keep his eyes closed, to return to the ignorance of sleep. But a movement of someone else in the room drew his attention. Zaluu?

He opened his eyes, discovering the red tint continuing to affect his vision. He turned his head. One of the young attendants sat at his room's table. The other bed remained empty. That, more than anything else, told him Zaluu was gone. He closed his eyes again, and an involuntary moan escaped his lips.

"Clanless, sir. Are you in pain? Should I summon the healer again?" The attendant's youthful voice intruded on his misery.

"No. No." Clanless hesitated before asking: "What happened?"

"Sir?"

"The barbarians. What happened?"

"Why, you stopped them, sir! They would have overrun the city if not for you! And the other fighters, of course."

"Are they… how many of us survived?"

The attendant didn't answer. Clanless opened his eyes again and looked up at him. "It's all right. You can tell me."

"You are the only survivor, sir."

The only one. He'd suspected as much, of course, but he'd hoped some of the others had lived, even though they'd fallen in the battle. "Badaar?"

"Oh!" The attendant brightened. "He's alive, recovering the same as you. But you're the only arena fighter left."

Clanless had never felt so desolate. He closed his eyes again and turned away.

"Some of the barbarians did break in," the attendant said after a few moments. "They tore some of these rooms apart. I've tried to return everything to normal in here. When the city guards arrived, they dealt with them, of course. Two of the, uh, other attendants were killed." He paused. "But the rest of us are alive. Thanks to you."

Despite his despair, Clanless let his curiosity ask: "What of the barbarians outside the city?"

"There aren't any. They all came here. And you stopped them. The entire city is celebrating your name! You're a hero!"

Clanless didn't say anything else. He didn't feel like a hero. All of the fighters went into the arena every week, knowing they might die. But none of them would have ever dreamed they would all die in one day. And he alone remained. He should have died too. Fighting and killing in the arena was one thing, but this had been different somehow. He'd killed more than ever. His stomach roiled at the thought.

"Sir?" The attendant had left the table and now knelt next to his bed. "My family lives just outside the arena. If you… if you hadn't stopped the barbarians, they would have killed us all." He swallowed. "I owe you my life, the lives of my parents, and the lives of my three little brothers and sisters."

For a moment, the memory of little sister Ot flooded his thoughts. Her little smile, her laughter, her wiggles as he carried her around the house, the smell of her after Mother bathed her… He wondered if the attendant's siblings were anything like her. And he wondered what Ot was like now. She'd be… seven years old by now? Eight? Nine? He struggled to remember.

"Can I get you anything, sir?" the attendant asked. "I was told to wait on your needs."

"No. I need… some time alone, please."

"Of course. I'll be right outside the door if you need me."

Clanless gave an affirmative grunt. He listened to the sounds of the attendant getting to his feet and leaving the room. Once the door closed, he sighed and sat up. His body was slow to obey his mind. Though he'd been healed, it would take quite some time for it to recover from the trauma he'd endured last night… if it had been last night. How long had he been asleep? The red tint to his vision indicated it couldn't have been long… unless he'd used the Taint so much, his vision had altered permanently.

He surveyed the room. Only one chair sat at the table; the other must have been smashed or taken elsewhere. Most of the books were gone from the shelves. With an effort, Clanless got up and went to examine his personal chest. All of his finer clothes, the ones Gogeku fussed over so much, had been torn and cut to shreds. Some of the blood from his larger crystal jar had been dumped out, leaving behind a huge stain on the floor. That stain would cost him months of freedom. The rest of his blood crystals, and most importantly, the paper receipts and Kekeen's note were unharmed. One of Zaluu's throwing knives lay on top of the papers. Clanless picked it up and turned it over, noting its cleanliness. Had Zaluu stashed it here before the fight? Or had someone found it after the battle and put it here?

With a morbid fascination pulling at him, Clanless walked to the other side of the room and opened Zaluu's chest. Folded neatly at the top he found his friend's cape—one of them, anyway; Gogeku constantly made more. He took it out and held it to his own chest as a tightness spread within. He'd let himself grow close to Zaluu against his own plans. This friend hadn't betrayed him, but it had still ended in pain.

He staggered to the center of the room and fell to his knees. Looking up at the red-shaded moon, he whispered, "I knew the prayer as a child. We said it every day. And I heard Zaluu repeat it here so many times. But—" He choked up for a moment. "But I, I can't remember it now. All I can think of is…" He closed his eyes and held the cape as tight as he could. "Blood is life. Blood is precious. Blood is power."

He lowered his head and finally, finally, the tears fell. They cascaded down his cheeks, one after the other. He couldn't remember the last time he had cried. In the privacy of the small cell of his clanhold's temple, maybe? He didn't know. Certainly not since he'd begun his training. He'd have been mercilessly mocked by the other boys. And then once he came here, he'd had no cause for tears.

Except when Kekeen left. Why hadn't he cried then? He should have. The tightness in his chest welled up and exploded up through his throat and mouth in an enormous sob. He crawled to his own bed and into it, where he rolled up in a fetal position, the cape clutched at his chest. More sobs shook his body. Alone, he let them come.

Alone.

ⵦⵦⵦⵦ ● ⵧⵧⵧⵧ

"The Hawk King is coming!" The attendant's breathless announcement erupted out of his mouth in the same moment he threw the door open.

It had been three days since the battle, and Clanless had left his room only when necessary. The red tint had diminished over that time until his vision returned to normal. He looked up from where he sat on his bed, but didn't say anything.

"Did you hear me?" The attendant practically danced across the room. "The Hawk King is coming! Here! To this arena! In the middle of High Winter even!"

"Why would he come here, of all places? Everyone is dead. I'm not going to perform for him."

"He's not coming to see a fight! He's coming to celebrate the victory over the barbarians. And to reward the heroes who stopped them. That's you and Master Badaar!"

For a brief moment, a flicker of hope erupted in Clanless's heart. But no. The Hawk King would never reward him with freedom, not when the Empire and its religion depended on the arena system so much. He took a deep breath. "How soon is he arriving?"

"Tomorrow!"

After the attendant left, Clanless finally turned to Zektel. Once he'd summoned her, he informed her of the imminent arrival.

"This is fantastic, dearest. It's the next big step in your quest! Recognition by the Hawk King will accelerate your career and lead to your freedom even sooner than we'd hoped!"

"I don't want to fight any more," Clanless said. "It's too much. I don't care any more."

"You can't think that way. Not now. Not when you're so close."

"It's not worth it!" He got to his feet and paced across the room.

"You're saying this because your friends died? Aldan, dear, you've known—"

"Nothing is worth it!" he interrupted. "I've accomplished nothing, except killing. I lost my family. I lost Kekeen. I lost Bain—I may have crippled him for life! And now I've lost Zaluu! And the others. It's just not worth it."

Zektel sighed. "You're not thinking clearly. Tell me, did you enjoy the time you spent building your relationship with, with that girl?"

"Of course."

"Did you enjoy the time you spent building your relationship with Zaluu?"

"Yes. What are you getting at?"

"If you hold to the task, if you keep working, then you can have all that in a lasting way someday! When you've won your freedom, you can build new relationships. And they won't have all of this arena stuff hanging over them! No more constant threat of death! True freedom, Aldan. Isn't that worth fighting for?"

He didn't know how to answer. She was right, in most ways. Even so… "It takes so long," he whispered. "I don't know if I can make it."

"That's no reason to give up! Fight harder! Make a bigger show than Orgina or the Hawk King himself expect! The greater your victories, the faster it will come! Your legend just exploded. People will be talking about you all over the Empire. They'll come for miles to see you fight now. And that Daghilch or whoever was trying to kill you? They won't dare to move against you. You'll be more popular than the Hawk King!"

Her words made sense, but did little to assuage the deep pain inside. Maybe, maybe he could do it. But not yet. He needed time.

"Are you listening to me, Clanless?"

"Yes. You're probably right."

"Ah, wisdom from you at last." She laughed, but he didn't.

Even with the pain and despair, curiosity gnawed at him. "Zektel… how did you show up in the battle? I didn't summon you."

"I'm always with you, remember? You were using your power so much, I used some of the blood splashed about to manifest myself. I might be able to do that during a regular fight, but by the time there's enough blood, it would probably be over."

He grunted.

"Your power was incredible, by the way. I've never seen anything like what you did there. No wonder the priests fear the Taint. I didn't count them, but you must have taken down near a hundred barbarians!"

"Who was the other voice?" Clanless asked abruptly.

"Other voice?"

"Before I passed out, I heard someone talking to you. Another voice."

"I'm sure I don't know what you're talking about."

He slammed his fist on the table. "Don't… lie to me now, blood-wraith! You were surprised by something in the fight, and then someone else was talking. I heard it!"

Zektel shifted in her pool of blood. "Very well. I didn't want to bother you with more complications while you were upset."

"Bother me."

"Yes, yes. The other voice was another of my kind."

Clanless stopped pacing. "Another blood-wraith?"

"I've told you there are others of us here, haven't I? At any rate, one of them was attached to the leader of the barbarians."

"What happened to it? After the fight?"

"I don't know. You lost consciousness. When you can't perceive anything, neither can I. I do know that I've sensed no sign of him ever since you woke up again."

Clanless sat and looked at her blood-image. "You've been guiding me, pushing me, for years now. Did that wraith guide the barbarians here?"

"I don't know. If he is anything like me, he was trying to achieve what was best for the man to whom he's attached."

"Did the barbarian have the Taint? He didn't use it against me."

Zektel paused. "I don't believe so. As far as I know, you're unique in that power. Maybe he never communicated directly with his… the man he worked with. I don't know."

Clanless rolled his eyes. "You don't know a lot."

"My memory is not what it used to be, dearheart. I can't recall much of my life before you."

"Hm." He sat on the bed again. At least this topic gave him temporary distraction from his grief. That was good. He needed to focus on other things, or he'd be overwhelmed again. "If the Hawk King offers me a reward, what should I ask for?"

"You mean besides your freedom?"

"He'd never agree to that. I shouldn't even try. What else could I ask him for?"

"The next best thing. Blood."

ᑕ ᑕ ᑕ ᑕ ● ᗡ ᗡ ᗡ ᗡ

Gogeku came to Clanless's room the next morning with a new set of fine clothes. He insisted on dressing Clanless and adjusting the clothes on the spot.

"We can't have you looking like a peasant in front of the Hawk King," Gogeku babbled as he worked. "We want everyone to represent this city well, not to mention Orgina and the entire organization here. And you are, after all, the, the only fighter… we have…" His voice broke, and he turned away, hiding his face.

Clanless ran his hands down the surface of the shirt stretched across his chest. "Geku, I… You've always kept me looking good, and I've never properly thanked you." He put a hand down on the short man's shoulder. "So thank you. I don't deserve it. You're amazing."

Gogeku sniffed. "Of course I am. I labor day and night to make the lot of you lunkheads presentable. It's just a shame, that's all, that you will be the last one. I never would have predicted such a thing." He turned around and cocked his head. "The shirt is still not sitting right on your shoulders. Part of the struggle of leaving one bare all the time. Let me check the back." He pulled his stool around behind Clanless and climbed onto it.

"I won't be the last," Clanless said. "Surely Orgina will find new fighters to get this place going again. And they'll need your help."

"No," Gogeku said from behind him. "No, no. I shall never do this again. I'm too old and too emotional now. I shall retire. I have a cousin in the capital who designs clothing for Clan Ghutalta. Perhaps he'll allow me to assist him."

"He would be lucky to get you."

Gogeku climbed down from the stool and came around to examine the front of the shirt again. "What a very kind thing to say. Thank you, Clanless." His eyes looked up and down the outfit. He shook his head and let out an enormous sigh. "You won't impress the Hawk King with these clothes, but at least you won't embarrass us too much. Alas, it's the best I can do on such short order." He walked to the bed and picked up the fur pelt lying there. "I assume you wish to wear this over it. I had it cleaned again. Remarkable how this fur has held up for so long. I've never seen anything like it."

Clanless threw the fur over his shoulder and fastened the chain. "It seems to be one of a kind."

Gogeku nodded. "As are you," he said quietly.

"What was that?"

"Nothing. I must be going." The little man gathered up his tools and stuffed them in his bag.

"Gogeku! I do believe you paid me a compliment!" Clanless grinned, his first smile since the battle.

"You must have heard me wrong." Gogeku picked up his stool and headed for the door. "You should go at once to the arena entrance. Badaar will meet you there. Beyond that, you're on your own. Try not to fall on your face in front of the ruler of the Sar Empire, if you please."

"I'll do my best."

"I suppose that is all we can hope for." Gogeku hurried out without another word.

Clanless ran his hand through the fur, still as soft as ever. If he ever won his freedom, he should go back and seek out Nukai. Perhaps he could find out more about the fur's origin. A simple wolf didn't seem likely any more.

He made his way along the halls, every silent step filled with thoughts of those who would no longer walk this path. When he reached the arena entrance, he found Badaar as predicted. The trainer's face brightened at the sight of him.

"There's the real hero," Badaar said, stepping up to meet him. He clasped Clanless's shoulder with his left hand. "You're the one who did everything out there. I don't know why they want me here."

"You survived," Clanless said, fighting down another lump in his throat, "and you—" He broke off as his eyes locked on to Badaar's right arm. It ended in an unfamiliar stump.

Badaar followed his gaze. "Ah, that. Healing magic doesn't regrow limbs, you know." He shrugged. "I'll be all right. I still have one good hand."

Clanless didn't know what to say. Gogeku leaving and Badaar crippled? This place would never be the same again.

A soldier appeared at the entrance, clad in gold and red. Two hawk wings swept back from the sides of his helmet. He gestured to the two of them. "Your presence is now required. Be advised. You should not speak to the Hawk King unless he asks you a question. It is an honor to be in his presence."

Badaar and Clanless walked together out onto the sands. A mild winter wind rustled their clothing. Clanless tried not to think about the horrors of the last time they'd been here. The blood and bodies had been cleaned up, but he could still see it all in his mind.

A pavilion had been set up in the center of the arena, covered in heavy cloth to shield it from the weather. Beneath it, a throne of sorts had been erected. A man sat on the throne, flanked by two more of the armored soldiers. Clanless noticed the hole in the wall had already been repaired. It wouldn't do to have the harsher winter winds rushing through to the Hawk King. A few other richly-clad men and women stood beneath the pavilion as well. Several were shivering; none looked comfortable. Two red-robed Daghilchs waited to the left of the throne, neither of them familiar. As Clanless and Badaar drew closer, he noticed Orgina standing near the throne. She rocked from foot to foot from nervousness or the cold; probably both.

Clanless hadn't known what to expect of his first sight of the Hawk

King. According to what he'd read, the man had ruled the Sar Empire for several hundred years. And yet he appeared as healthy and hale as a man in his middle years. He sat straight and tall on the throne, hands casually holding the arms of the chair. "He does have a large nose," Clanless said to himself with a slight smile. Zaluu had been right about that. But the king's eyes observed him with serious calculation, examining every inch of him before doing the same to Badaar and then returning to Clanless. This was not a man to underestimate in any way.

He wore a black outfit decorated with a colorful embroidered hawk on his chest. A white cape hung behind him. Instead of a crown, he wore a fur-lined helmet that rose to a sharp peak. As if in contrast to his darker clothing, the other nobility wore bright clothes: yellow, purple, blue. Orgina wore her usual dark red.

"And here are the heroes, I take it?" the Hawk King asked, his voice strong and resonant.

"They are, your majesty," Orgina answered with a short bow. "Allow me to introduce to you my trainer Badaar, and my last arena fighter, the man known only as Clanless." The two men also bowed.

"I have heard of you both," the king said. "I am pleased to see you are both recovered, thanks to the blood of clan Kurav." He got to his feet, revealing him to be no taller than an ordinary man. In fact, aside from his rich clothing, he appeared completely ordinary. He took several steps closer, his cape fluttering behind him. "In fact, I'd daresay half of the Empire has now heard of the weapons master and the arena fighter who held off an entire barbarian army."

Clanless wanted to say, "It wasn't an army," but reminded himself of what the soldier had told him.

"Badaar, master of weapons," the Hawk King went on. "You are already a Hero of the Empire. And this new feat tops even what you've done before."

"I did very little, your majesty," Badaar answered. "'Twas Clanless here who is the hero. Single-handedly, he took down dozens of the invaders. Without him, all would have been lost."

"Indeed." The Hawk King stepped in front of Clanless and examined him. "We have all heard of his deeds and his... talents."

"It is not a talent," said a Daghilch.

The Hawk King raised his hand toward the priest as if to silence him. "You see my dilemma." Clanless wasn't sure who the Hawk King was addressing. "I cannot proclaim an arena slave to be a Hero of the Empire, especially not with his... uncertain relationship with my priests. Therefore, it is my judgment that as the story is spread by our people, Badaar"—he turned back to the other man—"should be recognized as the primary hero here."

The unfairness of it bothered Clanless, but not enough to speak out. What difference did it make what people said? They already told many other stories about him that weren't entirely true.

"Badaar, I proclaim you Hero of the Empire a second time." The Hawk King smiled. "And for a second time, I ask you to join me in the capital. Your skills could be used to improve my soldiers, rather than those who fight for our entertainment."

Badaar bowed. "And for the second time, your majesty, I must decline." He held up his stump. "I am of much less value to you than I once was. And to be quite honest, I am tired. I do not see myself continuing this work much longer."

"It is your mind that is of value, not whether you possess two hands," the Hawk King said. "I will accept your decision, though it displeases me." He turned back to Clanless. "You, however, I can certainly reward, clanless one."

Clanless looked back at the Hawk King, trying to hold back any expectations.

"As I said, I cannot label you Hero of the Empire, but there is no doubt your story is spreading. You are a legend. And legends should be together. Therefore…" He trailed off and walked back to the throne before turning around again. "Therefore, Clanless, you will be coming back with us to Et-Baylak to join my personal Dohor of arena fighters. You will fight in the greatest arena of the Empire in front of crowds that will dwarf this place."

Orgina made a noise in her throat. The Hawk King turned to her. "I have not forgotten you, Orgina. I will pay you well for him. Bring me his bloodbond."

Orgina drew out the metal sheet representing her ownership of Clanless. He hadn't seen it since the Daghilch gave it to Kan all those years ago. The Hawk King held out his hand, but Orgina hesitated. "Forgive me, your majesty," she said at last, "but… Clanless is all I have left, the only draw for my arena. If you take him, I will have nothing."

"I understand your loss. Now transfer the bloodbond to me."

One of the soldiers offered a dagger to Orgina. She pricked her finger on its tip, then smeared her own blood across the metal sheet. "With my blood, I transfer the ownership of this bond. Let it be known throughout the Empire and under the moon's gaze," she recited.

The Hawk King took the sheet, pricked his own finger, and touched the plate. "I take ownership of this bloodbond." He looked it over before setting it on the arm of the throne.

"Fear not, noble Orgina," he said, turning back to her. "In addition to full payment for the slave, I will send word to the seven other major arenas requiring them to send you one of their top fighters. This will not restore your loss, of course, but it will give you a start in rebuilding. I have little doubt that you will overcome and thrive."

The Hawk King sat down and looked at Clanless. "Are you prepared to fight for the honor of your king, Clanless?"

"Yes, your majesty, except—" He stopped himself, not sure if he dared speak further.

"Except what? Tell me your problem, slave." The last word came out stronger, reminding Clanless of his place.

"I apologize, sire. I only wanted to say…" He dropped his eyes. "I have lost so many friends. May I have time to mourn them before I fight again? My body is healed, but my heart is still broken."

The Hawk King did not say anything for a few moments. Clanless felt sure he would now be punished for his effrontery. The king's face softened a little before he spoke: "I am not a monster, Clanless. I understand your loss. I've been in battles myself where many of my comrades fell, never to rise again. In this, you are not alone." He paused. "However, I am also pragmatic. Should you spend too much time in mourning, your skills may lose their edge, and that I cannot allow. I have a very special fight in mind for your first appearance in my arena. But take comfort in this: we are in the midst of High Winter. You will have at least a few weeks to prepare before the arena season begins. Only thus far does my magnanimity extend for now."

Clanless swallowed and bowed. The Hawk King waved dismissively. Badaar touched Clanless on the arm. The two of them bowed once more before turning and walking out of the arena. Once they'd left the sands behind, Badaar let out a relieved sigh.

"That was a near thing, Clanless," he said. "The Hawk King is not one to tolerate questions from his slaves. And for you to do so after Orgina already pushed her luck…" He shook his head. "You're fortunate he was in a good mood."

Clanless looked back out toward the pavilion. "He seemed… almost like a normal man. I don't know what to think of him."

Badaar ran a hand across his short hair. "Let me give you some advice, son. The Hawk King… I don't know what you've heard—or read—about him, but more of it is true than you'd expect. He is not a man to underestimate in any way. He is the most dangerous man you will ever meet."

"Is that why you won't go work for him?"

"Among other reasons."

"What do you mean?"

Badaar shook his head. "I've said enough. Just know that you can never trust him. And never turn your back on him." He put out his left hand. "Moon's stability to you, Clanless. May the goddess guard your steps."

Clanless awkwardly shook his left hand. "Farewell, Badaar. I hope you find the rest you crave."

He laughed. "Not if Orgina has her way. All new fighters? We'll be starting this place over from the beginning."

Clanless took a deep breath and took one last look out at the arena. He'd fought here countless times for over five years. But in its current state, all he could think about was the final battle. And those memories—the ones he could recall, anyway—were ones he didn't want to dwell on. He turned away and took the first steps toward the capital city.

Part Three

ET-BAYLAK

MESSAGE FOR YOU

As they exited Pasque House, the remaining two members of the Dohor showed up. "You left without us!" Hawking accused.

"Oh, king's son!" one of the girls called from the door. "I've missed you! Where have you been?"

"You know he's not really the son of the Hawk King, don't ya?" Hagh asked her.

"He's close enough," she answered with a shrug.

"It's your last night, Clanless," said the fifth fighter, his scarred face barely visible in the twilight. "Why didn't you want to celebrate with all of us?"

"Hagh and Sugh were here when I first arrived." Clanless didn't know why he felt the need to defend himself. "I just wanted to spend some time with the two of them."

"And a few ladies," Hawking observed.

"Just one stop out of many," Sugh proclaimed. "Now that you're here, join us! I believe I've worked up an appetite again! Let's go find something else to eat!"

Clanless opened his mouth to respond, when a young boy raced into the courtyard, eluding a quick grab from the guard at the door. "Yesun?" Clanless recognized the attendant as he skidded to a stop in front of him, panting from his exertion. "Again? What are you doing here?"

"Message for you." The boy thrust a folded note toward him.

Clanless opened the note and read the handful of words within. He looked back at Yesun. "Who gave this to you?"

"A storyteller. In the lower city." He peered past Clanless into the manor.

"A storyteller?" Sugh asked. "I haven't heard a good storyteller in months! Where is this one?"

"Not this time," Clanless said. "This is something I need to deal with alone." He pushed Yesun ahead of him. "And you're not supposed to be in here."

The door guard, who'd just caught up, scowled and shook his fist at the boy. "I'm going. I'm going!" Yesun protested.

"My friends," Clanless said, throwing his arms wide as he walked almost backwards after Yesun. "I will catch up with you later tonight. I have someone else I need to visit first."

The Dohor erupted in genial protests, but he waved them off. He followed Yesun out, where he caught the boy by his sleeve.

"Was she there?" he demanded. "When the storyteller gave you the note? Was she there?"

"Who?"

Clanless almost snapped an answer before he recognized the false innocence on Yesun's face. The boy was mocking him. He growled.

Yesun laughed. "No, she wasn't there. At least not that I saw. Or heard. But I didn't get to see much. The storyteller sent me out as quick as I could go." He patted his pocket. "Paid well too."

Clanless nodded and looked down at the note. Of course she was back in the city. Of course they would want to see him now. He opened the note again and looked at her signature in the light from the manor's outdoor lanterns.

Kekeen.

BEASTMAN

Then

"This is absolutely outstanding, dearheart!" Zektel's voice filled Clanless's head as he looked out of the carriage window at the passing countryside. The carriage shook from a strong burst of wind.

"Is it? I'm not sure. I'm not sure of anything anymore." He toyed with the blood vial on its chain around his neck.

"Of course it is! This has been the plan all along. Don't you remember?" Alone in the carriage for days, Clanless had turned to Zektel for conversation. Though a part of the Hawk King's convoy, he was nowhere near the king himself. He'd even slept in the carriage, well constructed and shielded from the winter winds and cold. "You'll be fighting in the capital city arena! The most prestigious place an arena fighter can reach! As part of the Hawk King's own Dohor, you'll have an even better life than you had in Ghoyor. And you'll be able to earn your freedom even faster!"

"How so? Will they let me siphon more blood from each fight?"

"Probably not. But you'll have less cause to spend anything you make there. Those who serve the Hawk King have every amenity provided for them."

"It's not like I spent a lot anyway." Clanless shifted his weight as the carriage began to ascend a steep hill. He'd seen maps of the Sar Empire, but distances were still hard for him to judge, having traveled so little in his life. He thought they must be near the capital by now, but had no way of knowing for sure.

"What did you think of him?" Clanless asked. "The Hawk King?"

"There's something strange about him," Zektel said. "I know you've said he uses all kinds of blood-magic. Maybe you could explain that a little more? What has he used?"

"From what I've read, it seems that each clan's blood can be used to create a different effect." The view through the carriage window had shifted to huge fields—dead now, covered with a thin layer of snow and ice, but undoubtedly full of grain during High Spring. Such fields were usually located near a city. "Clan Kurav's provides the healing. Clan Torov has the voice magic, I think. The Hawk King uses that, at least."

A small child ran along the side of the road, waving and playfully trying to keep up with the carriage. Clanless waved back. He did the same as a child, but never for a carriage a fine as this one. Even High Winter couldn't keep children indoors all of the time. The Empire's children learned to be strong against the winter from an early age.

"The Hawk King comes from Clan Shukan, though. And no matter what I read, I couldn't find out what their blood does. Zaluu didn't know either. I think… I think it extends his life. He's far older than he looks."

"What does the blood of your clan do?"

"I don't have a clan."

"You know what I mean. Clan Tokuur."

Clanless snorted. "It creates weakness. The military has tried to figure out a way to use it against the empire's enemies for generations, but with little success. It's mostly useless. And that's why Tokuur will never gain any prominence. Their blood just isn't useful, except for sacrifices." Even as he said it, he wondered. If the goddess gave the magic, why give one clan such a useless power?

"Back to the sacrifices. I still don't understand why they need so much, especially if, as you say, Tokuur blood doesn't do much for them."

Clanless shrugged. More and more buildings—homes and other structures—appeared in his view. They had to be near the city now.

"The capital is also the center of the moon goddess worship, isn't it?"

"Sure," Clanless said. "The highest-ranking priests live here. The Ghamba Lam rules over all of them."

"But he doesn't rule the Hawk King?"

"I don't know."

"Curious. At any rate, you'll have to keep an eye out for them. Your story will be well known here, of course. And with more priests around, there are bound to be some who don't like you."

"There it is!" Clanless pressed up against the carriage window. The road curved back and forth, and now he could see their destination: Et-Baylak, capital city of the Sar Empire.

"Impressive," Zektel admitted.

It seemed to Clanless that each time he'd moved in life, he'd found a place far beyond his expectations. First, Rochibal had been such a drastic difference from the clanhold. Then Ghoyor had blown that away. And now… Ghoyor looked like a hovel compared to what he saw.

Et-Baylak sat on top of an enormous hill, dominating the view for many miles in every direction. Its massive walls stretched higher than any other city in the Empire. Even the fiercest of winter winds would have no chance against these walls. Pinnacles, positioned every so often along the wall, stretched even higher. And yet, it was only the first wall. Clanless could see the tops of a second wall further inside the city, as if a second city had been built within the first. Most of the buildings that could be seen behind the walls were made of white stone, or perhaps snow covered them. It was difficult to tell in the low light. Dozens of spires and circular domes of every height strained to reach toward the moon.

"What do you know about the city?" Zektel asked.

"Only what I've read. The four most powerful clans are all centered here and compete with each other for control. The Hawk King rules from here. It's the center of the entire Empire."

"And yet…" Zektel's voice faded a little. The blood's efficacy must have been dwindling. "It's not on a coast. It's not on a major river. It's almost in the middle of nowhere. Why here?"

Clanless knew that one. "It's the exact center. Of everything. The most exact position for being directly beneath the moon. The exact center of the Empire itself. The priests even claim it's the exact center of the entire world."

"I'm sure the other empires and kingdoms would have something to say about that."

"Maybe." Clanless considered that. How many other empires and kingdoms were there in the world? He knew of their neighbor, the Melkute Kingdom, but no others, at least not by name. He'd fought against some foreigners, like the one with the pet monster, but he knew nothing about where they came from. The books he'd read seemed to lump everyone else into the same category as the barbarians.

Zektel made a couple more observations on the architecture as they approached, but her voice soon faded away. Clanless considered summoning her again, but decided not to use up any more blood.

The carriage made a final turn leading into the city. Clanless saw several of the gold and red clad guards just before they passed beneath the city's enormous wall. A few brief moments of darkness gave way to a sudden explosion of light as they entered the main street of Et-Baylak. His eyes took a few seconds to adjust to the brightness of the shining light of dozens of lamps reflecting from the bright white stone and snow.

Aside from the architecture, the outer ring of the city didn't seem much different from Ghoyor. But once they passed the second wall into the inner ring, everything changed. The wealth on display boggled his mind. He'd never even imagined some of the opulence he beheld: shopping districts larger than the clanhold he grew up in, massive homes that could have easily housed a dozen families at once—and might, for all he knew!—and looming over it all, atop the highest peak of the hill, the massive arena side-by-side with the Hawk King's palace.

The palace had not two, but three red-tiled roofs—or was it four?—all curving out to pointed corners. An enormous half moon with the clan Shukan symbol rested on the very top. Most of the homes they passed showed clan symbols of varying sizes as well, some on the roof or outer walls, some in fancy displays atop their fences. Clanless couldn't tell from the angle, but it looked as if the palace might be bigger than the arena; they were at least similar in size. He tried to see more, but the carriage turned down a long street with tall houses obscuring the view.

Clanless sat back against the carriage's cushioned seat. In a few minutes, the carriage slowed as it prepared to enter the arena grounds. Clanless took a deep breath, trying to prepare himself for this next phase of his life.

༺ ☾ ☾ ☾ ☾ ● ☽ ☽ ☽ ☽ ༻

"This is your room." The guide, a young woman scarcely older than Clanless, turned in a circle. "Does it meet with your approval?"

He looked around, stunned. The room was larger than the quarters he'd shared with Zaluu. "All of this is for me?" He felt stupid asking the question. Only one bed sat in the room, after all—though again, it was larger than any he'd ever slept on. He also had his own table and chairs and a large set of shelves (though no books). His chest from Ghoyor had already been placed at the foot of the bed. The case holding the moonblade sat on top of it. Apparently, he could keep it in his own room now.

The guide smiled and tossed back her long, black hair. She reminded Clanless of cousin Borde in some ways. "Yes, of course. The Hawk King takes care of his own. You'll see. There are many other... perquisites of serving the Hawk King this close."

Clanless was afraid to ask what that meant. He walked to the room's window—an actual glass window!—and looked out. To his disappointment, his view consisted only of a single wall of the Hawk King's palace. He couldn't even see much of the fancy tiled roofs. Still, it would be nice to let some air in from time to time—when High Winter ended, of course.

"What was your name again?" he asked, turning back to the woman.

"I am Qara of clan Dalbai." She spread her hands apart. "It is my honor to serve the Hawk King by attending to the needs of the Dohor. Every one of their needs, whatever they may be." Something about the table caught her eye. She stepped over to it and brushed some crumbs or dust away.

"So I can ask you just about anything, I suppose?"

"I will endeavor to answer any questions you may have." She inclined her head with a little tilt.

"How many members of the Dohor are there?"

"At present, there are only four, including yourself." Qara's perpetual smile bordered on a smirk. "The Hawk King is very particular about those whom he inducts into his elite." Her eyes roamed over his body. "If you are here, then you belong here. He only chooses the best."

"Only four? I guess that makes Arena Nights somewhat... short." Clanless sat on the bed, testing its softness and strength.

"Oh, no. There are many other events in addition to the Dohor fights. Arena warriors from across the Sar Empire come to test their strength and audition for a spot among your number. Sometimes, the Hawk King's soldiers step into the arena, seeking fame and glory for themselves. Or perhaps captured enemies are forced to fight. Our possibilities are virtually endless." She closed her eyes and massaged her temples. "Apologies. I am subject to frequent headaches. How else can I help you?"

"Who arranges the schedule? The fights?"

"The arena master is Badzorik of clan Torov. You will have an opportunity to meet him tomorrow, I believe."

"Who is the trainer?"

"Trainer?"

"The one who helps me prepare for the fights." Clanless gave a short wave. "To keep training and getting better."

"Ah, I see." Qara folded her hands together in front of her. "It is understood that by the time a fighter ascends to the Dohor, he is skilled enough to handle such things for himself. The Hawk King does not hire a specific person for the role you describe."

"Oh." Clanless supposed he could come up with his own workout regimen, but he'd always had someone do that for him. "I guess I have a lot to learn."

"That is one of the reasons I am here." She paused. "Before I show you the rest of the facility, I do need something from you." She took an empty crystal vial from a pouch on her belt. "I need a sample of your blood."

Clanless blinked. "My blood? What for?"

"It is a request from the Hawk King. He keeps samples of the blood of all his Dohor."

Clanless could think of no purpose for such a thing, but he couldn't refuse a request from the king. Once the vial was full, Qara put it back into the pouch and smiled at him. "See? We should have no difficulty getting along here."

She opened the room's door and gestured down the hall. "Everything you need for the daily routine is to the left."

Clanless stood up and joined her, looking out at the other doors.

"There are eight rooms here, though four are currently unoccupied, of course." Qara stepped out into the hallway. "Beyond them, you'll find the latrine and the baths. Beyond that, around the corner down there, is the dining hall. But you're welcome to bring your food and drink back to your own room, if you prefer."

Clanless's eyebrows rose. What an odd concept. Qara's tone indicated she found the practice annoying.

"The hall turns again to the left beyond the kitchen, and you'll find the practice grounds and the passage that leads to the arena itself. I will have an attendant explain the process for your fights. One or two of them will be available to assist you on Arena Nights; although, quite often other members of the Dohor assist each other instead."

That sounded… encouraging. Camaraderie among the Dohor? Clanless glanced back the other direction in the hall. "And to the right?"

Qara gave a short gesture in that direction. "It leads to the exit into the city."

"Oh. How of—" Clanless cut himself off. He didn't want to appear foolish asking about "permission" to go into the city. The Dohor seemed to operate on a much more independent basis.

"The Hawk King requires you to remain within the arena walls on event days, until the events are concluded," Qara explained, apparently recognizing what he wanted to know. "After that, and every other day, you are free to come and go as you wish. There are certain areas of the city we wish you to avoid, but that can be explained later. There are some eating establishments that we highly recommend, who are happy to give large discounts to the Dohor for the prestige your presence brings to them."

That was convenient.

"And we strongly recommend that you avoid the common brothels and restrict yourself to the Pasque House, the royal brothels. There is no charge for their services to our fighters, and they are the best in the city, if not the entire Empire. At least, so I am told."

Clanless didn't know how to respond to that, so he changed the subject. "Are there maps of the city? How do I find my way around? This place is enormous!"

Qara nodded. "It can be overwhelming, I suppose. I've spent my entire life within Et-Baylak's walls, so it's very familiar to me. At any rate, you needn't worry. You may request an attendant at any time to guide you through the city streets. In fact, it is preferable if you take one with you on all such excursions. Should you have, ah, difficulty in returning, the attendant can summon proper transportation."

Should he get himself stone drunk, she meant.

"How often do I, uh, see the Hawk King himself?"

"The Hawk King is present at virtually all arena fights, at least when the Dohor are competing. He has his own royal box where he entertains guests." She gave another of those head tilts. "Aside from that, you probably will not see him unless he summons you into his presence. And that would be a tremendous honor."

"I'm sure."

Qara waited a moment before asking, "Do you have any other questions?"

"I don't... I don't think so. Thank you."

She gave a little bow and turned to the right. "Should you need more, you can send an attendant to find me. Or...." She paused and glanced back. "My room is also this way. Near the exit. You're welcome to come to my door... at any time." Her smile might be saying more than her words, but Clanless pretended not to understand.

"I'll remember that." Clanless gave her a smile before she continued on her way. He turned back to his room—his own room! What would Zaluu have said about that? The thought put a damper on his excitement. He closed the door behind him and went to his bed. At least now he could rest.

Clanless woke without any assistance as the sun's pursuit began, a habit he'd long since mastered living in the arena. After dressing, he went to the dining hall. He found no one there but a server who was all too happy to fill up his plate. He sat alone at a table and ate.

A few minutes later, an enormous dark-skinned man entered the hall. Without a glance at Clanless, he obtained a plate full of food and left. So much for camaraderie.

After eating, Clanless unpacked the moonblade and made his way to the practice grounds. This early in the morning, High Winter's cold would be almost too much. But he needed some time outside. The practice grounds turned out to be sand, like a normal arena, but less than half the size. It made sense for the small number of fighters who used it.

Clanless stretched a little and began working through his favorite moves. He twisted and swung the moonblade in an upward arc, then turned and did the same in the opposite direction. Though he'd slept well in the new bed, all of his muscles felt stiff, perhaps an after-effect of the carriage ride here. After about five minutes, he worked out the stiffness, getting into a rhythm of movement that took him across the grounds.

He paused to catch his breath, swinging the moonblade to its usual spot on his shoulder. Sweat poured from his head in spite of the cold. He reminded himself to ask Qara about a haircut.

"Not bad," said a voice behind him.

He turned, trying to stay casual, and found another fighter watching him. Despite an impressive physique, the man had to be the oldest arena fighter Clanless had ever seen. His craggy face and wisps of hair had seen better days… long ago. He bent over and coughed loud and long. Clanless grew alarmed. "Are you all right?"

"Yah, yah." The older fighter wiped his mouth with the back of his forearm. "I cough more than's good for me. Except when I'm fightin'. No coughs then." He put out his hand. "They call me Hagh. From clan Gham-kiin."

Clanless shook his hand. "I'm Clanless."

"Knew that much from the brand. Is that all they call you then?"

"It is." He shrugged, bouncing the moonblade.

Hagh cocked his head. "Ohhhh. You're that one what fought off the barbarians, right? I heard a bit about that."

"It wasn't all that much."

"I'm sure. Welcome to the Dohor, anyway. Nice blade."

Clanless swung the moonblade down. "It's one-of-a-kind."

"So I see. That makes two of you dishonorable fighters here." He shook his head. "What's this place coming to?"

"The priests already hate me, so why should I fight by their rules?"

This time, Hagh shrugged. "It's your business. Just strange, that's all. But the Hawk King don't seem to mind harassing the priests a bit. Sugh's been here for months."

"Sugh?"

"Yah. He's got an axe. Bigger than yours. But he's bigger than you too." Hagh glanced up. "Sun'll be surrendering early today. Let's get out of the moon's gaze."

They walked back inside the building. "I'm guessing you use a mace?" Clanless asked.

"Two maces. The sisters. They're sweet. You met anyone else yet?"

"No. I saw a big man at breakfast, but he didn't talk. I'm guessing that was Sugh?"

"Probably. Plate piled high? He likes to eat in his room. Not sure why. I hear him talkin' in there sometimes. He's an odd one." Hagh coughed. "But we're all odd here."

Clanless pushed his hair back. "Have you been here long? What's this place like, compared to other cities?"

"Long enough. Been fightin' for over eight years now."

"Eight years? Are you close to winning your freedom?"

Hagh laughed, which turned into another cough. "You are still new, aren't ya? No one wins their freedom. I would've had to keep everything I earned for the past ten years to even get close!" He shook his head. "Life is good enough as it is. Why would I want to be free?"

Clanless wrinkled his brow. "To be free? To do what you want. Not be forced to fight and kill all the time."

"I like fighting. The sisters like it too. It's all we know."

"I'm going to be free," Clanless insisted. "It's the only reason I keep going."

"Whatever works for you, boy. As for the rest of your question..." Hagh gestured toward the arena. "This place isn't like other cities. The crowds are much larger and more bloodthirsty. They want to see death all the time. And the Hawk King's the worst of them. He keeps thinking of new and crazier ways for us to fight. We'll all end up dead eventually." He laughed again. "The fight he's preparing for you is proof of that."

"What fight? Do you know the schedule?"

Hagh eyed him. "They didn't tell you? It's already all over the city. Gonna be a record crowd come to see your first fight in a couple weeks.'"

"Why? Who am I fighting?"

"It doesn't happen very often." Hagh obviously enjoyed delaying the answer. "I've never seen it myself, but I've heard stories. In some ways, I envy you. You're getting a rare privilege."

"Hagh. Who am I fighting?"

Hagh's grin showed a couple of missing teeth. "They've captured a beastman."

☾ ☾ ☾ ☾ ● ☽ ☽ ☽ ☽

Clanless had tried to read everything he could find about beastmen back in Ghoyor. He didn't find much. Most people had never seen one; many regarded them as a myth. In general, they were regarded as horrible marauders, far worse than the barbarians, yet primitive and ignorant.

"They captured a beastman?"

"Aye. Keeping him locked up over yonder." Hagh gestured vaguely toward the arena. "They haven't done anything to him. Just keeping him away from folks and locked up. He's got his own weapons and everything."

Clanless considered for a moment. "Can we see him?"

"Nah. They'd never allow it. We almost never get to see our opponents before the fights."

"Tell me more about the fights here," Clanless suggested. "What should I expect?"

"I'll tell ya, but let's go sit down. No reason to stay out here right now."

They went back inside to the dining hall where Hagh regaled Clanless with tales of the capital arena. Clanless pretended not to notice that most of the stories involved a great victory by Hagh.

Over the next few days, Clanless adapted to life in Et-Baylak. Hagh became a quick friend almost right away; though Clanless hesitated to tell him much about his past (or the Taint). Sugh, despite early appearances, turned out to be friendly as well; though he couldn't help looking intimidating even when he didn't mean to.

The only other current member of the Dohor was a young fighter known as Silence, from clan Dariachin. He'd lost his tongue in an early arena fight, something else the healing magic couldn't repair. The others didn't ignore him, but struggled with communication of any kind. For his part, he rarely tried to engage with any of them, spending most of his time alone. Yet according to Hagh, Silence might be the deadliest of them all inside the arena. He fought with a mace, like so many others, but carried a chain with his off-hand. He used it to surprising effect both offensively and defensively.

Clanless learned little about the rest of the staff, consisting of attendants and cooks. The only other person he saw on a regular basis within the arena grounds was Qara. She continually asked him what else he needed, checking on the condition of his furniture, his clothing, and everything else. On the fourth such day, he made a request to have flatbread added to the dining hall's menu, solely because she kept asking what he wanted. When he walked into the dining hall the next morning, hot flatbread awaited him on the serving table. After a few more days, the easy availability of the bread made him worry he might eat too much of it.

As a result, he trained himself harder, despite High Winter's harshness. He put together all he'd learned from Kan and Badaar and devised his own daily regimen. Based on his own exhaustion afterwards, it equaled or surpassed what Badaar put him through.

"You work too hard in the cold," Sugh told him. "It is not good for you. Stay inside more."

"I have a fight to prepare for," Clanless said, counting down the days. "A beastman is waiting for me."

And then the day arrived.

((((●))))

Hagh took Clanless into the actual arena the day before his first fight, but it didn't prepare him for the crowd. Everything was on such a larger scale than Ghoyor. Not just the size of the arena, but the sound and enthusiasm of the crowd. The roars were almost deafening at times. The people had heard of him, of course. The presenter could barely be heard over them, extolling Clanless for his fight against the barbarians.

"You've heard tell stories of men who saved a clanhold from barbarians, but here is a man who saved an entire city!"

Clanless found it interesting to be compared to Daviland. Evidently, that story had reached the capital as well. The implication of the presenter's words were easy to see. Ignore Daviland. Here's an arena slave who did something bigger and better.

The nature of the crowd was different also. Though he couldn't make out much about the people in the higher stands, the lower ones were filled with wealthier, higher-class citizens than usually watched his fights in Ghoyor. There had always been rich people there, of course, but nowhere near these numbers. Clanless got the feeling that admittance to Arena Night in Et-Baylak cost a good deal more than it did elsewhere.

If that weren't enough, scattered around the lowest stands were a number of luxury boxes for the elite of the elite. Large spaces with only a handful of people, servers with food and drink and other amenities… Clanless couldn't imagine what it took to get into one of those.

And the largest and most elaborate of all these boxes belonged to the Hawk King. Clanless could see him now, standing at the front of the box while other dignitaries mingled behind him. Clanless lifted the moonblade in acknowledgement to the king, who gave a slight nod in return. The crowd roared again, and the presenter launched into a description of the terror of the beastmen and what the audience might be about to see. As he spoke, the opposite arena door opened. The beastman emerged to screams and derision from the crowd.

Clanless tuned it all out as the strange opponent approached. He loped across the sand in a smooth but unusual gait. Clanless braced himself, watching the creature's every movement. He needed to learn everything he could as fast as possible.

The beastman looked larger and more solidly built than even Sugh. While man-shaped, his arms appeared longer than human, hanging almost to the ground as he approached. His skin tone was a type of orangish-brown, contrasting with his pure white hair—and there was a lot of hair. It hung long from his head down his back and in a narrow beard in the front. Both forearms and shins were covered in the same white hair as well. He wore only a short black skirt of leather around his waist, and a necklace of some sort dangling from his neck. Both his hands and feet ended in animalistic claws. In his right hand, he held a sword. To Clanless's surprise, it looked like an exceptional weapon: curved like a scimitar, but with a handful of serrations on the back edge. He'd expected any weapon wielded by a beastman to be makeshift, a bone perhaps. Not an expertly-forged and shaped sword. Maybe there was more to them than people understood.

As if to punctuate that thought, the beastman stopped and stared at Clanless. His eyes gleamed brown with a hint of red. His ears rose into sharp points amidst the enormous hair. When he opened his mouth, it revealed lines of sharp teeth. And then he spoke: "We fight?" The voice, though guttural, was easily understood.

Clanless took a step to the right and started to circle. "Yes. That's why we're here."

The beastmen glanced around at the crowd, but also began to circle, mirroring Clanless. "They watch. See kill."

Clanless didn't answer. This fight grew stranger by the minute.

The beastman grasped his necklace with his left hand and held it up. Clanless still couldn't see it clearly. "You kill, then you take."

He blinked. "You want me to take your necklace if I kill you?"

"You take," the strange creature insisted. Then he pointed at Clanless. "I win, then I take."

The crowd grew restless at their slow pace, and made known their displeasure.

Clanless ignored them and darted his eyes around. "You take what?"

The beastman patted his own shoulder. "I win, then I take."

Clanless put his own hand up. "The fur?"

The beastman nodded.

"Sure. Why not?"

"Agreement made." The beastman stopped moving. "Honor is set. Now. We fight!"

With that, he lifted his sword high and charged, bellowing a cry no human voice could duplicate. Clanless braced himself. He rarely had an opponent charge so directly, but it gave him plenty of options. He planned to dodge the sword stroke and attempt to cut the beastman's feet out from under him with the moonblade's long reach.

To his surprise, the beastman dropped both hands—including the one holding the sword—into the sand. His momentum flipped him into the air and forward. His clawed feet slammed into Clanless's chest. Though braced in a strong stance, he couldn't resist the entire weight of the huge opponent. His back smacked into the sand. The beastman leaped off him, his claws leaving multiple scratches across Clanless's chest.

Clanless leaped to his feet, spinning to face his opponent from a new direction. The beastman moved faster than he'd anticipated for one so big. And those long arms did more than extend his reach. He had to take these things into account. He initiated his own charge, a short one. He kept his torso turned, with the moonblade held out to the side. At the last moment, he swung it in a wide arc across and upward. Such a move could usually at least tag an opponent who either underestimated the moonblade's reach or dodged up instead of down. The beastman did neither, backpedaling instead, just enough for the blade to miss him. He had to drop his left hand back into the sand to keep himself from falling all the way.

Seeing that, Clanless let the momentum of his blade's arc spin him in a circle to bring across another similar stroke, this time dropping into a crouch to swing at knee level. To his relief, the very tip of the moonblade caught a bit of flesh above the beastman's knee. A scratch meant he'd won.

But he couldn't win the fight too fast, not in front of this crowd and the Hawk King who'd brought him here. The people needed a show. For the next couple of minutes, he executed several of his signature crowd-pleasing moves. Only once more did he manage to cut the beastman, this time in a long slash across its back, cutting away a hunk of white hair at the same time. The beastman, on the other hand, gave him four or five more wounds from claw and sword. One gash on his thigh worried him a bit; if the fight lasted too long, he'd bleed out.

Clanless decided he'd put on enough of a show. When next he achieved some separation from the beastman, he clenched his fist and activated the Taint. He didn't need to use his fist, of course, but combined with his glowing eyes, it gave the crowd an indication that he was doing something.

The beastman gave a shiver and stared at him. He did not fall. He didn't show any sign of pain.

Clanless tried again. The beastman shivered again and cocked his head—actually almost his entire upper body. "What you do?"

The Taint didn't hurt him. He must have felt something, based on the shivers. But either it wasn't pain or... pain didn't bother him. Were the beastmen immune to pain itself? Or did the Taint simply not work on their blood? Regardless, he had to find a way to win without it. For the first time since early training, Clanless felt a touch of fear. He had no guarantee of winning this fight.

The presenter yelled something about Clanless and his magic power, but it didn't matter. Only the enemy mattered. Only survival mattered. Every moment of his training raced through his head. No more show. Fight.

With new urgency but careful precision, Clanless wielded the mighty moonblade in a series of attacks designed to wear down his enemy. But this opponent showed no signs of tiring. Even after being locked up for weeks, the beastman appeared to have boundless energy. He dodged or deflected every attack and countered with many of his own.

The enemy didn't tire, but Clanless did. Even without any measurement, he knew this had become his longest single battle ever. Only the fight with the barbarians had been longer. If he hadn't worked hard during the cold of High Winter, Clanless wouldn't have even lasted this long. The crowd appeared both pleased with the intensity and length of the duel and disappointed at the lack of anything spectacular.

And yet Clanless had never faced a more skilled opponent. Though it wasn't just skill with weaponry, but the beastman's inhuman abilities that made him so fearsome. He could jump higher, reach further, and sometimes move faster than any enemy.

The beastman rolled past him, underneath a swing of the moonblade. He jumped up before Clanless could spin around. Dropping the sword, the beastman leaped onto Clanless's back. The foe's powerful arms wrapped up and around his own, pinning them up, making the moonblade useless. The beastman's legs twisted around his thighs. The weight pulled him back. They fell together onto the sand. The beastman released with his left hand and grabbed up his sword where he'd dropped it. Clanless elbowed him with the newly-freed arm and activated the Taint at the same time. Though it only caused a shiver, it was enough for him to break free from his enemy's powerful hold. He rolled away, coughing in the cloud of sand that erupted from their movements.

He barely managed to get to his knees before the beastman leaped higher than ever. He came down toward Clanless, sword swinging in a massive overhand chop. If he'd been on his feet, Clanless could have simply dodged. But on his knees, he couldn't move fast enough. With no other recourse, he heaved the moonblade up with both hands as a shield. The two weapons collided with a massive clang that reverberated above the shouts of the crowd.

The fall and the impact staggered the beastman. Before he could recover, Clanless lunged forward, still on his knees. He swept the moonblade out at its greatest arc, releasing one hand while the other gripped it at the very end of the handle. The curved tip of the blade ripped across the beastman's knees, cutting deep. He screamed but did not completely fall. With his legs useless, the beastman held himself up on his long arms, glaring at Clanless. He still held his sword in one hand.

Clanless got to his feet, growing weaker from his own injuries. He had no doubt the beastman was still dangerous. He could almost certainly lunge forward and swing the sword before falling back onto his hands. Clanless wouldn't give him that opportunity. He took a quick breath and leaped forward himself. He spun and delivered a massive two-handed upward stroke into the beastman's chest. The impact of the blow lifted the beastman off his hands. The crowd exploded in a shout of appreciation.

Clanless let the beastman fall off his blade. Hagh said the fight was to the death, so he had to finish it. He stepped up beside the fallen enemy, whose limbs quivered as he struggled to move. He lifted the moonblade, its bloody surface gleaming in the sun's radiance.

The beastman managed to get his hand up to his throat, where he hooked a finger under the necklace. "You… take," he gasped. "Tell… wife… honor served…"

"Blood is life. Blood is precious. Blood is power," Clanless chanted. He didn't know why he did it, but it seemed appropriate in the moment.

As Clanless brought the moonblade down, the beastman croaked out "Blood… is all." And then the blade cut off any more words forever.

Though he knew the priests wouldn't want it, Clanless knelt and used the Siphon anyway. He wanted a sample of the beastman's blood. He wasn't sure what he would do with it, but blood that resisted the Taint had to be valuable somehow. While kneeling by the body, he pulled the beastman's necklace free. Once done, he stood and acknowledged the crowd with lifted moonblade. His hands shook while holding it up, but he'd lived. He'd won.

Only then did he notice: the impact with the beastman's sword had left a chip in the moonblade. It wasn't much—barely the size of a fingernail clipping—but it was the first time his weapon had ever taken any harm in a fight.

He faced the royal box where the Hawk King stood watching. Hagh told him what was expected. He ran a finger along the side of the moonblade, collecting the enemy's blood. Then he used it to draw a line across his own forehead as he looked up at the king. He followed it with a bow.

The Hawk King applauded, and the crowd screamed his title. Clanless, the newest sensation at Et-Baylak's arena, had arrived.

(((●)))

The healer had scarcely begun work on Clanless before the summons came. An attendant reported that the Hawk King wanted to see his new arena fighter "at once."

"Better go right away," Hagh advised.

"I'm a mess," Clanless said. "Blood and guts and—"

"Doesn't matter. The Hawk King isn't known for his patience."

The healer stood aside as Clanless struggled back to his feet. "I guess I'd better go. Lead the way." The attendant did so, guiding him on a long route around the entire arena. As another fight raged on, the noise of the crowd and the presenter filled their ears most of the way. At last, they came to a hallway decorated with a red carpet and ornate walls. The attendant asked Clanless to wait while he went ahead and slipped in through a pair of doors. Clanless caught a glimpse of the sun shining on people moving about inside. The Hawk King's royal box, no doubt.

A moment later, the Hawk King himself emerged through the doors and approached. Clanless bowed. The Hawk King stopped and folded his arms.

"That was quite a performance, Clanless. The people will be talking about it for some time."

"Thank you, sire."

"I was not complimenting you. I am, in fact, somewhat disappointed in you."

Clanless wrinkled his brow. "How so, sire?"

The Hawk King sighed and looked toward the ceiling. "I was told of this amazing power you possess: that you can boil men's blood within their bodies. I expected more of you."

"My… power did not work on this creature, sire."

"So if we were to send you back in, along with several human opponents, you would show us this power?"

"If that is what you wish."

The king thought for a minute. "No, we can wait until next week, I suppose. But you must understand one thing for certain, Clanless. One thing."

"What is that, sire?"

The Hawk King's stare possessed him. "I have expectations. When I have expectations, they must be met, regardless of the difficulty involved. Do you understand?"

"I… believe so, sire."

"See that you do." The Hawk King waved him away. "Now go clean yourself. I expect"—he emphasized the word—"you will not appear before me in such a condition again."

"Yes, sire." Clanless kept his gaze down, trying to understand. Should he have cleaned up before coming, even though it meant making the king wait longer? Hagh had implied haste was more important. Still, the king made the point of his "expectations." He would have to obey as best as he could.

When he looked up, the Hawk King had already re-entered the royal box. The attendant did not reappear, leaving Clanless to find his own way back. It took him almost twenty minutes to reach halls he recognized. He sought out the healer to complete his work and then made his way to the baths.

Soaking in the water alone, he remembered the beastman's necklace. He fumbled through the pile of his belongings and pulled it out. After rinsing the blood from it in the bath, he took a closer look. More blood. He scrubbed at it with a cloth.

The chain itself was unremarkable… except that such a fine chain implied a level of craftsmanship beyond what would be expected of the beastmen. Like the sword he'd carried, this evidence pointed to something more than the stories told. If such a simple thing was so wrong, what else about the beastmen might be wrong? The dying beastman spoke of a wife, implying family structures. He also spoke twice of honor… yet he fought with a bladed weapon. The beastmen believed in honor, but not in the same way. Curious.

He scrubbed away the last of the blood from the ornament hanging on the chain. It appeared to be made from a gold-colored metal. Clanless had read little about metals, save those used in the making of weapons. He didn't recognize this one. But the disc-shaped ornament itself displayed the carving of a circle with what looked like beams of light shining out from it. The sun or the moon? He couldn't tell. Within the circle, he could see an emblem of a single claw. Clanless turned it over and saw a strange combination of lines. Letters? If so, they weren't any letters he knew. Did the beastmen have their own language as well?

Clanless studied it a bit longer, but found nothing else. After another moment's thought, he put the chain around his own neck. If anyone asked, he'd taken a token from his slaying of a beastman. It fit with his personality. Orgina would have been pleased. He wondered if the Hawk King thought of such things at all.

NOTHING IS CERTAIN

Now

Yesun skipped on ahead of Clanless down the street. How did the boy have so much energy at the end of a long day? "Slow down," he called. "I'm not running all the way to the lower city."

Yesun looked back. "I thought you'd want to hurry. He said you would."

"He doesn't know everything, no matter how much he tries to sound like it." Clanless threw up his hands. "Why am I arguing with you? Let's just keep going."

Yesun pointed past him. "What about him?"

Clanless spun around to see a tall figure following them. He scowled. "What do you want, Bain?"

The fifth member of the Dohor made a noncommittal shrug. "I've a pretty good idea of where you're going. I thought I'd come along too."

Clanless planted himself in the street. "Why?"

"Lots of reasons. First and foremost, I'm curious to see how that old storyteller is doing after all these years. It is the same one, right? With the daughter you fancied?"

"Let me be, Bain. Not tonight."

Bain stepped closer and lowered his voice. "I think you've forgotten who you are for one more day. The Hawk King is still watching. Just because Daviland is in prison doesn't mean he isn't looking for the rest of his followers."

"What does that have to do with my—our—old friends?"

Bain snorted. "I'm not an idiot, Clanless. I think you would have learned that much about me, at least. Please don't make me tell you everything I know out here where someone might hear us." He glanced down at Yesun, who pretended to look the other way.

"Then why come with me?"

"Because now it will look like the two of us—old friends that we are!—are out celebrating together the night before your freedom, something that will appear completely normal to the watchers…" He lowered his voice. "As opposed to you running off to the lower city all by yourself."

As much as Clanless hated to admit it, Bain had a point. He'd kept himself clean and above reproach for two years to avoid the Hawk King's ire. His last night wasn't the time to ruin his record, especially not after the earlier threat from the Ghamba Lam. One false move and his freedom would evaporate like spilled water during the peak of High Spring.

Clanless threw his arm around the taller man. "Come then, old friend," he said loudly. "I have a desire to enjoy some food and drink that reminds me of my home!"

"Don't overdo it," Bain said, rolling his eye.

Yesun cocked his head, brow lowered. "So are we still going the same place?"

Clanless chuckled, though he felt no humor. "Yes, yes. Lead on."

Bain disentangled himself from Clanless's arm as they resumed their walk. "You're a fool, you know. You should spend your last night as a slave safe in bed. Then celebrate when you're free."

"Once I'm free, I'm leaving this city and going as far away as I can."

Bain shook his head. "Still a fool. You shouldn't be saying things like that out loud either."

"When have I ever taken your advice?"

"Almost never. And yet, if you had, you would have avoided some serious problems." He gestured to the street ahead. "Like the one you're marching into right now."

Clanless sighed. "I have only one problem, Bain. He's waiting in a cell for me to kill him tomorrow."

"He's not the problem, and you know it." Bain paused. "But he might be more of a problem tomorrow than you think."

"Why does everyone keep saying that?" Clanless threw up his hands. "I'm the greatest arena fighter this Empire—"

"Debatable," Bain interrupted.

"—this Empire has ever known. He's a beaten-up peasant leader. How could the fight possibly go any way other than the obvious?"

"Nothing is certain under the moon's gaze, save blood."

"What is that supposed to mean?"

Bain shrugged. "I don't know. I heard it in a tavern one night and liked the sound of it."

"Seriously?"

"Maybe."

They kept walking. The early evening air was pleasantly cool, though that would start to change tomorrow as High Winter arrived.

"What do you think of all Hagh's talk about Suirel?" Bain asked.

Clanless glanced toward the sky at the only moon he'd ever known. "Superstition has never helped me."

"The second moon isn't superstition." Bain paused. "But a lot of the stories around it are. You shouldn't ignore it, you know. Superstation has hurt you in the past because you don't know how to use it for yourself."

Clanless snorted. "You're always saying things like that, but here you are, right next to me, still a slave. What good has all your cleverness done you?"

Bain narrowed his eyes. "It's kept me alive so far. I don't have a magical power or a blood-wraith to help me like you."

Clanless couldn't argue with that.

"Besides," Bain went on, "I just might get my own freedom soon… without all the hard work of saving you've done."

"How are you going to do that?"

"By being clever."

PASQUE HOUSE

Then

Two hours after the final fight of the day, Qara met with the four arena fighters in the dining hall. "The Hawk King was pleased with all of your fighting today," she announced. "And he wishes you now to enjoy your life in his service. As such, he bids you all to spend the evening at Pasque House." She rubbed her temples before smiling at Clanless. "It will be the first time for Clanless here, so I expect the rest of you to show him what is expected."

"We will have no problem with this task!" Sugh exclaimed. He threw an arm around Clanless's shoulders and shook him. "We will show this poor boy the way he should go."

Clanless tried to protest. "It was a very hard fight. I am exhausted. Perhaps another—"

"You did not understand me," Qara interrupted. Her smile faded. "The Hawk King expects you to do this."

Ah. Expects. Clanless forced a smile in return. "In that case, who am I to argue against such a well-earned reward?"

"Now we're getting somewhere!" Hagh exclaimed, following it with a pair of coughs.

Silence, of course, said nothing, but he licked his lips with a grin.

Once they had eaten, the four arena fighters changed into nicer clothing and made their way out. For the first time, Clanless set foot on the streets of Et-Baylak. Even those were an improvement over the ones he'd walked in other cities. Each street curved upward in the middle, leaving lower ridges along each side for water to flow. The streets were made of stone, fit together with precision.

"Come, Clanless," Hagh said, leading the way. "The girls of Pasque House specialize in fulfilling your dreams. I hope you've thought of a good one for tonight."

"I never stop dreaming," Clanless answered to laughter from the others.

Pasque House turned out to be one of the magnificent manors he'd spotted on his way in to the arena. No sign identified it, but a single guard at the gate allowed them in without question. As they strode through a lush courtyard, Clanless caught a glimpse of a couple in a passionate embrace off to one side, barely hidden by the greenery. Sugh elbowed him with a knowing grin.

A young man opened the double doors at the end of the walkway, announcing, "The Dohor are here, my lady."

An elderly woman bowed as the four men entered an enormous lobby.. "Gentlemen. It is an honor, as always." She brightened at the sight of Clanless. "And our newest sensation! How delightful. Clanless, allow me to welcome you for your first visit to the Pasque House." She clapped her hands. "You shall have your choice tonight, of all those currently available!" The young man hurried away, calling down the hall. A few seconds later, girls poured into the lobby, smiling and giggling. All of them were clothed in skin-hugging silk robes of varying colors.

Sugh leaned in beside Clanless. "Just don't pick Erten," he whispered. "I've been dreaming about her for two weeks." He indicated a dark-haired beauty who smiled at both of them.

"Please, Clanless," the elderly woman said. "Choose one of my girls to delight you this evening." She came to his side and ran her hand along his bare shoulder with the brand.

He flinched at her touch. Her eyebrows went up. "Oh, this one will require a gentle touch, girls. Be prepared. It may be a long night."

"I certainly hope so," Hagh said.

Clanless thought to choose a girl around his own age, but as he looked them over, they all seemed younger. He didn't know what he'd expected, but surely a wider range of ages would be normal… wouldn't it?

"Come on," Sugh urged. "The rest of us are waiting our turn."

Clanless pointed at a girl who looked to be a couple of years younger, with pale hair that reminded him somehow of Kekeen. "You."

"Ah, Salkhi. One of our newest," the older woman observed. "I hope she meets with your approval." She patted him on the rear. "Should there be any problems, please let us know. Here at Pasque House, your wishes—your dreams—are our only goal."

Clanless nodded as Salkhi came forward with a shy smile and a twinkle in surprisingly blue eyes. She took his hand and led him from the lobby, followed by shouted suggestions from Hagh and Sugh that made his cheeks flame with heat.

Salkhi opened a door and glided into an ornate bedroom. An impressive canopy bed dominated most of the space. A cushioned chair sat to one side beside the largest mirror Clanless had ever seen. Salkhi released his hand and walked in front of the mirror. Turning, she untied her belt, and the silk robe fell away, revealing tiny undergarments. "Where would you like to begin, my lord?" she asked in a high voice, speaking for the first time.

Clanless swallowed hard. She was exquisitely beautiful, without question. Much of him longed for what she offered, but two things filled his mind: a nervous sense of fear… and Kekeen's face. He turned his eyes away and noticed a small table beside the door. A pitcher of water stood ready with a pair of drinking glasses.

"The Hawk King pays you for this?" he asked, running a hand along the wood grain of the table.

He felt the heat of her body as she came up behind him. "The House is compensated for you fighters," she said. "I'm not a part of that process."

"They don't pay you directly?"

Her cool hands touched his bare shoulder. Why did everyone always want to trace his brand? He tried not to jerk away. "I am a slave, my lord, much like yourself," she said. "I do what I am told to do. What would you like?"

"I don't know," he answered honestly.

"Perhaps I can make some suggestions then." She maneuvered in front of him, her body brushing against his in a deliberate manner. She reached up and deftly undid the clasp holding his pelt in place. "What kind of fur is this?" she asked. "It's gorgeous."

"Like you," Clanless wanted to say. "I think it's a type of wolf," he said instead.

She laid it carefully on the table then looked back up at him with a teasing smile. "You've made no move yet, my lord. Don't you find me attractive?"

"Very much so. I just…"

"What is it?" She wrapped her hands around the back of his neck, standing on her tiptoes because of the difference in their height. "Are you not a fighter in the bedroom as well? Come, the bed there can be our arena."

For a moment, he let her pull him in that direction. "I hope you're not as violent in this one, of course," she added.

He caught hold of her hands and pulled them loose. "Are some like that with you? Violent?"

She glanced away. "I don't talk about other men in here."

Clanless made a decision. "I will not be violent with you," he said. "In fact, if you wish it, I will never touch you again." He released her hands.

She stood still, her brow wrinkled, but a touch of fear appeared in her eyes. "I don't understand. Do I not please you?"

Clanless fumbled for a pouch he'd hung from his belt. He removed two blood vials from it and set them on the table. "I will pay you extra for the time we spend in here," he said. "But I do not... I have another girl that I love."

Salkhi's eyes darted to the vials and back. "You... don't wish to take me?"

"No. I mean, yes, I do! But... I won't."

"To stay true to this other girl?"

He nodded, though it was only part of the truth.

Salkhi ran a hand across his chest. "She is a lucky woman, this girl of yours."

He gave a weak smile. "I don't know if that's true."

Salkhi sauntered to the bed and climbed on it. "You're sure about this?" She leaned back, giving a full view of her body. "This is my job, you know."

"I'm... sure."

She shook her head. "The other girls will never believe this."

"Oh." Clanless thought for a minute. He took out another vial and added it to the first two. "This is yours as well, if you lie about our time here."

She giggled. "What should I say? How passionate you were?"

"Whatever works to make them think we, uh... enjoyed our time together."

Her mouth dropped. "You are... far too innocent for an arena fighter. Are you being serious about all this? This isn't some trick?"

"No." Clanless shook his head.

Salkhi laughed and sat on the edge of the bed. "So what shall we do with our time, if we aren't... enjoying it?"

"I don't know." Clanless sat on the cushioned chair. "Tell me about yourself."

"Men aren't interested in that kind of stuff. At least not usually." She rolled on to her stomach, feet in the air. "What do you want to know?"

"How did you end up here, if you're a slave? Can you buy your freedom?"

She studied him, as if trying to figure out if he was serious. "All right, we can play that, but you have to answer questions too."

He shrugged without committing.

"I'm a slave because my parents got into debt and sold me here." Salkhi traced a pattern on the bedsheet. "And freedom is a joke. No one ever gets free. Your turn. How did you get your brand? For real, I mean. Not the stories they tell in the streets."

"I have this magic power. The priests didn't like it, so they branded me and sold me into slavery. But I'm going to buy my freedom one day."

Salkhi looked up at him. "You are either the most naive man I've ever met, or… no, that's it. How can you possibly think you'll get free?"

He pointed to the blood vials on the table. "I don't spend what I gain from my fights. I keep it. I save it. And one day, I'll have enough. It'll be a few more years, but I can do it."

"If you're saving it, why are you giving it to me?"

"I already told you that. But maybe you can save it too. You might be free someday. Don't you want to be free?"

"Of course. But it'll never happen."

"Why not?"

She looked back down at the bedsheet. "Someday, a man will get too angry with me, and do something the healers can't fix. It's just what happens."

Clanless stared. "That's horrible!"

"It's part of the job."

"Do you… do you need healers regularly?"

She shrugged and didn't answer.

Clanless clenched his fist. He pushed down the bloodrush that threatened to rise up. "Have any of the other fighters hurt you?"

"I've only been with one of them: the quiet man. He was surprisingly passionate for a man without a tongue." She cocked her head. "What would you have done if I told you he hurt me?"

"I would have hurt him."

"Why?"

"Because it's not right. I won't allow it."

"You won't allow it?" Salkhi rolled over and slid off the bed. "Now you think you're the Hawk King?"

"No, I—I just don't want you to be hurt." His hand fumbled for his fur's chain. When he didn't find it, he toyed with the beastman's necklace instead.

"That's sweet." She smiled again and walked toward him. "I'm starting to think maybe I should drag you into the bed."

"I don't—I don't think you could do that."

She fluttered her eyelashes. "Maybe I have a magic power too. Would you like to find out?"

"I've already paid you. Should I take it back?" He got to his feet.

"No. Not unless you want me to tell everyone you're a eunuch."

"What? I am not!"

"I'm teasing, you big idiot." She put her hands on her hips and rolled her eyes.

He glanced at the door. "How long should I stay in here?"

"That depends. How long do you want people to think you took with me?"

"I don't know."

She laughed again and retrieved her robe from the floor. "We can go whenever you'd like."

Clanless watched her pull the robe on. "If I stay longer, does that mean you'll lose income, since another man won't… come in?"

"No. You're one of the Dohor. Everyone understands you get what you want. We're supposed to make you happy, whatever it takes."

"Then let's take longer."

"You're in charge." She sat down on the floor, leaving the robe gapping open. Clanless tried to keep his eyes on her face. "Let's take our time."

They talked a while longer. He told her about life in the arena, and she told him a little about life before the Pasque House. She came from Clan Dendsu, a respectable clan, but not among the richest. She'd grown up in another city, many miles from the capital, until her parents' debt led her to these circumstances.

Someone pounded on the door. "Clanless!" Sugh's muffled voice came through. "Finish her up already! We're hungry!" Laughter followed.

"I guess it's been long enough." Clanless got to his feet.

Salkhi scrambled up. "Oh, no, no, no. You can't go out like that. No one will believe you were with me."

He paused. "What do you mean?"

"You should be sweating, at the very least." She laughed again.

Clanless took the water from the table and splashed some of it on his face and neck. "Is that good enough?"

"Maybe. One more thing. You should rip my undergarments in half."

"What?" He turned around, saw her reaching down, and turned back quickly. "Why would I do that?"

"When you tore them off me, of course."

Her undergarment landed on his shoulder. He took the flimsy piece of material and glanced back to make sure she'd closed the robe again. "Just tear it?"

She cocked her head and raised an eyebrow. "Is that too hard?"

He ripped the material in two and tossed the pieces on the floor. "Good enough?"

She came up to him and leaned in close. "At least give me a kiss good-bye."

At this point, he didn't think of denying her. And he didn't want to. He leaned down, and their lips met. She pulled his head closer and kissed him deeper, letting her tongue do more than he expected. At last, she pulled away and sauntered over to the table. "A taste of what you missed," she said, gathering up the blood vials.

Clanless swallowed. "Save those," he told her. "Maybe you can be free one day too."

"Maybe. You can go now."

He reached for the door.

"Will I see you again?" Salkhi asked just before he opened it.

He glanced back. "I'm sure of it."

❨❨❨❨●❩❩❩❩

A day after the visit to Pasque House, Hagh invited Clanless back into the city with him. As they walked and talked, Clanless learned bits and pieces of his new companion's background. He'd been fighting in the arena for eight years, he'd said earlier, but he'd been a soldier before. He couldn't even remember how many years he'd fought the Hawk King's battles.

"Mostly barbarians," he said with a cough. "But you know about that type. Filthy lot. Heretics and pagans."

"I wouldn't have taken you for one of the devout," Clanless said, meaning it as a joke.

Hagh didn't laugh. "I'm not the most righteous of men, but I believe." He sighed and gestured forward. "That's why I go here every week after I've… indulged myself."

Clanless looked up and saw an impressive stone building, larger and more ornate than any of the opulent homes and shops in this region. Twin roofs with uplifted points at each corner led his eyes up toward a spherical structure made of crystal. The sun reflected from it into his eyes, and he turned away.

Hagh chuckled. "Too bright to look at when the sun's dominating, innit? At night, though…" He shook his head. "At night, the light of the goddess fills that crystal and it's somethin' to see."

Clanless followed Hagh up a series of stone steps to an enormous set of double doors, thrown open to all who would come. Inside, he saw a gathering area and a half-circle of pedestals, each holding a basin and a sharp knife. Blood-priests moved about the room. Three other supplicants were present, talking with the priests or praying alone.

Clanless stopped at the threshold. "Do your task, Hagh. I'll wait outside."

Hagh wrinkled his brow. "You can come in. It would do you some good to make a sacrifice and honor the goddess."

He shook his head. "They won't accept my blood." He tapped his brand. "The priests despise me."

"How do ya—" Hagh broke off and glanced around. "How do you seek forgiveness then? For, for things like last night? Or the arena itself?"

Clanless shrugged. "It's not something I can deal with. If the goddess is real—"

"No 'if' about it," Hagh interrupted.

"Assuming she's real then," Clanless said, "I just have to hope she'll understand when we meet."

Hagh nodded slowly. "I'll say a prayer for you, and maybe give a little extra blood."

Clanless smiled, thinking about Kekeen's prayers. "Thanks, Hagh. You're a good man."

Hagh snorted. "If I were, I wouldn't need to be here, now would I?"

"Moon's stability to you, old man."

"And t'you." Hagh turned and entered the temple. Clanless watched him go with a twinge of envy. Even as an arena slave like himself, Hagh had something he would never have. It reminded him of Zaluu.

A priest caught sight of him and glared. Clanless rolled his eyes and stepped back out of the doorway.

At the next Arena Night, the organizer pitted Clanless against a trio of barbarian mercenaries. They'd vowed vengeance against him for killing so many of their people. The vow—and the leather armor they wore in imitation of Bain—did them no good. He defeated them all with ease, making sure to provide a dramatic finish with the Taint. Surely, the Hawk King would be pleased.

Afterwards, the fighters visited Pasque House again, and Clanless spent a couple more hours with Salkhi. He enjoyed her company; though she was nothing like Kekeen. He talked with her about many things, but never beyond a superficial level. He didn't confide in her and didn't tell her about the Taint or anything related to it. She knew he possessed some strange power, as did everyone in the city, but he wouldn't talk about it. In some ways, it was the type of relationship Zektel had predicted he could have, but without the physical side of things. He still wasn't able to convince himself to go that far, either from loyalty to the memory of Kekeen, or from his own fear, something he couldn't even explain to himself.

Life in the capital turned out to be not much different from life in Ghoyor. The only real difference he found was wealth. So many rich people lived in Et-Baylak. But he soon discovered that if he traveled outside the inner city wall, he met people more like those he'd known for most of his life. And they were thrilled an elite arena fighter would deign to spend time with them.

Not that he spent a lot of time outside of the arena. As always, he worked hard and trained hard. He saved his blood, siphoning as much as he could from every fight. If he spent any at all, it was in the lower city eating houses, and what he paid Salkhi.

With so few others with which to train, he soon became close to Hagh and Sugh, at least to some degree. He still ached over the loss of Zaluu and didn't want to believe he could have a friend like that again. But these two persisted, like they wanted to spend time with him. Slowly, he began to relax around them.

Only Silence remained a mystery to him, for obvious reasons. He felt uneasy in the other man's presence. Hagh assured him he could speak normally around Silence ("He lost his tongue, not his ears!"), but it always seemed awkward.

Which is why, two months later, as High Spring reached its peak, he didn't know how to react when Silence insisted on taking him into the city.

HELLO, BROTHER

Then

"I don't understand what we're doing," Clanless told Silence as they passed through the gates into the lower city. "Where are we going?"

Silence only pointed down the street. Clanless shrugged and continued to follow him. What else could he do? The other fighter never asked for much of anything else.

But the deeper they went into the lower city, the more suspicious he grew. What possible reason could Silence have for coming this far? And why bring him? Memories of the brigands who'd kidnapped Koland returned. Was this another situation like that? Could the Daghilch have paid Silence to lead him into a trap? With a shock, he remembered Bain's words: how they'd promised him his freedom. He stopped in the middle of the street.

"I think this is far enough," he said. "I don't know what you're trying to do, but I've had enough."

Silence shook his head and pointed.

"No. You need to give me more than pointing, if you want me to go any further." He glanced up at the sky. "The moon is hidden. It's going to rain soon."

Silence rolled his eyes. He strode with firm steps away from Clanless several yards down the street. He stopped and gestured broadly at an eating house a few buildings down. Light and sounds of merriment spilled out from it into the street.

"Is that all? You've found a good place to eat?" Clanless resumed following him. If this was a trap, he thought he could handle it. He always carried Zaluu's throwing knife now, in case he needed to spill some blood.

To his surprise, Silence didn't go in through the main doors of the eating house but walked around to the side. The next building in line, an inn, was connected to the eating house with a covered walkway. They ducked under the shelter just as large drops began to fall from the sky. Silence opened the door and walked into a dimly-lit hallway.

Clanless joined him but didn't advance far. The sound of the rain hitting the walkway grew louder as it intensified. "What are we doing here? I thought we were going to eat."

Silence pointed to a room door before knocking on it. The door opened, but Clanless couldn't see the occupant from his angle. "Silence. Why are we here?" His hand tightened on the dagger's handle.

"I asked him to bring you here." The door opened all the way, and Koland stepped out into the hall.

Clanless's mouth dropped open. Koland turned to his companion. "Silence, you're welcome to stay, if you want, or you can go next door. The singer performing right now is exceptionally good."

Silence grinned and pushed past Clanless on his way to the eating house. "Singer?" Clanless fumbled with his words. "Is she—?"

"You'll see her soon enough, son," Koland interrupted. "For now, there's someone else here who wants to meet you." He gestured into the room.

His mind spinning, Clanless entered the room. It had been almost three and a half years since he'd seen the storyteller and his daughter. His last words to Kekeen were to ask her not to wait for him. She'd insisted she would. Had she held true to that? Did he want her to? She was here. Now. He would be seeing her soon. What should he say?

And who else would want to meet him? He contained his thoughts and looked around. The room appeared like any other inn's room: a single bed, a side table, and a couple of chairs. A hooded man sat in one of the chairs, tapping his fingers on the table. When Koland shut the door, the man stood and pulled back his hood. Clanless didn't recognize him. Over the years, he'd become skilled at evaluating a man's physique. What he saw now was a man who'd worked hard in his early life, perhaps on a farm or clanhold somewhere, and now... now he did something else. He wasn't an arena fighter or soldier, but he looked like he could handle himself in an ordinary fight. His curly brown hair and beard were entirely unremarkable.

"Hello, brother," he said with a gentle smile.

Clanless stared at him. For a brief moment, he thought… but no, if his mother truly had another son, he would be a small boy now. "I have no brother," he answered.

"We are both of clan Tokuur." The man spread his hands, palms up. "My name is Daviland, and I am thrilled to meet you."

"I have no clan." His answer came without thought, but he did recognize the name. Daviland. The one who wanted to overthrow the Hawk King. So Koland had found him again.

"The priests have told you that." Daviland took a step closer. "But words and a scar on your shoulder can't destroy family ties dating back generations. You are Tokuur, and you always will be."

Clanless snorted. "Family ties? What has clan Tokuur done for me in all these years?" He shook his head. "I have no ties. But I know who you are. Koland has told me about you, and I've heard many of the stories over the past few years."

"What have you heard?" Daviland folded his arms across his chest, still smiling.

"The heroic stuff, the stories people spread."

"They spread them about you as well."

"Of course. That's part of the point of being an arena fighter. It's how they get people to come—" He broke off. "Oh."

Daviland chuckled. "Yes, it works the same way in building a revolution. Stories get people to come. To join us. And we're in the room here with one of the greatest storytellers in the Empire." He gestured to the table and chairs. "Won't you sit down?"

Clanless took the offered chair with a look at Koland. "So all of the stories about him came from you?"

"Of course not," Koland answered, putting a hand on his chest in mock outrage. "I only spread them." He shrugged. "And maybe exaggerate a little bit here and there."

"A little bit." Daviland chuckled again. "You spin the tales masterfully, my friend, with little regard for the facts."

"Why am I here?" Clanless asked. "You wanted to meet me?"

"Yes, I did." Daviland settled into the chair across from him. "Koland has told me your story as well, and I think he kept to the facts on that one. Since we're of the same clan, and you have been so horribly mistreated, I wanted to meet you."

"What for?" Clanless folded his own arms now.

"For the same reason I meet so many other people across the Empire who have been abused by the Hawk King's systems." Daviland's eyes locked onto his. "To tell you there is hope. We can change things. We can all be free."

"I will be free. In a few years."

"But it could be sooner. And not just you, but everyone. Every arena fighter. Every slave of any other kind. Those the priesthood oppresses." He made a sweeping gesture. "I don't have to give you a big speech about the evils of this Empire. You've experienced it! And look at the opulence in the upper city here! Compare that with everywhere else you've lived. The Hawk King and his elite live in utter decadence while our people haul rocks to reinforce a wall in their home, fearful of winter winds and barbarian attacks."

"I'm not arguing with you. I hate the Hawk King. I hate the priests. But what do you want from me?" Clanless tapped his own brand. "I'm a slave. I can't do anything to help you. The bloodbond will stop me."

"Not if your master doesn't know what you're doing." Daviland cocked his head ever so slightly. "He doesn't know you're here meeting with me, does he? What would happen if he did?"

"Soldiers would surround this place. We'd never get out alive." Clanless shook his head. "But visiting places here in Et-Baylak is different from actively helping a rebellion."

Koland, leaning against the bed, spoke up: "Your friend Silence helps us. He's been a believer in our cause for almost a year now."

Clanless almost laughed. "What good does a man without a tongue do you? He can't exactly talk people into joining."

"He got you here, didn't he?"

"You asked him to. And you're ignoring the question."

"Silence has his uses," Daviland said. "He's helped us understand more of the arena system, for example, though I'm sure you could tell us more. We have other agents trying to help us understand more of the priesthood. And that, I believe, is of special interest to you."

"What do you mean?"

"Koland has told me about the attempt on your life back in Ghoyor. We think we've found out who was behind that attack."

"I already know that. It was the Daghilch who first branded me." Clanless gave Daviland credit: the look of surprise lasted only a split-second before he smiled again. But Clanless didn't let him speak. He turned on Koland. "And that attack was why you left! You took Kekeen away from me to keep her safe!" He lurched to his feet and pointed at Daviland. "This is how you keep her safe? By taking her to work for a man trying to overthrow the entire Empire? You call that safe?"

Koland gave him a level stare. "I am her father. Her safety is my responsibility, not yours. The only way that changes is if you marry her."

"You're doing a horrible job then."

"We're getting way off the subject," Daviland interceded. "Clanless, we need you."

"What for?" He furrowed his brow, fighting down the anger. "I can't be seen with you. I can't tell anyone I support you. And you can't tell anyone that I do. The minute that happens, I'll be summoned to the Hawk King's presence, and I'll lose everything."

"He wouldn't kill his most promising and highly profitable arena fighter."

"He wouldn't need to." Clanless put both hands on the table, resisting the urge to clench them both into fists. "At any point in time, he could send someone into my room. They could just walk out with everything I own, all the blood I've accumulated over the years. My hope of freedom would be completely gone. And then I wouldn't care any more. I'd die in the very next arena fight."

"But this is why we must resist!" Daviland's earnestness was almost contagious, despite Clanless's anger and fear. "It's not right that he can treat you that way!"

"Of course it's not right! But I can't do anything about it. Not now." He stood up. "A slave can't help you."

"Clanless," Koland said. "Please don't—"

"It's about the Taint!" Daviland burst out.

Clanless stared down at him. "What?"

"The Taint. Your power. That's why we need you."

Clanless looked at Koland. "You told him?"

"Everyone knows about the power you use in the arena," Koland said. "Davil already knew about the Taint and figured it out. When he asked, I confirmed it. That's all."

"I told you that in confidence!"

"Please." Daviland stood, reaching out a hand. "Do not blame the storyteller. It's me, Clanless. As he said, I've heard of the Taint, and your power sounded like it might be the same thing. I pressed him until he agreed. I can be quite persuasive."

"How can the Taint possibly help you? It's brought me nothing but pain and suffering."

"The blood." Daviland lowered his hand. "Haven't you ever wondered what the priests do with all the blood they take in sacrifices?"

"What are you saying?" Of course he'd wondered. Zektel had wondered too. They took far too much for any practical usage.

Daviland gestured broadly. "It doesn't matter if I assemble an army of the common people. I could recruit everyone in the lower city here, everyone in the clanholds, and many more. But we would still fall to the Hawk King's army because of the blood-magic! With all the enhancements they have available to them, a single soldier could be the equal of a hundred commoners, no matter how well armed they are."

Clanless didn't think the disparity was that large, but the concept made sense. He'd seen enough of blood-magic to know it could do amazing things.

"The priests, together with clan Berge, have huge stockpiles of blood, carefully preserved, and ready for usage at any time. This is the key to the Hawk King's power. If we could use the Taint against those stockpiles, we could take away that advantage, destroying their power!"

"Where are these stockpiles kept?" Clanless hated to admit it, but the plan did spark his curiosity.

"We don't know," Daviland admitted. "We're trying to find out."

"How do you know they exist then? Has anyone seen them?"

"They must exist! Where else could the blood go?"

"Maybe they just pour out the excess!" Clanless waved. "Maybe they swim in it. How should I know? The sacrifices are how they keep people committed to them. It doesn't matter what they do with the blood. Not really." He fumbled around and pulled a blood vial from his belt pouch. "Some of it goes here!"

"Clan Ghutalta controls banking and the economics of blood supply," Koland put in. "I've seen their process in person. The priests do not give them very much blood, certainly not in comparison to how much they take in on a monthly basis."

Clanless stuffed the vial back in his pouch. "Why are you even telling me all this and trying to recruit me, when you don't even know?"

"A revolution doesn't happen overnight," Daviland said quietly. "I have to lay plans in advance, balance the needs of my people, and keep them—and me—safe from our enemy as along as I can, while preparing for the battle to come someday."

Clanless shook his head. "I can't help you. Not now. Maybe if you find these stockpiles, we can talk again. But I'm at an enormous risk just being in the same room with you."

"I know. And thank you for listening to me. If you—"

The door swung open and Kekeen burst in, shaking water from her hair. "The rain is coming in sideways," she complained. "The roof over the walkway doesn't do any good. And the crowd's not going anywhere with this weather. Father, they want you over there for another story."

She threw her hair back, lifted her head, and her eyes found Clanless.

They stared at each other. Kekeen hadn't changed much in three and a half years, at least not in his memory. She remained as beautiful as he'd always believed her to be. Her face appeared a little less rounded, her features more sculptured. She was truly a woman now. Had he changed since then? Three years? He might have grown a little taller. A little broader. He had more scars; in fact, he was painfully aware of the visible ones, not sure what she might think of them.

"Aldan," she whispered. Wet spots sprinkled over the surface of her outer blue robe, shielding her inner yellow dress.

He didn't answer, not trusting his voice.

"Koland, my friend," Daviland said, stepping out from behind the table. "I would very much like to hear another of your stories. Let's go next door, shall we?"

Koland grunted and gave a warning glance to Clanless, which he barely noticed. The two men left the room. Still Kekeen and Clanless stood unmoving, apart from each other in awkward silence.

"You look beautiful," he said at last.

Kekeen laughed and shook her hair again. "I look drowned!" She smiled. "You look… stronger."

He shrugged.

"I heard about the barbarian attack," she said, taking a step closer. "It sounded horrible."

"It… was."

She cocked her head. "What's wrong? Aren't you happy to see me?"

"I am! I—" Clanless closed his eyes for a moment, trying to gather himself. "I'm sorry." He opened his eyes. "I'm… a little shaken up by"—he waved toward the eating house—"by the conversation with your father and, and Daviland."

Her face brightened. "That's right! You just met him for the first time! What did you think?"

"I think…" He spoke slowly. "That we haven't seen each other in over three years, and I'd rather talk about something other than… Daviland." While he said it, his mind bounced through so many thoughts and desires and dreams and failings.

"It's been that long." Kekeen looked down. She held her hands in front of her, intertwining the fingers. "It's… in some ways, that's hard to believe." She looked back up at him. "And in others, it seems like it's been even longer. I've missed you, Aldan."

"And I've missed you, more than anything." He took a step toward her, but at that moment, she jerked her head up, eyes wide.

"Oh! I have something for you!" She went to the bed and bent over to reach beneath it. She stood back up, holding a cloth bag, which she extended toward him. "I've been saving these for you."

Clanless wrinkled his brow, but took the bag. The familiar clink of crystal within let him know: "Blood?"

She nodded. "For your freedom."

He smiled. She couldn't possibly have saved much over the past three years, with her father's wandering lifestyle. The bag wasn't heavy. But the consideration moved him. "You're… very kind."

"So are you. You just won't admit it."

"What?"

"To everyone else, you're this ferocious killer." She waved toward the door. "They all imagine you as some kind of monster, taking delight in every kill. That's how they talk about you. But I know the real Aldan." She put her slim hand on the left side of his chest. "I know your heart."

He shook his head. "You're so different from all the other women." He thought of Salkhi, and even Qara with her flirtations.

"How so?" she asked in a low voice, looking up into his eyes.

"You're here giving me gifts and complimenting me." His eyes darted around the room before returning to hers. "All the other women I know would be pointing out how we're alone together in a bedroom."

"Do you think I'm not very much aware of that particular fact?"

Before he could answer, she'd wrapped her hands behind his head and pulled her own up to his. Their lips met. To Clanless, it was as if only a few moments had passed since they'd last kissed, sitting on the stage in Ghoyor. But that feeling sped away as he realized how much time had gone by, and how much emotion he'd held back for this particular moment. He wrapped his arms around her, lifting her from the ground so their faces could be at the same height. He held her close, kissing her as deep and as long as they both desired.

Part of him wanted to throw her down on the bed and see what happened next. Part of him was terrified at the very idea. And a third part was nervously aware that Koland and/or Daviland might walk back in through the door at any moment.

At last, his fear won over, and he broke free, letting Kekeen down to the floor. She gasped and wiped her mouth with the back of her hand.

"I guess you are happy to see me after all."

Clanless kept his hands around her waist. "Every time I see you, it's one of the only bright moments in my life of endless darkness."

She stared up at him, mouth agape. "How do you do that?" she demanded. "How do you say such perfect things?"

He laughed. "I told you: they just fall out of my mouth sometimes. I don't know where they come from."

She turned her head, looking at him through the corner of her eyes. "And yet the last thing you said to me was to find someone else. That I shouldn't wait for you."

"I did say that." He swallowed. "And I meant it at the time. I wanted you to be free, and not have to wait for so long. I wanted you to be happy."

"I'm happy right here and now."

"Me too. And, and I know it's selfish now, and I don't care. I want you to wait for me. I want you, Kekeen. I love you, and no other."

Her smile almost shattered his heart with joy. They didn't speak again for several minutes, though their mouths did communicate a lot.

Kekeen broke free this time. "We'd better stop," she said, pushing away. "Or my father will walk in on something he doesn't want to see."

Clanless glanced at the door. "I suppose you're right."

Kekeen led him to the table. They sat facing each other, hands entwined on the table's surface. Kekeen took a deep breath and let it out with a contented smile.

"How long will you be here?" Clanless asked. "How much can I see you?"

"I don't know. We're traveling with Davil as he makes plans and recruits people. I don't think we'll be here long." She gave his hands a squeeze. "But I hope it's a good long time. Are you… freer to leave the arena?"

He nodded. "I'm free in many more ways than before. But still a slave. I can't leave the city, or do anything that would cause problems for the Hawk King. He's my master now."

"Not for much longer, I hope. What did Daviland say to you?"

Clanless shook his head. "It doesn't matter. He tried to recruit me. But I can't do anything for him. I'm a slave. I keep trying to explain that to people."

"But if Daviland wins, you won't be a slave any more!"

"Do you truly believe he can do that?" Clanless gave her an intense look.

"Yes. Of course I do."

He released one of her hands and picked up the bag she'd given him.

"Then why give me this? Why did you save this up for me to help shorten the time it takes to purchase my freedom if you think Daviland is going to do it sooner?"

Kekeen pulled her other hand loose and crossed her arms. "I can have more than one plan."

"Of course." He smiled and set the bag on the table.

"I can!" She pointed at the bag. "If Davil succeeds, and you don't need that for your freedom, we can use it to help get our new life started!"

"Will blood still be the currency of the Empire if he destroys the priesthood?"

Kekeen hesitated only a moment. "I don't know. But the crystals themselves have to be valuable somehow, don't they?"

Clanless chuckled. "Maybe they are." He thought for a moment before leaning forward across the table. The necklace dangled as he grasped her hand again. "I will try to return tomorrow night. If you do not see me before sunset, it will be the night after. I think I will be here, but unusual things can happen. The Hawk King sometimes has 'expectations' of us."

"What does that mean?"

He hesitated. He would need to tell her about Pasque House eventually, but... "He sometimes wants us to make appearances at various places, so we're seen by the people. That kind of thing."

"You mean all of the fighters? I met the one who can't talk. What's his name?"

"Silence."

She snorted. "Right. I'm sure he picked that one out himself. Not much like your friend back at the last place, is he?"

Clanless looked down. He hadn't thought about Zaluu in a while.

"Oh." Kekeen realized the implication. "He... died in the barbarian attack?"

Clanless nodded.

"Then you did have help in that fight, right? Because the stories people tell claim you fought all alone."

"No." He shook his head. Interesting how even the Hawk King's attempt to shape that story hadn't worked out. People believed what they wanted to believe. "We were all there. But only Badaar—he was our trainer—and I survived."

Kekeen gave his hand a squeeze. "I'm sure Zaluu fought well."

"He was magnificent." Clanless tried to smile, but couldn't maintain it. "He died near me, but... I didn't see it happen. I didn't even know it had happened. I can't even remember seeing him."

"Would you want to see him die?"

"That's not what I mean." He tried to find the words. "I just thought… he was my friend. Shouldn't I have known… shouldn't I have realized it? When he died, I mean."

"Caring about someone doesn't create a magic link between them, as much as we wish it did." Kekeen bit her lip before continuing: "I try to tell myself sometimes that… that if you died in the arena, I would know it somehow. I would sense it." She shook her head. "But there's no reason to believe that. It's just wishful thinking."

"I wonder if there's a blood-magic out there that does create that kind of link." Clanless sighed. "That would be something."

Kekeen reached across the table and touched the hanging necklace. "What is that? I don't remember it."

"A memory of my first fight here in the capital. I took it from a beast-man I defeated."

"It's a beastman's?" She leaned closer to examine it. "I've never seen anything belonging to them. I didn't even know if they were real."

"Real enough. I have a scar on my thigh to remind me."

A soft knock was followed by the door opening slowly. "I'm coming in," Daviland called, taking his time. When he stepped in, he looked at the two of them and shook his head. Water cascaded from his curls onto his already wet shirt. "Not what I expected to find, I'll admit. You two are either the most discreet of lovers or…" He shrugged with a grin. "I'm not sure."

Kekeen giggled. "Wouldn't you like to know?"

Daviland gestured over his shoulder. "Your father wants you to return for one or two more songs. The crowd is a bit… edgy, I suppose, being trapped by the rain."

Kekeen stood. "We'll come right over."

Clanless joined her as they headed out the door. Daviland put out a hand to stop him. "Think about what I've said, Clanless. The Hawk King is not invincible."

Clanless nodded but said nothing. When he opened the exterior door for Kekeen, they both flinched at the downpour outside. As Kekeen had noted earlier, the rain came in almost completely sideways. "Here." Clanless removed his fur and put it over Kekeen's head. "It's amazingly proof against water."

She favored him with a bigger smile. "Careful, or I'll keep it," she warned before ducking out. They both ran across to the opposite building and hurried inside, mostly soaked. Despite her words, Kekeen removed the fur and returned it before hurrying over to the eating house's stage.

Clanless fastened the fur in its usual place. A murmur swept through the crowd as he entered. They recognized him, of course. Aside from the Hawk King himself, few were more recognizable in the city than the Dohor fighters. Silence gave him a wave from between two girls at a table in the middle. Recalling what Salkhi had said about him, Clanless chuckled to himself. He found a seat at another table, not far from the front. When a server hurried over, he asked only for a mug of his favorite, zokin.

"What shall I sing?" Kekeen called out. "Perhaps something bright to cheer us during this dark night?"

Several of the patrons called out song titles. Clanless stirred at a memory. *"The Day the Sun Surrendered!"* he called out. Several others echoed agreement.

Kekeen turned her smile on him. "Our arena fighter makes a request! Is it a good one?"

The crowd agreed (for the most part), and Koland started the music. Kekeen began the familiar words, her voice so familiar and yet even better, somehow, than the last time he'd heard it. By the second verse, much of the crowd had joined in. Clanless had known it would happen and didn't mind. He'd heard her sing and now could watch her as she moved and engaged with the people. He enjoyed the song too. It spoke of a love found, lost, then found again. In some ways, it described his relationship with Kekeen.

She'd waited for him. She loved him. Could there be anything greater in this life? If only he were free now! He could take her away, far away from Et-Baylak and arenas and Daviland and revolutions. She would be safe, and she would be his. His mind wandered as he watched her, imagining so much that could be, if things were different.

When at last the rain diminished and the crowd dispersed, Clanless and Kekeen had time only for a few brief words. The eating house owner wanted to clean up, while Koland and Daviland were already deep into conversation in the bedroom. Clanless stepped out into the sprinkling remnants of the earlier downpour and turned back for one more glimpse of Kekeen. She gave him her best smile and a little wave before she ducked back inside.

He turned to find Silence waiting for him in the street. Together, they took the long walk back to the arena. This time, Clanless didn't mind the distance so much.

Clanless tossed Kekeen's bag onto his table before stripping off his wet clothes. He hung the fur pelt up to dry, and threw the other clothes over his chair. An attendant would take them to be washed tomorrow. After pulling on a pair of his arena pants, he noticed the bag again. Curious, he opened it and dumped the contents out. Around a dozen crystal blood vials tumbled out.

But something was different. He picked one of them up and examined it. Instead of the usual green wax seal, these were sealed with gold. He'd seen that before, but not for a very long time. Was it…?

He took the vial out into the hall and made his way down to Qara's door. He knocked and waited. She opened the door a few moments later, wearing a night robe. "Clanless? It's the middle of the night. What do you need?" Her eyes swept over his bare chest.

"Oh." He shook his head. "I'm sorry. I forgot the time. It can wait." He turned.

"No, it's all right." She caught hold of his elbow. He flinched only a little. Her hand loosened its hold on her robe, letting it gap a little. "Do you need something?"

He held up the vial. "I received this tonight from, uh, a dealer in the market, as change when I bought something. But I think he gave me the wrong thing. Isn't this V-blood?"

Qara took the vial and held it up to the light. She squinted and massaged her temples. "It's gold-sealed. Voluntary blood for sure. And this symbol here. That's clan Shukan, the Hawk King's clan. This is the most valuable blood there is. I'd say he gave you the wrong one!"

Clanless took it back. "Thank you. I'm sorry for disturbing you so late."

She smiled. "My door is open to you any time, you know."

He nodded awkwardly. "Thank you again." He hurried back to his room, aware of her eyes following him.

Back in his bedroom, he examined the rest of the vials and counted them. He did the calculations in his head and sat down hard on his bed.

Where in the Empire had Kekeen gotten her hands on this much V-blood? And clan Shukan blood! If he understood properly, this bag alone knocked an entire year off his quest for freedom.

This was true love.

THE HAWK KING IS DISPLEASED

Clanless did return to visit Kekeen the next evening. The seasonable rain continued, creating the only negative aspect to the day. Clanless almost considered calling for a carriage to get back to the arena, but he decided against it. No need to alert Qara or anyone else about where he spent his time.

Unfortunately, someone knew his whereabouts. The next day, the Hawk King summoned him to the palace.

It had been over two months since he'd seen the king, other than the view from the arena floor to the royal box. This time, an attendant took him outside the arena and across to the palace next door. At least the rains had stopped for now. They entered through a side door, which still looked more ornate than any door Clanless had ever seen. Once inside, he felt like an idiot as he turned his head this way and that, trying to see everything. He couldn't help it, though. He'd seen wealth on display, of course. The Pasque House revealed more wealth than he'd imagined possible. But that paled compared to what he saw now.

The sheer density of the decorations overwhelmed his senses. Everywhere he looked, he saw marble pillars engraved with gold, red-trimmed lattice on the ceiling and some walls, and elaborately-embroidered tapestries filling any empty spaces. Gold decorated everything, along with copious amounts of the same crystal used to make blood vials. Every so often, he spied entire statues formed of the crystal. Some even had a dark red interior, as if blood had been sealed within.

The attendant led him to a pair of double doors made of a dark wood he didn't recognize. A hand-carved image of a hawk with outspread wings, inlaid with gold, spread across both doors.

"Please wait in here," the attendant said, opening the door and gesturing for Clanless to enter.

Left alone in the room, Clanless walked around, examining a variety of display pieces. Some looked as if they'd come from arena fights. Or maybe battles on the outskirts of the Empire? The Hawk King had done a lot of that in his early years. Clanless saw some barbarian weapons and clothing, at least one set of beastman claws, and a strangely horned animal skull. He leaned in to get a better look at the skull but pulled back when he heard the door opening.

The Hawk King entered, followed by a blood-priest who stayed next to the door. Dressed somewhere between a warrior and a nobleman, the king spread his arms with a smile... though it didn't seem altogether pleasant. "Clanless! Good to see my newest sensation doing so well!"

Clanless gave a bow, trying to remember if he was supposed to do anything else, like kneel or something. If so, the king didn't seem offended. He swept past him and paused next to the skull. "Ah, yes. That thing. I remember the day we killed it, out in the high hills beyond the northern desert. Those were the days, days of adventure and exploration, pushing the boundaries of this mighty Empire to all corners."

"It's fascinating, sire."

"Those days are over for me, Clanless." The Hawk King traced one of the skull's horns with his finger. "Now I fight different battles here, from the center of this Empire beneath the moon's gaze."

Clanless didn't answer, not sure whether his input was desired. With the king so near to him, he felt a sudden twitch and a sense of blood nearby. It was similar to what he experienced just prior to using the Taint, but... he couldn't pinpoint any actual bleeding on the king's part.

The king straightened. "Part of winning the battles here at home involves knowing what is transpiring in my realm, Clanless." He kept talking while facing the skull. "Most people think that means I'm watching for barbarian attacks, or consulting with the priests about the latest offerings and the amount of blood to allow into the economy. But it's much more than that."

The Hawk King walked around the skull display, putting it between the two of them. He looked over the top through the horns at Clanless and gave him an arched smile. "I have many people working for me, and a large number of slaves. And I keep track of what they're all doing."

Clanless froze.

"Yes, that means you. Your visits to the lower city have been noted. I am not altogether pleased, Clanless."

"I'm sorry, sire." Clanless lowered his head. "Have I shamed you?"

"Ordinarily, a tryst between one of my Dohor and a lower class girl would not matter in the slightest. Silence, for example, somehow has a dozen or more girls that he visits." The king chuckled. "But your visits come at an awkward time. There are rumors of rebellion, stories of a young clanholder who thinks far above his station. I cannot help but wonder: would Clanless, a son of poor clanhold farmers, be drawn to such a man?"

What could he say? Should he deny any knowledge of Daviland? How much did the Hawk King actually know?

"Regardless of the truth of the matter," the Hawk King went on, sparing him from responding, "I know that you will not now engage in any activity that would... displease me." He looked up toward the door, as if noticing the priest standing there for the first time. "Oh, and the priests have requested that I remind you of the conditions of your... banishment or whatever they call it. You are not allowed to father any children. You know this, correct?"

"I remember," Clanless said.

"Good, good. We wouldn't want to upset them. The current Ghamba Lam is so particular about things like this." The Hawk King shook his head. "I am glad we could resolve this situation so amicably."

"Yes, sire."

The Hawk King stared at him, piercing eyes over that beak-like nose. "Sometimes, Clanless, the... benefits granted to the Dohor may cloud their minds, make them forget the most important fact of their existence."

Clanless didn't answer again, afraid to speak.

"You are my slaves. You live one more day solely by my grace. Your purpose in life is to please me. This week, Clanless... I have not been pleased. Do you understand?"

"Yes, sire."

"Good. Keep it in mind." The Hawk King gestured to the priest who rapped on the door. "I have another... illustration of what I mean."

The door swung open. Silence entered the room, a curious look on his face. Spotting the Hawk King, he bowed at once. Behind him, the priest closed the door again.

"Silence! So good of you to come... but then, you have no choice, do you?" The Hawk King walked past him to the priest and held out his hand. The priest handed him two metal plates. Clanless recognized them at once: bloodbonds.

"I don't know if either of you are fully aware of the power I have over my slaves. Have you ever seen it demonstrated, Clanless?" The king held up one of the bloodbonds.

"No, sire." His own blood went cold. He'd heard stories throughout his life as a slave and had no desire to witness it.

The king put a fingertip onto the metal plate and twisted it. Silence jerked as if someone had yanked him upward. He stood frozen in an unnatural pose, looking like he might leap into the air at any moment... or fall forward onto his face.

"Completely, wholly at my command," the Hawk King murmured. To Clanless's horror, he drew a knife from his belt and approached Silence.

"Sire, I—"

"Be silent, like your companion here." The Hawk King walked in a circle around the frozen arena fighter. "Silence, I told Clanless I was not pleased with his recent indiscretions. With you, however, it goes beyond displeasure."

Clanless took a step forward. The priest cleared his throat. The Hawk King glanced back at him and sighed. He tossed Silence's bloodbond on to the floor and ran his finger over the second one. Clanless stiffened. He thought every muscle in his body had tightened, but that wasn't it. He'd heard the description before, but still had trouble grasping its truth: his own blood held him captive, kept him from moving even an eyelid.

"Can you see all right from there?" the king asked. He gauged the angle of Clanless's eyes to Silence and nodded. "Good, good. I wouldn't want my illustration to go unobserved because you glanced away." He turned back to Silence. "As I was saying, Silence, you have disappointed me. Gravely. I have reports that you were actually spotted in the presence of a man who seeks to undermine my rule." He shook his head. "Very, very disappointing behavior."

The Hawk King walked in a circle around Silence and came up beside him. "Ordinarily, I would have you taken to the dungeons where we could extract every bit of information from you that we desired. But there's a reason you're called by your current name." He opened and shut his mouth several times without a word, mocking the fighter's inability to speak.

Horror grew in Clanless's mind. He could do nothing, say nothing. Even the Taint couldn't help him here.

"Before you entered, I was telling Clanless here about what it means to be one of my slaves." The king put one arm around Silence's shoulders. "Your purpose in life is to please me. You live one more day solely by my grace." He paused. "That grace, for you, has ended."

He plunged the knife into Silence's stomach. Yanking it free, he stabbed again. "I apologize, priest, for the dishonorable waste here, but it serves my purposes." He turned back to Clanless. "I trust you understand."

Clanless could only watch as blood poured from the stab wounds, soaking Silence's pants and dripping to the floor where it formed a pool. Silence remained in the same pose, still unable to move.

The Hawk King cocked his head, looking back at his handiwork. "I don't know if he even feels it yet. I've wondered about that before. In a few moments, the loss of blood will override the bond's effect. But by then, of course, he'll have lost too much. Is that when the pain begins, do you suppose? All at once? Or does he feel it already? Either way, I suppose he can't scream."

Still Clanless could do nothing. The Hawk King wiped his knife on Silence's shirt. "Your next fight coming up… prepare well, Clanless. It may be more challenging than you expect."

As predicted, the bond's effect wore off a few moments later. Silence emitted a low moan and toppled over. He rolled over on the floor, his hands clutching at his stomach. Blood continued to pump out, spreading across the floor in every direction. The metal plate of Silence's bloodbond shifted on the smooth floor as the pool of blood expanded past it.

The king started toward the door. After the priest rapped on it again, both doors swung open. An attendant held the door as the priest left. The king followed him, but paused at the exit.

"Oh, one more thing, Clanless. There will be two new members of the Dohor arriving in a couple of days. I decided three is not enough. Or two." He handed the bloodbond to the priest. "Release him once the other is dead. I suggest summoning some guards, just in case." With that, he left the room, leaving Clanless to watch as Silence's life flowed away.

((((●))))

Once the priest freed him, Clanless retreated to his room, trying to erase the horror of the scene from his mind. He'd watched men die in the arena countless times, but this was different. Silence had been killed for displeasing the Hawk King, unable to even react to his own murder. Clanless debated his course of action for hours. The Hawk King must have someone watching him, observing where he went, at the very least. If he understood the conversation right, they didn't know he'd actually met Daviland, but only been in the same area. Otherwise, he'd be lying in his own blood beside Silence. Maybe. Someone knew his movements.

He considered talking it over with Zektel, but he knew what she would say. As usual, she'd urge him to forget about Kekeen and move on. The Hawk King was right, he should focus on his fighting, and so on. He didn't care.

He couldn't go back to see Kekeen, not while Daviland was there. That much he knew. Yet he couldn't just… stop. He couldn't disappear on her without any explanation. He would have to get her a message. But how?

At first, he thought about sending it with Yesun, the attendant who usually assisted him. But as much as he liked the boy, how did he know he could be trusted? He might be the very one reporting on Clanless's own movements.

Who did that leave? One of the other attendants? While he knew a couple of them by name, he didn't know much more. He certainly didn't know them well enough to discern whether he could trust them with something so personal… not to mention secret from the king.

In the end, he could think of only one person he might be able to trust, someone he could visit without arousing any suspicions, and whom he could pay to deliver his message.

Salkhi's bedroom changed little between his visits. Her outfits, always provocative, changed, of course. She led him in, as always, before sauntering toward the bed by herself. "Our usual arrangement?" she asked with a flirtatious look over her shoulder. "Or is this different, since you came alone, without the other Dohor?"

"I need to ask something else of you." Clanless took out his note and fumbled with it while he spoke. "Are you able to go out? Into the city, I mean?"

She cocked her head at him. "Sometimes… I get a day off once a week. Tomorrow, in fact. Why?"

"I need someone to deliver a message for me." He held up the folded note. "In the lower city."

"Ohhh, intrigue." Salkhi sashayed back to him. "Who's it for?"

He pulled the note away from her reach. "I'll pay you well to do this, and keep it secret."

She folded her arms and pouted. "After all we've meant to each other, you think I'd only do it if you paid me?"

"Would you do it if I didn't pay?"

"Probably not," she admitted. "So who's it for?"

"There's a singer performing at an eating house on Badbayar Street in the lower city. Her name is Kekeen."

"A girl? Is this the one you talked about? The reason you won't sleep with me?" Salkhi reached for the note again.

Clanless let her take it. She fanned herself with it as he pulled out a blood vial. "Do this for me, and this is yours."

Salkhi gasped, eyes wide. "That's V-blood!"

Clanless nodded. "Please. This is important to me. Can I trust you, Salkhi? To do this without telling anyone?"

Her eyes darted from the blood vial to his face. "You're really serious about this. About this girl. Why do you need me? What's the big secret?"

"I can't go see her right now, and she doesn't know." He indicated the note. "I explain it to her there."

Salkhi tucked the note into the pocket of her robe and held out her hand. Clanless dropped the vial into her palm. She looked it over with care. "This is the real thing."

"I don't know how much your freedom costs, but that's a start," he suggested. "If you keep saving—"

"Clanless, you big idiot." She swatted him with the belt of her robe. "You're talking about finances when this is a case of true love here." She plopped down in the cushioned chair and crossed her legs. "Tell me every-thing."

"Why would I do that?"

She held up two fingers. "First, because we need to kill some time, as usual. And second…" She leaned forward. "You're asking me, your whore, to deliver a message to your real lover. Don't you find that a little odd?"

He wrinkled his brow. "But you're not my whore…"

Salkhi rolled her eyes and sat back. "Clanless, dear. It's what everyone believes. I've told enough stories of you by now, and you only come to me, so everyone thinks you're obsessed with my bed and my body." She made a long gesture at herself. "Not that anyone would blame you, of course."

His face grew hot. "It's not, she's, um…"

Salkhi laughed again. "You can tell me. I already make up lies about what happens in here. I'm not going to spread around anything you actu-ally do tell me." She shook her head. "Considering how much blood you give me, I owe you that much, at least."

Since she'd taken the chair, Clanless wandered over to the bed and leaned against it. "I told you she's a singer. We met when I was in training to be an arena fighter." He paused, considering his words. "She's come back into my life only three times since then. But she's… she's perfect."

"You've been around her that little, and you're in love? She must be something."

Clanless looked down. "I don't know how to explain it."

"You don't have to. Now that I know a little bit, I can ask her. I'm sure she'll tell me." Salkhi's eyes gleamed with her smile.

"What?" Clanless looked back at her. "No, you don't… you don't need to ask her. I'll tell you more."

"Clanless. We're girls. We talk about guys. It's all right."

Salkhi and Kekeen talking about him? He didn't know what to think about that.

"I'm guessing you'll want me to bring a message back from her?" Salkhi went on.

"Uh, yes, that would be appreciated. The day after tomorrow is Arena Night. I'll come back here that evening." Recalling the Hawk King's warnings, he added, "If all goes well."

"Sure. And then we can have another thrilling and arousing talk." Salkhi jumped up from the chair. "So thanks for the business again, big guy. Come back any time."

He rolled his eyes, shaking his head as he moved toward the door. "You're something else."

"With you around, I have to be."

（（（（●））））

"The two new fighters arrived late last night," Qara informed Clanless and the others as they waited for the fights to begin. "They won't be joining us just yet."

Clanless rocked on his heels, nervous energy filling him before his fight. "What can you tell me about my fight? I've been told nothing so far."

"The Hawk King wished it so." Qara folded her hands together in front of her and looked down. "But at this late moment, I feel I can tell you that your opponent will not be human."

Animal then. The Hawk King had warned him it would be challenging. What then? Certainly not wolves again; the king would know how he'd done against them before. A feline predator of some kind, maybe? Something even more exotic?

"As Badzorik informed you all earlier," Qara went on, "Hagh is up first, and then Clanless. Sugh will fight after that."

"Saving the best for last this time!" Sugh proclaimed, flexing his muscles.

"You say that every time you're last," Hagh said with a short cough.

"Because it's true every time!" Sugh always laughed hardest at his own lines.

Clanless had told them about Silence, but the other fighters didn't seem as affected. Then again, they hadn't watched him bleed to death.

"I'll leave you four to it," Qara said. She exited in a hurry, never around when the actual fighting happened. Clanless wondered if she was squeamish about their injuries and healing. Like everyone in his position, he'd long since gotten used to the sight of gaping wounds and shattered bones. But he understood those who weren't. He didn't know how much he'd be able to bear now. The image of Silence trying to hold in his own blood wouldn't leave his mind.

Sugh nudged Hagh and gestured toward Clanless. "What do you think? Big cat?"

Hagh shook his head.

"What then? Some kind of feral dogs?"

Hagh shook his head again, this time with a cough.

"Running out of choices here, my friend. How can we make a friendly wager if you won't pick one?" Sugh complained. "Me? I choose cat. A really big one. With stripes or spots."

"Three," Hagh said, holding up fingers.

"Three vials?" Sugh asked. "On what? Just that I'm wrong? Come on, you've got to make your own prediction!"

"Take it or leave it."

They bantered back and forth a few more minutes until they received the signal for Hagh to enter the arena. He straightened up and charged out onto the sand. Clanless watched him go, fascinated by the change that came over the older man when a fight began. Sometimes Hagh coughed so long and so loud, Clanless worried he might fall over dead in the process. But once his feet hit the sand, it seemed almost like his health changed with the rest of him.

He fought against a pair of barbarian warriors of some kind. It didn't look like he would be having any trouble. Clanless glanced back at those around him. In addition to Sugh, a blood-priest, a healer, and four attendants stood off to the side. None of them were interested in engaging Sugh in his wagers either. The big man finally called to Clanless.

"What about you? What do you think they'll send out against you?"

Clanless looked back to see Hagh smash the head of his final opponent. "I don't know. But it'll be something difficult. Something I've never fought before, maybe."

"Have you fought a big cat?"

"No." Clanless chuckled. Hagh had used his Siphon, and now stood for the crowd's adulation. Not long now.

A few moments later, amid the roars of the crowd and the shouting of the presenter, Hagh jogged back to join them. "Sands are still wet," he gasped. "Different." He nodded to Clanless. "Watch your feet."

Clanless heard the presenter talking about him before the signal came. He gripped his moonblade and walked purposefully out on to the sand. Hagh was right. The sand's surface felt different under his feet. Water squished up between his toes. But he'd been practicing in these conditions for most of the week. It shouldn't affect things too much. In fact, it might hinder the creature he fought, if it wasn't used to this environment.

The crowd cheered his arrival. In his short time here, he'd already become their favorite. That might wear off over time, as he became as familiar to them as the older fighters, but for now, they loved him and couldn't wait to see him again. He lifted the moonblade with both hands, turning in a circle as he walked, acknowledging their cheers.

"Today," the presenter boomed, "our Clanless will be facing an opponent like no other. We've been promising you something new, citizens, and here it is! From the high hills it comes! Behold!"

The high hills? The home of the beastmen? Surely they hadn't caught another one. But no: the presenter said something new. Clanless turned toward the opposite arena door and waited with the crowd to see what came out. He wasn't prepared for what he saw.

A two-legged creature slightly larger than himself burst out of the doors and raced onto the sand. It paused at the cacophony of noise, looking up and around at the crowds. Clanless squinted against the glare of the sun, trying to understand the creature. The general shape, especially the head and whip-like tail, reminded him of small lizards, but he knew of no lizard whose back legs were long enough to allow it to balance on them alone. He also didn't know any lizards with claws and teeth that size. In that regard, it reminded him of the strange beast he'd fought with the foreign sorcerer.

The creature spotted him at last and hissed. It bent its head forward, its back creating a perpendicular line to the ground, from nose to tail. It advanced with slow, stalking steps. As it drew closer, Clanless could see that it was covered in longer scales, almost feather-like with ragged edges. He walked to meet it, fingering the handle of his moonblade and considering his options.

The other lizard-like beast he'd fought had been immune to the Taint. Maybe that's what the Hawk King had meant by "challenging." The other one had also been four-legged and relatively slow. This one looked built for speed and predation. He analyzed its attack possibilities in a few seconds. The teeth were the first danger; with a jaw that size, it had the potential to tear off one of his limbs if it managed to bite him, or do even worse to his head or torso. Avoiding that would be crucial to surviving. The three claws on its hands looked sharp, but not especially dangerous. The claws on the feet were another matter: longer and curved. The central claw on each foot arced upward in a vicious scythe-shape. Assuming the creature could kick, those claws could do massive damage. Much more to avoid than the single weapon carried by a human foe. This would not be easy.

Clanless crouched in a ready position, lowering his center of gravity. He held the moonblade in front with both hands, weaving it back and forth toward the creature. It would charge soon. He knew that much. Already its movements were faster than its initial stalking.

The creature picked up speed. As he'd expected, it was fast… very fast. It raced across the arena, having no difficulties with the wet sand. Its claws gave it better traction than human toes could ever provide. Clanless braced himself, letting the bloodrush build up within, tuning out the crowd and presenter. He briefly wished for a shield.

The beast leaped from about a dozen feet away. It flew through the air, all four limbs outstretched, claws at ready. Clanless dropped to his knees and swept the moonblade up as the monster passed right over him. He nicked its leg, but the tail smacked down on him. Clanless moved his head just in time. The impact on his left shoulder hit almost as hard as a mace strike.

He scrambled back to his feet, slower because of the wet sand. He activated the Taint, but as expected, the creature showed no reaction. Instead, it circled to the left. It took a quick look at the cut to its leg before focusing on Clanless again. Now it knew this opponent had a claw of its own. It would be even more careful. Or would it? Clanless had read up about the hunting styles of some animals, especially wolves, but he'd never even heard of this creature. He had no idea of its thought processes.

This time, the creature advanced in a slow and methodical way. It continued to circle to the left, so Clanless responded by circling to the right. He needed the time, anyway. His left shoulder had almost gone numb from the first strike. He tried to loosen it up, rotating his arm while he held the moonblade with one hand.

When the tightening of their circle drew close enough, Clanless charged several feet forward himself to get the creature's reaction. It scrambled a little bit at his first movements, but then settled in to wait for him. It lowered its head even further, snarling upward at the man who threatened it.

Clanless waited. He'd moved close enough to prevent it from executing another of those leaps. How would it attack now? He wasn't ready to go on offense himself yet; he needed to understand it better.

The creature stepped forward, closing the distance between them until it was only a couple of feet away. Clanless considered attack options. In its current pose, the lowered head was his only target. But he suspected that if he lunged forward and swung down at it, he'd be opening himself up to a swifter counterattack than he could handle. Better to be the one counter-attacking in this situation. He could be patient.

The beast couldn't. Few animals could, in this unusual environment, with the noise and the single target. The head swayed back and forth, and then it lunged forward. The head came up, mouth wide. The forward claws spread outward in both directions. Its chest became an obvious tar-get. Clanless sidestepped and swung in and up from the right. He missed the chest, but caught the creature in the lower jaw, gouging a serious gash through skin and bone. The crowd roared its approval. But the creature somehow kicked at an angle with its left leg. The largest scythe-shaped claw cut an equally serious gash in Clanless's left thigh.

He gasped and staggered back, regaining his footing as fast as possible. But the creature no longer even looked at him. It paused a dozen or so yards away, lifting its head as high as it could, tail down. It appeared to be looking up at something. The crowd?

Suddenly, the monster dropped its head and took off running, straight toward the arena wall. Clanless chased it as best as he could, though it out-distanced him in seconds. Why would it run away? With a sudden clarity of thought, pushing past the bloodrush pounding in his ears, Clanless real-ized: with the way this thing could leap, it just might be able to jump high enough to get over the top of the wall… and into the crowd.

He ran harder. For the moment, the wet sand actually helped him, providing a stronger support for his fast-moving feet. But his thigh burned from the cut as blood poured down his leg.

"Don't worry, citizens!" the presenter shouted. "That creature can't possibly get to you!" Despite his reassurances, the crowd in the beast's path panicked and scrambled over one another, trying to escape.

Clanless knew he wouldn't get there in time. He didn't have that kind of speed. He could think of only one thing to do, and it might cost him his life.

The beast leaped, long and high. It slammed into the arena wall, well short of the top… but it latched on with its claws. To everyone's horror, it took a step upward, its claws cutting a new hold into the wall. Only a couple of feet separated it from the stands. The panic above escalated to sheer terror.

Clanless paused a few feet away. He had no choice, not if he wanted to save those people. The Hawk King's soldiers would never reach that spot in time. Only one thing could stop the creature now: the moonblade.

He took a deep breath, lifting the blade back over his head. He aimed as the creature took another clawing step upward. Its head crested the wall. Clanless threw the moonblade with all his might. End-over-end it flew and embedded itself in the creature's back.

With a scream, the beast fell from the wall, crashing down into the wet sand. But it wasn't dead. It scrambled to its feet, but staggered sideways, unsteady. It hissed at Clanless.

The moonblade remained stuck in its back.

"Clanless saves the day, citizens!" the presenter cheered. "But at what cost?"

Weaponless, Clanless backed away. The crowd noise grew deafening as the creature limped toward him. Were they cheering for his death or hoping he would find a way to overcome an impossible situation?

He watched the monster as it moved. He had two options he could see. He could try to stay out of reach, dodge and run as needed, hoping the creature's injuries took a toll on it over time. Or he could try to find a way to get to his weapon. The latter, as impossible as it seemed, might be his best bet: the creature kept moving despite having a two-handed sword lodged in its back!

If he charged it and managed to leap high enough, he could plant a foot on top of its head and get to his moonblade from there. It would take absolute precision. The creature couldn't realize what he was doing until too late.

Too late to try it this time; the creature charged at him, jaws snapping. It wasn't nearly as fast now, but with no weapon, Clanless couldn't do much to stop it. He waited until the last moment, then dove to his left. The creature's right-hand claws raked across his back, gouging three furrows. A yell of pain escaped his lips, drowned out by the crowd's roar. The cuts were painful, but not life-threatening. Unless, of course, he couldn't finish this fast enough and lost too much blood.

He rolled and came to his feet as the creature circled back. This time, he had to try it. The creature lowered its head as before, almost inviting his plan. Clanless shifted his feet, preparing. Because of the injury on his thigh, he would need to use his right foot to kick off with the most strength. Then left foot on its head. At that point, he should be able to reach the moonblade.

It screeched and limped toward him, a little faster this time. He met it with a charge of his own. As planned, he leaped off the right foot just before they met. His left foot slammed down on the creature's snout. But then the plan went wrong.

As Clanless lunged toward the moonblade, the creature twisted its back in an almost serpentine fashion. Its jaws snagged Clanless's extended right foot.

His hand closed around the moonblade's handle just as the creature yanked him back. He pulled the blade free, but it went flying from his grasp as he went the other direction.

Teeth tore through the ligaments in his foot, ripping everything in between his bones and breaking a few of them at the same time. The creature whipped him around in the air to screams of genuine horror from the crowd, and at least one scream from his own throat. His ankle snapped. The jaws couldn't hold what was left of his foot. Clanless flew across the sand and bounced on its surface. He came to an abrupt stop, foot and ankle mangled, bleeding into the wet sand.

He pushed up on his hands, fingers sinking into the sand. Water gathered around him. The moonblade stood where it had landed, protruding from the sand, ready to be grasped… twenty feet away. The creature stood an equal distance away. The two of them and the blade formed a narrow triangle. Clanless crawled toward the blade, dragging his useless foot. The creature shook off its own discomfort and started toward him. Ripping the blade free from its back must have done more damage: it was clearly hurting and moving slower.

But it would reach Clanless before he could reach the moonblade.

Gritting his teeth, he pulled himself across the sand as fast as he could. The moisture pulled him back. If it had been dry, he might have made it. He might have had a chance.

The creature came nearer. It roared this time, a sound of triumph. It knew its prey couldn't get away.

Jaws opened. Clanless lifted his left hand to ward them off. If the creature took his arm, maybe he could still get to the blade…

Something slammed into the creature's head, knocking it aside. Clanless ducked his own head, shielding it from a sudden flurry of movement. When he lifted his eyes, he couldn't believe it.

Someone else stood above him, wielding a pair of spiked maces in rapid succession. He slammed blow after blow into the creature's head and side. Already struggling, it couldn't withstand the assault and fell back. The other fighter lifted both maces at once and brought them down on the creature's head. Clanless heard the skull shatter.

"What a fantastic twist, citizens!" the presenter screamed over the crowd's shouts of disbelief. "Clanless was doomed, failing to stop the monster, when out of nowhere… the newest member of the Dohor charged onto the scene!"

The new fighter lifted one of his bloody maces into the air to screams of approval. Clanless gasped, recognizing the weapons at last.

"From the arena of Mantukhai…" The presenter's voice kept going.

The fighter tore off his leather helmet and grinned down at Clanless, a horrible scar decorating his right cheek and the socket where his right eye had once been.

"People of Et-Baylak, please welcome… Bain!"

((((●))))

Clanless screamed as the bones and sinew in his foot knit back together. The healer grumbled aloud about the amount of blood he had to use.

"You use as much as you must," Hagh growled. "He deserves every ounce you have!"

Clanless could tell Bain stood behind Hagh. He wanted to say something to him, to understand how this had happened, but the pain overwhelmed his senses.

The healer's dour voice penetrated his agony: "He's missing a toe."

"What do you mean?" Hagh asked.

"The fourth toe. It's not here. The magic can't make it grow back."

Clanless pulled himself up enough to see his foot. The gap in his blood-covered foot was obvious. The creature must have torn it off, or even eaten it in the process.

"Now he is not just Clanless, but toeless!" Bain said from behind the others.

"The damage was severe," the healer continued. "It will take time to regain full use of this foot. Perhaps two weeks."

"No!" The syllable escaped Clanless's lips. He couldn't take two weeks off. Bad enough he didn't gain any blood from this fight, but to deny him two more? And even worse: how would he be able to see Kekeen if he couldn't walk?

"You will be able to limp about," the healer clarified, moving on to deal with the wound on his thigh. "And perhaps move further with a crutch or cane. But arena fighting will not be possible, unless you wish to die at once. Give yourself time to adjust to the change. It won't be easy."

Clanless groaned and let his head fall back. The pain of healing washed over him again from his thigh.

Hagh coughed. "Sugh is doing fine," he observed. "The crowd isn't impressed though. How could they be, after that last one?"

Clanless forced himself to roll over so the healer could get to the wounds on his back.

"Clanless! Are you conscious enough to hear what I'm sayin'?" Hagh moved next to him.

"Yeah," Clanless managed. He gritted his teeth as the healing blood poured over his back.

"This one here saved you out there. His name is—"

"Bain," Clanless gasped. "I know."

"You two've met?" Hagh looked back at Bain.

"We trained together," Bain answered. "As kids."

"Stranger things have happened under the moon's gaze," Hagh muttered. "But rarely without cause. This is no accident: you two knowin' each other."

Outside, the crowd's noise swelled. Hagh cursed. "What'd you make me miss out there?" He hurried back to the arena door.

Bain waited until the healer finished his work before moving next to the table where Clanless lay. "You're going to be all right," he said in a quiet voice. "Nothing keeps you down for long."

Clanless pushed himself up on his elbow. "What are you doing here, Bain?" He twisted to look up at his old friend. Shool Baina hadn't changed much since their fight over three years ago. He'd grown a little taller, perhaps, and had traded the goatee for a ponytail in back. The only major change was the scar… which Clanless had given him.

"The Hawk King needed new fighters," Bain said with a shrug. "He asked for me, since I'm the best Mantukhai had to offer. He also brought in a guy who's supposed to be the best from Naran. I suppose we should be grateful about that since Yeltek went there, if I remember right. Fights with chains, if you can believe it." He leaned in a little closer. "Also, this guy claims to be the bastard son of the Hawk King himself. I've already forgotten his real name because I keep calling him Hawking. It's too much fun. I've already told these other two to call him that, so you should join us."

Clanless stared at him, trying to follow his words through the fading haze of his pain. Hagh was right. This couldn't be a coincidence. Why

Bain? Did the Hawk King know about their connection? Their history? And if not, who else might have manipulated this? The last time they'd fought, Bain said the priests offered to free him if he killed Clanless. What was he after now?

"Why'd you save me?" he managed to ask.

"It didn't look like anyone else was going to do it, and it didn't seem very fair out there. If they catch any more of those beasts, they should let two people fight it. Too dangerous." He shook his head with a little smile. "Or maybe a voice told me to do it."

Clanless winced as he sat up. He needed to get off the table soon, in case Sugh needed healing. Blood trickled off his body, pooling on the table and under it. The blood-priest standing on the other side of the room sniffed, no doubt horribly offended at the waste.

Bain turned to look at him, then back to Clanless. With only one eye, he had to turn his head further than everyone else. "You're a mess. Come show me where the baths are in this place, and we can both get cleaned up. I went from rain-soaked carriage to my bed to here. I probably stink as much as you do."

Clanless pointed down the hall. "That way." He slid off the table but almost fell when his feet hit the ground. Bain caught his shoulder. "Careful. Remember what that snooty healer said about your foot."

Clanless wiggled the toes on his left foot, the four he had left. He'd never thought much about that particular toe, but its absence felt bizarre. He took a step. It was painful and awkward. He couldn't balance quite right. He hoped he could get used to the change. He began to understand what the healer had meant about an adjustment time. As if he needed something else in his life to worry about right now.

Leaning heavily on Bain, he guided the way to the baths. Both of them shed their gear and set about cleaning off the blood and grime of the arena. When sufficiently washed, Clanless settled back to relax in the waters. He glanced over and saw Bain, eye closed, doing the same nearby.

"I thought you wanted to kill me," he said after a few moments.

Bain opened his eye and looked at him. "The blood-priests wanted me to kill you in the arena. That was years ago."

Clanless pointed to his face. "And that?"

Bain shrugged. "You did what you had to do to survive, like you always do. I've moved on, Clanless. You should too. It doesn't bother me."

"Are you telling me the truth?"

"Probably not. I've told you not to trust me. But if I wanted to kill you, would I have just saved your life? Speaking of trust, how's your wraith friend?"

"Same as always."

Bain snorted.

A moment later, the other two fighters entered. Hagh and Sugh loudly proclaimed the stupidity of the fight Clanless had been given, and praised Bain for saving him.

"Truth is, I was about to run out myself," Hagh said as he sank into the waters. "But youngblood here beat me to it."

"Where's the other new one?" Sugh asked. "Should we round him up before we head to Pasque House?"

"It would only be right," Hagh said with a cough. "But maybe Clanless won't feel like such a long walk?"

"Try to keep me back," Clanless said, but his thoughts remained on Bain. Why had he run out into the fight? Despite Hagh's claim, that didn't happen. Everyone knew all arena fighters were living on borrowed time. Anyone could die in any battle. Interfering with one, even if the thought arose, could lead to severe consequences. Yet so far, no one had arrived to reprimand Bain. And the presenter had known his name. Had the Hawk King set the whole thing up?

KOLAND

Now

Yesun pointed to the eating house and stopped, waiting expectantly. Bain tossed him a blood vial, and the boy took off, leaving them behind.

Clanless took a deep breath. "This was a mistake," he muttered.

"I think I told you that several miles uphill from here," Bain said.

Clanless growled, stepped forward, and thrust the door open. He stopped in the doorway, transfixed.

She stood on the stage, eyes closed, swaying ever-so-slightly as she sang, a soft and gentle tune guided by an occasional strum from the older man and his instrument. Two years. It had been two years since Clanless last saw her. He thought he'd given up, moved on, when she didn't return to him a year prior. But...

He didn't know this song, didn't recognize the lyrics. But it pulled at his heart like one of Hawking's chain weapons. The pull worked its way up his throat, impeding his breathing.

"You do realize you take up the entire doorway now, don't you?" Bain asked from behind him.

Clanless stepped further inside. Bain slipped past him and stopped, also watching Kekeen. "If the goddess had a voice, would it be any sweeter than this?" he whispered.

Kekeen finished the song, but lowered her head without spotting the two of them. The crowd applauded, but sporadically, as if they weren't sure whether to cheer or to cry. Clanless wanted to do both, but did neither. Bain clapped.

Koland, sitting in his usual spot on the stage, launched at once into a different tune. Clanless recognized this one; he'd heard her sing it multiple times now. He'd always meant to ask if she or Koland had written it, since it spoke so much about stories.

"Touching a story, grasping a cloud," she sang as she hit the chorus. And she finally lifted her head. Her eyes locked with Clanless's, and the words stopped coming. They stared at one another across the room, ignoring the crowd and everything else.

Koland kept playing. When Kekeen didn't resume, he nudged her with the butt end of his instrument. She jumped as if bitten, to a few chuckles from the crowd. Most, however, had turned to see who had capture her attention. Whispers erupted across the room as, one by one, each table recognized the two Dohor. A server hurried to greet them, gesturing toward one of the only open tables and babbling something about honor. Clanless and Bain took a seat. Bain ordered drinks, but Clanless never took his eyes from Kekeen.

"My friends!" Koland called, taking control of the room again. "While my daughter recovers her voice, allow me to regale you with a story I discovered on the western borders of our great Empire!"

Kekeen left the stage, but slipped off into the shadows near the kitchen. Clanless started to get up, but Bain put a hand on his arm. "Wait. They sent for you, right? Just wait."

"Two friends set out on a journey," Koland began with the pluck of a single note. "Their city was ruled by a cruel tyrant, who ignored the laws of the Empire and enforced his own wicked desires."

Clanless almost growled. Was Koland going to tell a thinly-disguised allegory about Daviland?

"The two friends sought out the aid of a mysterious sage who lived alone in the wilderness. Though both wished to overthrow the tyrant, they differed on how to go about it. They hoped the sage would give them wisdom to decide the proper course of action."

The server arrived with their drinks. Bain took a long draught at once. Clanless nodded his thanks to the server, but didn't touch his mug.

"The sage listened to their tale of woe. They described life under the tyrant. One friend, who we'll call Geremun for now, suggested using the tyrant's own tactics against him, paying back his followers for the crimes they'd committed."

Some in the crowd murmured their approval.

"The other friend, Ogdai, disagreed. He wanted to take the fight to the tyrant alone. 'To strike at his followers would only inflame them all against us,' he argued. 'We need to bring some of them to our side!'" For each of the speakers, Koland altered his voice a bit, giving them a distinct sound.

"'We can't trust any of them!' Geremun said. 'They all must pay!'

"The sage listened to them argue for some time before he spoke. 'Do you have the capability to strike, either at the tyrant or at his followers?' 'We have what we need,' they told him. 'We have followers. We have weapons.' The sage considered their words, then turned to Geremun. 'Do you know the hearts of all those who follow your tyrant?' he asked.

"'Of course I don't! How would I know that?' he protested. 'Then do not be so swift in judgment. They may follow only because they have no hope of anything different.'"

Clanless snorted. "We're the followers, it appears," he said to Bain.

"Really? I thought I was the villain."

Koland plucked another note. "Geremun stormed away, angered by the sage's words," he went on. "Ogdai watched him go. 'That one is filled with anger and fear,' the sage said. 'If he does not control it, it will surely lead him to sorrow and pain.' Ogdai prepared to leave, but first asked the sage if he had any other words of wisdom to share. The sage pondered for a few minutes, before speaking a cryptic word: 'Sometimes, to save all, you must surrender.'"

"What does that mean?" asked a young listener at the front table.

"Exactly what Ogdai asked!" Koland said. "But the sage would say no more. So he returned to his city, spent weeks gathering his followers, and preparing for a daring strike against the tyrant. But when the moment came, when Ogdai arrived at the tyrant's home, ready to put an end to his rule, he found disaster."

Clanless continued to search the shadows for any sign of Kekeen. Her absence troubled him. The note, in her handwriting, said she had to see him tonight. Then why hadn't she returned? Why didn't she come to their table?

"Ogdai discovered Geremun in waiting, working with the tyrant and ready to defend him. During the time Geremun spent preparing, his friend had used the tactics of the enemy… and become the enemy in the process. The tyrant had admired his abilities and convinced Geremun to join him in the end. Worse still, he'd revealed Ogdai's identity to the tyrant, who immediately seized Ogdai's family and held them captive against his arrival.

"Ogdai saw his family as hostages and Geremun facing him, sword drawn. In that moment, he wavered. What should he do? His followers were outside. They could storm the home at his word. The tyrant would die, but so would his family and friend."

"I really don't think we're in this story," Bain observed.

"In that moment, Ogdai remembered the words of the sage. And so… he surrendered and dropped his weapon." Koland plucked another note and sat silent, looking down. Protests came from several of the listeners.

Koland looked up. "The story doesn't end there, of course. What kind of storyteller would I be if I left my listeners like that? Have some faith, citizens." His eye caught Clanless. "Have some faith," he repeated. He looked back around at the crowd. "The tyrant exulted over his victory. He laughed at the futility of the attack against him, explaining that his own guards were even now surrounding the faithful followers outside to ambush them. None of them would escape. Ogdai despaired. What good had his surrender done? The tyrant had won, and they would all die."

Bain set his mug down on the table a little too hard. Several people nearby gave him dark looks for the noise.

"In that moment, Ogdai looked into the eyes of Geremun… and there he saw despair as well. His friend had not foreseen this, did not want it. Not really. Even as the tyrant stepped up to cut his throat, Ogdai spoke: 'Save them, Geremun. There is still hope.' They were his last words. The tyrant laughed as his body fell dead on the floor."

Several of the crowd moaned.

"But the tyrant's laughter stopped. He looked down to see Geremun's sword buried in his chest. Within moments, Geremun released the captive family and charged out to warn the followers. The ambush failed, and the tyrant's forces were defeated." Koland paused. "So the words of the sage came true. By surrendering, Ogdai saved all."

"But he died," complained the young listener.

"Sometimes, sacrifice is necessary," Koland said. He got to his feet. "We'll take a short break, friends, and return in a little while. Enjoy your food and drink!"

"I don't think that was one of his best," Bain observed. "Not very inspiring."

"Is that why I'm here? To hear some vague moral in a story?" Clanless shook his head. "This is pointless. Why did I come?"

"Do you want me to answer that? I can, you know. It's completely obvious."

"No."

A server refilled Bain's mug, then bent next to Clanless. "Your presence is requested in the back room," he said in a low voice.

"There's a back room?"

The server pointed. "Through the kitchen, to the right."

Clanless got to his feet. Bain made as if to join him. "Should I come?"

"No, wait here. I'll let you know if I need any help."

Bain snorted. "Help? With that kind of danger? Not what I had in mind."

Clanless ignored him and made his way into the kitchen, aware of the stares and whispers that followed him. If this didn't get back to the Hawk King somehow, it would be a miracle. He found the door to the back room and hesitated for a moment. He almost snarled at himself for doing so, shoved the door open, and stepped inside.

NOBLE DEEDS

Then

Clanless detested leaning on a crutch, but what choice did he have? The other four Dohor walked a little slower to accommodate him on the way to Pasque House. None of them complained. Hagh and Sugh were too busy extolling the virtues of the House to Bain and Hawking.

Having met the other new fighter, Clanless could see why Bain gave him the nickname. He insisted on his supposed connection to the Hawk King, but cautioned them not to spread the story. "It's not public knowledge." Only a few close friends knew about it... which apparently included all of the Dohor, and from the sounds of it, soon all of the women at Pasque House. By labeling him Hawking, Bain was mocking his claim in a way the new guy either didn't realize or didn't mind. He accepted the label without protest. His real name, the one used by the presenter during fights, was Qaliyun. But none of the Dohor company ever called him that.

Hawking was the shortest and broadest of the Dohor. His face bore a passing similarity to the Hawk King, if Clanless squinted. He also had an odd pair of scars, remnants of a botched healing from one of his earliest fights—or so he claimed. The scars began on either side of his neck and ran down his chest, curving off to either side, almost mirror images of each other. Clanless had never seen anything like it.

The presence of these two changed everything... or rather, their presence plus the absence of Silence. Hagh and Sugh were doing everything they could to make the new men feel welcome, but Clanless kept his own mouth shut most of the way. He found he missed Silence, missed his grin and his genial presence. Death was an ever-present possibility for arena fighters, but not like that. Not murdered while unable to respond.

"As the new ones, you can choose any girl you want," Sugh told Bain and Hawking. "Except one, of course. Clanless would not appreciate you taking his favorite."

"Favorite?" Hagh snorted. "Not favorite. Only."

"Oh, really?" Bain raised his eyebrow. "What does your singer think of that?"

"Singer?" Sugh asked. "Who is that?"

"He's talking about a girl we both used to know," Clanless said. "It doesn't matter now."

When they arrived at the House, Salkhi was busy with another client. Clanless chose to wait, despite the efforts by other girls to attract his attention. One of them even sat by him on a couch in the lobby, insisting on keeping him company while he waited. He politely refused her advances, but she didn't seem to mind, chatting to him about arena fighting. She hadn't seen the day's fights, but she'd heard about the monster he'd fought.

"Weren't you scared of it?" She reached out to touch his brand. With an effort, he kept himself from flinching.

"Fear is always there, a little," he told her. "Everybody get scared, even me. But I can't let it control me. Then I'd be running for my life all the time." He smiled. "I don't think the crowd would enjoy that as much."

"What was your worst fight?"

His mind immediately flooded with images of the battle with the barbarians. "When I fought the beastman," he lied.

"I saw that one! We all did! That was your first one here. I think every one of us wanted you after that." She leaned a little closer. "Salkhi is so lucky."

"I like Salkhi."

At that moment, a tall man in tailored clothes walked through the lobby. As he pulled on his gloves, he glanced at Clanless and nodded in greeting. Clanless nodded back, noting the man's carefully trimmed hair and mustache. He'd seen many such rich men entering and leaving Pasque House.

The girl beside him sighed. "That was Salkhi's client. She should be ready for you soon." She got up from the couch with a lingering brush of her hand against his shoulder. "You know the room." She sauntered away to search for someone more receptive to her charms.

Clanless pulled himself up with the crutch. He should give Salkhi a few minutes, he knew, but he was anxious to hear from Kekeen. He moved down the hall toward her room, deciding to wait outside the door until she emerged.

When the door opened, a blood-priest emerged instead, putting the cap on to a large vial of blood. He looked up, saw Clanless, and scowled before hurrying away down the hall. Clanless stood still a moment until he realized the implications. He rushed into the bedroom.

Salkhi stood by the table, barely wearing anything, washing blood from her left arm. "What happened?" Clanless demanded.

She looked up with a gasp. Her eyes were red and tears still worked their way through her makeup. Clanless clenched his fist. "Did that man hurt you?"

"You're not supposed to be back here yet." She turned back to the towel and basin of water in front of her and resumed cleaning her arm.

Clanless limped closer. "Did he hurt you?"

Salkhi sighed. With her arm clean, she began drying it. "This happens, Clanless. I tried to tell you that our first night. Sometimes, the men get rough. That's why we have a healer on staff."

"What did he do?" Clanless could barely control his voice. His fist shook.

Salkhi tossed the towel and looked up at him. "You actually care, don't you? Even with your beloved singer, you actually care about me."

"Of course I do! That doesn't mean... You're my friend. I care about my friends."

"If that's what you tell yourself." Salkhi patted his arm, and turned back to her stand. She picked up a washcloth and looked in the mirror. "Ugh. I look terrible. Close the door, will you?"

Clanless growled to himself as he swung around on the crutch. He limped back and closed the door. When he turned around, Salkhi had finished wiping her face clean. "I suppose I have plenty of time to fix my makeup, since you're not really here for me," she said, dabbing at her eyes one more time. "Men aren't supposed to see us doing makeup. Destroys the illusion or something."

"That man—"

"Your girlfriend is so sweet!" she interrupted. "I can see why you're loyal to her." She picked up her robe from its crumpled spot on the floor. "But I learned something very important from her!" She pulled the robe on before looked at him with a twinkle in her eyes. "You haven't even slept with her! Can it be that the powerful Clanless is the only arena fighter in the Empire who's still a virgin?"

"You're avoiding my question." He desperately wanted to hear about Kekeen, but he still trembled over the sight of the blood on Salkhi's arm.

"And you're avoiding mine." Salkhi climbed onto the bed and stretched out on her stomach, facing him with her chin on her hands. "So let's move on. I met her, of course. Kekeen. We had a lovely talk."

He limped a step closer. "My message?"

"Why are you using a crutch?" She cocked her head. "What happened?"

"It's an arena injury. It'll take time to fully heal. What about the message?"

"Yes, I gave her the message." Salkhi rolled her eyes. "Of course I did. She read it on the spot. And then we talked. You didn't tell me you met her when you were only thirteen!"

"There's a lot of things I haven't told you." Clanless's eyes kept straying to the basin with bloody water and the stained towel. The bloodrush pounded in his ears, despite his attempts to push it down. He closed his eyes and took a deep breath through his nose.

"She sent a note back." He opened his eyes to see Salkhi looking at him with lowered eyebrows. "Are you all right?"

"Yes. Yes. Where's the note?"

She slid off the bed. "I was going to tease you and say you'd have to search me for it, but you're worrying me right now." She walked to the mirror and plucked a folded piece of paper from behind it. "Here it is."

Clanless took the note and limped to the padded chair. He sat and began to read, stumbling over a few words:

"My dearest Aldan, I was so relieved to receive your message (though you do need to work on your handwriting). Salkhi is so cute! I'm glad she's your friend. I understand why you can't come see me now, but I can come to you. Or at least, I can come to the upper city. I'll come alone, without anyone else who might cause a problem. There's an inn on Neghii Street where my father has performed in the past. I will be there two nights from now. Please come. I must see you. I love you. Your beloved Kekeen."

He read it over twice more. She was right to come alone, but even so... he worried over her safety. The Hawk King might still make the connections. He would have to be careful. He folded the note and slid it inside his shirt.

"Good news?" Salkhi asked from back on the bed. "The usual lovey stuff, or did she promise to do something to you? I suggested she should, you know, to see what kind of reaction she got from you."

"Thank you, Salkhi," he said. "You've been a huge help to me."

She shook her head. "You paid me, remember? Plus, we're friends now. At least, that's what I told your girl. She thinks I work at the arena."

"You didn't tell her about this place?"

"Nah. That would have required too much explanation." She chuckled. "And I'm not sure she would have believed me."

"She said you're cute." Clanless touched the note.

"Did she? I'm not surprised. I am cute, you know. Most people think that, even if you don't."

"I never said I don't think you're cute!"

Salkhi sat up and spread her arms. "Hello! Half-naked woman sitting on a bed here. And yet you don't do anything. In fact, you pay me extra not to do anything. That sort of says something to a girl."

"But... I've told you. Kekeen. And now you've met her." Clanless pointed vaguely.

"And now I don't believe you any more. You said you're staying true to her, but you've never been with her!"

"Not yet. I want to marry her!"

Salkhi sighed. "Fine. Don't tell me the truth."

"Why is that so hard to believe?"

"Because it doesn't make sense!" She pointed to herself again. "You have the opportunity. People already believe you're obsessed with me. But you won't get in this bed. And you haven't gotten in her bed either. There's another reason here." She waved both arms. "I know there are people who believe in being true for moral reasons, but what good is that if people already think you've done it? You had me tell stories, for the moon's sake! I want to know the truth!"

Clanless stood up. He limped to the bed and put both hands on it. At this height, Salkhi's face was actually a little above his. He looked up at her, breathing hard. She recoiled a little bit.

"You don't need to be afraid of me," he said. "I'm not getting in bed with you because I don't want to hurt you."

"It doesn't have to hurt," she whispered.

"What did that other man do to you?"

"What?"

"The man who was just here. What did he do to you?"

Salkhi threw her head back with an exasperated noise. "We're back to that? It's not your business, Clanless." She grinned. "Or should I call you Aldan?"

"Tell me what he did, and, and I'll pay you an extra vial."

Salkhi folded her arms across her chest. "You told me you'd hurt someone if they hurt me. Is that why you want to know?"

"Maybe. Why won't you tell me?"

She lowered her eyes. "It's part of the job," she whispered. "We're not supposed to talk about it."

"You should expect better. You're a person, not something to be mistreated and discarded. It shouldn't be that way."

She looked up at him for a moment, pain in her eyes. She lowered them again, slumping her shoulders. "But it is."

"Tell me what he did."

Salkhi rubbed her left arm. "He held my arm too tight, and it... it broke."

Something snapped inside Clanless. The bloodrush roared back so hard, he felt sure Salkhi could hear it. He could barely contain himself enough to speak: "He broke your arm?"

She nodded.

Clanless turned and stormed out of the room. Or rather, he used the crutch to get out as fast as he could.

Someone was going to burn.

◖◖◖◖●◗◗◗◗

Clanless hadn't spoken with Zektel in over a week. But he needed her advice now. Back in his room, he poured out some blood and summoned her.

"Oh, now you want to talk to me..." she began.

"Save it!" he snapped. "You know what I want. What I need to do. How can I do it?"

"You want to do what? Hunt down this man? Hurt him for what he did?"

"Yes."

"And how do you propose to do that? Do you not think he will recognize a muscle-bound branded taichin whose eyes glow? And limps?"

Clanless growled, clenching his fist. "That's why I'm asking you for help!"

"We both know why you want to do this, Aldan." Her voice softened. "You don't have to pretend with me. The broken arm—"

"Just tell me what to do!"

"All right, all right. You know, your friend Shool Baina would be ideal to help out on something like this."

Clanless sat on his bed and looked down at his own trembling fist. "He's not my friend."

"Really? He's known you longer than anyone else."

"I don't trust him." Clanless looked up toward his window. "The Hawk King bringing him here, right after he gets upset with me and kills Silence? It can't be a coincidence."

"You may be right, though I fail to see how it helps the king. What does he gain from it?"

"Someone else to spy on me, for one thing."

"Aldan. Dear. Everything is not about you, you know." Zektel stretched her blood form. "The Hawk King is controlling an empire. He's not spending all his time obsessing over one of his slaves."

Clanless said nothing. Too much anger roiled within him. Kekeen. Daviland. Silence. Bain. The nobleman.

Zektel sighed. "All right. So let's say you track this nobleman down to his home. What do you propose to do then?"

"Cut him. Burn him with the Taint."

"You can't do that. Use the Taint on him, and everyone will know it was you. Unless you kill him, of course."

For a brief moment, Clanless considered the idea. "No," he said at last. "I won't kill him. I want him to learn, and he can't do that if he's dead."

"Then you can't use the Taint."

"Fine." He didn't have to use it, anyway. His own physique far outstripped the nobleman's.

"And don't think I haven't noticed how you're not discussing the singer with me," Zektel said. "Or the problem with the company she keeps."

"That doesn't matter right now."

"Of course it matters: it will affect when you do what you're doing. And…" She paused. "And if you believe you're serious about this girl, you must consider what she would think of what you're planning."

What would Kekeen think? "She's siding with a man who wants to end all slavery and oppression. I think she'd be understanding of my stopping the mistreatment of another woman."

"If you say so." Zektel's form shifted. Sometimes she looked so much like a real woman, Clanless wondered if she'd once possessed a human form. "Now then, you first need to find this man's home. And when you go to him, you'll need a disguise. At the very least, hide your face and brand."

"I can do that easy."

"And you should wait a few days for your foot to heal further. The limp could identify you."

Clanless almost snarled at that. She was right, of course, but he hated the idea of waiting. What if this man went back to Pasque House and hurt Salkhi again? What if he killed her? Would he even be in trouble if he did? The Hawk King's laws did not protect slaves as they did citizens of the Empire. If he needed any proof of that, Silence's fate sealed it.

"Aldan… what are you thinking?"

"About changing everything. About killing the Hawk King."

"Don't be ridiculous."

"I could, you know. Kill him. One of these times he meets with me. I could catch him by surprise."

"You're a fool if you believe that."

Clanless's head flew up. Zektel almost never talked to him with such bluntness.

"You don't understand what the Hawk King is," she went on. "You've gotten so used to the wonders of blood-magic, you've forgotten their power. I know you remember when you broke your arm as a child. What happened after that? How long did it take to heal?"

"Weeks. Months." He didn't like to think about that time.

"And Salkhi's broken arm. How long did it take to heal it with the blood-magic?"

"You know the answer," he growled.

"It's a wonder! A healing that normally takes weeks took minutes. That's amazing!" Zektel's form shrank; her magic was fading. "The Hawk King's blood grants him extremely long life. And then there are the other ones. You've fought people who have their strength enhanced. Their speed."

Clanless grunted. The speed ones were annoying.

"The Hawk King has all of that. All of it! Who knows how often he uses the magic or has it used on him? And there are more we don't even know about! The old joke the boys made of you being a taichin? He really is one!" She shook her head, blood dripping down. "You might be able to seriously wound him if you caught him by surprise, as you say. But kill him? I don't think so. He's too powerful. But someday, perhaps… after you're free, we might be able to do… something."

Clanless sat silent. Zektel shrank a little more.

"I'm the greatest arena fighter in the Empire," he said after a few moments.

"Yes, you are. But—"

"Let me finish." He held up a hand. "I'm the greatest arena fighter in the Empire, and you're right. I can't beat the Hawk King. So what hope does someone like Daviland have?"

Zektel didn't answer this time.

Clanless nodded. "You've put it into perspective. Thank you. Now. The nobleman. How can I find him?"

((((●))))

Clanless approached the inn Kekeen had named. He wore a borrowed cloak with a hood covering his head and hiding his brand, the same cloak he planned to wear the next night when he went hunting. Even so, he couldn't help looking all around him on the street, wondering if anyone were spying on him. He couldn't hide the limp… yet.

The girl at Pasque House had asked him about being afraid in the arena. No fear within those walls compared to the fear that gripped him when he thought about Kekeen in danger. And he couldn't protect her from the danger of the Hawk King… unless he pushed her away, far away. Could he do that?

He reached for the inn's door. A voice called to him from the alley: "Over here!" Kekeen waved to him and stepped back out of sight. Clanless again looked around to see if anyone watched before he followed her into the alley. Kekeen was being more careful than he'd expected; with dark clouds obscuring the moon, the darkness would hide them well here.

She almost leaped into his arms, embracing him with all the strength in her slim body. He returned the embrace, kissing her and whispering his love.

After a few moments, she pulled back. "I didn't know whether you'd make it," she said. "Everything is so crazy right now." She studied him in the darkness. "You were limping. Are you all right?"

"It will heal. Don't worry about it. Are you all right? Your father?"

"We're doing well. Davil has—"

"Don't say his name," Clanless interrupted. "It's too dangerous, even here." He glanced around again. Was there someone else waiting in the darkness? Koland?

"He says we'll have to leave the city soon," Kekeen said a little quieter. "Like you said: things are becoming dangerous."

"More than you know." Clanless shook his head. "The Hawk King knows too much. You need to get away from that man and stay away from him."

"What? No, we can't do that!" Kekeen pulled back. "He's our hope. He's the one who can change things so you can be free!"

"It's not going to happen. The Hawk King is too powerful! I'll earn my freedom on my own, just like I planned."

"I… no." She shook her head firmly. "My father will never give up. And neither will I. It's bigger than just you, Aldan."

"Listen to me." He gripped her tighter. "The Hawk King killed Silence. Right in front of me."

Kekeen gasped and put a hand over her mouth.

"I couldn't stop him. I couldn't do a thing, and neither could Silence. The Hawk King controls our bodies in any way he wants. We're toys to him!" He paused, letting it sink it. "He knows, at the very least, that this rebel has been in the lower city, in the same area that I was visiting. He knows who I've visited. That means he knows who you are. And your father. It won't take him long to make the next step, if he hasn't already!"

"If he had, we would have all been arrested already," said another female voice from the shadows. Clanless tried to see through the darkness. His hand strayed to Zaluu's throwing knife. Was this one of the Hawk King's spies?

"Oh, Aldan." Kekeen's smile returned. "You won't believe the luck. We met at a gathering of Da—that man's supporters. And so I brought her with me, because I couldn't travel alone, and you both would—"

"Who is it?" Clanless stepped to the side, positioning himself to protect Kekeen if needed.

"Aldan. It's me." A woman stepped into view, smiling and folding her hands in front of her. Clanless took a step back and almost fell on his injured foot.

Borde.

Before he could say anything, she rushed forward and embraced him. He returned the hug, looking over the top of her head at Kekeen, who beamed at him. His cousin. After all this time. How was this possible?

"You've gotten so tall," Borde murmured, pulling back. "And wide, of course!"

"Borde. How… what did…" He didn't know what to say. Memories rushed back, of his boyhood crush on his older cousin who seemed so beautiful. Of their play and work together. And.. and that was all he needed to remember now. Seven years. Or was it eight? She'd grown, though not as dramatically as he. Her hair was even longer than he remembered, though her face held the beginnings of wrinkles, from age or… something else? "What has happened to you?"

"What has happened to me? I should ask what has happened to you!" She laughed, though it didn't sound very happy. "I mean, I know part of it, of course. You've grown up. You've been fighting in the arena all this time?"

"I have. What of—" He swallowed. "What of my family?"

"They were fine, the last time I saw them." She paused. "That was… a long time ago. Your baby brother was still so small. He must be working with your father by now."

"You left the clanhold then." Clanless felt foolish for stating the obvious, but he didn't want to think about a brother. "And your husband. Did he find a job in the city like you hoped?"

Borde looked down. "He's dead, Aldan. We were married less than a year before he was caught outside the hold by a barbarian raid."

"I'm… so sorry."

Borde shrugged. "We had our time. We were happy for a while. I left the clanhold soon after." She looked up with a gentle smile. "And now I've found a man who makes me happy again."

"Isn't this fantastic?" Kekeen exclaimed. "The goddess must be smiling at us, to arrange this so perfectly! To think that I would find your cousin, Aldan. And we'd all be connected by Daviland!"

"I'm not connected to him," Clanless insisted, his thoughts returning to the present. "I can't be. You don't understand. If I even visit the area where he's rumored to be, the Hawk King will probably have me killed… if he doesn't just kill me himself! He killed Silence! He almost had me killed in the arena last week!"

"He doesn't know as much as you think," Borde said. "If he did, we would all be in prison now."

"Maybe he's just waiting for the right timing. I don't know. You don't know him like I do."

"Think it through," she kept going. "He warned you about being seen where this 'rebel' had been seen. That doesn't mean he knows where to find him, or anyone associated with him. He only knew Daviland had been seen. He warned you to keep you away, just in case you were thinking about it."

"He didn't just know that." Clanless pointed at Kekeen. "He knew about Kekeen. He even reminded me of the conditions of my banishment, that I can't have children. He knows how many lovers the other arena fighters have. He knows my history and who I'm connected with in the past. He knows things he shouldn't have any way of knowing, unless he has spies everywhere watching us." He paused. "Or there's another magic I don't know about yet." He hadn't considered the possibility until that moment. Could there be a blood-magic that gave knowledge somehow?

"Regardless," Borde said, "we'll be leaving Et-Baylak within a few days."

Clanless noted her use of "we." "Then you're a part of all this? You travel with him?"

"Sometimes. When I can."

"I won't leave again without saying goodbye," Kekeen broke in, catching hold of his arm. "We can meet here again."

Clanless almost chuckled. "Meeting in a dark alley." He scratched his head. "I guess that's the best we can hope for."

"Some lovers have far less," Borde said. "It's... good to see you, Aldan. I'll go inside and let the two of you be alone for a bit."

Kekeen squeezed his arm. "Don't you want to know anything more about your family?"

"She told me all I need to know. They're safe and well." He looked back at the other woman. "It is good to see you, Borde. I hope we do get a chance to talk again, when I'm free."

She nodded with a smile and hurried around the corner to the inn's entrance. He almost called her back, almost asked for more. He'd been too stern, too quick with her. All because of Daviland.

Kekeen moved up against him again. "That wasn't as... great as I'd expected it to be. Are you all right?"

Clanless looked down. "I'm scared, Kekeen. I'm frightened. Not for myself, but for you." He looked into her shadowed face. "I couldn't bear it if something happened to you. Especially if it was my fault. The Hawk King killed Silence in front of me to make a point. What if he decides to go after you for the same reason?"

"Now you're sounding like my father when we left Ghoyor." She ran her hands up to the sides of his face. "Why can't you let me worry about me?"

"Because I love you. You're... you're a part of me. When we're together, it's like my life is completely different than when we're not. I want that to last. I want to be with you forever."

She smiled. "There you go, saying the right things again."

"But it's why I worry about you. I want you to be safe."

"Dear Aldan. I can't be always safe. I could run away and live a quiet life in a clanhold and still be killed by barbarians, like Borde's husband." She brushed back a lock of his hair. "I won't live in fear of what might be. Let me live for what I believe. And if I suffer or die for it... at least I will at first live."

"I don't know. I don't know if I can live with that."

"You can't control me." Her smile faded. "I'm not some toy you pull out now and then to enjoy. This isn't about whether you can live with it."

Clanless winced. "You're right. It shouldn't be about me."

"There you go."

"But you'll have to forgive me if I don't like this man you're following around," he added in a hurry. "He's the reason you're in danger. He's the reason you're running away from me again. I can't be happy about that."

Kekeen lowered her eyes. "I guess… I guess you would see it that way." She looked back up. "But he's a good man, Aldan. Like you. They're calling him the Chosen One now. And he wants to help people."

"He takes you from me, Kekeen."

"So that he can free you, so we can be together!"

He tried not to show it, but his anger against Daviland grew throughout the conversation. Clanless was rational enough to know that his anger against the man who'd hurt Salkhi might be shaping his emotions, but he didn't care. Daviland was taking Kekeen away. Daviland was the sole reason the Hawk King was suspicious of their relationship.

"Let's talk about something else," he suggested.

For the next few minutes, they ranged through various less important topics, like the food at the arena, or why Koland still didn't want Kekeen to dance at their performances. All too soon, Clanless noticed more people leaving the inn and realized how much time had passed.

"I have to get back to the arena," he said reluctantly.

Kekeen glanced toward the inn's door. "Borde is probably wondering when I'll ever come back."

"I wish we could run away together," he said, realizing he'd said it before in this very conversation.

"As do I." She gave him another kiss. "Our time will come, Aldan. It will come."

"Until then." He lifted her off her feet again in an embrace he wished would never end.

((((●))))

Clanless wrapped the cloak's hood tighter around his face. Another day of rain helped with his disguise, giving a reason for the extra clothing. His foot hurt with each step, but at least his limp wasn't obvious any more. He'd done everything he could to disguise his identity, even letting his facial hair grow for three days to further obscure his face.

It had been far easier than he expected to find the man he wanted. A small payment of blood to his favorite attendant, Yesun, produced the desired results. He'd been able to make discreet inquiries at Pasque House, discover the nobleman's identity, and track down his home. Clanless stood down the street from it now.

Waiting in the rain, he reminded himself of Salkhi's broken arm. Despite his discomfort and doubts, he needed to be here. The soaking rain did little to cool him down. Anger continued to roil about in the pit of his stomach: anger over the Hawk King's power, anger over the murder of Silence, anger over Daviland's influence on Kekeen, anger that she would be leaving him again, anger over the rich and powerful who got away with things, and anger over all that had happened to him throughout his life.

The nobleman's wife and daughter had left in a carriage half an hour earlier. Based on Yesun's observations of the man's habits, he would be coming out soon, on his way to Pasque House yet again. He wouldn't make it this time.

Clanless shifted his weight, wincing a little from his hurt foot. Who would have thought that losing a toe would change a man's balance so much? It had been days now, and while he could hide the limp, he still experienced odd sensations.

The nobleman's front door opened at last. He emerged, glanced up at the sky and the slowing rain, and pulled his own hood up over his head. He hurried down a short flight of stairs and out into the street.

Fortunately for Clanless, his target didn't use a carriage to get to Pasque House. Perhaps he was trying to keep his visits secret. Taking a carriage would involve a driver, who might talk. A short walk of a few blocks, even in the rain, was worth it for the pleasures that awaited.

Clanless waited until the man was almost beside him. He caught him by the arm and yanked him into a narrow passage between two estates. The owners couldn't agree on a single wall style, so both had built their own, leaving a small gap between.

"What are you—?" The nobleman caught a glimpse of the knife in Clanless's hand. "Hel—" he started to yell. Clanless clamped a hand over his mouth while the other held Zaluu's knife close. His old friend would have approved of this use of his knife.

"Keep silent if you want to return to your dry home alive." Clanless tried to add a nasal gruffness to his voice, though he doubted it mattered. His voice wasn't the thing most likely to identify him.

The man fumbled for a pouch inside his cloak. "Here, it's all the blood I have on me," he said, offering it forward.

"I'm not here for that," Clanless growled. "I'm here because you've hurt someone. I'm going to hurt you in return."

The man's eyes widened, but he didn't try to scream again. His breath accelerated. "I, I never hurt anyone. I'm a good man, with a reputation. I have a good name here."

"Because people don't know how you act behind closed doors. You abused a woman at Pasque House last week. You broke her arm."

A stifled laugh erupted from the man's throat. "Her? She doesn't count."

Clanless sheathed the knife and seized the man's left arm. He twisted it, forcing the nobleman to his knees. "Doesn't count? She's a person!"

The nobleman winced and tried to pry his arm free. "She's a slave!"

Clanless twisted the arm further. The man cried out. "Ah! Listen, listen. I thought the healer would take care of her. If not, I'll gladly pay whatever is needed."

Clanless leaned down toward him. "Do you have a healer in your home?"

"N-no."

"How long will it take to send for one?"

"A-an hour. No more." His eyes tried to seek out those of Clanless in the shadows. A glimmer of hope shone through them.

Clanless grabbed the arm with both hands and brought it down on his knee with an audible crack. The nobleman screamed until Clanless seized his mouth again. "Now you know how she felt," he hissed. "I hope this lesson is enough."

The man made inarticulate sounds behind his hand. Clanless couldn't tell if he was still trying to scream or beg forgiveness.

"Should you ever go near one of those girls again, I will hear of it." Clanless released him and shoved him down into the mud. He pulled out the knife and made sure his victim could see it. "And next time, I won't break something you can heal. I will cut something off." He lowered the knife to make his point. "Do you understand?"

The man nodded, holding his arm and whimpering.

Clanless left him there, stalking away into the rain. Somehow, his anger hadn't diminished a bit.

((((●))))

Kekeen smuggled a note to Clanless (with the help of Yesun), asking to meet her again in the same place. As the sun finished its retreat, he made his way to the inn. He longed to see her again, but he knew this would most likely be the end. Daviland would leave the city and take Kekeen with him.

She greeted him alone in the alley, and they embraced like lovers who cannot stand their moments apart. Once they both caught their breath, he glanced around. The moon shone without clouds to hide her face this night. No one else waited in the shadows. "Are you alone?" he asked.

"My father is inside," she said, gesturing at the inn with her head. "He won't interrupt us."

"You're leaving then."

She nodded. "I don't want to. But it's too dangerous for us in the capital. We need to go somewhere else for now."

"To build his rebellion."

"Something like that. I don't know the details."

"He'll fail, Kekeen. There's no chance." He had to convince her somehow. "The Hawk King has ruled for hundreds of years. Anyone who's even spoken against him has vanished. What hope does some clanholder have?"

Kekeen pulled away from him and ran a hand along the rocks forming the lower part of the inn's wall. At about three feet, it transitioned to wooden planks dyed with a red stain. It probably looked much nicer in the sun's light.

"Hope is a funny thing," Kekeen said. "As a child, after my mother died, I began traveling with my father everywhere. I sought out people my own age wherever we went, but they were few and far between." She looked back at him with a gentle smile. "But then one day, I saw four boys all together watching me, and one of them wouldn't stop staring."

"I couldn't help it," he said.

"I'd never had the opportunity to talk with four at once. What a treat! And yet, I discovered I only wanted to hear from one of them."

"Kekeen…"

"Let me finish. When the boys left that night, I discovered something. I needed something new in my life. I needed hope." She stepped back next to him, looking up. "I looked up at the moon and prayed to the goddess. I knew the boy I'd met was marked for death. I knew death would be pursuing him every day." She reached into her sleeve and pulled out a familiar but very well-worn scarf. "I looked at this every day, and every day I prayed to the goddess. And so… I found hope. That hope stayed with me for a year until I saw you again. And then again for two more years. And then even longer. Hope is the only thing I could hold in my heart, believing you still lived."

Her smile took his breath away. He wanted to look at it forever. "Don't you see, Aldan? You shouldn't be alive. When I mentioned you in passing to my father in those first months, he would tell me not to expect to see you again. Arena fighters do not live long, he reminded me. And if they do, they become horrible people. Yet here you are: alive and…"

"Maybe not so horrible?" he suggested, though his mind flashed to what he'd done to the nobleman.

"Beautiful," she whispered.

He kissed her again, deeply, but she pulled away sooner than he liked. "Do you understand? Hope is the only reason I had to believe you lived. And you did! And now I have hope that, that the Hawk King will be defeated one day. I can't give up on hope. It's all I've had. All I have."

He studied her for a moment. "I guess I understand. A little."

"Haven't you experienced hope in your life, Aldan? Hope that we would be together someday? That you'd be free?"

"I've made my own hope." He worked through it slowly in his head before saying it: "My future freedom is because of my work, because of my savings. It's all because of what I've done."

"And what about us? Did you have any hope for us?"

He hesitated. "Most of the time… No. Not much. After the first time we met, I never thought we'd meet again. The second time, your father took you away, but you left the note. That gave me hope, I suppose. For a while. But then you came back and left yet again, and that time… I lost hope. I lost it until you showed up here, a few days ago."

"And now?"

"Now I don't know. I want to have hope, but I can't see it. I can't see the Hawk King ever being defeated. And if you stay with Daviland, then I don't know what will happen to you. What if I gain my freedom, and he's still out there? Would you come back for me? Would you give up his cause? For me?"

"You could join us," she countered. "You could help us. We could be together, and fight together."

"What do you know about fighting?" As soon as the words escaped his mouth, he regretted it.

Kekeen pushed away from him. "I know enough! I know you don't give up when things look bad. I know a fight isn't over just because something went wrong."

"I'm sorry. I shouldn't have said that."

"What do I know? What do you know?' she snapped, ignoring his apology. "What do you know about never having a home to call your own? What do you know about putting on a smile and pretending to be happy for crowd after crowd? What do you know about drunks pawing at your body as you pass by? What do—"

Clanless grabbed hold of her arm and pulled her back to him. "I'm sorry. I'm sorry," he kept repeating. She flailed her fist at his chest without any power before burying her face in it. Sobs shook her body against him.

What could he do? What could he say? She was leaving him… again… and he'd upset her. He'd give anything to take back the words that spawned this. At the same time, his heart ached for what she'd said of her life. He'd never considered that it might be difficult; she always seemed so happy and joyful in her performances.

"I believe, Aldan," she said at last, wiping tears away. "I have to believe. I have to have hope. It's how I live."

"I'm sorry," he said again.

She looked up into his face, her eyes moving back and forth as though searching for something. "Maybe you can't hope," she said. "Maybe that's been taken from you, like so many other things."

"I don't know."

"But if you can't hope, if you can't believe… can you even love?"

"I love you, Kekeen."

"You say that, but do you? Do you understand what it means?"

"I know that everything is different when you're around." Desperation rose in his chest. He had to say the right things now. "I don't feel anything like this from anyone else. Look!" He grabbed her hand and put it against his brand. "If anyone else touches me like this, I flinch away. Not with you! You're different. You bring me… joy. You bring me happiness. Without you, I don't have those things. And now it's being taken from me, not by circumstances, not by the arena or the Hawk King or the priests… but by this one man. This man who comes between us."

Her mouth opened. "I'm not in love with Daviland!"

"I'm not saying you are! Goddess, I can't say things right tonight at all! Please, please believe me. I love you!" He closed his eyes and held her close. "I love you!" His voice broke.

For a few moments, they stood still beneath the moon's gaze, saying nothing. Their hearts raced together. Their ragged breaths escaped together.

"Aldan…" Kekeen began at last, "dear Aldan. I love you too. I'm sorry. You bring me joy too. More than I've known."

He took another deep breath, and his heart sang. She did still love him.

"But I have to go. You can't stop me. I have to fight for what I believe."

He opened his mouth, but again she pushed on, not letting him speak: "I'll be fighting for you, whether you believe it or not. I'm fighting for us. You're just going to have to accept that."

"You believe there's hope, and I don't," he said, an idea occurring to him. "Let's put it to the test."

She wrinkled her brow. "What do you mean?"

"One year. You stay with him for one year." She started to object, but he hurried on: "At the end of the year, when High Spring nears its end again, if he hasn't made significant progress, if there's no more basis for this hope, then you come back here, to me."

"But you won't be free yet," she protested.

"No, but I'll be closer. And you can stay here, in the city. We'll find you a place. And we can see each other almost every day!" As he conceived the plan, Clanless got more and more excited. His words spilled out faster and faster.

Kekeen thought for a moment. "But if he's made progress, if my hope is stronger…"

"Then stay with him."

She nodded and then smiled. "My hope will be stronger."

"You'll forgive me if I hope it's not."

"I will try." She poked him in the chest with a finger. "If you try to find some more hope."

"I will… do what I can."

She leaned against him again, her head turned to one side. "Oh, Aldan. Why is the world so messed up? Why can't things be simple?"

"Ask your goddess, I suppose."

"She's not—" Kekeen broke off with a chuckle. "Never mind."

They stood quiet together for a long while, enjoying each other's warmth and presence. At last, Kekeen stirred. "I want to stay here forever," she whispered. "But my father will come out soon, wondering what's happening."

"You said he wouldn't interrupt us."

"Even he has his limits." She giggled and pulled away from him a bit.

"One year," Clanless reminded her.

"One year," she repeated. "And my hope lives on."

He kissed her to avoid answering. And because he wanted to. More than anything, he didn't want this moment to end.

THE YEAR OF WAITING

Clanless trained hard for the next week, pushing himself to eliminate any trace of a limp or imbalance from the foot injury. He ran back and forth across the training grounds many times a day, remembering Kan's door-to-door runs… especially when Bain joined him.

He didn't know what to think about his old friend. Bain behaved amiably enough, swiftly getting to know the other fighters. He treated Clanless as though nothing bad had ever happened between them. His rescue in the arena played well with the crowds, who were eager to see him fight alone. He performed well at the next opportunity. Sugh joked he would soon displace Clanless as the most popular if he kept this up. Perhaps that had been the Hawk King's intent?

At any rate, Clanless convinced Badzorik, the arena master, to allow him to fight again the next Arena Night. He almost laughed when Badzorik informed him he would be fighting as part of a two-man team… with Bain.

Together, they took down an entire squad of elite soldiers, hand-picked for the battle. After a stern warning, they made sure to leave the soldiers all alive at the end. Fighting without killing was almost harder, especially with a larger group of opponents. The Taint helped, of course.

Badzorik allowed them each to have a single combat afterwards, a simple one-on-one with a desperate criminal. Clanless appreciated the opportunity to finally siphon some more blood for himself, though his attitude had changed. He found himself reciting the blood prayer with each kill, maybe in memory of Zaluu… maybe because Kekeen's hope rubbed off on him. Maybe the goddess did hear him.

Following the fights, Bain joined him in the dining hall. The other fighters had already cleaned up, eaten something, and moved on.

"Are we going to continue being awkward with each other?" Bain asked after a minute of silence.

Clanless shrugged, spreading butter over his flatbread. "I don't know. You tell me. Why are you even here?"

"I'm here because the Hawk King bought my bloodbond from my former master." He sighed and lifted a cup of tea. "And let me tell you: this is luxury like I haven't known since I was a child."

Clanless wondered how different things had been in Mantukhai, but didn't want to ask. "Did the Hawk King say anything to you about me?"

"About you? No, not that I remember. Why would he?"

Clanless didn't answer. He rolled his flatbread into a cylinder and took a bite.

"Look, we have lots of other things we can talk about, you know."

"Like what?"

"Like why you like that stuff so much." Bain pointed at the flatbread in his hands. "It's just bread."

"But it's flat."

"But you don't eat it flat." Bain's brow wrinkled. "You fold it or roll it up."

"To keep the butter inside."

"Then why not eat bread that's… not flat?" Bain held up a fluffy roll.

Clanless took another bite, chewed and swallowed. "I don't think I can explain this to you."

"Can you explain your blood friend, then?" Before Clanless could respond, Bain pushed on: "In the years since we met, I've tried to learn more about blood-wraiths. Would you like to know what I found out?"

Clanless rolled his eyes at him. "More old nursery tales?"

"No, not this time." Bain smiled at the reference. "I sought out the wisest loremasters of Mantukhai during my time there. I really wanted to know."

"You're going to tell me whether I want to hear it or not, aren't you?"

"Probably. Did you know there are references to the blood-wraiths dating back hundreds of years?"

"So since the Hawk King was a boy?"

Bain snorted. "Older than that, even. From what I could find out, they latch on to people for as long as it serves their purpose. They don't leave unless the person dies, or they find someone else that would give them more of what they want."

Clanless frowned in spite of himself, not wanting to give Bain any credit on this topic. Even so, thinking Zektel might leave him wasn't pleasant. "So what do they want?"

"That's the part I can't figure out," Bain admitted. "The stories don't seem to agree either. Some say they want power over men. Some say they want the blood-magic. Some say they're just trying to cause trouble for the fun of it."

"Zektel is after none of those. I think I'd notice that."

"One thing did seem clear," Bain went on. "They latched on to people with ambition, people who were going somewhere. And they turned that ambition into something else, something… corrupt."

"My only ambition is to win my freedom."

"But to do that, you have to become the greatest arena fighter in the Empire, right?"

"Some would say I'm already there."

Bain chuckled. "I won't argue that… for now. But that comes from ambition, don't you think?"

"So do you think I'm corrupt?"

"No. And that's the curious part to me. She hasn't really used you for anything, has she?"

"She's done nothing but help me."

"She hasn't tried to steer you toward a more—I don't know—dark path?"

"No." But she had worked to make him not care about his opponents in the arena, to put aside everything but the goal of freedom. Was that dark?

Bain shook his head. "Like I said, it's curious. She must have some kind of agenda, but none of that seems to come up with your life so far."

"What do you even mean by corrupt? How do blood-wraiths corrupt people?"

"Like I said, this is all vague, and some of it is certainly unreliable. Somewhat like me, I suppose."

"You keep saying things like that, and I'll actually believe it."

"Good. You should. But in the stories, these wraiths would turn an ambition for a good thing into an evil thing. And the more ambitious someone became, the more they'd be able to twist it. Huh. Maybe that's why it hasn't happened with you."

A thought occurred to Clanless. "Do you think the Hawk King has a blood-wraith on his side?"

Bain set down his tea. "Now there's an interesting idea. Why do you say that?"

Clanless shrugged. "You're talking about ambition. He had enormous ambition, and it paid off. He's the ruler of the Empire."

"Very, very true. Thank you, Clanless. You've given me something else to ponder."

"Glad I could help." He tossed the final bite of flatbread in his mouth and got to his feet. At that moment, Yesun burst into the room.

"The Hawk King requests your presence, Clanless."

ᗢ ᗢ ᗢ ᗢ ● ᗣ ᗣ ᗣ ᗣ

Yesun led Clanless on the now more familiar route around the arena. The sounds of the crowd and voice of the presenter could not be heard this time; all of the fights were over for the day. Apparently, the Hawk King remained behind with those in his box, discussing important matters… or just continuing to celebrate.

Why would the king want to see him now? Had he heard about the meeting with Kekeen? What if Clanless walked into the box and found her there, a prisoner?

Another attendant met them in the ornate hall outside the royal box. "The Hawk King will be out shortly," he said. "He bids you wait here for now." Clanless nodded, and the royal attendant slipped back inside.

Yesun waited with him, to guide him back afterwards. After a moment, a short man in dark blue clothes exited the box. He glanced at Clanless, revealing a lined face with a heavy beard, before hurrying off in the other direction.

"Who was that?" Clanless asked.

"I think it was an ambassador from the Melkute Kingdom," Yesun said. "They often dress in blue."

Clanless had done some reading on the kingdom to the north, but much of it had been couched in terms of dangerous enemies waiting to attack the Empire. He knew few facts about them. Apparently, they were friendly enough to negotiate with the Hawk King.

Three Daghilchs exited together next. Clanless searched their faces as they walked by, but he didn't recognize them. For their part, they knew him, of course, and glared openly.

"They really don't like you," Yesun observed once they'd gone.

"I'm aware," Clanless said.

Maybe this had nothing to do with Kekeen. Maybe it was about his performance in the arena. Or his connection with Bain. Or any number of other things.

Another younger man slipped out and hurried away in the other direction without even a glance at them. "That was the Hawk King's son, Prince Ghouk," Yesun said.

"Huh. Doesn't look like Hawking at all, does he?"

Yesun stifled a laugh.

The royal attendant emerged and beckoned Clanless forward. "Enter, but wait until the Hawk King speaks to you," he whispered.

Clanless stepped into the royal box, his first time inside. It was larger than it appeared from the arena floor, able to comfortably sit several dozen people. Tables with food and drink filled even more space. Three or four noble families remained with the Hawk King, though they appeared to be in the process of leaving.

Clanless stood to one side to allow room for them to exit. One of the families approached: a nobleman with his wife and daughter. As the man turned to call one last farewell to a friend, the daughter, a young girl on the edge of womanhood, caught sight of Clanless.

"Look! It's him! It's Clanless!" she exclaimed. She pulled her mother toward him. "Where's your moonblade?" she asked. Both looked him over with admiration, as if they examined a slab of meat hanging in the marketplace.

Clanless smiled down at the girl. "It would not be right to carry a weapon into the presence of the Hawk King."

The father caught up to them. "Come along, Tavuu. Leave the arena fighter alone."

Clanless looked up and froze. The nobleman's left arm rested in a sling hung from his neck. It was him.

"Considering how often you enjoy other views, you shouldn't fault us this one time," the wife complained as she turned to follow him.

The nobleman kept going without another look at Clanless. He apparently made no connection between the arena performer and the angry man who'd assaulted him in the rain.

The daughter looked as if she wanted to argue, but followed her parents obediently. She glanced back and winked at Clanless before they went through the door. He relaxed and let out a quiet sigh.

"Clanless!" the Hawk King exclaimed. "So good to see you!"

He turned and bowed to the king as he ascended to the top of the box. Two other noblemen walked behind him, watching the arena fighter with curiosity.

"You recovered quickly from your fight with that creature two weeks ago," the king observed with his arched smile. "That was a terrifying moment. We all thought we were about to lose you."

One of the noblemen murmured agreement.

"It was a near thing, sire," Clanless answered. What did the king want from him? He'd set up that fight to punish Clanless; he'd even said as much.

"Yes, well, it's a good thing our newest fighter intervened. What did you think of Bain, Lord Ulakan?"

"He fights with reckless abandon, your majesty," the nobleman on the king's left answered. "Very entertaining."

"Indeed, indeed. Ah, Clanless, you haven't met many of the other leaders of the Empire, have you?" The Hawk King gestured to the men at his sides. "This is Lord Ulakan of clan Ghutalta and Lord Ezen of clan Torov." He craned his neck, looking back behind them. "Lord Ghayaktal was just here, wasn't he?"

"He and his family just left, sire," Ezen said. He gestured toward the door.

"Ah, what a shame. He would have enjoyed meeting you," the king said. Were his eyes watching Clanless for reactions? Did he know? Clanless kept his face as impassive as possible.

"These three effectively run the entire city of Et-Baylak," the Hawk King went on. "As such, they have a strong interest in the success of this arena. It produces an enormous income for the city."

Clanless nodded, wondering where this was going.

"And that takes us back to your last solo fight, Clanless. These three were concerned. You've been an excellent entertainer, a superb attraction for the people. We wouldn't want that to end too soon."

"None of us do," Lord Ezen added.

"I will not fail you, sire," Clanless said.

"See that you don't." The Hawk King turned, waving dismissively. "You may go."

Clanless left the royal box and found Yesun waiting for him. What had been the point of this meeting? Was the Hawk King again flaunting his knowledge of Clanless's actions? Or was the injured Lord's presence a coincidence? Either way, Clanless vowed to keep his head down and not do anything else risky until he won his freedom.

（（（（●））））

The weeks passed, surprising Clanless. After Kekeen's departure, he'd expected time to slow to an absolute crawl. He trained, he fought, he visited Salkhi, and he did little else. As the days wore on, Bain and Hawking fully integrated into the Dohor. Despite his misgivings at Bain's presence, Clanless soon fell into an easy camaraderie with them, if not complete friendship.

It also didn't take long before Clanless again became the most popular arena fighter. People soon forgot his failure with the lizard creature. Or if they remembered, they passed it off as a bad day, or proclaimed it an unfair fight. With that popularity, however, came more difficulty. Like Orgina, Badzorik struggled to find opponents worthy of Clanless. More often than not, he would throw him out against a much larger group of opponents. Every so often, Clanless would fight someone new, someone with blood-magic powers. Regardless, he defeated every foe he faced. Even without the Taint, he was better than any of the other Dohor... except perhaps Bain.

From what he could tell, Lord Ghayaktal never visited Salkhi again. In fact, he wasn't seen at Pasque House throughout the year of waiting.

High Winter came, his one-year anniversary as one of the Dohor. A year ago, he'd been in mourning for Zaluu. But he pushed on through whatever the Hawk King threw at him. His single-minded quest for freedom kept him going... that, and the hope of Kekeen's return.

When possible, he sought out news of Daviland. In this, Yesun proved to be his greatest ally. The boy soaked up information wherever he found it. He listened to the gossip in half a dozen eating houses across Et-Baylak, both upper and lower city, and gleefully repeated every morsel to his audience of one. Sometimes, Bain listened in as well, expressing interest in the goings-on outside the arena. Clanless suspected Bain had his own ways of getting information; he often asked questions that indicated a greater knowledge than he professed.

Daviland's name had become well known by then. Rumors swirled through the city. He was in the west. No, he was in the south. No, he'd made an alliance with a foreign land and would soon arrive at the head of an enormous army of sun worshippers. Most of the stories were easy to discount. But sometimes, a gleam of truth might slip through.

On one of the last days of the sun's surrender, Yesun burst into Clanless's room. He scowled at the intrusion; he'd warned the boy about entering without knocking. Keeping Zektel a secret depended on it.

"He's a hero!" Yesun blurted.

"Who is?" Clanless lay on his bed, the warmest place in his room. Thanks to the cold, he had no desire to get up.

"Daviland! He saved the people of Dolkot!"

Clanless turned his head. "Where's Dolkot?"

"It's a city in the west." Yesun hopped from one foot to the other in his excitement. "They were attacked by barbarians, just like you were! But they didn't have you there to save them. They're way out on the edge of the Empire. But Daviland was nearby. He and his people came to the city's rescue. They defeated the barbarians and drove them back. They're saying he killed dozens all by himself!"

Clanless frowned. That last bit was probably an exaggeration, but something must have happened for there to be so many details.

"The Hero of Dolkot! That's what they're calling him now!" Yesun went on. "Everybody's talking about it."

Clanless sat up. The event as described wasn't enormously significant, and yet… it would rally supporters to Daviland's cause. Clanless didn't much care whether the cause grew, as it had no hope, but he did care that Daviland appeared to be making progress. It would give Kekeen hope, and that was not to his liking.

Three days later, the Hawk King announced a new treaty with the Melkute Kingdom. He promised new trade and opportunities for all. The king's representatives pointed out the treaty would allow him to spread his military around to protect against new barbarian attacks. For a time, the news made people forget about Daviland. Clanless couldn't help but wonder if that had been the Hawk King's plan, if he had deliberately held back the news of the treaty until the right moment.

As he counted up his earnings, Clanless began to experience some of the hope Kekeen talked about. The end was in sight. He wouldn't buy his freedom this year, but possibly the next. He had only to survive his arena fights and avoid displeasing the Hawk King.

News of Daviland faded away, aside from rumors of his location. As the weeks of the new year passed, Clanless allowed himself to experience a little more hope. If Daviland wasn't accomplishing anything, Kekeen would return.

The Dohor all turned out to be more skilled than any fighters he'd known in his earlier homes. Hagh, Sugh, Bain, and even Hawking fought week after week without significant loss. Every couple of months, one of them might lose a non-lethal battle, but nothing worse than that. Even then, Clanless couldn't help wondering if the losses had been intentional, to give the crowds the impression of vulnerability. After all, if they were all impossible to beat, wouldn't the crowds get bored? Then again, they never failed to scream and cheer at his own fights, regardless of how hard or easy his victory.

Two months after Bain and Hawking's arrival, the Hawk King brought in yet another fighter: Derbish. He didn't seem to fit in with the rest of the Dohor very well, displaying a bloodthirstiness none of them shared. Clanless tried to be pleasant with the man, but couldn't find anything in common. It was just as well. Derbish was killed in his third battle. After that, the Hawk King showed no inclination for adding to their number.

As High Spring rose and the designated time neared, Clanless visited a number of eating houses in the upper city, searching for news of Koland and his daughter. Yesun gladly did the same for locations in the lower city. Neither of them heard anything.

The time arrived: one year to the day from the last time he saw Kekeen. With no word, Clanless visited the inn where they'd last met. He lingered in the alley next door for hours. Kekeen did not appear. Thinking he got the date wrong, he did the same thing the next day. Still no sign of her.

Arena Day followed, and he fought hard against a challenger from the Melkute Kingdom. From Clanless's point of view, the warrior was no different from any other he'd fought in his career. He fell the same as any.

That night, he visited the inn a third time, with no results. Only then did he accept the truth: Kekeen wasn't coming back. She'd stayed with Daviland, wherever he might be.

（（（●））））

"You don't know what's really happened," Salkhi told him.

Clanless had ranted to Zektel for hours until she'd told him to go see Salkhi instead. "You never like what I have to say about the singer, anyway." So he'd gone to Pasque House, angry and depressed.

"She's not coming back," he grumbled from his seat in the padded chair.

"Maybe she is, and maybe she isn't." Salkhi sighed. "She could have been many miles away and is still trying to get here. Maybe her father wouldn't let her travel alone. It could be anything."

"You're right. Maybe she's dead."

"That's not what I meant."

"Maybe she's fallen in love with him instead. Maybe her father convinced her I'm too dangerous. Who knows?" Resentment ran through all of his words.

Salkhi rolled her eyes. "You're behaving like a child."

"That's what Zektel said."

"Who's Zektel?"

He'd never let her name slip out before. "She's someone who works in the arena."

"She's right then. You're being childish."

"How? Because I expect her to honor her word?"

Salkhi threw up her hands. "How do you know she's not? That's the problem with your agreement! You can't even know if she's honoring it, because you aren't there! Maybe Daviland is on the verge of something huge. You just don't know!"

"She could at least have sent a message."

"Maybe she did. Maybe it hasn't gotten here yet. Maybe it got lost. There are a million possibilities."

Clanless smacked his palm on the arm of the chair. "I let myself hope."

"What?"

He shook his head. "I shouldn't have done that. I let myself hope. I let myself believe it would work out. It never does. Something goes wrong. Every single time."

"Is that what you think?"

"Yes," he snarled. "Every time something good or decent comes into my life, it's ripped away. Every friend I have dies. And every chance I get with Kekeen is destroyed. My life has been cursed ever since I was sold into slavery."

"You're pathetic."

He got to his feet. "Why am I even here?"

Salkhi slid off the bed and put her hands on her hips. "You sit back down! You're not leaving this room that soon, or else our arrangement is over. And I'll tell everyone whatever I want about you."

"Maybe you should. It can't make things any worse."

She stepped in between him and the door. "You think you have a cursed life? At least you only have to worry about the arena once a week, and you even get a break during High Winter!" She gestured around at the room. "This is my arena. I have enemies enter it sometimes every day of the week. And yes, any one of them could kill me, as you well know. At the very least, they take something from me that I can never get back. And friends? You think I have friends in here? We're both slaves, Clanless. But compared to me, you have an ideal life!"

Clanless stared down at her. Anger and shock over her defiance faded into shame. Of all the people to whom he could complain about his lot in life, she was the last one to whom he should speak.

"I'm sorry."

"You should be." She didn't move.

Clanless sat back in the chair. Salkhi watched him for a moment, as if making sure he wasn't about to jump back up and run for the door. When he didn't, she returned to her spot on the bed.

"So it's been a year," she said.

"Since she left," he clarified.

"Which means you've been coming to me for something like a year and—what? Three months?"

"Something like that."

"You'd think after all this time, we'd understand each other better."

He let out an enormous sigh. "No. You understand me just fine. I'm the one who can't figure things out."

"I'm not going to argue with you."

He snorted.

Salkhi looked down. She started to say something, but stopped herself.

"What is it?" Clanless asked.

"I guess I need to know..." She paused again, then blurted it out: "Is this going to change things for us?"

His eyes widened. "What do you mean?"

"If you're not pining over your singer any more, are you still going to visit me? And pay me the way you have been? Or will you start expecting something else?"

"I... No. I hadn't even thought of that. I'll still come, when the Hawk King expects it of me." He shook his head. "And after what you just said, do you truly think I would want something else from you? I don't want to be one of your enemies, Salkhi."

"Good. I have enough of those."

"Friends then?"

"That's what we told Kekeen." She raised a finger. "But don't think I didn't notice you refer to another girl as 'working at the arena.' That's also what we told her about me."

"I didn't tell her that! You did!"

"Let's not quibble." Her eyes twinkled. "So who is this mystery girl then? What's her job at the arena, if she really has one?"

"She's the manager of the Dohor," Clanless growled. "She's the one in charge of keeping our side of the arena running. She's not important."

"Important enough to tell her what's going on with the girls in your life, apparently."

"Will you let it go? Please?"

Salkhi shrugged. "I'll bring it back up when I want to annoy you again. But you're still not answering me completely. You don't want to be my enemy, but... are we just friends? Or more than that? Maybe?"

"You know I—"

"No," she interrupted. "I don't know. I don't understand. It costs you nothing. You're not even trying to be true to her any more. You just made that much clear."

"It's more than that. I just... I can't."

"After over a year, don't you at least owe me the courtesy of a real answer? There's probably not another man in Et-Baylak that would turn down the opportunities you've been given. I could probably seduce the Hawk King, if given the chance."

Clanless rubbed his hands over his eyes, both to hide his anxiety and to stop staring at Salkhi's thinly-clad body. He didn't know how to tell her. He didn't fully understand it himself. "When you... proposition me," he said at last. "I enjoy it. I like it. But... there's something else. I feel... terror. I don't even know why."

She stared at him. "You're scared of me?"

"Not just you. Being physically close to someone. Anyone. The only one who doesn't terrify me is Kekeen... most of the time."

Salkhi jumped off the bed, approached him, and reached out toward his bare shoulder. He flinched, as he almost always did. She nodded. "That's why you do that."

"Do what?"

She cocked her head. "You don't even know you're doing it? You jerk a little bit when I touch you, or I'm about to touch you." She pointed at the brand. "Is that the reason? Because of what they did to you?"

"I don't... I don't think so. I think it's something else. Maybe even before that." He ran a hand through his hair. He knew the fear. He knew what he did. He just didn't know why. Or did he? An image of a dark figure bending over... He jerked to his feet. The image vanished.

"What is it?" Salkhi asked.

"I don't know. I should... I should go."

"But... you'll be back?"

He nodded. "When the Hawk King has expectations. I'll be here."

BROKEN HEARTS

Now

Koland sat at a small table, eating a late supper. Kekeen stood beside him. Both looked up as Clanless entered. Koland wiped his mouth and nodded. "I'm glad you got our message—" he began.

"What is this?" Clanless burst out. "I'm literally a day away from freedom, trying not to cause any problems. Just being here is risking everything if the Hawk King finds out!"

"You know exactly why we asked to meet you," Koland answered calmly.

"You can't kill Daviland!" Kekeen exclaimed.

Clanless nodded. "That's it, isn't it? You didn't want to see me at all. You just want to save your precious Davil." He turned back to the door.

"Aldan, wait!" Koland called, getting to his feet. "It's not what you think. We have a lot to discuss."

"Why?" Clanless stood with one hand on the door, ready to yank it open. His entire body trembled, surprising him. "Why should I listen to you?"

"You're angry," Koland observed. "I suppose you have reason to be. Kekeen didn't return after a year."

"It's been two years! And not even a message in all that time." He almost opened the door.

"I tried!" Kekeen's voice sounded closer. "I sent a message, but it never got to you. I didn't even know until last week. The messenger—"

"I don't care about the messenger," he cut her off.

Her hand brushed against his back, then settled on his shoulder. "Do you… do you still care about me?"

He turned to face her, his gut roiling. "I don't know how to answer that. What do you want from me? It's not enough that you have to risk my freedom; now you want me to sacrifice my life?"

"No, no. I don't want you to die." She held her hand up a moment after he turned, then let it drop to her side. "But I don't want you to kill him either."

"It's one or the other, Kekeen. That's how the arena works. I either kill him or he kills me. I have no choice."

"There are always choices," Koland said softly.

"Name one," Clanless challenged. "Name one choice where Daviland and I both walk out of the arena alive and free."

"We have a plan," the storyteller said. "When Suirel appears in the sky, the Empire will fall. A lot of things need to happen, but it can work. And we need your help both tonight and in the arena tomorrow."

"I am one victory away from freedom. One siphon full of blood. That's all it will take."

Koland extended his arm and pulled back his sleeve. "Then take some of mine."

"It doesn't work that way. It has to be blood from the arena."

"Why? Isn't voluntary blood more valuable than involuntary?"

Clanless didn't answer. He couldn't think of an answer.

"I think there's more to the blood system than they've told us," Koland went on, rolling his sleeve back down. "There are too many inconsistencies. But that's not important tonight. As I told you, we have a plan. The Hawk King will fall. Tomorrow. But only if Daviland lives through the fight."

"If he lives, I die." Clanless shook his head. "You can't ask that of me. I've fought for over eight years for this. I can't throw it all away now."

Koland sighed. "I know that, son. You're not a part of this. I would lay down my own life for the cause, but I can't lay down yours. And I can't ask you to die for a cause that is not your own."

"Then I have to kill him. And win my freedom." His eyes darted to Kekeen. Did she still care? What did it matter? She wouldn't want him if he killed her hero.

"If you help us tonight, then tomorrow, the fight may not matter," Koland said.

"What do you mean?"

"We may achieve victory tonight. Or more likely, we can achieve it to-morrow, but we might need you to stall the fight, make it last long enough for our people to strike."

"You think you have enough people to defeat the Hawk King, his sol-diers, the priests, and all their blood-magic?"

"Most of the lower city is ours, and at least a quarter of the upper city. We have the numbers." Koland walked back to his table and picked up his drink. "But the blood-magic would overcome numbers. You're right about that. And that's why we need you." He took a sip.

Clanless understood. "You need the Taint."

Koland nodded.

"It's what Daviland talked about the night we met. You've discovered where the priests are keeping the blood, and you want me to Taint it."

"Essentially, yes."

The door opened behind Clanless. He moved out of the way as Borde rushed into the room. "You're here!" she exclaimed. She threw her arms around him. He awkwardly returned the hug, but his eyes flickered to Kekeen again.

"You can't kill him, Aldan. You can't!" Borde pleaded.

He patted her back. "It's not so simple, Borde."

She pulled back and looked up at him. "Yes, it is. I love him."

Clanless blinked. "You—"

"I love him. When the Hawk King is defeated, we plan to be married."

"Oh." He looked back at Kekeen, who wore a sad smile.

"So you can't kill my beloved. I don't care about anything else right now. You can't kill him!"

Koland took her arm. "We're discussing what can be done, Borde. We'll do everything we can to save him."

"Promise me, Aldan! Promise me you won't kill him!" She shook Ko-land's hand off.

"It's not... I can't promise that."

The slap caught him completely off guard. "What happened to the kind man you were becoming?"

He caught her hand before she slapped him again. "He died, Borde. Part of him died when his family stood by and let the priests take him away. The rest died in the arena. Or maybe it was even before that."

"What do you mean?"

"You knew what was happening. How could you not?"

"What?"

"Never mind." He shook his head, not even sure himself what he'd been talking about. Why did she bring out such strange feelings? "Koland, if you want my help, you have to talk. I don't have all night." He glanced to the side. "And Bain is waiting out there."

Borde pulled herself free and stalked to the other side of the room.

"Yes…" Koland also glanced in the direction of the dining room. "Not sure about that one. Can we trust him?"

Clanless hesitated. "I don't know. He knows some of what's going on, but I don't know how much. And I don't know where his loyalties lie… other than to himself."

"Then let's leave him out of it, as much as possible." Koland returned to the table and sat down. "I have a map here. Once I finish eating a little something, I can go with you."

"You expect me to just sit around and wait for you to eat?"

"No." Koland picked up his fork. "I expect you to talk with my daughter."

Clanless's eyes shot to Kekeen, who immediately lowered hers. "Do we have anything to talk about?"

"We must," she said without looking up. "I need to tell you why I didn't come back."

"Very well." He folded his arms.

"Not in front of everyone," she protested.

Borde made a huffing noise and left the room. Koland merely waved. "Go talk in the corner. I won't listen. Much."

Clanless rolled his eyes and moved to the corner of the room. Kekeen followed him, but stood apart. "Did this… did this destroy everything between us?"

"I don't know what to think. We made an agreement, Kekeen. You didn't keep it."

"But I did keep it!"

"You didn't come back."

"No… because that wasn't what we agreed!" She took a tentative step closer. "We said I'd come back if I lost hope in Daviland, if—"

"If he made progress," Clanless interrupted. "If he did enough to make it clear he could win."

"And he has! We're right on the verge of it even now!"

"And a year ago? You knew enough then?"

She hesitated, but only a moment. "Yes."

"I don't believe you." He shook his head. "I have no reason to believe you. From everything I heard, nothing changed during that year."

"You weren't with us! How would you know?" Her hands jerked up with a short gasp. "No, no. I'm doing this all wrong. I'm not mad at you. You're mad at me. And I'm trying to, to explain so maybe you won't be." She took a deep breath. "You heard of Dolkot, didn't you?"

He nodded.

"That was the turning point. We heard they were in trouble and were close by. Daviland led a small band of his followers, and they saved the city! It changed everything! People started to understand the difference between him and the Hawk King. They understood that Davil actually cares about the people."

"Having people is not enough. You know that. There have been uprisings before. The Hawk King is too powerful." Clanless wasn't sure why he was arguing now, but he'd been on the defensive since his arrival and couldn't stop.

"This will be different. I told you I had hope. I have even more now."

He let out a single laugh. "Now? When your leader is in prison, fated to die tomorrow?"

"Yes! Because it's all working together. Even your involvement—"

"And that's why you came now. That's the only reason you sent for me." His voice came out more harsh than he expected, but he continued. "It's not about me. It's not about us. It's only about him. If he weren't here and in trouble, you never would have come back. You never would have contacted me."

"I—"

"Can you tell me I'm wrong? Do you know what that means?"

She opened her mouth, but didn't say anything.

"That means that if Daviland hadn't been captured, then tomorrow I would fight some other poor soul, kill him and win my freedom." He stared into her eyes. "And then I would have left this city, and we would have never met again."

Kekeen winced. She knew he was right. "You wouldn't have come looking for me?" she whispered.

"How would I know where to look? Every week, I hear new rumors about where Daviland is. More importantly…" He swallowed; the next words would hurt both of them. "Why would I look for you? You didn't come back for me."

She put a hand over her mouth. "You… you don't mean that."

"Why wouldn't I?" The words were more savage than he'd intended, but they came anyway, torn from the depths of his shattered heart.

Kekeen's eyes welled up. She didn't answer.

Clanless tore his eyes away from her. "Koland! Are you finished yet?

Let's get this over with!" It was, perhaps, the cruelest thing he'd ever done.

BLOOD RAID

As Clanless and Koland made their way out through the dining area, Bain got to his feet. "What's happening?"

"Koland has something to show me elsewhere in the city," Clanless told him, still trembling from his conversation with Kekeen. He tossed his fur pelt to Bain. "Can you return this for me? I'll see you back at the arena."

"Are you sure?" Bain glanced at the storyteller. "You might not want—"

"It'll be fine," Clanless cut him off. "Goodbye, Bain." He stepped outside and pulled on the cloak he used to disguise his appearance. It wouldn't do to be recognized on this kind of trip. Without his fur and with his brand covered, he might be any other man on the street… a large man, but just a man.

Koland didn't speak from the moment he got to his feet until he and Clanless were several blocks away from the eating house. "Words said in an instant of anger can lead to years of regret," he said without preamble.

"Is it your business?" Clanless didn't want to have this discussion.

"The happiness of my daughter is always my business." Koland paused in the middle of the street. "While you are justified in some of your anger, you took things way too far."

"Where am I wrong?" he challenged.

"You left no room whatsoever for Kekeen's belief in the cause we serve."

"I don't believe in your cause. Or your leader."

"That doesn't matter." Koland pointed at his chest. "She does. She has a belief, a hope, because that is part of who she is. And you forced her to choose between her beliefs and you. Even your 'agreement' left no room for compromise."

Clanless walked past him. "Are we going to visit this blood repository or not?"

Koland resumed his pace. "If you love Kekeen, you have to love all of her, not just part of her. Her belief in the value of each individual is what led her to you," he went on. "And it's that belief that led her to commit to Daviland's campaign. It's a part of who she is. If you manage to strip that away from her, she won't even be the woman you love any more."

"If you keep talking, I will reconsider this trip," Clanless said. Koland fell silent.

The storyteller spoke the truth, of course. Yet for all his life, Clanless had endured pain. And since he'd been thrown into the arena, he'd been able to strike back against anyone who hurt him... most of the time. It had become instinct, he considered. In the arena, you either hurt them first or hurt them harder. With that as the constant backdrop of his life, he had reacted to Kekeen in the same way but with his words. He'd hurt her. He knew that. But she'd hurt him first.

"What happened to the kind man?" he muttered to himself.

"What was that?" Koland asked.

"Nothing."

At that moment, someone ran up behind them. Clanless whirled, reaching for the knife in his belt. He relaxed when he saw Borde slow to a stop next to him. "I'm coming with you," she announced.

"If you wish," Koland said. "We only need Clanless here, but you're welcome to walk with us."

She fell into step with them and kept silent most of the way, much to Clanless's relief.

Koland led the way into the upper city. Everywhere they walked, they saw people preparing for the celebration tomorrow... or getting an early start on the revelries. Merchants added extra decorations to their places of business, advertising their wares in sometimes-strained connections to the season. Larger homes—at least some of them—also sported new decor, usually stylized depictions of the moon capturing the sun or snow falling from the sky.

A stiff breeze already descended into the streets, ripping some of those decorations free and sending them tumbling along. The winds ordinarily wouldn't start this early, but the chaos moon supposedly made this upcoming High Winter worse than normal.

The sun had long since retreated for the night, taking its warmth with it and abandoning the sky to the brightness of the moon. Clanless glanced up at it and wondered: if the goddess had answered Kekeen's prayers to keep him alive, why was this happening now? Did a being like that truly care about individuals in this world? And how would she feel about what they were planning to do now?

Kekeen believed in the goddess. But she fought against the blood-priests. Clanless had a much tougher time separating the two, though he supposed he'd done more of that the past couple of years. "Blood is life. Blood is precious. Blood is power." The mantra still fell from his lips after every fight and sometimes in the mornings when he awoke. But if the blood were so precious, what did that say about the Taint? His life seemed filled with contradictions.

Why was he doing this, anyway? He didn't believe in Daviland's rebellion and didn't think it would succeed, even with his help. He felt no obligation to Kekeen any more, not for this, at any rate. In one sense, he relished the opportunity to do something against the priesthood. And maybe it was as simple as being asked. Kekeen, Koland, and Borde all begged him to do it. And while he wouldn't surrender his chances at freedom tomorrow for them, he could do this much.

"It's not much further," Koland said, interrupting his musings. Clanless glanced around. He recognized the area of the city. The palace and arena weren't far from here. Pasque House was even closer. In fact, he'd walked through some of this with Hagh early in his time at Et-Baylak.

"The temple," he said aloud, remembering. "Is that where we're going?"

Koland nodded, visible in the moon's light and the many lanterns that decorated this area. "It should have been obvious to us. The biggest temple in the biggest city, with the most powerful priests and their leaders present almost every day."

The Ghamba Lam. Of course. At the thought, Clanless almost stopped in his tracks. The priest had predicted he'd be asked to use the Taint tonight. "A great task," he called it. And he'd told Clanless to do it. He wanted the blood supply tainted! But why? Was he against the Hawk King somehow? Was it a trap? Clanless opened his mouth to tell Koland but stopped himself. He needed to think. What possible reasons could the Ghamba Lam have for telling him to do it? And how had he known?

He must have a spy within Daviland's people. It would explain how Daviland had been captured. But if true, then the spy likely knew of Clanless's own meeting with Daviland two years prior. No, that couldn't be right. He'd have betrayed Daviland then, cutting him off before he grew too powerful.

How would the Ghamba Lam profit from the Tainting of the blood supply? It would limit the military response to Daviland's uprising, throwing the city into chaos. The Hawk King might very well lose, especially if the priests were against him somehow.

But that made no sense. Daviland wanted to overthrow the priests too! The Ghamba Lam wouldn't be participating in the destruction of his own order.

"Aldan," Borde said in a tone so low he almost didn't hear her. "Forgive me for earlier. I had no right to talk to you that way."

He grunted in response, not trusting his words at this point. From the situation with Kekeen to the confusion over the Ghamba Lam, his emotions and thoughts were in a turmoil. Better to keep his lips sealed as much as possible.

The closer they drew to the temple, the more people they saw coming and going. "The blood donations are accelerating tonight," Borde pointed out. "They won't be taking more tomorrow, so they've encouraged everyone to come tonight."

"It works to our advantage," Koland said. "It's easier to avoid notice in a crowd."

Once they arrived, his words proved true. The three of them merged with the crowd ascending the stairs. Clanless stared at the crystal sphere at the top. Hagh had been right: the moon's light infused it, creating an alternate moon, one that had descended from the heavens to bless those who came to this temple.

But at the top of the stairs, Koland peeled off to the right, splitting away from those entering the main doors. Borde and Clanless followed him around the narrow walkway as it turned along the side of the temple.

"Nothing to hide us here," Clanless pointed out.

"But no one's looking over here." Koland continued along the narrow path. "They're all focused on the front. If we went in that way, we'd draw unwanted attention to ourselves when we tried to go past the priests and their work. There aren't any ways to slip past them inside."

"But there are out here," Borde said. Clanless couldn't tell if she were stating or questioning.

"Down here." Koland glanced around before sitting down on the edge of the walkway. He slipped down, hung by his hands for a brief moment, then dropped down into the dark. Clanless waited a moment, then followed. He caught Borde as she dropped, helping her avoid the harder landing. Then he looked about.

They stood in a side garden to the main temple. A path led through a lush array of trees, unusual both for the city and the general climate, to a statue of the goddess perched on the moon. A flame burned within the moon itself, shining out through dozens of holes on every side, providing an unusual sort of illumination to parts of the garden. Where they stood lay in darkness.

Koland ignored the garden and faced the wall of the temple, where the path ended. "There's a door here," he said, "but it's not easy to find."

Clanless pushed against the stone, but nothing moved.

"It has a hidden latch," Koland explained, feeling along the wall.

"What if there's a priest right behind the door when you open it?" Clanless asked.

"Then I'm afraid I'll need you to remove him before he recognizes you."

"I don't kill outside the arena."

"Render him unconscious. I don't care. Ah, here it is." Koland's hands moved in the dark, followed by a click-thump sound. Clanless helped him push the stone again. This time, it moved inward easily, revealing a door and doorway much slighter than anticipated. No one met them; in fact, the passage ahead appeared as dark as the path behind.

"How did you discover all of this?" Borde whispered.

"Slow and careful infiltration of the priesthood," Koland answered. "Now I suggest we keep quiet through the hallway. The priests should all be busy up top, but we can't be sure."

"I hope there's light somewhere."

"In the blood chamber, yes. Quietly now."

Koland crept forward. Clanless gestured for Borde to follow, while he brought up the rear. They made their way down a short hall before it met a larger one. A dim and flickering light came from far to the left, but Koland turned right. A few feet later, they found steps descending into the darkness. Clanless assumed the priests must carry lanterns themselves, unless some blood-magic let them see in the dark. He'd started to believe almost any type of power might exist.

Descending stairs in the dark was a treacherous task, but they made it to the bottom without any major stumbles. Here, Koland had to search around for another latch. Once he found it, they swung open another door only to be blinded by a sudden eruption of light beyond it, a light strangely mixed with red. At the same moment, Clanless's other senses were overwhelmed with the presence of blood. The smell filled his nostrils. The coppery taste exploded through his mouth. The other two didn't react;

they couldn't sense it like he did.

Clanless blinked until his eyes adjusted. He stepped into an enormous chamber and stared in awe and a bit of fear around him. "Goddess," Borde whispered.

The chamber stretched longer than the temple above it. While the front area resembled a massive man-made chamber in any palace or elaborate structure with carved panels decorating the walls, the back half of the chamber appeared to be a cave, hewn from the rock itself. Two smaller passages stretched away into darkness.

The light came from a dozen lanterns attached to the walls. But the enormous storage containers in front of them, six on each side of the chamber, reflected and amplified the light. The containers were formed of crystal, the same crystal used in the currency vials. They were shaped almost like drinking mugs, but with a spherical base that required supports to keep them upright. Blood filled the interior of most of them, some more than others. Clanless approached the nearest one, tilting his head back to see the top, at least twice his height. Wooden platforms surrounded each crystal, with stairs in each corner of the room.

"Shukan, Ghutalta, Kurav, Torov," Koland said, pointing at each of the first four containers. "And so on. One for each clan." He turned around. "Can you do it? Can you… Taint them?"

"I don't know," Clanless answered, staring. "I've never done this much before." Except maybe during the fight against the barbarians. He had no idea how much he'd done then. He put his hand against the crystal. How much blood could this contain? Hundreds of gallons at the least; maybe even a thousand!

"The longer we are here, the longer we risk discovery," Koland pointed out in a quiet voice.

Clanless nodded and climbed up the nearest set of stairs to the right. Borde followed, to his irritation. Her presence aroused… strange feelings. He would expect some kind of nostalgia, maybe a longing for what he'd lost, but it wasn't that. He tried to analyze his feelings, though it took some thought. He felt edgy, as if he expected a threat to appear at any moment, and not because of their location. It made no sense.

Koland moved to the doorway they'd entered and kept a watch on the stairs.

From the platforms, Clanless saw that the crystal containers were sealed on top. Of course they would be; otherwise, the blood would decay. The crystal somehow kept the blood fresh within. Kekeen said something once about the value of the crystals. Did they provide the true magic, and the blood only transmitted it? The priesthood kept so many secrets.

"How does this work?" Borde asked. "Do you just… snap your fingers or something?"

"The blood needs to be exposed to the air." In all the times he'd used the Taint, that seemed to be the deciding factor.

They both stepped closer to the nearest container, the one Koland had labeled Shukan, the Hawk King's clan. Borde pointed to a metal handle that appeared grafted into the crystal. Clanless grasped it and turned. A type of crystal lid, about a foot across, screwed out of the container.

"This must be where they pour it in," Borde observed.

Clanless set aside the lid. The sensations of the blood washed over him, making him take a step backward. The taste and smell would not have been more overwhelming if someone had poured a bucket down his throat. He choked and coughed, bending over double.

"Are you all right?" Borde reached a hand out toward him.

He waved her away. "Give me a moment," he managed. He sounded like Hagh. His eyes watered, and his gorge rose. He fought back against the sensations. If he could handle eight years in the arena, he could handle this. He swallowed, gritted his teeth, and straightened up.

He stepped back and held out his hand over the container's opening. With a thought, he activated the Taint. The heat behind his eyes exploded, stronger than he'd ever felt it. Borde gasped and stepped back, staring at his face. Flames erupted out of the container, searing his palm. He leaped back, almost falling from the platform and letting out a short cry of pain.

Idiot. When he used the Taint on a small amount of blood, he saw a spark or two. Whatever the Taint was, it involved burning of some kind, burning away some part of the blood itself. With this much blood, that burning became a much more violent thing. He examined the skin on his palm. Three or four blisters were already forming. The pain he could bear, but he'd have to wear a glove tomorrow to wield the moonblade. He couldn't very well go to the healers and ask for help. They'd want to know what happened.

"Did it work?" Koland called from nearby. He'd come halfway up the stairs. "What happened?"

"I think so," Borde said. "Was it supposed to do that?"

"It's fine," Clanless answered. "Open the next one."

This time, he stood well back from the opening when using the Taint. While he avoided the flames, the second usage drained him more than he expected. As the heat from his eyes faded, his entire head grew fuzzy. The rest of his body didn't feel much better. When Borde moved to the third container, he held up a hand. "I need a minute."

"We don't know how much time we have," she protested.

"I need a minute," he repeated. He glanced back where they'd come. "Put the lids back on. I don't want them discovering the bad blood until much later." For that matter, once the sabotage was discovered, wouldn't they immediately suspect him? Who else could do this to their blood? He growled to himself for not thinking of that sooner. Too late now.

After a few moments' rest, they moved on to the third container. After Tainting it, Clanless could barely remain on his feet. He leaned both hands on his knees, taking deep breaths. This made no sense. He'd used the Taint more than this before. Borde again reached out, this time putting a hand on his shoulder. He shrugged it off, straightened up, and moved to the fourth container. "Open it," he ordered, his voice ragged.

Koland left his watch position and joined them on the platform. "Aldan, don't overdo it."

"Time," he grumbled.

"Yes, we don't have much time, but it won't do us any good if you collapse, and we can't get you out of here."

"One more, and then I'll rest." That would be a third of the blood, at least.

Borde unscrewed the fourth container and stepped back. Clanless lifted himself up, reached out, and activated the Taint. The force of it erupting out of him, burning his eyes, threw him back this time. He hit the wall and fell onto the platform. He rolled on to his back, gasping. His consciousness swam through murky waters.

"Aldan!" Borde cried.

Koland fell to his knees beside him. "Aldan?" Clanless saw a dark shape bending over, reaching toward him, speaking his name in a soft but strong voice… His fist shot out in a wild swing and struck Koland on the side of the face. The storyteller flailed backward, almost tumbling off the platform. Borde caught his arm and steadied him.

"Clanless! Ahh!" Koland gripped his chin. "You nearly took my head off!"

Clanless scrambled back on his hands and feet. "No, no. Not again. Stay away."

"Aldan? What's wrong?" Borde asked while keeping her distance.

His vision and consciousness cleared. Horrible memories flooded in, threatening to overwhelm him. "No, I don't. He didn't…" He buried his face in his hands and trembled as if he'd just emerged from frigid waters.

Koland got to his feet, but didn't move any closer. "Aldan. Did someone hurt you? Maybe a long time ago?"

Clanless lifted his face and stared. "How did you know?"

"I've traveled many miles in my life and listened to the stories of hundreds of people." He rubbed his chin again. "Through all of it, I've seen some things repeated. I've learned things about people. I should have seen it sooner with you, though."

"Seen what?" Borde asked.

Koland shook his head. "You struggle with physical touch, physical forms of affection, don't you, son?"

"He called me 'son,' too," Clanless murmured, looking back down.

"Your father?" Borde exclaimed.

His face shot up, anger contorting his features. "No. Yours," he spat through gritted teeth.

Borde staggered back as if slapped.

"Uncle Sejikdi," Clanless said. "I tried not to think of him for so long. I think I genuinely forgot it. Or at least pretended to. And then you showed up." He shook his head. "The memories kept pushing their way up, and I kept pushing them back down."

"Clanless. Look at me," Koland said in a firm voice. Clanless lifted his eyes to meet the storyteller's. "What happened to you was horrible and wrong. I'm so sorry. But we need you. Right here. And right now. And if we take too much time to deal with your pain, the priests will find us here, and everything will be ruined." He held out his hand. "What do you say?"

Clanless looked up at the man. His thoughts were a horrifying jumble of the present and the past, of using the Taint, of flinching away from physical contact, of his uncle slipping into his room in the dark of night... He closed his eyes and let himself tremble again, but only for a moment. And then he took the pain and shoved it into the darkest recesses of his mind, and locked it away. In his mind, another hand turned the key. He opened his eyes, took Koland's hand, and pulled himself up.

"Open all the containers," he told them. "I'll do it all at once and get it over with."

"Are you sure?" Koland asked, wrinkling his brow. "Doing only one took a lot out of you."

Clanless shook his head. "I'm limiting myself. I'm shutting it off too quick, and that's ripping energy out of me. I think. I need to just let things go."

Koland let Borde open the remaining containers on the right side while he went to those on the left. Clanless descended and stretched himself out on the floor in the center of the room. While the other two worked, he lay still and stared at the ceiling. He'd locked the memories and pain away, but the trauma remained. He couldn't ever get rid of it. And maybe locking it away wasn't the best thing to do, but he'd been doing it since before the Taint. He didn't know how to stop. In fact, he didn't think he could truly control it. Did that make sense?

"They're open," Koland called.

Clanless inhaled deeply through his nose. And then he let the Taint flow without restraint, just as he'd done that horrible day with the barbarians. The already-overwhelming perception of the blood shattered his senses. He could see, hear, smell, taste, feel nothing but the blood. Somewhere in it all, he thought he heard a brief cry of pain. His own blood seemed to boil within him, not in pain, but in reaction to the Taint's power.

"Oh, Aldan, Aldan…" Zektel's voice whispered in his head. "I've tried to help you lock away the pain all this time. Don't you see? That's what has given you strength, the strength to fight, to endure the arena all these years, and still remain yourself."

"You knew," he replied with his thoughts. "You were there even then."

"Yes, but I couldn't speak to you yet, or I would have. All I could do was help you contain it."

Amidst the blood-sense filling everything, he struggled to understand. "You've been affecting my mind? My thoughts? All of my life?"

"Only a little bit. Here and there. When you needed to forget something. When you needed to focus on the present, not the past. When you couldn't think of the right thing to say…" Her voice faded, washed away in a never-ending sea of red. Did red have a sound? Blood did. A pounding. A constant beating. The bloodrush.

Clanless gasped. His head shot up from the floor. His hands flew out and braced himself to keep from falling right back. His clothes were wet, his skin slick with sweat. How long had he been lying there?

He blinked, and discovered he could see again, though everything retained a red tint. The room hadn't changed. Where were Koland and Borde? He climbed to his feet and grabbed one of the wooden supports, his legs wobbling. He felt as though he'd fought half a dozen arena battles in a row. He lifted his head and searched the room.

Koland lay still on the left platform. Borde wasn't moving on the right one. Clanless groaned. Had the Taint affected them too? He hesitated a moment, then clambered up the stairs on the right.

"Borde?" He took her shoulders and gently shook her. She moaned and moved her head. "Are you all right? Can you hear me?" Her eyes opened. A tremor ran through her body, and she let out a breath.

"I, I think I'm all right. Is that what the Taint feels like?"

"I guess. I don't know what you felt." He let her go. "I'll check on Koland, and then we need to get out of here."

((((●))))

Koland turned out to have struck his head on one of the crystals when he fell. After helping Borde re-seal all of the containers, Clanless carried Koland out. The cool night air in the garden helped revive him enough to guide them out of the temple grounds and back into the streets.

"I did what you asked," Clanless said. "Whatever happens tomorrow is now out of my control."

"Please," Borde said. "Don't kill him."

"I'm not asking you to die, Aldan," Koland said, holding the side of his head. "All I ask is that you don't end the fight too soon. Things will be happening. It's the height of the celebrations. That's when we'll be moving in."

"And what?" Clanless shook his head. "I just make the fight last until someone throws the Hawk King from his royal box?" He gestured back toward the temple. "Even with this, I don't see that happening."

"Maybe not that dramatic." Koland chuckled, then winced. "But we'll see what transpires. Just… keep in mind that we're fighting for all of us."

"And I'm fighting for me, remember? It's my freedom."

Koland nodded. He hesitated before adding: "And about what happened back there, with your memories…"

Clanless ran a hand through his sweaty hair. "I don't know what you're talking about."

Koland studied him in the dim lights of the street. "No. I don't suppose you do. Farewell, Aldan. I hope we meet again tomorrow or the day after." He took a step away then paused. "Should I say anything to Kekeen for you?"

"Tell her…" Clanless took a deep breath and let it back out. "Tell her I, I'm sorry."

Koland nodded.

Borde stepped up and embraced him. Clanless returned it awkwardly. "I'm sorry too," she whispered. "I didn't know. Not for sure. I wondered where he went sometimes, but…"

"What are you talking about?"

She sniffed and wiped her eyes. "Never mind."

He stared down at her red-tinted face. "Borde. I haven't… I haven't been fair to you either. I'm very happy to see you again. I hope everything works out for you… somehow."

"Only if Davil lives tomorrow." She shook her head.

A strange conviction swept over Clanless, a desire to once again be the kind man she'd asked him to be, something more than a killer in the arena. He started to speak, but stopped himself. Except he wasn't the one stopping his mouth.

"Don't say it," Zektel's voice filled his mind. "Don't you say it. We've come too far."

"Are you controlling my voice?" he thought back.

"I'm warning you, Aldan. Tomorrow is everything we've worked for. I went along with this little side mission because it's ultimately pointless, but don't you dare reconsider now."

"Aldan?" Borde looked up at his face, confused at his frozen silence.

"Let go of my voice, Zektel."

"Only if you agree with me."

"You do not control me. Let me speak, or I swear I will never summon you again."

She made an exasperated sound in his head. His lips could move again. He shook himself and looked back at Borde. "I'm sorry. I was having an argument with myself."

"Clever," Zektel grumbled.

Clanless took hold of Borde's shoulders. "Your beloved will not die by my hand," he said.

"You absolute, incomprehensible fool," Zektel snarled.

Borde embraced him again. Koland nodded wearily. "We must go," he said.

"Aldan, don't you die either," Borde whispered before pulling away.

He watched the two of them hasten away down the street, mingling into the celebrating crowds.

"How, exactly, are you going to summon me if you're dead?" Zektel asked.

"I won't die."

"Two men enter an arena in a death fight. One of them has to die."

"Better that it's me, then." Clanless turned in the direction of the arena. "At least Daviland has something to live for." When he said the words, he suddenly found that he believed them. A peace settled over him, a peace calming all the turmoil he'd felt for the past several hours.

But Zektel's actions troubled him. He couldn't remember everything that happened in the temple, but he remembered her admissions. She'd been manipulating him all of his life, affecting his thoughts, his words, and who knew what else. She'd just now tried to keep him from speaking.

"I have always been here for you," she said in his mind. "You have had no better friend than me for your entire life."

"Maybe. But you tried to control me. Friends don't do that."

"The way you tried to control Kekeen?"

He growled as he hurried down the street. "You never liked her anyway."

"True. But only because I saw it would end in tragedy for you. And it's hypocritical of you to accuse me of trying to control you—for your own good, I might add—while you do the same thing to your friends."

"Why are you even still here?"

"You used the Taint longer and for more blood than ever in your life. I may be able to speak with you for a long, long time."

"Then be silent for a while. I need to think."

"Whatever you wish."

Could Zektel hear his thoughts when he wasn't specifically "thinking" at her? He didn't believe so, but the concept disturbed him.

He reviewed the night's events. He'd ruined things with Kekeen, probably forever. He'd struck at the blood-priests in a way that would make them hate him even more, if they determined his fault. A twinge of pain reminded him he'd burned his hand. And he'd ended the night by promising not to win his final fight tomorrow.

The palace and arena loomed ahead of him, lit by a thousand torches and lanterns. The other Dohor might be back already, or they might not. On this night, anything was possible. He spared a quick thought for Bain. He'd no doubt returned already.

But he was nowhere to be found within the arena, and Clanless's fur pelt had not been returned. For a brief moment, Clanless considered returning to the lower city eating house. Bain might have stayed to hear from Kekeen again, or even to talk with her. They knew each other, after all. Would she turn to him after the harsh words Clanless had spoken to her?

He berated himself. Such thoughts were ridiculous… and might come from Zektel. Could she do that much? He hated even thinking about it.

With nothing else to do, Clanless put out the lights and got into bed. For a long time, he lay awake, staring into the darkness. Tomorrow. Everything would end tomorrow, one way or the other.

WORDS OF WARNING

Bain must have come back during the night. When he woke late the next morning, Clanless found his fur pelt hanging on one of his chairs.

Everything in the room was a different shade of red. After the barbarian fight, the effect on his vision had lasted several days. It would probably be at least that long this time.

After eating a late breakfast, he headed to the practice grounds to warm up for the day. He found Sugh and Hawking working out. They acknowledged his arrival but kept busy with their own routines.

Clanless tugged a glove on his burned hand. He'd asked Qara to bandage it, which she'd been happy to do. She'd offered to summon a healer, but he turned her down. He'd blamed a mistake with a lantern to Qara, but a healer trained in understanding wounds and hurts would know better. He could deal with it for one arena fight.

His last fight. If he won, he could buy his freedom from the Hawk King afterwards. He'd never have to fight in an arena again. And if he lost... he'd be dead. If Daviland didn't kill him, the Hawk King would kill him for failing. And he'd told Borde he would not kill Daviland. Even if he won the fight and then refused to kill his opponent at the end, the Hawk King would kill him for defiance. Probably. Koland claimed something would happen, a revolution or something, if he could only make the fight last long enough. He didn't see much hope in that path.

Kekeen consumed his thoughts even more than the fight. How could he have been so cruel to her?

"What are you thinking, Aldan?" Zektel's voice filled his head.

"I'm thinking that regardless of the fight, I ruined my one chance at happiness last night."

"Regardless of how she felt before, she made it clear that she doesn't care about about you now."

"Did she?"

"If her precious Daviland hadn't been captured, she wouldn't have even come back. It's a hard truth, I know, but she admitted it. She doesn't care for you. Why should you care about her any more?"

"I can't just turn off what I'm feeling. I've cared about her—loved her—for years." While he continued the discussion in his head, Clanless went through a series of exercises with the moonblade. His burned hand was uncomfortable, but bearable.

"Lock it away, at least for today. You can do that. Do you need help? I can make sure you don't remember it for a while…"

"I don't… No. I don't want to forget her!"

"Just for today."

"No." Though he protested, he did consider it. It would be easier to fight without the memories of Kekeen pulling at his emotions. And yet, he'd always been able to put things aside during a fight, to focus. Besides, it was his last fight and an easy one. He didn't need focus to defeat Daviland… or to let him win.

Qara entered the practice grounds. "Badzorik is ready!" she called.

Clanless grabbed a towel and wiped sweat away. The other two joined him as they headed for the dining hall. Badzorik didn't always give them a thorough explanation of the day's fights, but this was a special event. Everyone needed to know their parts for today.

Bain and Hagh waited in the dining hall already. The latter gave Clanless a short nod of greeting. All of the fighters took seats and looked to the arena master. Badzorik shuffled through several pages before looking up and beginning: "As you all know, today is a very special occasion for the Empire."

"There's something special about today?" Hawking asked, receiving only a glare from the arena master in response.

"This will be unusual in that the fights will take place once the sun surrenders and Suirel appears," he went on. "It won't be too dark, but the arena will be well lit with torches and flames anyway. You will all be fighting in turn. Qaliyun will lead off…"

"Who?" Sugh asked.

"He means Hawking," Hagh answered with a cough.

"If I may proceed?" Badzorik asked with another glare.

These explanations usually proceeded in a similar fashion. The fighters couldn't resist their own editorial comments and jokes, while Badzorik perpetually failed to see humor in any of them. The explanations of the fights continued this time, until he got to the one that mattered.

"And then the main event: Clanless will be fighting against the rebel Daviland."

Hagh muttered something under his breath.

"Easiest fight of the day," Sugh said.

"Nevertheless, the Hawk King wishes this one to be an elaborate event," Badzorik said. "Do you understand, Clanless? You're expected to kill him, of course, but… not too quickly."

"That's the hardest part of the whole thing," Hawking inserted.

Clanless gave a half-shrug to indicate his agreement. If he followed Koland's instructions, he'd make the fight last, but for a different reason.

Badzorik dropped a piece of paper. As he bent to pick it up, the other fighters started talking to each other about their fights, assuming he was done. He cleared his throat loudly. "There are one or two more things…"

Hagh coughed, almost as if in mockery of Badzorik's throat-clearing. Bain snorted.

Badzorik looked at his paper. "The Hawk King has been seeking every way possible to increase the entertainment value of today's events, as you well know. There will be many other events transpiring before the fights, and more afterwards. In addition, he has arranged for something more during the last fight, the one between Clanless and this Daviland person."

Clanless looked up. Something more?

"The Hawk King has sought out a singer to perform during Clanless's fight. She will be with the king in the royal box, using blood-projection like the presenter."

Clanless thought his heart might stop. "Who is the singer?"

Badzorik shrugged. "I do not know the girl's name. Apparently, someone in the Hawk King's family heard her sing in an establishment somewhere, and suggested her. Someone from the lower classes, I understand. It is seen as a good way of appealing to those people, even as their so-called hero is killed."

"You don't know it's her," Zektel said in his head. "And even if it is, what difference does it make?"

"It makes all the difference," he responded. "The Hawk King knows everything. He took her and is making sure I know it. If I don't kill Daviland now, he'll kill her too."

"Did you say something?" Sugh asked.

Clanless blinked. "No." He hadn't said any of it out loud, had he?

"And finally," Badzorik said, looking at the last sheet of paper, "an unprecedented attack took place last night. It seems that rebel forces were able to damage the blood storage used for healing. As such, there will be limited to no healing available following the fights today."

The Dohor exploded with questions and outrage. "How did this happen?" "Who did it?" "What do you mean by 'limited'?"

"Limited is limited," Badzorik replied testily. "I know only what I am told, and I have told you that much."

"Are you sayin' there's a chance we might not be healed?" Hagh demanded.

"I am saying what I have told you." Badzorik sniffed. "If I were you, I would do my best not to be injured."

"Maybe you'd like to handle my fight," Hawking said. "Then you can do your best."

"We get wounded all the time out there," Hagh argued. "If we don't have healing, any one of us could die, much sooner than the Hawk King would like."

Badzorik folded his papers. "Are you questioning the will of the Hawk King?"

Hagh coughed more violently than usual.

"Of course not," Bain put in. "But you must admit it puts a damper on our enthusiasm to fight. Why should we risk permanent injury for the sake of longer entertainment? We should end our fights as fast as possible."

"I would—" Badzorik began.

"The Hawk King would, naturally, be displeased by such actions," Qara cut in. "Healing magic is a privilege you are given, by his grace. You would all do well to remember your true status." Her eyes flashed.

The fighters grumbled, but didn't challenge her. Clanless sat still, mind whirling. The blood destruction had been discovered, of course, but they were only reporting the lack of healing blood. Maybe Koland had been mistaken. Could all of that blood have been from Clan Kurav? That would mean there were eleven other storerooms of equal size, one for each clan. That couldn't be. And yet... where did all the blood from the constant sacrifices go?

But his mind skipped past all of it to the one topic that mattered: the singer. Kekeen. It had to be, no matter what Zektel said. He was trapped. They all were.

"Clanless isn't worried, at least," Sugh proclaimed, clapping him on the back. "He has the easy fight!"

He pushed a smile to his face. "No, not worried at all."

☾☾☾☾●☾☾☾☾

Clanless returned to the practice grounds. Though he needed no great preparation for this fight, he did it anyway. Over and over, he pushed himself through every exercise he knew. He ran. He lifted. He swung his blade in every combination imaginable. He worked through the warmth of the sun's pursuit, until the sweat coated every inch of his body and ran down his skin in tiny rivers.

He didn't notice the visitor until he took a break for water. At first, he struggled to remember where he'd seen that face. The royal box. The prince.

"Your highness," he said with a nod.

"Impressive," Ghouk said, staying within the shade of the nearest wall. "Have you done this every day in your time here?"

Clanless shrugged. "More or less." He took several more swallows of water, enjoying the coolness within.

"Then it is no wonder you're the best." The prince leaned against the wall with folded arms. "It will be a loss for the Empire when you leave the arena."

"I will leave it tonight, one way or another." Clanless picked up the moonblade and prepared to resume his practice.

Ghouk looked at his hand and picked something from one finger with his thumbnail. "It is a loss," he repeated. "Both to the Empire and to my family. I've looked forward to the day when my father's slaves would become mine. I have... different ideas."

"Is there something you need, your highness?" Clanless swung the moonblade over his shoulder. "If not..." He gestured to the practice grounds.

"You may resume your oh-so-exhausting rituals in a moment, Clanless." Ghouk straightened and walked out into the sun. "My father sent me here to speak to you."

Clanless inclined his head. "As always, I am ready to hear the words of the Hawk King."

"Your master."

"And my king."

Ghouk picked up one of the practice maces and took a few swings with it. As Clanless expected, he showed some proficiency. He'd had some training in his privileged life. "I'm sure you've heard of the singer in the royal box tonight."

Clanless tightened his grip on the moonblade. "I have."

"My father at first thought that news alone would be enough for you." Ghouk held up the mace, closed one eye and stared down the length of it with his other. "I, on the other hand, pointed out to him that you might need a more direct message. You haven't always been the smartest of the Dohor, though arguably the mightiest."

"Say what you came to say."

Ghouk looked up at him. "She is an acceptable beauty, for a commoner. And her voice is…" He made a genuflecting gesture toward the moon. "Like the goddess herself. Although, you know, she has found it difficult to sing in the Hawk King's presence. The poor girl is quite overwhelmed with the honor we've bestowed upon her."

"Why are you telling me this?"

Ghouk cocked his head and looked off to the side. "I wonder… after her performance this evening—and your own, of course—I might bestow my own… honor… upon her. I did say she was a beauty, didn't I?"

Clanless took a step toward the prince, almost without thinking.

Ghouk smiled. "That got to you, didn't it?" he whispered. He pointed the mace at Clanless. "We know of your infatuation with this girl, fighter. I'm not being subtle here, like my father. If you fail to kill the rebel tonight, she dies." He licked his lips. "But maybe not right away. It would be good for her to receive some pleasure before the end, don't you think? Word is you have trouble in that regard."

"STOP!" Zektel's voice exploded in his head. Clanless flinched. Had he started toward Ghouk? He couldn't even remember with the echoes of that shout reverberating through his skull.

"If you attack the king's son, it will destroy everything," she continued in a quieter tone. "Everything we've worked for, and everything you want with the girl. Hurt him, and you guarantee her death."

Ghouk, who'd raised the mace defensively, snorted. "It seems I've struck close to the moon with that one," he said. "At any rate, the message is delivered. I'm sure we can all expect you to do your duty this afternoon." He glanced skyward. "The sun is about to surrender. It won't be long now."

"I will do what I must," Clanless growled.

"Good, good." Ghouk returned the mace. "I'm sure you'll make us all proud."

Clanless knelt beside the entrance to the arena. The sun's surrender happened right on schedule, and the events began. Bain now fought some champion from a distant land, not that it mattered. He would win, of course, and then the presenter would call for Clanless. And then what?

"Zektel, what do I do?" he asked in his head.

"I can tell you only what I believe. What I've always said. You need to fight. Fight like everything depends on it. Kill him. And then take his place as the leader of the rebels. You will be the 'Chosen One' yourself. You will succeed where he fails."

"But Borde... and Kekeen..."

"Your cousin has not been a part of your life for almost a decade. It's not fair of her to show up now and make demands of you. And if you truly love Kekeen, you'll do everything you can to save her life. And that means killing this man."

"I don't know. I don't know if I can."

"You are the greatest Dohor, the greatest arena fighter this Empire has ever seen. If you can't do this, no one can."

Clanless remained silent for a few minutes. Another thought occurred to him. "Hagh!"

"Right here. Having second thoughts on fightin' the Chosen One?"

"Pray to the goddess for me, Hagh. I don't know what's about to happen."

"I've been at it." A series of short coughs followed in a staccato.

Clanless nodded and stood. The crowds were cheering Bain. It wouldn't be long now.

"Looks like he avoided serious injury too," Sugh observed. He looked to the blood-priest standing nearby. "Does that mean you have enough healing magic for Clanless if he needs it?"

The priest returned his look with a level gaze and did not answer.

"You don't need him," Zektel said inside. "You don't need anyone. You are the real Chosen One. Chosen for this very moment to win this fight and ensure your legacy forever."

"The Hawk King's legacy, maybe."

"Yours will be greater than his. You will take his place one day. You'll set all the slaves free. You'll change the Empire forever!"

Bain was jogging back toward the entrance. One last thought occurred to Clanless. "Zektel, does the Hawk King have a blood-wraith with him?"

"Why do you ask?"

"It feels strange when I'm near him. You discovered another one with the barbarians that one time. Do you sense one with the king?"

She didn't answer for a long moment. Bain had almost reached them. "Yes. Yes, I believe he does."

"What about the Ghamba Lam?"

"No. At least I don't think so. That one is strange."

"I noticed."

Bain came to a stop, dropped his maces on the floor, and bent over, breathing hard. "Getting cold out there already. But the smoke from the fires is stifling."

"We all noticed." Sugh patted him on the back. "Clanless! They're chanting your name!"

Clanless swung the moonblade up over his shoulder. He took a deep breath and walked out into the arena.

THE DAY THE SUN SURRENDERED

Fire filled the arena. Torches sputtered in the breeze every few feet around the wall. Even as Clanless walked out onto the sand, attendants were running around the edges, replacing any torches that had gone out. An inner ring of pillars had been erected in the center of the arena, each one topped by a metal bowl of fire. Once the fighters entered that ring, they could see almost nothing beyond its boundaries, though those above presumably could see everything.

Clanless couldn't help but take a quick glance up. The sun had surrendered, as it always did this time of year. But there… high in the sky above and to the right of the moon: a second moon, smaller and darker, though tinted by red like everything else he saw. Suirel. The chaos moon. For the first time, Hagh's mutterings about destiny and the chaos moon's arrival gave Clanless pause. He shook his head and strode forward.

The crowd chanted "Clanless!" over and over, just as Zektel had promised they would, so many years ago. She'd been right about so many things. Maybe she was right now. He lifted the moonblade in acknowledgement of their chant. They erupted in greater applause and cheers.

"As promised, citizens, here to complete tonight's fights: Clanless the indomitable. Clanless the unbeaten. Clanless the greatest arena fighter of all time!" The presenter's magic-enhanced voice boomed above the chants. But then a different voice replaced his.

"Hear the words of the immortal Hawk King." The crowd quieted at their ruler's voice. "Tonight, my servant Clanless fights for the last time.

Should he win tonight, he will purchase his own freedom and become like all of you. But we will never forget him, will we?"

The crowd roared their agreement.

"Tonight is no ordinary fight either. You have all heard rumors of his opponent. Tonight, we see how much of a 'hero' he really is. Behold the man who dares challenge far above his station. Behold Daviland!"

The crowd, unsure about how to react, split into cheers and derision.

Clanless watched Daviland walk into the inner ring of pillars. He looked no better than he had the day before: disheveled, bruised, limping a bit. He carried a simple short sword in one hand and a buckler in the other. "It's not too late, Clanless," he called.

"Yes, it is," Zektel murmured. "Don't listen to him. Kill him quickly, and take his place!"

"I don't know…"

In that instant, an image of a decapitated man filled his mind. He saw himself inserting the Siphon into the remains of the man's neck. Clanless almost stumbled. "What was that?"

"A memory to remind you. You've killed hundreds now, dearheart. Don't fade now."

Clanless felt sure he'd never cut off someone's head. Not like that. Had he? He didn't remember it at all.

"But that is not all!" the Hawk King continued. "Tonight, we will enjoy the spectacle of this fight with a musical accompaniment instead of the usual presenter!"

The crowd stirred with various reactions. Few knew what to think of this. Daviland turned his head toward the royal box with a wrinkled brow. He hadn't been told about this part.

"From the midst of the common people, your king has found a rare jewel: a singer whose voice cannot be matched. She will sing for us now, as these two warriors meet for the first and last time!"

Kekeen had never watched him fight before. He certainly wouldn't have chosen this battle for her to see.

"Focus," Zektel whispered. "Focus."

"What song could best match this momentous occasion?" the Hawk King asked. "I knew there could be only one answer. My lady… you may begin. Clanless, Daviland: may the will of the goddess be done."

Clanless took a step forward but no further. The voice he'd hoped and dreaded to hear began to sing. Even enhanced by the blood-magic, he could hear the slight tremor of nervousness and fear in her voice. And of course it was that song.

"On the day the sun surrendered,
I met my love around the bend..."
Daviland turned back toward Clanless, mouth open. "Kekeen?"

Clanless growled and started forward. Enough of this. He had every reason now to kill this man. He'd been ordered. It would win his freedom. He could save Kekeen. Why should he even hesitate? Borde would understand... someday. He stalked toward Daviland as the song continued.

"Yes! Kill him!" Zektel whispered.

"In the shadow of the goddess
We pledged our love would never end..."
Some of the crowd joined in the song, perhaps finding it an entertaining addition to the fight, after all.

"Clanless!" Daviland lifted his buckler and dropped into a guard position. "He's using her, isn't he? Threatening her if you don't kill me?"

Clanless delivered a reckless two-handed stroke. Daviland protected himself with the buckler, but the force of the blow drove him back several steps.

Kekeen's voice cracked a little as she started the second verse: *"On the day the sun surrendered..."*

"She wouldn't want this, Aldan!" Daviland shouted. "No matter what happens, she wouldn't want this!"

"He has no right to call you by that name," Zektel hissed. "Kill him!"

"I left my love to find a home..."

"Nyaarggh!" Clanless delivered an uppercut that tore the buckler from Daviland's arm. It ricocheted off one of the pillars and landed in the sand a dozen feet away. Daviland responded with a quick thrust of his short sword. Clanless sidestepped, dodging with ease.

"So that we could stay together..."

Clanless drove Daviland back and around, swinging blow after blow. Somehow, the smaller man continued to elude him.

"Kekeen wouldn't want you to kill me," Daviland tried again. "And she wouldn't want me to kill you."

"Like you have a chance!" Clanless sneered. He paused, standing several feet away, breathing hard. Where was the bloodrush? Why couldn't he feel right about this?

"What does it matter what she would want?" Zektel asked. "She rejected you. She doesn't love you."

"Oh, side by side no more to roam." With the pause in the fighting, Kekeen's voice gained strength.

"You've already lost." Clanless pointed at Daviland. "You're bleeding."

Daviland nodded, acknowledging the cut on his side. "So are you," he said just loud enough to hear.

Clanless glanced at a scratch on his upper left arm. "What does that—"

Daviland lifted his sword straight up and brought it down in a swift motion, pointing at Clanless.

Pain—a burning sensation—exploded in his bleeding arm then shot up into his chest. The Taint? How? The pain spread throughout his entire body, and he staggered.

The crowd erupted in shock, and Kekeen's voice faded.

Clanless's vision turned dark, erasing the red tint. A sensation of falling overtook him, and he collapsed to his knees.

"You're not the only one, you know," Daviland said, moving closer. "Stay down, please. All I need is a sample of your blood…"

Clanless fought to stay conscious. "Stay awake, stay awake, stay awake!" Zektel's voice hammered in his head. The presenter said something he couldn't hear—or was that the Hawk King? As Daviland came near, Kekeen's voice sang again.

"On the day the sun surrendered…"

In desperation, Clanless activated the Taint himself. His eyes burned. Daviland stiffened and staggered. "It doesn't have to be this way," he groaned.

"I lost my love to my best friend…"

Clanless had always hated this verse of the song. Losing a love wasn't something to sing about.

Daviland fell.

But Clanless was in no condition to do anything about it. He pulled himself to his feet, leaning on the moonblade. "Now! Get him!" Zektel insisted.

"Be quiet!" Clanless growled.

Daviland rolled over and grabbed his fallen sword. "So that's what it feels like…"

The pain from the Taint combined with the bloodrush pounding in Clanless's ears. There it was at last. He saw Daviland's lips moving as the other man got to his knees, but he couldn't hear it, or Kekeen's singing. Zektel's voice intruded through the chaos: "It's hasn't been much of a fight, but you may as well end it now. He played his one trick. Kill him."

Clanless pulled up the moonblade and took a step forward. The pain faded. Whether Daviland's Taint power wasn't as strong, or whether his body could handle it better, it didn't matter. Zektel was right. He should end this.

"On the day the sun surrendered," Kekeen's voice burst into his head. He hesitated. He knew she was in danger. But hearing her voice constantly reminded him of her goodness, her kindness.

"I found my love in shadows dim…"

Daviland got to his feet. "The Hawk King will fall," he managed to gasp.

Clanless lunged forward, but the effects of the Taint were stronger than he'd thought. His swing went far too wide. Daviland tried to respond with his own swing, but almost dropped the sword.

"You can do better than that!" Zektel's voice resonated with another image in his head: two more arena fighters lying dead on the sand, horrific wounds bleeding out. He didn't remember them at all. Where were these coming from?

"On the day the sun surrendered," Kekeen sang out louder than ever. Wait. Hadn't she skipped some lines?

Clanless stepped back, trying to regain his strength. Daviland did the same. Somehow, he found the fallen buckler and retrieved it.

"I saw my love across the sand…"

Clanless blinked. That wasn't part of the song. Kekeen was making up new lyrics. Did… did she mean him?

"No, no, no," Zektel said. "Don't listen. Just kill him. You can apologize to her later, with tears and everything. She'll listen to you."

"With the blade he wields so strongly…"

Daviland came at him now, charging with more speed than Clanless would have expected. The Taint should have drained him more, as it had Clanless himself. But what was Kekeen singing?

"Ignore her!" Zektel screeched. "Protect yourself!" An image of a large hand twisting the arm of a small boy appeared in his head. The arm snapped with an audible crack, even as Daviland's sword ricocheted off one of his bracers.

Clanless dodged and parried a series of blows from Daviland, his head swimming. He'd broken his arm carrying a rock to the back wall, hadn't he? Or had that been Uncle Sejikdi too? How much had Zektel locked away in his head?

Kekeen's voice rang out louder than ever: *"You will know him by his brand!"*

Clanless froze. She did mean him. She loved him still. She was telling him, through her song.

"Kill him!" Zektel roared.

"I can't."

An image of Zaluu lying broken and bleeding flashed into his head. "You didn't save him. Save your girl now. Kill him and take his place!"

"No. I can't."

Zektel's voice grew even harsher. "Koland thought you locked the memories away. He's wrong, Aldan. I did. I protected you. You owe me." Yeltek's guts spilling out filled his mind. Jik's face filled with fear. Tunt's voice echoed in his ears: "You're the villain now."

"It's not too late, Tunt," Clanless whispered. He stepped toward Daviland but left himself wide open.

"I'm sorry," Daviland said as he stabbed. His sword bit into Aldan's stomach. "Oh!" Kekeen exclaimed before her voice was cut off. Clanless fell to his knees, his hand clutching at his gut. Blood poured out around it. Daviland stepped back.

"Don't give up!" Zektel cried. "You can still do this. Use the Taint! Use the Taint!"

"No…" Clanless whispered.

"You fool! I'll leave you, Aldan. I will not go down with you. Kill him!"

Daviland watched him with wary eyes. Zektel was right. He could use the Taint again, right now. It would stagger Daviland, allow Clanless to lunge forward and end this with his own blade. All it would take is a thought.

"If I leave you, all of your pain comes back," she warned. "You've forgotten so much more than you know." Another bloody image of a fallen warrior. Jik's smashed shoulder. Uncle Sejikdi's face. "I've kept it locked away. You don't want that, Aldan." A shadow above him, reaching down. "Kill him!"

Even without the Taint, he could do it. If Daviland took one more step, he'd be in range of Clanless's one-handed sweep. It would be easy.

The crowd noise was deafening, but a commotion came from the royal box. Remnants of the blood-enhanced voices, maybe. Shouts.

Aldan slammed the moonblade down into the sand and lowered his head. "For Kekeen. And Borde," he whispered.

Daviland took the step closer. "I still need your blood." He fumbled at his neck and pulled at the string there. A vial hung from it, already full of blood.

"Goodbye, Aldan. You failed me, but there's another opportunity here. I'm sorry." Zektel's voice didn't sound sorry at all. "If Daviland has the Taint also, then he is a far better host for me than you've ever been. He's willing to do whatever it takes. You aren't."

His eyes widened. If Zektel went to Daviland, she might manipulate him in any number of ways. "No. Don't."

Daviland bent and held the vial to the bloody wound. "It's the catalyst, you see. The Hawk King knew. He should never have allowed us to be in the same place."

His words made no sense. Clanless tried to warn him about Zektel, but his mouth wouldn't move.

Daviland dumped the blood over his own head and stood. He turned and pointed his sword at the royal box. "The reign of the Hawk King is over!" he shouted.

"And my reign begins," Zektel said.

Bain said the blood-wraiths "latch on to people with ambition."

Clanless both heard and felt a tearing, a sudden wrenching as if every bit of blood in his body were being yanked forward. Something separated itself from him, moving away. His body fell backward.

In the same moment, images filled his mind. Horrible images of terrible moments in his life, moments he'd… forgotten. Pain, physical and emotional, flooded over him. How? How could these things be? What had Zektel done? He saw moments of absolute brutality from his own hand in the arena, over and over again. Things he couldn't imagine himself doing. He saw Zaluu on the ground, his body torn apart by barbarians. And yet, his eyes still moved as he begged: "Help me…" And he saw Uncle Sejikdi coming to him in the dark…

As his consciousness fled away in despair, the last thing Aldan saw was Daviland, standing tall and strong. The rebel leader, the chosen one, looked back at him one last time. He crouched, as if about to launch himself into the air.

And his eyes were rimmed in red.

WAKING UP

Clanless swam in darkness until a light drew him in. As he approached, he realized the light came from the moon itself. He'd never seen it so large and clear, with so many distinct shapes and lines on its surface. Almost he thought he saw cities and roads. But that couldn't be true. For a moment, he caught a glimpse of Suirel, the chaos moon, beyond it all. If light filled the regular moon, darkness filled the second. A chill swept over him.

A brighter light emerged from the moon, so bright he lifted his hand to shield his eyes. After a moment, it faded enough for him to peek out. Suirel was gone. The light coalesced into a human shape, though he couldn't make out any details. Regardless, he knew who it must be.

"Goddess," he whispered, surprised to discover he had a voice in this place… wherever it might be.

"Oh, Aldan. How you have suffered, without even knowing it." Her voice echoed in his mind, somewhat like Zektel's had done. But this voice came with peace and comfort. A warmth suffused his body, as though he'd been wrapped in blankets. It drove away Suirel's chill.

"How I have wished for this day."

"You… you know me?"

"I have known you for your entire life. Once I understood you, I chose you for a purpose. I saw your early mistreatment and how you persevered. And so, I gave you the power your people call the Taint, knowing you would be the right one." The light moved, as though she shook her head. "But one of the others latched on to you right away. And so, I stepped back. I could not reveal myself to you while she was there. I suppose I gave up then. I even considered starting over with someone else."

A pause. Clanless closed his eyes for a moment, enjoying the warmth.

"And then this girl started praying for you. I took notice again. I saw your struggles, and how your heart did not change too much, even with that one influencing you. You frustrated her to no end, by the way."

Clanless opened his eyes. He frustrated Zektel?

"So I stepped in from time to time, prodding, helping you when you did not notice. Did you truly think you survived all those years because of your own power?"

He felt ashamed, dirty even, to have believed it.

"Once, I had to speak to your friend directly to send him to save you. You would have died in the arena that day."

Clanless sucked in a breath. "Maybe a voice told me to do it." Bain.

"And now that she is gone, I can speak to you… but only for a few moments, here and now. Soon, my connection to your world will wane."

"Why?" he croaked. "You're the goddess!"

"That does not mean what you believe it to mean. I was… assigned this role, to oversee your people, the people below the moon's gaze."

"Assigned?"

"I'm afraid I haven't done a very good job." The goddess sighed. "The wraiths have become a serious problem."

"Zektel."

"That is the name she gave you, is it not? An attempt at familiarity. They have learned much over the years."

"I don't understand."

"That is all right. You do not need to understand at this time." She appeared to turn to the side, as if distracted by something. "There is war in the heavens."

"Suirel?"

"Him?" She continued to look to the side. "He is… a part of it, yes. But your fate is no small part of it as well."

"Is that why I am here?"

He imagined a smile on the glowing figure as it turned back. Her voice sounded like smiling. "No. But I wanted you to know these things. You have been in my thoughts for some time."

"Oh." He never would have imagined a goddess thinking about him.

"And I am very sorry to say that you will feel horrible when you wake up."

"Because the healer didn't have enough blood?"

"No. Because you will be remembering all the things the wraith kept from you." The shining figure shimmered with some kind of movement. "You need to know it is not your fault. It is not your fault your uncle abused you. It is not your fault Zaluu died. It is not your fault you forgot these things."

He thought for a moment. "But I did kill all those other men."

"Yes. You made that choice. But it was a choice between killing or being killed."

"I still made the choice."

"And you must live with that. Farewell, Aldan. For now."

"Wait! I have so many questions!" He blurted the first two that came to mind: "Why did you choose me? Why do you require blood sacrifices?"

"The blood…" Her voice grew faint. "…is certainty."

The light vanished. The moon remained behind for a few moments. Then it too faded away. Clanless sought its glow for a while longer but soon lost himself in the darkness.

❨❩❨❩❨❩●❪❫❪❫❪❫

Clanless didn't want to wake up. Though his consciousness returned, it came with new memories. He'd never realized how much Zektel influenced his mind, how much she'd locked away. He moaned without even realizing it.

"I think he's waking up," said a voice, not sounding pleased with the idea. Someone was with him. He wasn't still on the arena floor? Even as he thought it, he recognized the comfort of a mattress, not sand. The comfort vanished when pain from his gut made itself known. He convulsed.

"He's bleeding again!" said another voice. "Hold that cloth tight!"

"I'm trying!"

"Has no one found a healer with blood available?"

At this point, he knew he'd heard at least three different voices. But the physical and emotional pain were too much for him to concentrate on identities. If only he could lose consciousness again, slip back into the darkness without thought and memory… Uncle Sejikdi's face loomed above him. His eyes snapped open.

Instead of his uncle, he saw Kekeen looking down at him, face full of concern. The other voices belonged to Hagh and Sugh. He thought he caught a glimpse of Yesun running out the door. He lay in his own bed in his own room. A single lantern burned atop his table. He grasped all of this in a few seconds as his eyes darted about. His head rolled with his eyes and he lost focus. The smell of his own blood and sweat overwhelmed his nostrils.

"Aldan. Can you hear me? Look at me, please," Kekeen pleaded. Her hands pressed to either side of his face and held his head still.

His eyes focused, blurred, then focused again on her face. Her beautiful, wonderful face, marred by an ugly gash on her forehead above her right eye. The blood had clotted over, but it also needed healing, or she'd be left with a scar. It seemed a horrible loss amidst everything else.

"Hang in there, lad," Hagh said from his other side. He must be the one keeping pressure on the wound. "You can do this."

"I, I, ah, I…" He tried to speak, but couldn't seem to form the words.

"Where is that healer?" Sugh shouted, stomping out of the room.

Vision blurring again, Clanless coughed. Then darkness claimed him once again.

❨❨❨❨●❩❩❩❩

The next time he woke up, Clanless took a deep breath and evaluated his circumstances before doing anything else. The pain from his gut had lessened, though it still sent throbs of agony cascading through his torso. The lack of yelling and shouting might be a good sign. He allowed his eyelids to crack open.

Kekeen sat on the bed beside him, the picture of exhaustion. Her head hung down, and her eyes were half closed. Someone had bandaged her forehead. The red dress she wore must have come from the Hawk King. A couple of tears and wrinkles may have ruined its finery, but Kekeen herself could not have been more beautiful in his eyes.

"You're still here," he whispered, surprised to hear his own voice.

She turned with a gasp, eyes flying open. "You're awake!" She leaned in close, her hair falling around her face. Only a few minutes later did Clanless realize she'd been leaning over him on the bed, and he'd felt no fear. He hoped that much didn't change.

He tried to reach up to touch her face, but she grabbed his hand. "Don't try too much," she warned. "Bain said you almost bled out before they dragged that angry healer in here."

He had received at least partial healing, then. "What… happened?"

"The Hawk King is dead," she said. She brushed back some of her hair, but it fell right back down. "One of the lords protected me in the booth for a few seconds before Daviland arrived. He killed the king, just like the prophet said he would!"

One of the lords? Clanless deeply hoped it wasn't Lord Ghayaktal. That would be awkward.

"H-how?"

"Davil leaped all the way into the booth! He must have used some kind of blood-magic. The fight with the Hawk King…" She shook her head. "They both ended up falling back down into the arena. Davil killed him almost right next to you!"

The Hawk King used all kinds of blood-magic. Daviland must have tapped into multiple types as well. That single vial of blood he'd used…

Kekeen glanced toward the door. "Things are still pretty chaotic out there. A lot of fighting is happening between the Hawk King's soldiers and our people. But Daviland is in control in the palace. Everything should clear up… eventually."

Clanless wanted to ask more, but his eyes became heavy again and slipped closed. His head jerked, and his eyes flew back open.

"You don't have to stay awake," Kekeen said in a hurry. "If you need to rest, you should." She looked toward his stomach. "The priest healed you, but not all the way. He didn't have enough blood."

"Goddess," he whispered. "I saw her."

Kekeen cocked her head. "You saw the goddess?"

"Her hand was on him!" Hagh's voice came from the doorway. "How else can ya explain his survival?"

Kekeen sat up and smiled at the fighter as he came to the bedside. "Moon's stability to you, Clanless." Hagh shook his head. "You've been through it. Told ya not to fight the chosen one. Suirel tried to claim ya, but you're still here."

Clanless wanted to laugh, but it hurt. Everything hurt. Hagh grabbed a tall glass of water and brought it to Kekeen.

"You can rest now, though," he added. "Don't worry yourself over anything."

"He's right," Kekeen said. She gave him a careful drink of the water. "You don't have to do anything. You can rest and heal as long as it takes."

"No fights." Hagh turned his head and coughed. "Never again, if we don't want to."

Clanless tried to lift his head. "What?"

"You're free," Kekeen said. "All of you!"

"As far as we know, anyway," Hagh said. "The Hawk King is dead. And unless he found a way t' pass on our bloodbonds, we're all free men now."

"Could he do that?" Kekeen's brow wrinkled. "Pass on the bloodbonds?"

Hagh shook his head. "There's a process. Like everything else, it requires blood. And he's dead, so he can't do it. Just in case, Bain and Sugh are looking for them in the palace now."

Clanless looked up at Kekeen. "You were right." Daviland had freed him. In fact, Daviland had done everything: beaten Clanless in the arena, killed the Hawk King, rescued Kekeen, overthrown the entire Empire… "I've done nothing," he realized.

"None of it would have happened without what you did last night," Kekeen pointed out. "Borde told me how you ruined their blood supplies."

"What's that?" Hagh asked.

"He—" Kekeen broke off as Bain and Sugh entered the room. "I'll explain later."

"He's awake!" Sugh boomed. "Praise be!"

"The bonds?" Hagh asked.

"No sign of them." Bain shook his head. "Maybe the Hawk King had them on his person. If so, they're buried with him wherever Daviland's followers took the body."

"I suspect the Ghamba Lam," Sugh said with a shrug. "He was in the booth."

"You shouldn't speak evil of that one," Hagh said. "He still serves the goddess."

"What does it matter who was in the booth?" Bain asked. "The Hawk King died in the sands!"

As the conversation continued, Clanless found his own ability to keep up slipping away. So many new memories had flooded his mind—all of them bad—he was having a hard time sorting through even recent memories. They all blended together in anachronistic ways, creating odd match-ups like Uncle Sejikdi and Zaluu, or Tunt and Silence. He thought he needed to tell the others something, something important. But he couldn't grasp it.

His eyes wandered to the moonblade hanging in its usual spot on the wall, seeking something stable. He traced its form, from the well-worn handle to the chip in the blade from the beastman. But it only raised more questions. Would he ever need it again? For so long, it had been a part of him. Could he just leave it there on the wall now? To hang forever alone? He wasn't sure about that.

Freedom. He'd worked for it for so long. Now what should he do? Go back to the clanhold to see his family? It would be nice to see his parents, his little sister, and the little brother he'd never met. But he didn't think he could face his uncle… not without either cowering in fear or murdering him. He wasn't sure which would be more likely.

What would he do in Daviland's new Empire? Would it even be an Empire anymore? He couldn't think of any kind of job he could do after years of arena fighting. He didn't know anything else. The arena system would be gone, of course. So what did that leave for him?

His eyes returned to Kekeen's face, watching her mouth move as she talked with the other fighters. Whatever happened, he would stay with her. That much he knew.

For now, as he fell asleep again, that was enough.

((((●))))

The next day, Clanless grew strong enough to sit up. When Kekeen left him for a while to get some sleep of her own, he called Hagh in. He pointed toward the chest at the end of his bed. "Open it."

Hagh raised an eyebrow but opened the chest. He whistled. "I knew you had a lot of blood stashed away, but this is…" He shook his head. "I guess you really were about to buy your freedom. Now what are you going to do with it all?"

"I want you to take it. The certificates too," Clanless said. He glanced at the door before continuing: "Go to Pasque House and ask for the owner. Then use whatever it takes to buy Salkhi. Once you have her bloodbond, set her free."

Hagh pulled out a bag full of blood vials and looked at Clanless uncertainly. "You don't want to do that yourself? It would mean more to her."

"I don't want to wait another day." Clanless shook his head. "Anything could happen to her, especially with the healing blood in short supply right now."

Hagh nodded. "And this blood may not be worth as much in a few days, I suppose."

Clanless agreed. No one knew yet what Daviland would do about the blood economy. Would it continue as it was? What would happen with the priests? Daviland had said he would bring it all down, but now he faced reality. Word had already spread about a meeting today with the Ghamba Lam.

"Just get her free, Hagh. And then give the rest to Yesun's family."

He headed for the door. "I'll be sure they know it comes from you."

Clanless almost told him not to do that. But he doubted Hagh would listen to him. He took a deep breath and winced at the pain in his gut.

At least he'd accomplished something worthwhile. Salkhi would be free.

He stared up at the moonblade again. Its shape and scored surface made him think of his vision after the fight. The goddess knew about him, had given him the Taint, and wanted him to know it. And she worried about the blood-wraiths for some reason. And Suirel, the chaos moon, had something to do with it all.

Zektel. She'd shaped his whole life from the moment the Taint first appeared. She'd claimed to be part of him at first but gradually let it slip that she was far older. Maybe some of what Bain said about her had been true, after all.

He wanted to scream. She'd betrayed him, used him for her own purposes, and then abandoned him. But he wanted her back. He looked toward the plate he used to summon her. Maybe if he used the Taint, she would come back to him. She'd been his only friend, his only confidant for most of his life. He didn't know if he could live without her.

And now she possessed Daviland. Would he listen to her? Follow her advice?

She'd said another blood-wraith possessed the Hawk King. If their goals were aligned, would things change in the Empire at all? He needed to tell someone, let them know about Zektel.

But who would he tell? The only one who even knew about her was Bain. Since their training days, he'd never told another soul. How could he go to someone now, like Koland, and tell them he'd been possessed all his life by a creature who now possessed Daviland? Who would believe him? Even if they did, they couldn't do anything about it. And he didn't want them to; he didn't want her hurt.

She'd betrayed him! He shouldn't care about her... but he did. He pushed down the impulse to scream again. If he did, someone would rush in and offer to help. They couldn't help him. No one could.

The memories she'd unlocked still threatened his every waking moment. He thought he was doing better at sorting through the past and present now, but there were so many. They faded in and out. Some he couldn't quite grasp yet. Some would not go away. His uncle. Zaluu's death. And all his own killing. So much killing. The goddess told him most of it wasn't his fault, but the killing was. He'd killed and killed and killed, even sometimes when it wasn't strictly necessary for the fight. And he'd been cruel too. He could have killed some of his opponents in seconds, but he made it last, for the sake of the crowd and his own reputation.

He'd been a monster. And people had cheered him for it. Maybe Kan had been right all along: "People want to see the villains, because deep down... they want to be one." He'd been a villain. A tool for the Hawk

King. And people had loved him. Did a monster, a villain such as he, even have a place in this new world?

In answer to his thoughts, the door opened and Kekeen entered. Seeing him up, a smile spread over her face, the smile he'd adored since he first saw it eight years ago. He did not deserve this. He did not deserve her. But if she stayed, if she wanted him…

She knelt beside his chair and took his hand in both of hers. "Is there anything I can do for you, Aldan?"

He smiled, knowing only one answer would be right.

"Sing for me."

The Beginning

For more information on Clanless & his world,
upcoming books, and more,
visit timfrankovich.com

(Sign up for the newsletter and
you'll get access to free short stories)

If you enjoyed this book, please post a review on Amazon,
Goodreads, B&N, or wherever you find books!
There's no better way to spread the word.

On the Day the Sun Surrendered

Lyrics & theme by Tim Frankovich. Musical notation by Bradford Eide.

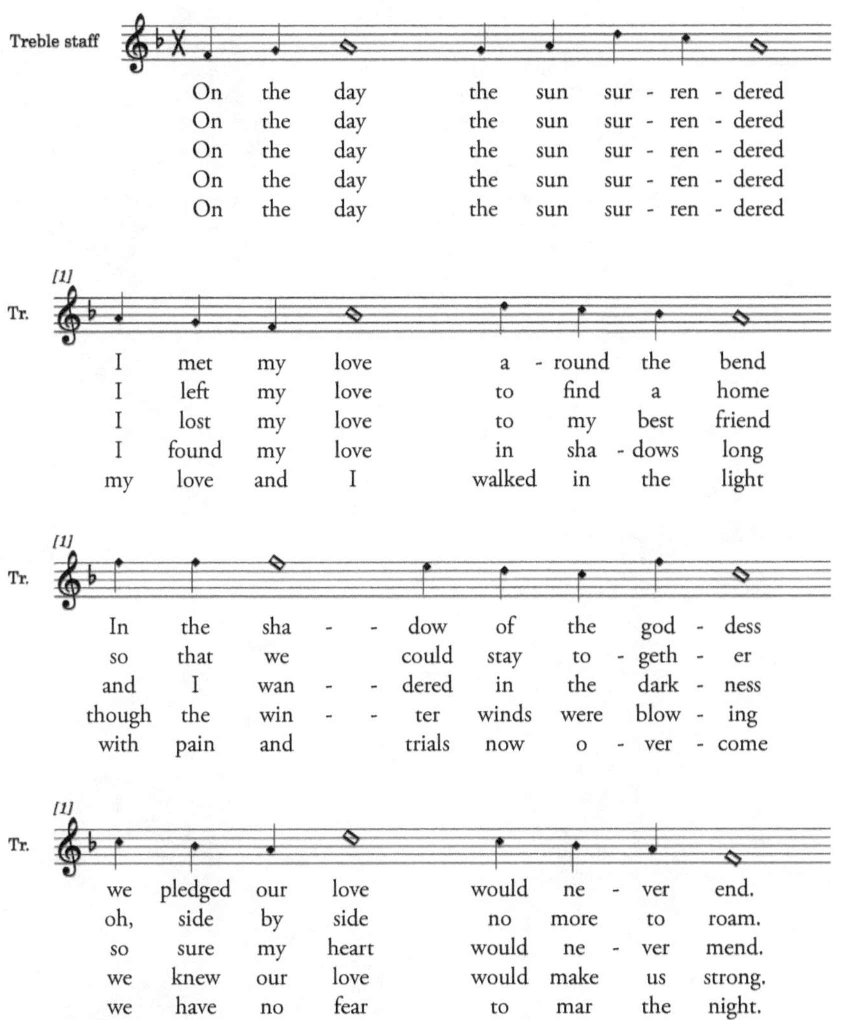

Clans of the Sar Empire
(Taken from notes by the arena fighter Clanless)

The Sar Empire consists of twelve clans of various levels of power and influence.

Clan Shukan - One of the four most powerful clans, vying for power within the capital. The Hawk King comes from this clan, which gives them the greatest prestige. They also have a great deal of influence over the priesthood. Owns a large portion of the city.
Blood-magic: Life extension *(I think)*

Clan Ghutalta - Second of the most powerful clans. Controls most of the banking system within the capital, and has significant influence over the priesthood.
Blood-magic: Unknown *(Not sure why no one—including Bain!—will tell me)*

Clan Kurav - Third of the most powerful clans. Has arrangements with many smaller clans to bring in their goods, thus controls much of the market within the capital.
Blood-magic: Healing

Clan Torov - Fourth of the most powerful clans. Owns the largest portion of the city, and has bits of control throughout everything. Diversifies their influence, but is always scheming to increase it.
Blood-magic: Voice

Clan Zavi - Their richest family owns a mansion in the capital, but their primary influence is over the harbor city and the shipping industry.
Blood-magic: Speed *(seems odd)*

Clan Shasin - While they only have small influence over the priesthood in the capital, this clan virtually controls religion in most of the other cities and quite a few clanholds.
Blood-magic: Unknown *(why are people so secretive?)*

Clan Dendsu - Richest members own a couple of large homes in the capital and another city. But they control the largest amount of farmland in the country, via several clanholds.
Blood-magic: Unknown *(again!)*

Clan Dalbai - Operates the arenas in all of the cities. (Shares capital city arena management with Clan Torov.) Has some influence within the priesthood to help them find new gladiators.
Blood-magic: Endurance *(I think)*

Clan Berge - Military-focused. Highest officers are all from this clan. Also maintains a very large blacksmith guild throughout the land.
Blood-magic: Strength

Clan Tokuur, Dariachin, Ghamkiin - The low clans, agricultural, mostly live in clanholds.
Blood-magic: Tokuur is weakness (?). No one seems to care about the other two.

Acknowledgements

Before I started writing this book, I knew I needed to do a lot of brainstorming and planning. I had so many ideas, but I needed to bring them all together. The world of Clanless and the Hawk King is vast and intricate. How did it all connect? What role did each clan play in the greater tapestry? What was significant about that geostationary moon?

With that in mind, I wanted to make sure I made things realistic. I could easily say, "the moon doesn't move," and leave it at that. But I wanted more. I could envision the effects on culture and beliefs of the people who gazed up at it. But I wanted to know what effects it would have on climate and wildlife. And so I turned to people much smarter than I am: NASA Flight Engineer Kjell Lindgren (though I had to wait for him to get back from the ISS), and Dr. Sonny White of the Limitless Space Institute (Seriously, this guy is smarter than all the rest of us put together. Check out their website at: https://www.limitlessspace.org). Any of the brilliant science-y parts come from them. Any silly mistakes are mine.

I'm grateful for brainstorming sessions with Tys Grenz, who helped with connecting everything, and John Hart, who is great at finding loopholes in magic systems (and game rules). Many thanks to Stephen Tallman and Allen Perkins, as usual, for their excellent beta reading feedback. And thanks to the continued support of the Apex Writers Group, especially the Science Fiction & Fantasy subgroup.

Thanks to Scott Foster for advice and help with the chapter artwork. My initial attempts were lame. It's much better now, thanks to Scott.

Extra-special thanks to Bradford Eide for creating the musical notation for *On The Day the Sun Surrendered*, and to Chris Vaughn for connecting us and pulling it all together. I plucked out a tune on a keyboard, and they ran with it.

I feel extremely blessed to know all these people, who have all helped me create this book. This is the power of community, and a testament to the Creator of all of our stories.

The path to this book's publication has been long and winding. Original-ly, I hoped to publish it by the end of 2022. And then I injured my hand in mid-October and needed surgery. As I write this, five months later, I can *almost* type at the same rate as before.

But the delay ended up being a good thing in the long run. It allowed for some more serious editing and revision work. Unable to plunge into my next book right away, I had a lot more time to think about this one. This, combined with all the people listed above, made the final story much stronger.

The story, however, is not over. Watch for more about Clanless soon…

About the Author

Tim Frankovich has been exploring fantastic worlds since third grade, when he cut up a grocery sack and drew a Godzilla-meets-superheroes story. Since then, he's gotten a little bit better at the writing part (not so much with the drawing).

His goal as a writer is to transport readers to another world, make them care deeply about characters in dire situations, and guide them deeply into life itself.

At the moment, he is probably suitably conscious somewhere in Texas with his beloved wife, awesome kids, and a fool of a pup named Pippin.